A
SEASON
FOR
DEATH

RAY HARRISON

A Sergeant Bragg-
Constable Morton Mystery

BERKLEY BOOKS, NEW YORK

This Berkley book contains the complete
text of the original hardcover edition.
It has been completely reset in a typeface
designed for easy reading and was printed
from new film.

A SEASON FOR DEATH

A Berkley Book / published by arrangement with
St. Martin's Press

PRINTING HISTORY
St. Martin's edition published 1987
Berkley edition / July 1989

ISBN: 0-425-11639-5

A BERKLEY BOOK ® TM 757,375
Berkley Books are published by The Berkley Publishing Group,
200 Madison Avenue, New York, New York 10016.
The name "Berkley" and the "B" logo
are trademarks belonging to Berkley Publishing Corporation.

PRINTED IN THE UNITED STATES OF AMERICA

10 9 8 7 6 5 4 3 2 1

To Jan and Nigel

PROLOGUE _____

James Morton patrolled slowly along the Lichtentaler Allee, keeping in the deepest shadows under the trees. To his left, he could hear the gurgle of the Oos River—little more than a stream at this time of year, trickling along its cobbled bed. There was no denying that it was an attractive feature of Baden-Baden, with the weeping beech trees and carefully tended gardens on either bank. A little contrived, perhaps, but unrepentant; bubbling cheerfully along towards the theatre and the spa buildings, content to be at the service of the rich and elegant of Europe. During the day, the Allee was a constantly changing parade of fashionable ladies—beautiful and plain, shapely and gross, strolling along on the arm of their escorts, intent on seeing and being seen. In the course of one afternoon's duty at the Trinkhalle, where his royal master was attending a reception, Morton has seen one plump, red-haired matron strut by three times, each time in a different dress! That seemed to be the essence of Baden-Baden nowadays; the provision of a graceful, restrained back-drop to the display of opulence. When Morton had been told of the trip, he had looked forward to some modest play at the tables; only to find

1

that the casino had been closed by the joyless hand of German protestantism. Not that this prevented gambling; it merely transferred it to hotel suites and private houses. But at least the politicians could claim that the town no longer lived on immoral earnings!

Morton reached the road junction and glanced up Gunzen-bachstrasse; the German detective was nowhere in sight. He stepped into a patch of moonlight and took out his watch. Almost two o'clock in the morning. The house was still in darkness—apart from the glow in the bedroom window. Morton gave a snort of self-mockery. It was bizarre that he, a detective-constable in the City of London police, should find himself doing guard duty in a German spa town. It was certainly not what he had expected, when he had accepted the six-month tour of duty with the Prince of Wales's household police. He had scarcely taken up duty, when the Prince had been asked to be a member of a Royal Commission on the Aged Poor. The offer had been accepted with alacrity. No doubt it was both surprising and gratifying for him to be given a job of some importance, instead of merely opening new hospitals and holding garden parties. He had bustled about elatedly, vowing to attend every one of the commission's sessions, and declaring that he would happily forego his summer holiday in France next year. Then self-interest had reasserted itself and he had announced that, in compensation, he was going to Baden-Baden for the final race meeting of the eighteen ninety-two programme. Inevitably, of course, there was a further consideration—and she must be unusually attractive, for him to give up his stag-shooting in Scotland!

Morton began to pace slowly back along the Allee. The late September night was cold, and he was glad that he had brought his heavy ulster. It was almost three years since he had done a spell of night duty, on the beat. Some officers preferred it; there was none of the daytime tangle of horses and carts, no throngs of clerks and messenger-boys. At night the City of London was another world, its buildings gaunt and empty, its streets deserted. After midnight there was almost a presumption that anyone still about, was up to no good. Well, perhaps it was not so very different here!

If he had had any choice in the matter, Morton would have preferred to stay in London. But the Metropolitan police sergeant, who was in charge of them, had brusquely overruled his protests. It was the first time that a member of another force had been seconded to his squad, and he seemed to take it as a personal slight. The knowledge that Morton had been appointed at the prince's own insistence, had even strengthened his determination. He had pointed out Morton's fluent command of German and French, and asserted that he had never had a constable so well qualified to accompany the prince on foreign trips. Moreover, he had said with a smirk, Morton would easily pass for a gentleman, with his accent and easy manner; he was the obvious choice. As a result he had been spending his days at the race-track, his evenings outside some private gambling-room or other, and a good part of each night in the Lichtentaler Allee. At least the heir to the throne had plenty of stamina! Though he was passing his time more pleasantly than was his personal detective.

Morton halted at the path that formed the western boundary of the property, and looked around him. Nothing stirred. The gas lamps glowed along the river bank, the carriage still stood under the trees, its driver dozing on his box. Everything was in order. He turned and made his way into the darkness of the path.

One could hardly blame the sergeant, he reflected. It was he who was the oddity. In a sense, life was getting back at him for his lofty resolve to be of service to his fellow men. As a young man with very considerable personal wealth and a growing reputation as a sportsman, one would have expected to find him at the centre of the social set, not grinding away at the routine duties of a policeman. To the sergeant, it must appear to be condescension; do-gooding of the worst possible kind. At times, Morton could accept that that was uncomfortably near the truth. After experiencing it for a year, he had genuinely become sated with the vacuous routines which passed for enjoyment among the leisure classes, and had been looking for a more satisfying way of spending his life. He had been arrogant enough to voice his dissatisfactions at a dinner-party where the Commissioner of the City Police, Sir William

Sumner, was also a guest. With some scepticism, Sir William
had invited him to join his force, and make his way from the
bottom, strictly on merit. He had accepted the challenge, and
in four years had progressed from uniformed constable to
detective constable! But at least it was purely on merit. He
flattered himself that Sergeant Bragg, his gruff and down-
to-earth mentor, was beginning to regard him merely as a good
policeman, rather than a socialite playing at it. Most of the
time, Morton could convince himself that he was just as
committed as the ex-army men who made up the bulk of the
force, and had little better open to them. But he had reservations, there was no denying it. He had gone into the force with
a strong determination to succeed; but at the same time, he had
promised himself that the moment he ceased to obtain any
satisfaction from it, he would resign. Acknowledging that he
had this escape route had so far made him the more persistent
in finding a quixotic contentment with a policeman's lot. But
he had always seen that function in idealised terms—protecting
the vulnerable, upholding the law, curbing the aggression of
the strong. His present duty was at best an unwelcome
interlude. He would, of course, go through with it; but if he
failed to get back under Sergeant Bragg at the end of his tour,
then he would probably resign. He remembered Bragg's
sardonic smile when they parted. In all probability, the
sergeant had a good idea of what was entailed; he had no doubt
thought it would do him good!

There was a certain irony in the notion that he, the scion of
a wealthy and ancient family, would be spending the weeks
around Christmas at Sandringham, the prince's country seat—
probably sharing a room over the stables with an equerry, or
the valet of a guest. His days would be spent toiling across the
fields, helping to gather the slaughtered pheasants; putting up
the tent where the ladies would be compelled to come, to
applaud and take luncheon. Well, he would certainly get a
servant's-eye view of the proceedings. To that extent it might
be helpful in the future, but he could hardly believe that it
would be enjoyable.

At the end of the hedge that ran to the south of the grounds,
Morton met the German detective. They exchanged a few

muttered observations, but the man was uneasy, anxious to be back on his rounds. He had the harder part, of course. There were greenhouses, outbuildings and stables at the rear of the house. Any intruder, or would-be assassin, would approach from that side. Morton wondered what the man thought of being detailed to guard the middle-aged, short, rotund heir to the British throne, on an adulterous visit to a French *demi-mondaine*. It was certainly not to be taken lightly. The Russian nihilists had become very active of late, and had taken to exploding dynamite bombs by means of electricity. The British royal family was linked in marriage with the Tsars: what greater *action d'éclat* could they achieve than to blow to pieces the heir to the greatest empire the world had ever known?

Morton turned and retraced his steps towards the river. In the still, cold air nothing moved. The lights of the carriage flickered near the bridge; it was now half past two . . . He began to wonder what he could undertake, if he were to leave the police force. Now that he had played cricket for England on their last Australian tour, he could look to spend more time in the game. In many ways he would welcome that; though it would not absorb all his time and energy. His thoughts turned to The Priory, his childhood home. But there was no opening for him there. His parents resolutely pretended that his elder brother Edwin, paralysed by a bullet while soldiering in the Sudan, was managing the estates. It was patently untrue, but the fiction gave him something to live for. Morton sighed irritably and turned back along the Allee. There was, of course, no reason why he should not get married—apart from the fact that the only girl he admired enough clearly had no intention of marrying anyone. Moreover, he resented the implication that he should be content with the role of begetting the future heirs to The Priory. There seemed to be no escape from his dilemma . . . He glanced towards the front of the house, and saw a light glowing bright in the hall. The door opened, and he caught a momentary glimpse of dark hair and a creamy skin; then the door closed and the Prince of Wales walked briskly down the steps towards him. Morton blew briefly on his whistle and the German detective appeared round the side of

the house. Now was the moment of greatest risk. Morton heard
the carriage starting towards them. He peered into the deep
shadows, but all was motionless. The Prince hurried unspeak-
ing into the carriage, and it moved quietly away. The German
detective was now walking alongside one door, and Morton
took up position by the other. At least, by three o'clock he
ought to be in his cramped little bed at the top of the hotel,
while his master undressed, yet again, in the palatial suite on
the first floor.

CHAPTER ——————
—————————— ONE

Detective Sergeant Joseph Bragg strolled up Ludgate Hill in the evening sunshine. He felt content, even pleased with life. After a cold and depressing winter, the late April sun had suddenly blazed down all day; and, according to the *Standard*, they were in for a long period of good weather. It was amazing how quickly the women had responded to the change. Yesterday wrapped up in heavy coats, this evening they were clad in bright cotton dresses. But soon they would find it chilly, as the sun went down. For his part, he decided, he would give it a few days, before shedding his woolen vest. A young woman was walking briskly towards him, her breasts bouncing under her cotton blouse. It made you glad to be alive!

For once, he had bested Inspector Cotton, as well. The miners were striking in the north, and there had been the usual near-riots on the picket lines. The police up there had asked for help from other forces, and Cotton had wanted to send one of Bragg's constables. He had managed to fight him off, on the grounds that, with Morton seconded to the Marlborough House squad, he was already short-handed. Now Morton was due back on Monday, and they had forgotten all about the idea. He glanced up at the dome of St Paul's Cathedral, the gold cross gleaming in the last rays of the sun. If only they could clear away the few buildings at the top, there would be a spectacular view of the cathedral, all the way up Ludgate Hill. As it was, the nearer you got to it, the more it was obscured. He pulled out his battered watch. He just had time for a pint of beer at the Goose and Gridiron, before going home for supper. He could listen to the bell-practice for a bit, as well—though not for too long! Last time, he'd become so caught up in it, that his supper had been spoiled. Mrs Jenks, his landlady, hadn't forgiven him for a week! He crossed in front of Queen Anne's statue, her eyes resolutely averted from the cathedral, and went into the public bar.

He took his beer over to a bench by the open door. The pub was quiet. Most of its customers were clerks from the offices around. There was no way you could get near to the bar at lunchtime; and it was the same, for a good half-hour, when work finished at six o'clock. Now there were only a few stragglers; the rest had gone to catch their trains back to the tidy new suburbs and their rosy-cheeked wives and children. Till six o'clock next morning, that is; then they'd be starting back to the daily grind once more. Well, that wasn't for Joe Bragg. Much better the grimy terraces in the greatest city in the world, where there was constant bustle, always something new, where you could really feel alive . . . The bells were beginning . . . a gentle murmur, all seeming to strike together, then gradually each bell becoming distinct, separated from the others, as they rang more slowly.

Bragg stretched himself, then took out his pipe and lit it. He had had enough of living in the country by the time he was fourteen. Mind you, that had been real country, not a garden suburb. A little church and a few houses, in deepest Dorset; that was Turners Puddle. Not even a pub! . . . Now the bells were ringing evenly, in a descending scale. If you listened carefully, you could count twelve distinct notes. Any moment they would start their changeringing and, in the complicated pattern, you would not know how many bells there were—or care for that matter, as you were enveloped in their cheerful, rich resonance . . . There they went . . . Bragg concentrated, determined to unravel the pattern at least for a few moments . . . No, he had lost it already. Much better to lean back and allow the sound to wash over you . . . It was all so perfect, so, well, celestial in a way. You would never think that there were men up there, pulling ropes. If anything could lure him back to churchgoing, it would be the bells . . . Suddenly, there was a discordant clangour, as two bells sounded together. For a moment the others went on ringing, then came to a stop in an ugly jangle. The unexpected silence was oppressive, disquieting. Bragg put down his glass, and went outside. He gazed up at the bell-tower, but nothing seemed amiss. He was about to go back inside the pub, when he saw a man burst out of the west door of the cathedral.

'Help! Help!' he shouted.

Bragg ran across and grabbed him by the arm. 'I am a police officer,' he said. 'What has happened?'

'It's the dean!' cried the man. 'He's got tangled up in the rope.'

'Is he badly hurt?' asked Bragg.

'I think so. He's up by the roof.'

'Right,' said Bragg decisively. 'You go and find the beat constable, and bring him here. How do I get inside the tower?'

'Through All Souls chapel, just to the left, there's a small archway in the corner.'

Bragg hurried up the cathedral steps, and through the heavy wooden doors into the chapel. It was gloomy, in the fading light, but the open doorway was a dark blotch to the left of the altar. Beyond it was a narrow spiral staircase, where Bragg had to slow down lest he should lose his footing. He crossed a stone landing to another spiral staircase, which brought him to the ringing room. Inside was a huddle of men, shocked and pale.

'I am a police sergeant,' Bragg said. 'Is there anyone in charge here?'

A bulky man with a heavy moustache came forward. 'I am James Pettit, the conductor of the band,' he said.

'What happened?'

'I hardly know,' replied Pettit, his eyes drifting upwards to the rafters. 'He must have become entangled in the rope, somehow.'

Bragg peered at the dark outline in the shadows. All he could see was a pair of boots projecting from a black cassock, and above that the white blobs of the hands.

'Did anyone see what happened?' Bragg reiterated.

There was a dull shaking of heads.

'We were just beginning a touch of Stedman Cinques,' Pettit explained. 'The dean was ringing the tenor, and in that method the tenor keeps in the same position, beating the time, as it were. The other ringers would be concentrating on each other.'

'I see. Well, we will get him down as soon as the constable arrives. I would like Mr Pettit to stay behind, but the rest of you can go home. If you recollect anything about the accident, let me know through him.'

The ringers began to put on their coats, then one of them strode over to Bragg.

'I'm Horrex, the steeplekeeper,' he said with a slight cockney accent. 'I look after the bells. You can't get him down with the bells like they are, you'd get killed.'

'Why is that?'

'You will have to release the other end of the rope and lower him.'

'Oh, my goodness!' exclaimed Pettit. 'We shall have to ring the bells down.'

'I don't understand you,' said Bragg.

'At the moment, the bells are standing with their mouths upwards, kept just off-balance by a stay. The slightest touch on one, and it could swing down and crush you . . . Come along, gentlemen, let us bring them down as quickly as possible.'

The ringers turned back reluctantly, and each took his place on a circle of large wooden boxes. They took hold of their ropes, and watched Pettit for the signal. Dazed as they were, they pulled off in order; but the ringing quickly became a discordant clashing, as the lighter bells sounded ever more rapidly until they were stilled. As the last bell ceased, there was a clatter of boots on the staircase and a policeman appeared, his helmet reverently in his hand.

'Ah, there you are, constable," said Bragg. 'Lend me your lantern, will you?'

He shone the light upwards, and could make out the head lolling sideways.

'He looks bad,' murmured Horrex.

'For my money, he's dead,' replied Bragg bluntly. 'Constable, find the beadle, and tell him to inform the coroner. Then come back and give me a hand . . . Everyone else go home, except for Mr Pettit and Mr Horrex.' He shone the lantern upwards again. The dean's body was suspended within a foot of a huge oak beam which supported the ceiling.

'How high is this room?' he asked.

'Thirty feet,' replied Horrex.

'And how long is the rope?'

'About seventy feet.'

'So if we release the other end of the rope, we should be able to lower him to the ground. Is that what you are saying?'

'Yes. But there's not much room up there, and he's a heavy man.'

'I reckon I could hold him, if you can deal with the rope. Is there room enough for the two of us to squeeze in?'

'We can try,' said Horrex.

'Good. Mr Pettit, the constable will be back in a moment. Will the two of you stand by here, to take the weight as we lower him down?'

Pettit looked up apprehensively. 'Yes . . . yes, I am sure we can manage that.'

'Right. Let's get on then.'

He followed Horrex up the spiral staircase, which became progressively narrower until his shoulders were rubbing the sides. Then he found himself in the open air; in a high-vaulted chamber, with a great circular aperture in each wall. Up here in the tower there was still some vestige of daylight, and Bragg could make out several large bells, crammed in a heavy timber frame at floor level.

'What are the wheels for?' he asked.

'They are mounted on one end of the bell's headstock—you could think of that as the axle—and the rope is attached to the rim of the wheel. You start ringing with the bell in the raised position. You pull on the rope, and the wheel swings the bell down, through an arc, until you check it.'

'And when you next pull, it goes back to where it started from?'

'That's right . . . The tenor bell is in that far corner.'

Bragg shone the lantern to where Horrex was pointing. The top of a bell was visible beside a large wheel. A piece of wood jutted upwards from the headstock; around it, and around the wheel and the bell, was a tangle of rope.

'That's funny,' Horrex muttered.

'What is?'

'Nothing. I expected it would have been the stay that broke . . . I shall have to disconnect the rope from the rim of the wheel, before we can untangle it. The rope goes down to the ringing room through a hole, over there. If you can take the weight, I will be as quick as I can.'

Bragg crawled along one of the beams and, squatting down with his back to the wheel of the next bell, pulled on the rope to ease the strain on the knots. Horrex had been right, the dean was very heavy.

'I've got the rope off the wheel,' Horrex grunted. 'It won't be long now.'

It could not be any too soon, thought Bragg. He was bending half-forward, and twisting to one side in the confined space. He could feel a sharp pain growing under his shoulder blade and the rope was cutting into his hands. He hauled upwards, in an effort to straighten himself, and heard a dull thud as the dean's head hit the ceiling.

'Just this last knot, and it will be free,' said Horrex . . . 'That's it. Now I will hold him, while you stand up. You will get a better purchase then.'

Bragg eased himself upright and, taking a fresh grip on the rope, began to lower the dean to the ground. There came a shout from below and the rope went slack. Bragg released his end and it disappeared through the hole. They clambered back to the doorway, and went gingerly down to the ringing room. The body of the dean lay on the floor, the bell-rope biting into the flesh of his neck, his eyes staring out of a purple face.

Bragg felt his heart. 'He's dead all right,' he pronounced.

'Constable, will you see that the body is taken to the mortuary—rope and all? Mr Pettit, perhaps you would be good enough to inform the authorities. Has he any family?'

'Why, yes, he has a wife . . . I will go to see the senior residentiary canon. He will know what is best.' Pettit gave a final glance at the body and hurried out.

'Now, Mr Horrex,' said Bragg, 'something surprised you up there. I want you to come up again, and show me what it was.' He led the way up the narrow staircase, until they were once more crouched over the tenor bell.

'You see this piece of wood sticking upwards?' asked Horrex. 'This is called the stay. When the bell is in the ringing position, with its mouth upwards, the stay is pointing down, and touching what we call the slider . . . Here, you will see it better on this one.' He twisted round to a small bell behind them.

'You mean that flat piece of wood below the bell, at right-angles to the wheel?'

'That's right. It pivots on a pin at one end, and can slide about twelve inches in a slot at the other end. The stay catches on the slider as the bell comes to the top, and pushes it across until the ringer checks the bell. Then when the bell is swung round and up the other way, the stay pushes the slider back again. We normally leave the bells in the standing position. To achieve that, the ringer allows the bell to go just a fraction beyond the point of balance. Once the slider is pushed to the end of its travel, it holds the bell at rest.'

'What is the weight of the tenor bell?' asked Bragg.

'A little over three tons.'

'Good God! I am surprised anyone can move something that size. And you say that it can be held up by a wooden stay, that tapers to no more than three inches square?'

'It has worked all right for centuries.'

'So what was puzzling you?' asked Bragg.

'Well, the slider is fairly heavy, and made of oak; the stay is ash. The idea is that if anything goes wrong, the stay will break first, allowing the bell to go round in a complete circle. That prevents damage to the headstock.'

'But that didn't happen this time?'

'No. Could you shine the lantern downwards? There's the

slider . . . See, it has split at the pivot.' Horrex stretched himself along the beam, and groped beneath the bell. 'Got it.' He pushed himself backwards on to his knees, and brought the stout piece of timber into the light of the lantern. One end had been wrenched apart and the smashed piece hung drunkenly down.

'And you say that this doesn't happen often?'

'I have never seen it before. What is more, I could have sworn it was perfect yesterday. I'm a master carpenter, which is why I became steeplekeeper.' He smiled briefly. 'We rang the bells down after service on Sunday, so that I could check them, and grease the bearings.' He turned the slider over in the lantern-light. 'Hey! Look at this!'

'What?'

'Chisel marks! On either side of the pivot-hole.'

'Are you sure?'

'Of course I'm sure! See for yourself!' He thrust the wood into Bragg's hands, and began to scramble back along the beam. Bragg followed him ponderously and came up with him in the ringing room. He was kneeling before an open cupboard, peering into a wooden box. 'Look!' he cried. 'Somebody has been at my tools. I never leave them like that. See the handle of that chisel? Somebody has been hitting it with a hammer!'

'Is the cupboard normally locked?' asked Bragg.

'No. The grille at the entrance to the ringing room is locked when we are not here, and that has always been enough.'

'Who holds the key?'

'Mr Pettit has one key, and the other is with Mr Wilkins the dean's virger.'

'I'm afraid I shall have to ask you to let me have a written statement of the circumstances,' said Bragg heavily. 'It looks to me as if the dean was murdered.'

By noon next day, Bragg had been formally appointed coroner's officer for the case. He decided that, even though the cause of death appeared to be obvious, he would start, as usual, by hearing what the pathologist had to say. He hurried along the congested streets, their rutted surface already dusty in the

warm sun, and went up the steps of the Golden Lane mortuary.
Dr Burney received him with his usual loose smile.

'Ah, Sergeant Bragg! I was expecting you. The coroner was
along an hour or so ago, and said he would be asking for you
on the case.'

'I was called to the scene almost as soon as the incident
occurred,' said Bragg. 'I helped to get him down.'

'Well, it seems a straightforward enough case,' Burney
remarked turning to the corpse, supine on his slab. 'I must
confess that it is outside my experience—as an accidental death,
that is.'

'Why do you say that?' asked Bragg quickly.

Burney gave a sly grin. 'Death was caused by a fracture-
dislocation of the cervical spine. See,' he took up a probe and
pointed. 'I have dissected out the second and third vertebrae.
There is an almost complete rupture of the spinal cord.'

'I am not surprised, with a three-ton bell at the other end of
the rope.'

'That would certainly account for the severe laceration of the
tissue.'

'Are you saying that it was not an accident, sir?' asked
Bragg.

'By no means, but this is precisely the type of injury caused
by judicial hanging.'

'Hmn . . . Well, I don't think any of the ringers is a
hangman, but I am not satisfied it was an accident.'

'Indeed, sergeant?' Burney's slack mouth sagged open in
anticipation.

'I cannot understand yet how the facts link up, but the
mechanism of the bell the dean was ringing, had been
interfered with before the practice.'

'So you think it was murder?'   .

'I don't know. The obvious candidate for splitting the
bell-slider was the man who drew my attention to it.'

'Well, I have found nothing in my examination which is
inconsistent with accidental death.'

'Are there any factors which might have contributed to it?'
asked Bragg.

'You mean, did he have apoplexy while ringing? No, the

dean was in robust health. There was not even any indication
that he might have been indulging in *vino sacro*, and thus
impaired his judgement!'

'And what about the rope?'

'It was merely a simple loop around the neck. The initial jerk
of the rope upwards would have been enough to fracture the
spine and embed the noose in the surface tissues. The weight
of the body would have kept it in place thereafter.'

'At least he was killed instantaneously?'

'Oh yes, sergeant. There is not the slightest doubt about
that.'

Bragg found Wilkins, the dean's virger, in his little house in
Amen Court. He answered the door with a napkin tucked in his
ample waistcoat, and Bragg accepted an invitation to join him
in some cold pie and pickles.

'This is a bad business,' he said, as he poured Bragg a glass
of beer. 'I can't even say how I'll be fixed myself. It's a
personal appointment, and the new dean might have his own
ideas about whom he wants as his virger.'

'What is the dean's job?' asked Bragg, spearing a gherkin.

'Well, he runs the cathedral—not only arranging the services
and that, but seeing it is kept in repair, and properly furnished.
It's really his cathedral, not the bishop's.'

'And you?'

'I'm his right-hand man on the secular side, as you might
say.'

'You hire and discharge the cleaners and so on?'

'The dean always had the final word on that. My job was to
oversee all the lay staff, and report to him.'

'What sort of a man was he?'

'Dean Hadley was a real gentleman. Strong-willed, mind
you— you have to be in that job—but fair. I've never seen him
lose his temper . . . I reckon he really loved the place. He
never seemed to be at home; always pottering around, thinking
of ways to improve the cathedral.'

'How could he be a bell-ringer, as well as take part in the
services?' asked Bragg.

'Oh, he wasn't a regular ringer. He used to take a turn

sometimes, to keep his hand in. Mind you, he'd been very keen when he was younger.'

'I see. What time do you lock up the cathedral at night?' asked Bragg, changing tack.

'Six o'clock. Sometimes it is a bit later, if there are more than usual at evensong. They like to look around a bit afterwards.'

'And last night?'

'About five past six.'

'You are sure about that?'

'Yes, I am always the last out.'

'What about the night before?'

'Monday? It was on the dot, that night.'

'I am told that Mr Horrex, the steeplekeeper, checked and greased the bells on Monday.'

'I wouldn't know about that,' said Wilkins dismissively. 'They have their own key to the west door.'

'You have no control over their comings and goings, then?'

'Dear me, no! They're an uppity lot. They get very upset if you interfere in their affairs. Sometimes you would think St Paul's exists just to hold their bells!'

'Is there friction between the ringers and the cathedral staff, then?'

'No, not really. They just go their own way.'

'And did the dean put up with that?'

'Oh, he was one of them. He didn't seem to care that half of them are atheists. As long as he got his bells rung, they could do what they liked.'

'So, how many keys are there to the doors of the cathedral?'

'There are keys to all the doors, but the only ones in use are for the west door and the dean's entrance, in the south-west tower.'

'Where are the keys kept, that are not in use?'

'In the safe, in the dean's office.'

'Who holds the key to the safe?' asked Bragg.

'The dean, normally, but the senior canon has got it now. He will have to stand in, until the new dean is appointed.'

'Suppose he lost the key to the safe?'

'We could get a new one from Chubbs inside a couple of days.'

'Has the canon checked the contents of the safe?'

'Yes. I showed him where everything is, this morning.'

'Were you with him when he opened the safe?'

'Yes. He took everything out, so I could tell him what it was.'

'And the keys, were they in order?'

'Oh yes.' Wilkins gave a self-satisfied smile.

'So, we are concerned with the keys for just the two doors. How many are there for the dean's entrance?'

'The dean has one, and there is another in the key-cabinet in my office.'

'Is that all?'

'Yes.'

'And what about the west door?'

'I have one, the bell-ringers have one, and there is a spare in my key-cabinet.'

'Have you let your key out of your possession in the last few days?' Bragg asked abruptly.

'Never! At night it sleeps on my bedside table.'

'Where is this office of yours?'

'Upstairs on the south side of the cathedral, near the library.'

'Is that open to the public?'

'No. You get to it from the vestibule of the dean's entrance.'

'And nobody could slip into the vestibule, and up the stairs, while you were not looking?'

'No. The door from the nave is kept locked.'

'Is this key-cabinet kept locked?'

'It is.' The virger fished under his napkin, and drew out a small shiny key.

'And it has not been forced open, or anything like that?'

'No.'

'Has anyone else got a key to the cabinet?'

'Only the dean.'

'Has anyone asked you for the key to the cabinet in the last few days, or for a key from it?'

'No.'

'Hmn.' Bragg pondered for a while, chewing the ends of his ragged moustache; then he roused himself.

'Let's think about the staircase up to the bell-tower,' he suggested. 'Is the door in the little chapel kept locked?'

'It is.'

'Who has the keys?'

'The ringers have one, the only other is in my key-cabinet—we have to give the staircase a clean occasionally!'

'Does the same apply to the grille at the entrance to the ringing room?'

'It does.'

'Is there any other way into the bell-chamber?'

Wilkins considered for a moment. 'There is a door off the spiral staircase, that gives on to the west gallery, but it is always kept locked.'

'How many keys are there to that?'

'Only the one—and it's in my cabinet.'

'Is the door still locked?'

'Well, it was this morning at eight o'clock. I can vouch for that,' said Wilkins huffily.

'And how do you get to this west gallery?'

'Up the staircase, from the vestibule in the dean's entrance.'

'Which the public does not have access to?'

'That's right. Now, if you don't mind, I must get back. If the arrangements for the dean's funeral are not perfect, I wouldn't want to meet him in heaven!'

Bragg spent an hour that afternoon wandering around St Paul's, inspecting the side chapels, looking for places where a man might hide. On the ground floor there were comparatively few. It was not like a medieval cathedral, with lots of chapels and chantrys. The walls were comparatively unobstructed—that is if you ignored the grandiose monuments to long-forgotten generals and sea-captains. That left only three chapels—one of which gave access to the bell-tower. He decided that, during the next few days, he would visit the church at six o'clock, and see for himself how the virgers went about clearing it. Then he sauntered down Fleet Street to the Temple, where Sir Rufus Stone, the coroner for the City of London, had his chambers.

When he was admitted, Sir Rufus was engaged in replacing some weighty legal tomes in his bookcase.

'Ah, Bragg. I was hoping to see you . . . Just a moment, while I tidy up. I have to earn my living somehow, to allow me the luxury of administering justice in the City for a mere pittance.'

'I hope you won, sir.'

Sir Rufus turned his leonine head. 'Of course I won, Bragg,' he said fiercely. 'Do not be flippant!'

Bragg suppressed a smile. 'I came to see you about the dean of St Paul's, sir.'

'A sad affair.' The coroner took his usual pose in front of the fireplace, where, despite the warmth of the day, a few coals glowed dully. 'I knew him quite well, Bragg. We often played whist together . . . I shall have to find another partner now.'

'What kind of man was he?' asked Bragg.

'Oh, quiet and reserved. Not a lot to say for himself, but he could finesse like the devil himself.'

'How is his wife taking it?'

'I cannot say. We did not know them socially—though I have met her at garden parties, on occasion. You have seen Burney, I suppose?'

'Yes, sir. His report will be consistent with there having been an accident, all right.'

'What do you mean, Bragg? Are you suggesting it could have been anything else?'

'It could have been murder.'

'Murder?' Sir Rufus's eyes widened in incredulity. 'But at least another eleven people saw it happen! You are being fanciful, man.'

'Perhaps. But the accident only happened because the slider on the bell broke; and the slider broke because it had been split open with a chisel.'

'Are you sure, Bragg?'

'The steeplekeeper had checked the bells, only the previous night. He swears it was in perfect order then.'

'But Hadley was not a regular ringer. How did the perpetrator know he was going to be ringing at that practice—and, moreover, that he was going to be at that particular bell?'

'I cannot yet say, sir. But equally, I cannot ignore the evidence of the slider.'

'I suppose this steeplekeeper's word can be relied on?' remarked Sir Rufus dubiously.

'He tells me he is a master carpenter, so he should be able to recognize chisel marks when he sees them.'

'Well, I see no reason to postpone the funeral, because of these speculations of yours, Bragg . . . Dammit, I cannot for the life of me see who would benefit from his murder. So far as I am aware, his wife is his only relative, and she would doubtless inherit his estate. I take it you would agree that she can be ruled out.'

'Having been up in the bell-chamber,' said Bragg, 'I think any woman could be ruled out.'

'And it is not as if anyone could kill him in order to succeed to his office. Although the chapter of the cathedral theoretically choose the dean, in fact they elect—as a pure formality—the nominee of the Crown. I cannot see Mr Gladstone being influenced overmuch in favour of any place-seeker.'

'Then, if he was murdered, it must arise from his private life.'

'Unless they got the wrong man, Bragg. Do you know if someone else was due to ring that bell at the practice?'

'I have not got around to asking yet, sir.'

'Well I suggest you do,' Sir Rufus glared. 'I want the perpetrator of this outrage caught. It would still be murder, even if someone else was the intended victim—or manslaughter at the very least . . . Yes, Bragg. We will expose the truth of this affair to the light of day!'

CHAPTER _____
_____ *TWO*

Catherine Marsden descended the stairs jauntily and went into the breakfast room, where her father was staring moodily out of the window.

'Is mamma not down yet?' she asked, glancing at the pristine table.

'Now, you know that she does not come down on the morning after the press viewing, until I have vented my spleen on someone or something else.'

'Then, let me offer myself as the sacrificial victim,' she said with a smile, and picked up the neatly folded copy of *The Times*. 'What do they say?'

'I have not ventured to read it yet.'

'Well, if you will stop prowling, I will put you out of your misery.'

Her father sat down reluctantly, while Catherine turned the pages.

'Here it is,' she announced brightly, and began to skim through the first paragraphs. ' "This year's Summer Exhibition at the Royal Academy can hardly be said to be of vintage quality",' she read. 'Typical of *The Times's* Olympian approach! . . . They are complaining about the poor hanging of the exhibits, and the fact that several well-known artists are not exhibiting at all, this year . . . Ah! Here you are! Are you ready?'

'Let me know the worst.'

' "Mr William Marsden has exhibited six canvases. Among them is a portrait of a young woman, entitled *The Opening Flower*. It is a painting of great sensitivity and subtlety. The subject holds a rosebud to her cheek" . . . Papa! It's not my picture? The one you did last autumn?'

'It is!'

'Oh, how could you?!'

'I thought it was rather good. Go on.'

' "The subject holds a rosebud to her cheek",' Catherine continued reluctantly, ' "and one is invited to suppose that she displays the sensations conjured up by inhaling its fragrance. Here one must take issue with the imagery implicit in the title. This is no demure innocent on the threshold of life, but a self-assured beauty." ' Catherine lowered the paper and glared at her father's delighted face.

'Is that all?' he asked.

She turned back to her reading. ' "There is a zest in the skin tones, a hint of challenge in the sensuous mouth and the mocking eyes. This is a remarkable and somewhat disturbing painting, which is undoubtedly the most intriguing canvas in the exhibition." '

'What about the other pictures?'

'Nothing about them,' Catherine replied shortly. 'It goes on to Pratt after that.'

'Huh! Typical of a newspaper. Still, they did us proud on the portrait.'

'Papa, I am very annoyed with you!'

'Annoyed?' he asked, feigning astonishment.

'Why did you not tell me that you were exhibiting it?'

'It never occurred to me that you might object. How was I to know that it would provoke such a notice?'

'It was that stupid title, which gave the reviewer his opening. He would not have been able to resist it.'

Mr Marsden reached over the table, and squeezed her arm. 'I am sorry. One has to do it, because the public look for a moralistic story in everything. It seemed to be the obvious title; perhaps I did not give it enough thought.'

'I wish you had not submitted it at all,' said Catherine chidingly.

'Nonsense! It is the best thing I have ever done. And the critics clearly agree with me. It is time we got away from these vapid pictures of callow young women, and painted what is really there. Think of Goya and Velasquez—every facet of their sitter's personality is on the canvas, king or peasant, like it or not. Compare them with the insipid society portraits we churn out nowadays.'

'I do not see why you have to use me to salve your artistic conscience, papa,' said Catherine crossly.

'Come now, in forty years your grandchildren will gaze on it, and know exactly what you were like at their age.'

'I sincerely hope not! Journalists only use the word "sensuous", when they would prefer to say "sensual" but dare not.'

'Journalism is your business, and painting is mine,' said her father cheerfully. 'I tell you, that portrait is you to perfection— and I am proud of you both.'

Morton strode up the stairs to Bragg's office with a light heart. It was good to be back in the old surroundings; good, also, to have a worthwhile job again, instead of being nursemaid to pampered royalty. At the end of his tour, he had spent a week on leave at his parents' home in Kent. But even this had not been totally satisfying. His mother was taking a house in Curzon Street for the season, since his sister Emily was at last to achieve her ambition of being presented at court. The Priory was in turmoil, with frenzied packing of linen, crockery and silver. His father, Sir Henry Morton, had successfully maintained that his duties, as Lord-Lieutenant of Kent, would not allow him to accompany the ladies; so Morton had been pressed into agreeing to act as escort, whenever his duties would permit. Much as he detested society functions, he was looking forward to it. His Aunt Amelia was bringing Violet over from America for a London season, and Morton had a warm regard for his amiable and amusing cousin. All in all, life had taken a decided turn for the better. He rapped on Bragg's door and entered.

'Come back for some real work, have you?' a sly grin peeped from under Bragg's moustache.

'You could say that.'

'Was it not to your liking, then?'

'I wrote my letter of resignation twice, then tore it up.'

'I reckoned that you would go in as a royalist, and come out a republican.'

Morton laughed. 'Not quite, but it was certainly not my idea of police work . . . It is odd, though, how different people really are from their public representation. Our well-beloved Princess Alexandra turns out to be something of a tyrant, who beats her maids with a hairbrush; while the Prince of Wales is, in fact, exceedingly kind and considerate.'

'I don't suppose it will make much difference to me, whichever way they are . . . Right, lad, the only thing of any substance on our plate, at present, is the case of Dr Hadley, the dean of St Paul's.'

'I read about his death in the paper. Are you the coroner's officer?'

'I am, and it is not as straightforward as you would think.'

'From the account in *The Times* it sounded as if it was a pure accident.'

'Well, everything points that way. He was ringing the tenor bell with eleven more people in the room. They had been ringing for five minutes or so in a perfectly normal manner, when somehow the rope gets entangled around the dean's neck and jerks him up to the roof.'

'Surely someone saw exactly what happened?'

'No, lad. It seems impossible, but none of the other eleven will admit to having seen it.' Bragg fumbled in his pocket for his tobacco pouch, and began to cut thin slices of twist with a juice-stained pocket-knife. 'It seems,' he went on, 'that they were doing change ringing, and that particular method called for the dean's bell to beat the time, while the others rang in different positions around his.'

'I have watched the ringers at home, on occasion,' said Morton. 'It has always struck me as an exceedingly difficult art.'

'As I understand it, the others were following a different bell every time,' said Bragg.

'I see . . . So they would be concentrating on the person they were going to follow. That seems reasonable.'

'Except that every time round, someone had to follow the dean.' Bragg began to rub the tobacco lovingly between his palms. 'You might accept that, since the tenor didn't move in the sequence, no one needed to watch him particularly. But they stand around in a ring on crates, and there cannot be more than three feet between each ringer. On their own account, there must have been one person concentrating on each of the ringers on either side of him.'

'So you are not content with their explanation?'

Bragg took his pipe from the ash-tray, and began to feed the shreds of tobacco into its bowl with his finger.

'On its own, the fact that they did not see what happened is no more than surprising. But when we went up to the bell-chamber, to release the rope and get him down, we found that a bit of the machinery had been tampered with. Horrex, the steeplekeeper, had checked it the previous night, and says it was all right then. Bring me that piece of wood from the cupboard, lad.'

Morton walked over to the corner, and took it from the bottom shelf.

'Right,' said Bragg. 'Hold the broken ends together for the moment, will you? Now this is called the slider. It fits directly under the bell, and parallel with its axle. It pivots on a pin that goes through the hole there, and the other end is free to move a foot or so, between stops on the opposite side of the frame. Follow me?'

'Yes.'

'Now, there is a length of ash wood, called a stay, sticking up from the top of the bell. When they are doing change ringing, they start with the bell resting with its mouth up. In that position, the stay is pointing downwards, and has pushed the slider across, the full length of its travel. In that way the bell is held, just off balance.'

'I am surprised that something so flimsy can stop the swing of a bell,' said Morton. 'They must be enormously heavy.'

'The one that killed the dean is over three tons. But it's a matter of balance, they tell me, and it seems to work. Anyway, when they start, they pull the rope and the bell swings down. It rings just before it reaches the top again. Between strokes, the ringer checks the bell at the top of its swing. So, although the stay touches the slider, it does not push it across as far as the stop.'

'And on the next stroke, the stay would push the slider back again a little way.'

'That's right.'

'So, what went wrong on this occasion?'

'Turn it over, lad. See those marks on either side of the hole? What do they look like to you?'

'Chisel marks!' exclaimed Morton . . . 'and along the grain. Weakened like that, it could only be a matter of time before it broke. What would happen then?'

'The bell would go over the top in a circle, and from what I saw last Tuesday, it would wind the rope right up.'

'But not necessarily take the ringer with it?'

'I don't know, lad. Perhaps not . . . Then there is the other side.' Bragg laid a match across the bowl of his pipe, and sucked noisily. 'Wilkins, the dean's virger, who seems a bright enough chap, keeps a tight hold on the keys of the cathedral. There were only twenty-four hours between Horrex's checking the mechanism, and the start of the practice. So far as I can make out, during the whole of that time the keys have been locked up in Wilkins's office—apart, that is, from the set held by the ringers themselves.'

'Would only they have the necessary knowledge to tamper with the mechanism?'

'One would assume so . . . And, of course, we must proceed on the basis that whoever did it must be regarded as having intended the results of their actions.'

'When is the inquest?' asked Morton.

'Next week sometime, I expect. Sir Rufus is hopping mad, going on about bringing the truth to light—more because he has lost his whist partner than anything else, I reckon.'

'It all seems rather problematical,' said Morton doubtfully.

'Not the way Inspector Cotton sees it.' Bragg put his pipe in the ash-tray. 'According to him, Horrex is our man. He has the knowledge, he admits working on the bells the night before, and he would have concealed the broken slider if I hadn't gone up with him. Any magistrate would give me a warrant, according to the Inspector.'

'So why not arrest him?'

Bragg ruminated for some moments, staring out of the window. 'No, lad. It won't do. I was with him when he brought the broken slider from under the bell. He only saw the chisel marks when he turned it over. I could swear he was taken by surprise . . . Another thing. He was upset, because whoever did it had used his chisel and damaged the handle. Horrex is a master carpenter. I don't believe a craftsman of that standing could bring himself to ruin a boxwood handle with a hammer, to save his life. Come on, lad, let's go and poke about a bit.'

They strolled along the sunlit streets, till they were standing in St Paul's churchyard, gazing up at the bell tower.

'Amazing that they can get twelve bells in there, isn't it?' remarked Bragg. 'They are packed in a great square frame of oak, and not much more than a foot apart. It was no easy matter to get between them to free the dean's body, I can tell you. It would have been a job for you, if you had been around.'

'And, since I have not got your partiality for murder, it might have all gone unnoticed.'

'By the time you are my age, lad, you will have as jaundiced a view of humanity as I have. Come on, let's see if we can find the dean's virger.'

They walked slowly round the nave, and at the end of the tour Bragg had not added to his list of possible hiding places.

'We must be here at half past five this afternoon,' he said. 'I want you to sit by that pillar there, on the south aisle, and I will be here. I want to see how carefully the virgers check that everybody has left the building, before they lock up. Now, grab that fellow in the cassock there, and ask him where his boss is.'

They were taken down to the crypt, where Wilkins was supervising the preparations for the dean's funeral.

'I didn't think they buried people inside churches any more,' Bragg remarked.

'I have never known it before,' said Wilkins, 'and I have been here twelve years. But the dean was very highly regarded, and everyone seemed to want it—and since the present cathedral is barely two hundred years old, there's still plenty of room.'

Morton wondered what qualities had been possessed by the deceased prelate, that his compeers should deem him worthy of being interred beside Nelson and Wellington.

'That door at the entrance to the crypt, Mr Wilkins,' remarked Bragg. 'Is it locked at night?'

'It is, sergeant.'

'So, if anyone stayed behind and hid in here, when you closed up, he would not be able to get out?'

'Not unless he had a key.'

'Who does have?'

'There are only two. I keep one, and the other is in my cabinet.'

'The same old story, eh? Now, when I wrote my notes up last night, I found I'd forgotten to ask you about the door from the nave to the dean's entrance. You said it was kept locked, if you remember. Who has the keys to that?'

'I have one,' said Wilkins, 'and the other is in my cabinet.'

'I make that three thundering great keys you carry around with you,' said Bragg disbelievingly.

In answer, Wilkins dived into the pocket of his cassock, and brought out three large keys on an iron ring. 'All present and correct, sergeant,' he exclaimed with an impish smile, then glanced back self-consciously at the gaping hole in the paving slabs, where the dean was to be interred.

'Can we see this key-cabinet of yours?' asked Bragg.

'Of course.'

Wilkins led them up the stairs from the crypt, across the

floor of the nave, to a pair of immense doors in the south-west corner. He once more took the keys from his pocket and, with Bragg watching intently, he unlocked them.

'You could hardly slip in and out of here unnoticed,' Morton remarked, as they went through.

'They match the pair on the other side—the entrance to All Souls chapel, from where you reach the bell tower,' said Wilkins, carefully locking the doors behind them.

He took them up an elegant staircase, that seemed to spiral up the walls of the tower without visible means of support. Then he led them along a corridor, at the end of which they could see library shelves through an open door. A few paces short of this he stopped and, opening a low door, took them into a small chamber against the south wall of the cathedral. Morton strolled over to the narrow window. The ground was many feet below, and the window did not open.

'I notice that you do not lock your own office,' said Bragg.

'No, I've always left it open, in case the dean needed anything.'

'Other people come up here, surely?' Bragg persisted.

'Oh yes. Cleaners and staff have to, of course, but the door to the nave is always locked after them. If we didn't, the place would be full of tramps—and besides, there are some valuable books up here.'

'And what about the canons and so on?'

'The clergy are here a good deal, of course, for meetings and so on. They would generally use the dean's entrance.'

'You are not going to say that he pops up and down like an office-boy, to let them in.'

'What he does . . . did, was his responsibility,' said Wilkins shortly.

'So at least, it is possible that the dean's entrance could be left unlocked, and someone might pop through it, and get up here.'

'I suppose so.'

'Right, now where is the cabinet?'

The virger went over to an alcove and drew back a faded green curtain. Behind it was a substantial oak cupboard, fitting the niche tightly, the door flush with the wall. It was secured with a stout lock, and there were no signs of damage to the woodwork.

'Open it,' Bragg demanded.

Wilkins produced the key from his waistcoat, and unlocked the cupboard. Inside were rows of brass hooks, mostly labelled and with keys dangling from them.

'Thank you, you can close it now,' said Bragg equably. 'Now then, can you think of anyone who might have had it in for the dean? Anybody who might have played a trick on him to get his own back . . . a trick that went wrong?'

Wilkins shifted uncomfortably from one foot to the other. 'Well, there was Dick White . . . he was real vexed when the dean sacked him, and swore he hadn't seen the last of him—but he was just sounding off.'

'When was this?'

'It will be a year ago this Whitsuntide. He had been getting very slack and unreliable. I'd complained to the dean about him scores of times, but he would just smile and pass on. Then, that day, Dick should have put out the special Whitsuntide cope for the procession, and he'd forgotten. And the dean dismissed him on the spot.'

'Did he?' exclaimed Bragg encouragingly.

'Against my better judgement, I promised Dick that I would see if I could get the dean to change his mind, but he was adamant.'

'It all seems a long time ago,' said Bragg. 'Thank you, anyway. Now, there is one other thing you can do for me. Can you tell me where the bishop lives?'

'The Bishop of London?'

'Yes.'

'Fulham Palace, but I can save you a journey. He is conducting the funeral tomorrow, and he has come in to prepare for it. He is in the dean's room now. I will ask if he can see you.'

After an interval, they were conducted through the library to a comfortably furnished study beyond.

Bishop Temple rose from the desk and held out his hand.

'I am so sorry that you have to be involved in this sad affair,' he said in a rich vibrant voice. 'However, you have your duty to do.' He waved them to sit down. 'There is some question of the mechanism's having become defective, is there not?'

'That's right, my lord,' replied Bragg. 'It seems beyond doubt that it was interfered with, though as to whether that was done with the intention of causing the death of Dean Hadley or not, we still have to establish.'

'Oh dear.' The bishop placed the palms of his hands gently together, and to Morton the movement seemed momentarily graceless—an automatic, empty gesture repudiating the dean. He realised that the elaborate funeral in the crypt was a deliberate attempt by the church authorities to counteract any breath of scandal.

'You must have known the dean very well,' Bragg remarked.

'Not so well as did my predecessor. I was only elevated to the bishopric three years ago; and there is less contact between bishop and dean than you would think.'

'Would you say that he had any enemies?' Bragg asked.

Temple fixed him with his large brown eyes, a look of benevolent sincerity on his face. 'I cannot conceive of the existence of any such person,' he said. 'He was such a kindly man.'

'That's not how some people have described him,' said Bragg shortly.

'He was a quiet, withdrawn person,' the bishop went on as if Bragg had not spoken, 'exceedingly efficient in his duties, yet without the canker of ambition; an unassuming man, for one so highly placed—almost an ascetic . . . It was as if his life was devoted to praising God through the well-being of St Paul's.'

'You make him sound like a saint, my lord,' said Bragg gruffly.

'Perhaps that would be altogether too high an attribution,' Temple smiled engagingly, 'but I cannot believe that anyone would deliberately set about to kill him.'

Catherine ran up the steps of her parents' Park Lane house, and unpinned her hat in the hall. It had been a good day, she decided, and tomorrow promised to be even better. She had

been deputed to attend the funeral service of the dean of St
Paul's, and write an account for the Wednesday edition of her
paper. Since the *City Press* was only published on Wednesdays
and Saturdays, it was not often that it could be really topical;
so Mr Tranter, the editor, was determined to do full justice to
this solemn occasion. She had left the office early, and bought
some new black shoes. She would have to wear her black
dress, she decided, with perhaps a soft grey scarf, to show that
she was only an onlooker.

'Is that you, dear?' her mother called from the sitting-room.

'Yes, mamma.'

'There is a mountain of post here.'

'For me?' Catherine asked, in delighted surprise.

'They are addressed to both of us,' said her mother, 'but as
I did not recognize the writing on any of them, I left them
unopened.'

Catherine began to slit the envelopes. 'Oh!' she exclaimed in
disappointment, 'they are invitations—and from people I have
never heard of . . . There you are, a dance at Mrs Albert
Henderson's in Knightsbridge on the tenth of May, a drum at
Lady Vigo's in Eaton Square on the thirteenth . . . Oh, my
goodness! Mamma!' her voice became incredulous. 'We are
invited to a dance at Devonshire House on the fifth of May.
Oh, I would love to go to that!'

'Oh dear!' her mother cried in alarm. 'It is that wretched
portrait. I knew in my bones that this would happen.'

'Now, come along, mamma,' said Catherine bubbling with
excitement. 'We just have time to get new gowns . . . Please
do not look so put out, it will be fun!'

'You know that I feel uncomfortable at these great society
functions. I am happy enough in the houses of our friends, but
at Devonshire House there will be hundreds of others, pushing
and treading on one's toes; and the morning after we shall not
recall who was there, nor will they remember us.'

'Poor mamma!' There are another five that I would die to go
to. See!'

'I think it is thoroughly silly that you are not allowed to go
to them on your own. After all, you go to work in the City
every day, and into some of the most dreadful places in the

course of your job. I am not expected to chaperon you there.'

'It cannot be helped. The convention is that I am an innocent maid, who needs protecting from the world by her adoring and anxious mother.'

'I hope it is not wholly a convention, dear.' A faint smile rose to her mother's lips. 'Certainly I can attest to my anxiety.'

'You will accept, won't you?' Catherine pleaded.

'I suppose your father will be delighted,' said Mrs Marsden, in mock petulance.

'Then he will not mind the outlay on a new dress or two . . . Please, mamma!'

'Well, I did see some rather nice material, in Kate Reily's in Dover Street . . ."

'Then you will?'

'Oh yes, if you want it so much . . . And I was looking forward to a quiet summer . . . I suppose I shall have to start leaving cards again on all and sundry.'

'You will love it, you know you will,' said Catherine exultantly.

'I no longer have your name on my cards, since you had your own.'

'You will have to get some new ones printed . . . Now, what kind of dresses should I wear?'

On leaving the cathedral, Bragg and Morton had snatched a hasty lunch in a pub and gone back to Old Jewry. While Morton was writing out his notes of the morning's interview, Bragg went to report to Inspector Cotton. He came back ill-tempered, having been roundly told that he was wasting his time.

'Thank God that sod can only advise me, and not order me what to do,' he exclaimed, as he banged the door behind him. He picked up his pipe. 'Any new ideas?'

'I do not think that we can make too much of the dean's entrance being left unlocked,' Morton said tentatively. 'Anyone hiding in that part of the cathedral would be unable to reach the nave, and thus the staircase from the All Souls chapel, because of the locked door.'

'Yes, but can we accept Wilkins's word that it is always

locked?' asked Bragg darkly. 'It would be damned inconvenient.'

'That is true. On the other hand, the obvious point of entry, when the nave is open to the public, would be through the west door. It must, at the very least, be probable that when he locks up for the night, Wilkins does what he professes to do, and checks that the door to the vestibule of the south-west tower is closed.'

Bragg struck a match irritably, and jabbed it into the bowl of his pipe. 'Where does that leave us?' he asked.

'From your notes, it appears that there must be a doorway from that rather elegant staircase on to the west gallery. An intruder might get on to that from the dean's entrance.'

'You are right, lad. We ought to check that it is kept locked—I can't see it being used much, can you?'

'No. In any case, you did ask about the door at the other end of the gallery, the one that gives on to the staircase up to the bellchamber. Wilkins was insistent that it was still locked on the morning after the accident.'

'I wonder if Wilkins is our man?' Bragg ruminated. 'On the face of it, they got on well together, and it is at least possible that he will lose his job, when a new dean is appointed . . . You know, what we haven't got a smell of yet in this case, is motive—and damned little opportunity as well. I suppose it has to be one of the ringers . . . Come on, lad, let's go through the motions, and see if Wilkins is as good as his word.'

They strolled to St Paul's, and arrived at twenty minutes to six; then they took up their places in the nave. Wilkins was nowhere to be seen, but several of his cassocked acolytes were working their way from the east end, shepherding the few sightseers out. In time, they too were herded down to the west door, and Bragg had to produce his warrant-card to prevent their being ejected. Five minutes to six; the virgers had shed their robes of office and, transformed into mere human beings again, had departed through the west door. Only one remained, standing by the door, his cycleclips pinioning his trousers. As they watched from the shelter of a massive pillar, Wilkins came into view. He walked slowly down the choir and into the nave, glancing about him as he went. He searched the north and south transepts, then proceeded down the central aisle. When he neared the west end, he went across to the south aisle and looked into the Wellington chapel, then paused at the door leading to the dean's entrance, and checked that it was locked. Then he made his way to the north aisle, and inspected the two chapels there. Apparently satisfied, he moved towards his assistant, and caught sight of the policemen.

'Ah, Sergeant Bragg!' he exclaimed. 'Did you get on all right with the bishop? A real nice man he is.'

'Yes, thank you, Mr Wilkins. Is everything ready for tomorrow?'

'It will be. They say Mr Gladstone is coming—and him the prime minister. That shows what they thought of Dr Hadley.'

Bragg heard Morton snort in derision, then suddenly the bells began to peal.

'Hello,' he remarked. 'I didn't expect them to be here.'

'They will be ringing tomorrow,' said Wilkins, pulling out his watch. 'Well, gentlemen, I have to lock up now . . .'

'We'll go and have a chat with Mr Pettit,' said Bragg. 'I expect they will let us out.'

'Suit yourself, sergeant. Goodnight.' Wilkins ushered his assistant through the west door and, going out, locked it behind him.

Bragg led the way into the All Souls chapel. The door beside the altar gaped wide. They climbed the stairs and, peering into the ringing room, watched the taut ropes move up and down, till the bells' sound sank to a murmur, then was stilled.

Seeing them in the doorway, Horrex crossed over. 'We shall be ringing a half-muffled peal tomorrow,' he said. 'I have to fit a pad of leather on one side of each clapper. We have been ringing down,' he added.

'Why do you normally leave the bells standing up?' asked Bragg.

'It isn't very pleasant to hear a peal of twelve being rung up, or down—as you will realise when we ring them up again, after I have finished.'

As he turned towards the staircase, Bragg grabbed him by

the elbow. 'You said that it would be dangerous to work in the bell chamber, with the bells standing up.'

'Courting death, I'd say.'

'So, whoever chiselled the slider, knew that the bells would be down.'

Horrex raised his eyebrows. 'I suppose that must be so.'

'When did you decide to service the bells?'

'After ringing for evensong, on Sunday. The rope of number three was beginning to fray. So we stayed on till after the service, and then rang them down.'

'So, at that stage, only the twelve of you knew that the bells would be down.'

'Us, and any bell-ringer within ten miles, sergeant.'

Horrex disappeared up the stairs, and Bragg crossed to Pettit.

'I would be glad if I could have your address, sir,' he said. 'Just in case we need to contact you.'

Pettit gave him an uneasy look, then pulled a card case from his pocket. 'Here is my private address,' he said. 'I work as a loss adjuster, at 57 Cornhill. You can find me there any weekday.'

'You know about the slider, I take it,' Bragg remarked.

'I should think everybody in London does,' replied Pettit sourly.

'How did it happen that the dean was at the practice last Tuesday? He was not a regular ringer, I understand.'

'No. He is a member of the society, and used to ring regularly till he came here. He was too out of practice to ring for a service, but he has often stood in on a Tuesday, when someone was missing.'

'Who asked him to ring last week?'

'He suggested it himself. He came to see me after service on the Sunday afternoon. He particularly wanted to ring the tenor.'

'Why was that?'

'He had heard us ringing down, and wanted to ring it up again. Being so heavy, it is no easy task; and as a strong man, he enjoyed the challenge.'

'I thought it was a practice.'

'That is true, sergeant. The dean was going to hand over to Tom Fewtrell, before we began to ring the changes; but Tom decided to cry off and visit his daughter instead—she's just had her first baby.'

'And was the dean enjoying it?'

'I suppose so. His timing was off. He was a bit late in the rounds, then, just as it happened, he was early.'

Bragg gazed around the ringing room. 'These boxes you stand on,' he said. 'They are all of different heights. Why is that?'

'They relate to the size of the wheel on each bell,' said Pettit. 'The idea is to prevent coils of loose rope gathering around your feet, when you pull down. As the rope on the tenor is longest, so that box is the highest.'

'It sounds a dangerous pastime, to me.'

'It can be, to the novice.'

'Watching you just now, I noticed that, as the bell sounds, you catch the rope on that fluffy striped bit and stop it.'

'The sally, you mean? Yes. The momentum of the bell is almost spent when it rings. We check it, and hold it on the balance for a moment, till the next pull.'

'You did not see the slider that was broken?'

'No. I gather you took it away.'

'Suppose someone did not check the bell as it reached the top, would it break the slider?'

'It might, though the stay ought to break first.'

'I'm thinking that, with the dean being so rusty, he might have made a mistake, and it was an accident after all.'

'I am sure it was an accident, sergeant, despite the marks on the slider. But the dean would not have made that kind of mistake. He was one of the finest ringers in the world—you cannot be a member of the society otherwise. Most towers in the country would have been honoured to have him, rusty or no.'

Violet Harman dabbed some cologne behind her ears, smoothed her dress, and walked over to the window. It was exciting to be in London at the start of the Season. Below her there was a constant stream of hansoms, broughams—even a landau pulled by a pair of sleek chestnuts. Everywhere was good-humored bustle; and she was to be part of it for three whole months! She and her mother had barely set foot in The Priory, before Lady Morton was whisking them up to Curzon Street. They were not to return to Kent until a few days before they were due to leave for America again. And James would be squiring them around as he had promised! The moment they had arrived here, Emily had insisted on taking her to Hyde Park, where society would be enjoying the afternoon sunshine. They had strolled under the trees, looking at the ladies' fashions, acknowledging the bows of smartly dressed gentlemen. It had been wonderful! They had even seen the Princess of Wales drive by in her carriage, smiling and waving.

It was true, of course, that she had come out in Boston three years ago. Her father had given a grand ball on her eighteenth birthday; but, beside this breathtaking display, it all seemed rather provincial. She frowned in self-reproach; such a thought was disloyal, and the ball had been the event of the season . . . Then she tossed her head defiantly. She was determined to have the most marvellous time. She glanced at herself once more in the mirror, then went downstairs.

'You look charming, dear,' her aunt greeted her.

'Thank you,' she said with a smile. 'I assumed that we would not be receiving visitors this evening.'

'Not unless James can be called a visitor. He promised to call in, if he could.'

'Oh, good!' She turned away to the far end of the room, where Emily was sitting at a low table, poring over papers and magazines. 'What are you doing?' she asked.

'I am making a list of what is on. Listen! In June alone, there are recitals by Paderewski, Sarasate, and Madame Adelina Patti. In two weeks' time the opera starts at Covent Garden with Madame Melba in *Lohengrin* . . . Let me see what they are doing on the eighteenth of May. It is a tradition that one goes to the opera, on the evening after being presented at Court . . . Ah! It's *Carmen*. How absolutely wonderful!'

'Do the débutantes all go together?' asked Violet.

'No!' Emily replied animatedly. 'You make up a party yourself. Mamma will have to do the arranging, of course, but

I shall say whom I want. She will have to be present, or some other chaperon; and since papa is not here, she might want James to come also. Apart from that, we can ask whom we like.'

'Am I to be included?'

'Of course! We shall just have to see whom we meet . . . It would have been better had my presentation been later in the Season. Some girls are almost ready to announce their engagements by then. It is always informative to see who is with whom, at the Opera.'

'Goodness! You do sound determined to find a husband.'

'Of course I am. That is what the Season is about. Mamma would not let me be presented at eighteen; she said that I would make a better choice with more maturity. Now I am twenty-one, I have to make up for lost time!'

'Is that not all rather calculated?'

Emily opened her eyes wide in astonishment. 'What else could it be? There are always many more girls than young men; so, if you want to be married, you cannot afford to be a wallflower.'

'You will have plenty of admirers, with your money.'

'Now who is being down to earth?' Emily crowed. 'Anyway, I want to be a great society hostess . . . It will have to be at least a lord, maybe even a duke—and we will find a marquess for you!'

'What would that make me? A marquisite!'

'What are you laughing about?' enquired Amelia from the other end of the room.

'Emily was just explaining English titles to me, mamma.'

The girls went over and joined their mothers.

'Did you find it difficult, when you came over from America, Aunt Lottie?' asked Violet.

'I did indeed! And since your grandfather was the ambassador of the United States here, we were constantly mixing with the aristocracy. Your father would have been rather too young to remember, but I used to go to receptions and be totally confused over whether I was expected to offer my hand or curtsy. They are so obsessed by etiquette over here—particularly the Prince of Wales.'

'You only curtsy to royalty,' announced Emily.

'If you insist on ruining other people's anecdotes like that, dear, you will not deserve to get a husband,' Lady Morton said, reprovingly.

Violet was moved to rescue her impetuous cousin. 'Who was that charming young man, who passed the time of day with us in the park?' she asked.

'Lord John Whitmore.'

'And whit more could you wish for, than him?'

'A great deal more. He is the second son of an Irish peer.'

Violet laughed uncertainly. 'But how do you know these things?'

'The stud book! One never goes anywhere without it.' Emily crossed over to the bookcase, and from the bottom shelf drew a great red tome. 'There you are, *Debrett's Peerage and Baronetage*. There is no gainsaying that. See! We are in it.' She turned the pages rapidly. 'There, that is the coat of arms of the Morton baronetcy; here are details of the present baronet— papa, whom he married, and his children—Albert Edwin born eighteen sixty, James Eversleigh Kerwood born eighteen sixty-five, Emily Jane born eighteen seventy-one.'

'It is kind of chilling to be set down in print, in that way,' said Violet. 'I do not think I would like it.'

'Emily exaggerates, dear, as usual,' said Lady Morton. 'Though I must confess that it is useful to know where you are with likely suitors.'

'I have often wondered,' said Amelia with a teasing smile, 'why you were content with Henry, when you might have had almost anyone you chose. After all, Jenny Jerome was not so much after your time, and she got Lord Randolph Churchill. And Alva Vanderbilt is talking about hawking Consuelo around next year, till she gets herself a coronet.'

'But, my dear,' replied Lady Morton, 'I could afford to let my heart decide for me; and I have never had cause to regret it. I would recommend that these young ladies should follow the same course.'

There came a tap at the door, and Morton entered, smiling broadly. He greeted them, then kissed his aunt's hand, and placed a brotherly peck on Violet's cheek.

'I do believe that Parker is enjoying acting as doorman,' he remarked. ' " 'Tis my job to say whether the ladies is at home, or not at home," he told me. "And tonight they is not at home, 'cept to you, master James" . . . I count myself privileged!'

'I think that you have broadened out a little, since last May,' said Amelia.

'Even servants of royalty live well, aunt. And how is Uncle Josh? Stilll rattling around America on the train?'

'I fear so. I sometimes feel he will hardly notice we have been away!'

Morton took a seat beside Violet. 'And what have you been doing, cousin?' he asked.

'The usual social round. But last October we went down to New York, for the fourth centenary of the discovery of America,' said Violet excitedly. 'They had a big parade and procession. There was one car in the form of a monster's head, and Mr Edison had fitted it out with three thousand electric lights! It was as bright as the moon! Papa was most impressed.'

'Which probably means that he has bought some Edison stock,' remarked Morton with a smile. 'Have you ladies decided what your programme is to be?'

'I have begun a list,' said Emily . . . 'Oh, James,' she went on excitedly. 'Did you know that the portrait they have been making all the fuss about is Catherine's?'

Violet saw a guarded look come over his face.

'Yes. It was mentioned in the *Observer* on Sunday,' he said.

'Have you been to see it?'

'I did drop in, last night.'

'Is it as good as they say? We must go!'

'Oh yes,' he said lightly. 'It is Catherine all right; the Catherine we all know and . . . admire. Now, do you require anything of me this evening, mamma?'

'No, dear. Tomorrow we shall be leaving cards on our acquaintances; so in a few days we can expect to receive some invitations. And we must make plans for giving a dance ourselves . . . I do wish this house was a little larger. Perhaps we could hold it in a hotel, or some rooms. I hear that is done frequently, nowadays. Could you make some enquiries for me, dear?'

'Of course. Now, unless there is anything else, I will wish you goodnight.'

'There is one thing,' Violet broke in brightly. 'As I am not looking for a husband, I would much prefer not to be thought of as eligible. Since it seems that everyone will already know that the Mortons are not exactly penurious, I would like you all to give it out that we are poor relations, visiting from America.'

'What, in the gowns you have brought?' exclaimed Emily.

'I shall say I borrowed yours! Promise me . . . please! I just want to enjoy myself.'

Lady Morton smiled. 'We promise,' she said.

CHAPTER _____
_____ THREE

On the morning after the funeral, Bragg and Morton called at the deanery. It was a large house, on four floors and they had to ascend a double flight of steps, to get to the imposing front door. It was a considerable time before their ring was answered; then a short plump woman in a cook's apron appeared.

'Police,' Bragg grunted. 'Is your mistress at home?'

'She is in the sewing room.'

'Would you tell her that we would like to see her, please.'

'Then you had better wait inside.'

She ushered them into a long room, at one side of the house. At the end, a window overlooked the courtyard. The dome of St Paul's loomed beyond the delicate new leaves of the plane trees by the gate. From time to time, as the breeze caught the branches, one could see the north-west tower and the blank holes of its bell-chamber.

'I wonder how she has taken it,' Bragg murmured, surveying the austerely furnished room.

'According to Miss Marsden's account, in this morning's paper, she bore up well.'

45

'She will be glad to get away from here, though, I should think.'

There was a discreet cough behind them, and they turned to find a small woman standing by the door. She had grey hair, wire-rimmed spectacles and wore deep mourning.

'You wished to see me?' Her voice was quiet and flat, as if it had lost all timbre. She walked, almost soundlessly, to a chair by the fireplace and sat down. Morton raised an enquiring eyebrow at Bragg, for she had not thought to invite them to sit.

'We are just tidying up the coroner's file,' said Bragg, subsiding into a chair opposite her. 'And I have brought over the dean's effects.' He pulled an envelope from his inside pocket and, tearing it open, slid the contents on to a side table. 'Watch, pen-knife, pocket-book, keys, handkerchief, small change . . .'

She glanced briefly across, then her eyes dropped to her hands again. They were clasped, but to Morton it was hardly the clasp of mourning; there was no pressure, no seeking of reassurance or comfort. To him, the grasp seemed reposeful, relaxed. Nor did Mrs Hadley's face display indications of grief; it was pallid, showing neither emotion nor interest. Yet it was not the numb incomprehension that he had encountered in some cases of sudden death; rather, she was incurious, indifferent, a husk long since empty.

'I was saying that you would no doubt be leaving here,' said Bragg in a sympathetic voice.

'Yes. They would like me to vacate the house within a month . . . There will be redecoration to do.' Again the voice was colourless; there was no hint of resentment against a fate that had dealt her such a savage blow.

'Where will you go?'

'My sister has written to say that there is a suitable cottage near her. In all probability I shall take it.'

'What part of the country is that?' asked Bragg encouragingly.

'It is a small village on the banks of the river Wye, near Hereford . . . We originally came from Gloucester,' she added.

'I wouldn't have thought it, from your accent.'

A thin smile crossed her lips, but she did not reply.

'Will you be able to manage all right?' Bragg asked.

'Oh yes. My husband's stipend was two thousand pounds a year, and we lived very simply.'

'Then, that is one comfort,' said Bragg warmly.

'Yes.'

'Have you not got any children to go to, for a bit; to help you to get over it?'

'No, we were not blessed in that way. My husband felt that indulgence of the flesh interfered with his devotional life. That is my one regret.' Even now, the voice expressed no emotion.

'We have been looking into the accident, for the coroner, of course.'

'I gather that I am required to appear at the inquest.'

'I fear so. But I can make it less upsetting for you, if you can tell me a thing or two now.'

'I would be grateful for that.'

'You no doubt know that the mechanism of the bell broke.'

'Yes. A similar accident occurred in a parish where my husband was curate, many years ago.'

'Did it now? . . . It may seem an odd thing to ask, ma'am, but did your husband have any enemies?'

She considered the question in a detached way. 'No. I can think of no occasion which could have given rise to enmity, in even the most choleric person. The dean was a calm, reserved man. I cannot recall his losing his temper over any-thing . . . It was rather like living with Christ himself.'

'I see. Was he preoccupied, in the days before his death? Did he seem at all worried, or disturbed?'

'No, but even had he been worried, he would not have revealed it to me. He used to wrestle with his problems on his knees, before his Maker.'

'Can you recollect any changes in the pattern of his life recently, anything unusual?'

For the first time, a spark of animation showed in her face. 'There was one incident, that seemed rather odd. I was driving in a hansom cab, near Tottenham Court Road. It would be, perhaps, a little over a month ago. I saw a man go into a tobacconist's shop in Cleveland Street. I was certain that it was the dean, although he was not dressed in clerical garb. My husband was of very striking appearance.'

'Why should it surprise you?'

'Well, the dean did not smoke.'

'Perhaps he was buying cigars as a present for someone,' remarked Bragg.

'However, I was wrong.'

'You asked him about it, then?'

'Yes. I told him at dinner, and he denied having been near the West End at that hour. He was very short with me.'

'That's that, then,' said Bragg dismissively. 'I take it your husband had a study at home. May we have a poke around there?'

'I am afraid that you may find it very untidy. My husband found the noise of the parlour-maid very distracting, and insisted on discharging her. He said that he would give her wages to charity—the Mission to the Jews, I think he said.'

'Don't worry, ma'am,' Bragg replied genially. 'We are used to a bit of dust.'

The study showed little evidence of disorder. Some letters had been piled precisely on the desk, under a glass paper-weight. On a side table, there were a few pages of manuscript and three or four books of reference. The bookcase itself held a collection of religious texts and commentaries, the collected sermons of John Donne, one of the dean's predecessors, with a few volumes on architecture and ecclesiastical sculpture. There was nothing in the least unexpected.

'Was she what you imagined?' asked Bragg, as he began to go through the desk drawers.

'Not remotely. She seemed almost untouched by it.'

'The bride of Christ, eh?' remarked Bragg coarsely. 'Well, she's not much of an advertisement for the joys of heaven.' He pulled out his pipe, and looked around for an ash-tray, then put it back in his pocket.

'He was obviously preparing a sermon for St Mary Magdalene's day,' said Morton, turning over the manuscript pages. 'He seems to have had considerable sympathy for that erring lady.'

'That's the stock in trade of these parsons; sympathy and

understanding, but where does it get you? . . . There is nothing here.' He picked up the waste-paper basket, and emptied its contents on to the top of the desk.

'Hello!' he exclaimed. 'What's this?'

Morton went across. Bragg was extracting a bundle of envelopes from a large piece of crumpled newspaper.

'It looks as if he didn't want the charwoman to become curious, when she was emptying the basket.' He slipped off the rubber band. 'All printed in capitals,' he said, 'and all addressed to *THE VERY REVEREND, THE DEAN OF ST PAUL'S.* Is that what they called him?'

'I imagine that that would be the proper mode of address,' said Morton, crossing behind Bragg and looking over his shoulder. Bragg took the top envelope, and pulled out the letter. It was also printed in capitals.

REVEREND SIR,
    MAY I BEG A FURTHER CHARITABLE CONTRI-
BUTION. THE SAME AMOUNT WOULD BE WEL-
COME. I AM SURE YOU COULD ARRANGE IT BY THE
THIRTIETH.
    I HAVE THE HONOUR TO BE,
    YOUR MOST OBEDIENT SERVANT.

'That's a damned odd begging letter,' said Bragg. He pulled out the other letters. 'Look! They are all virtually the same— and not one signed.'

'One gets the feeling that he had little option but to comply,' said Morton.

'There is a bank book in the middle drawer. Get it, will you?'

Morton took it out and opened it. 'The dean obviously had an account with the Bank of England,' he remarked, handing it to Bragg.

'Yes, but his pass-book has not been made up for a year . . . What was the date of the first of those letters, lad?'

'The letters themselves are not dated; the postmarks on the envelopes go from . . . yes, the seventh of April last year, to the fourth of April this year.'

'Were they all sent at the beginning of the month?'

Morton shuffled through the pile, 'Yes, none later than the tenth.'

'And is there one for every month?'

'There seems to be,' said Morton going through the pile again. 'No, we do not have one for October last year; apart from that, the sequence is complete.'

'I wonder what happened to that one,' Bragg muttered.

'The symbol, at the head of the letters, seems rather crude,' said Morton. 'It appears to have been put on with a rubber stamp. Obviously it is not a very wealthy charity!'

'Let me see.' Bragg took one of the letters and, holding it at arms' length, peered at it.

'You really will have to get some spectacles,' said Morton laughing.

'Nonsense! You are the eyes, I'm the brains. What does it look like?'

'It has been done with some kind of stamp—perhaps a cork, that has been cut away in the centre to outline a shape.'

'And what does it look like?'

'A curved sword, above a short, rather wavy, bar.'

'Hmn,' said Bragg pensively . . . 'Is that the lot here?'

'I cannot think of anything else, sir.'

'Right. Then we will commandeer this, just in case.' He picked up a photograph of the dean from the table, and slipped it into his pocket.

It was mid-morning when they reached the Bank of England, and the banking-halls were crowded.

'Can you see young Gibson?' Bragg asked. 'He owes us a favour, if anybody does.'

'There he is.' Morton pointed to the end of the counter. 'He seems to have moved up in the pecking order, since the business of the counterfeit notes last year.'

'I expect he grabbed a good bit of the credit,' said Bragg with a sardonic grin. He went to the head of the queue that stood by Gibson's counter, and attracted his attention.

'I would like a word,' he said.

'Give me a few moments,' replied Gibson in a guarded voice. He beckoned to a uniformed messenger, who thereupon diverted new customers to other counters. After several minutes, Gibson's last customer had been dealt with, and he disappeared. Bragg was beginning to prowl restively, when he reappeared behind them, and took them along a corridor to a small office.

'What can I do for you?' he asked, waving them to chairs.

'It's the dean of St Paul's,' said Bragg bluntly.

'What about him?'

'We want to have a quick look at his bank account.'

'But I cannot do that!' exclaimed Gibson, horrified.

'I felt sure you would be able to, now you have gone up in the world,' replied Bragg, meaningfully.

'What possible reason could you have for seeing it?' asked Gibson.

'We believe that the dean was the victim of criminal activity. His own pass-book has not been made up for a year, so we cannot confirm it from that. Obviously, we could get his executor, whoever he might be, to ask for the information. But by the time all the rigmarole has been gone through, the scent will be cold.'

'There is a strict rule that no one, not even the police, is to see a customer's account without his express authority.'

'It might be a little difficult to get, where he is,' said Bragg cheerfully.

'Not the least of my problems,' Gibson went on in a worried tone, "is that his account is in a ledger which contains the accounts of other customers.'

'But then, you would be with us, to see that we didn't peer into their affairs.'

'I was beginning to feel that I might be able to leave you alone with the ledger, for a few moments,' said Gibson hesitantly. 'Obviously, that is not what you would wish.'

'Well, it would be so much quicker if you could explain things to us . . . I am sure the chief cashier would approve— though he might not want to know about it officially.'

'Oh dear,' exclaimed Gibson despondently. 'If he found out, and did not approve, my career would be ruined. You realize that?'

'Never fear. We will not let you down. The coroner has got the most wide-reaching powers, it is just that we don't have the time to use them.'

'You are acting for the coroner, are you?'

'Yes, of course. Do you want to see my letter of appointment?'

Gibson looked at them doubtfully for a moment, then disappeared out of the room. He came back with a large ledger, which he deposited on the table before Bragg.

'We must be quick,' he said urgently.

He opened the book at a page headed 'Hadley, Robert George, DD.' Beneath it there was a series of entries recorded in immaculate copperplate writing.

'What period are you concerned with?' he asked.

'From the beginning of eighteen ninety-two, up to date,' said Bragg.

Gibson turned a few pages. 'There is where last year starts.'

'These are the payments in, on the left, are they?'

'Yes.'

'I take it these quarterly receipts of five hundred pounds would be his stipend?'

'It would certainly appear so.'

'There is not much else on that side of the ledger, is there?'

Gibson turned back to the beginning of the account, and scrutinized the top of the page. 'This is where we make any general notes,' he said. 'The small credit arose from a holding of Consols. I see that he sold them in March this year.' He turned to the current page again.

'As regards the debits,' remarked Bragg, 'we have a series of withdrawals of ten pounds every month. Can you say how that was taken out?'

'I imagine it would be in sovereigns, for housekeeping.'

'Can you just check back for us, to see if that pattern held in eighteen ninety-one?'

Gibson sighed irritably, and turned back a page. 'Yes, it did,' he said.

'So, the only other regular withdrawals of substance, would be the series of two-hundreds?'

'So it would appear.'

'These would have been withdrawals of notes?'

'Very probably.'

'Could you find out what they were—denominations and serial numbers?'

'It might be done, but it would take time, and I could not possibly undertake it without a proper request from the executor.'

'Never mind. Can you confirm that the withdrawal at the beginning of March last year was the first?'

'I anticipated your question, when I looked back just now. It was.'

'Would the dean get a pension, I wonder?' Bragg mused.

Gibson seemed startled. 'I presume so,' he replied.

'Well, he hadn't got much in the bank, had he?'

'The latest balance is one hundred and ninety-three pounds, twelve shillings,' said Gibson. 'There will presumably be further stipend due, from Lady Day to the date of his death, which would be around a hundred and twenty pounds . . . After legal and executors' cost, his widow will be left with around three hundred pounds only.'

'Are you sure of that?' asked Bragg in concern.

'Why, no, I am making certain assumptions, such as that he did not have a hoard of gold sovereigns under the bed. We know that he does not own the deanery, and since he was not due to retire for some time, I assume that he has not acquired another residence.'

'What about accounts with other banks?' asked Bragg.

'Had there been any, we would almost certainly have known, and made a ledger note at the head of the account.'

'What about other investments?'

'In general terms, the same would apply.'

'So, for a man in his position, he was not well off?'

'He was a poor man in anyone's terms, sergeant.'

They took a cab to Tottenham Court Road and, after asking the constable on the beat, found Cleveland Street. The tobacconist's shop was in a terrace of grimy Georgian houses. The window was crammed with pipes, bowls of shag and flake to tempt the palate, and boxes of cigars. The door gave directly into the shop, and there was no other entrance at the front. The paintwork was clean washed, the brass doorhandle shone, the windows of the upper floor were curtained—and yet somehow it engendered a feeling of disquiet in Morton. Perhaps its aura of respectability was the very reason, for the street itself was narrow, the pavements ill-swept.

They concealed themselves in an entry, opposite the shop, and settled down to keep observation.

'I don't much care for this dean chap,' observed Bragg, 'though I admit I am prejudiced against parsons. Yet I reckon he was better than most. I get the feeling that that bank account belonged to somebody who knew he would retire on a pension big enough to meet all his needs. A stipend of two thousand pounds a year is a hell of a lot of money, even for someone in his position—and from what we saw this morning, they didn't spend a lot on ordinary living.'

'I would imagine that Mrs Hadley could make ten pounds a month meet the wages of the remaining servants, run the household, and even leave a margin for personal expenses!' said Morton.

'If we had been able to examine the account properly, I think we would have found that he had always given a lot to charity—though why anyone should want to convert the Jews, I can't imagine. They always struck me as having a perfectably serviceable religion already.'

'Then we get the monthly series of payments,' said Morton, 'which ran down what little he had saved, very rapidly.'

'Right. It's my guess that he knew the writer of the letters . . . I know it's not necessary. He could have destroyed the first letter. But as I see it, the first demand for a "charitable payment" must have been made personally.'

'The first two hundred was paid in March, certainly,' said Morton.

'Then after that, all that is needed is a letter . . . I think we must assume that the withdrawals were in notes. No one, nowadays, would walk around with two hundred sovereigns in his pocket. Then, of course, the dean has to deliver them to his blackmailer . . . I wonder if he wrote a letter back, each time.'

'There were no notes to that effect on the letters he had received, or on the envelopes.'

'At all events, he draws out the notes, and puts them in an envelope, And, let's say, he takes a cab to Tottenham Court Road, then walks along here, and delivers it to that tobacconist's, to be collected.'

'And at the end of March this year, his wife, quite coincidentally, takes a hansom along Cleveland Street, and sees him entering the shop.'

'It must be that, mustn't it?' declared Bragg. 'Wives don't mistake anybody else for their husband—not after they've been wed for half a lifetime.'

'I wonder what hold the blackmailer had over him,' said Morton.

'It was a powerful one, you may be sure.'

'Do you think that the bishop knew?'

'What makes you say that?'

'It is just a feeling that I got, when you were questioning him . . . I suppose it is not beyond possibility that the dean would confess—in a sacerdotal sense—to his superior. The bishop would then be in a dilemma. If the transgression was secular, and venial, he might have been willing to allow the dean to continue in office. Certainly the premature retirement of someone so vigorous would have raised questions.'

'This is all of a parcel with you feeling that the burial in the cathedral was to outweigh any rumour.'

'There was certainly an underlying discomposure in the bishop's manner.'

'Well,' Bragg stepped out of the doorway, and glanced around. 'We are doing no good here. I am going in to buy some tobacco. Give me a minute, then come in and distract the assistant's attention—choose some cigars, or something. I want to get a look round the back, if I can.'

'Could I speak to the duty Inspector, please?'

Bragg placed his warrant card before the Metropolitan police sergeant manning the desk.

'Just a minute.'

He took the card and disappeared down a corridor. A few moments later, a huge bouncing man in his shirt-sleeves came, hand outstretched.

'Joe! How are you, my old mate?'

They shook hands warmly.

'Come on, then, let's have a chat.' He led the way to a sparsely furnished office, at the back of the building.

I didn't know you had been promoted from sub-Inspector, Bill.'

'January last year!'

'Well done! I knew you'd make it.'

Bill turned to Morton. 'I joined the Met in the same month as your sergeant joined the City Police. We got to know each other when he was at Snow Hill and I was at Clerkenwell. The two beats ran alongside one another, at the back of Aldersgate Street station. Many a yarn we've had on nights, in that entry in Blyne Street.'

Morton grinned. 'Then I need not feel so guilty, myself.'

'How long have you been at Goodge Street?' Bragg asked.

'Ever since I was made up.'

'You know it well, then?'

'I should do. Why?'

'We have what seems to be a blackmail case on our hands. The bloke who was being rented was seen going into the tobacconist's in Cleveland Street. I wondered if you could tell me anything about the place.'

'Why don't you ask your victim?'

'I can't. He's dead.'

'I see,' said Bill shortly.

'We've had a bit of a poke around. I went in for some twist, and then young Morton came in and made a diversion. I turned out the back way, by accident, as it were, but I didn't get very far. There's a short passage, with a door to the yard at the end, and a gate that would lead you out to Conway Street. The stairs that take you to the upper floors must come down to the passage. I say "must come down", because you can't actually see them. There's a damned great oak door at the bottom— with a peep-hole, moreover.'

'Oh yes?' remarked the Inspector guardedly.

'What is it, Bill? A gambling club?'

'This is a tricky one, Joe. We've had a stop on that place for years. No uniformed policeman is allowed anywhere near it.'

'I bet you've looked it over, though, in your Sunday suit,' said Bragg.

'Well, I did buy some cigarettes there once.'

'Come on, Bill. You know more than you are letting on.'

'I shouldn't be talking to you at all, without permission from the Assistant Commissioner. If it gets out, I can say goodbye to my pips.'

'At least you can tell me about the premises. Am I right in what I saw?'

Bill sighed resignedly. 'Yes. There is a door that closes the shop off from the passage. When the shop is not open, that door is locked.'

'And the back door to the yard is left open?'

Bill nodded.

'Blast it!' exclaimed Bragg, 'all you are doing is confirming that we ought to be suspicious, without telling us what is going on.'

'I know,' the Inspector smiled briefly. 'I tell you, Joe, this is redhot.'

'Then, if it's so tricky, why hasn't the City force been warned off?'

'I doubt if anybody in the Met knows, outside of this division.'

'Well, if you haven't officially told me,' Bragg said roughly, 'I don't officially know. So I can take a few of the lads and turn it over.'

'That would drop me right in it,' replied Bill heatedly. 'You having been in here this afternoon.'

'All I want,' said Bragg determinedly, 'is enough information to make sure we aren't wasting our time. I promise to do nothing, until I have cleared it with you first.'

'You would have to go right up to the AC, before taking any action at all.'

'Right. I accept that.'

'Very well, Joe . . . Above the shop is an LBH club.'

'What is that?' asked Morton.

'Lend your Brother a Hand.'

'A charity?' exclaimed Morton in surprise.

Bill and Bragg began to laugh uproariously.

'No, lad,' Bragg spluttered. 'It's not a charity—it's a male brothel!"

A pimply youth showed the two policemen into Pettit's office, with ill-concealed curiosity.

'We won't take up much of your time, sir,' said Bragg. 'There are just one or two things.'

'I will do all I can to help, naturally,' said Pettit guardedly.

'First of all, those boxes you stand on, when you are ringing; what are the two leather loops, near the front edge, for?'

'Why, they are provided for the ringer to put his feet through. Not everyone uses them—indeed I do not do so myself.'

'What is the point of them, then?

'They are traditional, and like so many traditional things, one does not analyse the reasons for them. Perhaps they prevent one from accidentally stepping off the box—though they could hardly prevent one from overbalancing if one missed the rope.'

'How do you mean?'

'Let us say that the bell has been pulled off the backstroke. The rope comes down from the roof of the ringing room, by reason of the velocity of the bell alone. So, it accelerates to the bottom of the swing, and thereafter slows down. Even for an experienced ringer, it takes great concentration to judge the precise moment to check the rope—particularly after five thousand-odd changes, or three hours ringing! For a learner, this is compounded by the fact that the rope, being free in its whole length, does not necessarily come down in the same place. There can easily be a difference of a few inches in its position, though the sally is clearly visible, of course. It is not uncommon for a novice ringer to fail to grasp the rope.'

'And if that happened, the bell would go right over, and break the stay.'

'That is correct, sergeant.'

'Was the dean using the toe straps, that night?'

'I cannot say. He was wearing his cassock . . . but one must presume not, since they were undamaged.'

'Looking at the slider again, I realized that being just a

length of oak, with a hole drilled centrally at one end, it is the
same top and bottom.'

'Ye . . .,' said Pettit doubtfully.

'What I am getting at, is that it could have been taken off,
and put back with the chisel marks underneath. If we assume
that the wood was not actually split through, then Mr Horrex
would not have seen the damage when he checked the bells.'

'I see.'

'And that would mean we have to consider anybody who had
access to the bell-chamber, not only from Monday night, but
from the time you rang the bells down on Sunday evening.'

Pettit pursed his lips. 'That would seem to be the case,' he
said.

'Since Mr Horrex looks after the bells on his own, it seems
that one man alone could have tampered with the slider. Now,
it seems unlikely that you could get a hammer and chisel to it
while it was in position. Who else had the experience and the
equipment necessary to remove and replace it?'

'Anyone at all, with a knowledge of bells,' said Pettit in a
relieved tone. 'You just push one end in the slot, and drop the
other over the pivot. A child could do it!"

'Suicide?' exclaimed the coroner angrily. 'You must have gone
off your head, Bragg!'

'All the evidence points to suicide, sir.'

'Pah! At your age you should have an ingrained contempt for
evidence. Why should a man in his position commit suicide?
Dammit, man, I was playing whist with him only the week
before!'

'He appears to have been blackmailed for over a year. His
money had run out, and when a fresh demand was made at the
beginning of last month, he did not have the resources to pay.'

'Why the devil did he not say something to me about it? Had
he informed the police?'

'No sir. He was obviously convinced that failure to pay
would most certainly lead to exposure.'

'You talk like a penny dreadful, sergeant . . . "Death
before dishonour".'

'I think you have hit the nail precisely on the head, sir. Our investigations are not yet complete, but we have reason to believe that the dean was a practising homosexual.'

Sir Rufus's jaw dropped. 'Hadley a sodomite? I do not believe it!'

'According to his wife, she saw him going into premises that we now know contain a male brothel.'

'Good God! . . . But that is no evidence of suicide! You cannot commit suicide in front of eleven other people, without someone noticing it!'

'They noticed more than they realize, sir. They just haven't put it together.'

'So let me hear your evidence, Bragg,' said Sir Rufus truculently.

'We know that Dean Hadley was a very experienced ringer, if a bit out of practice. He was a strong man, and quite capable of controlling the tenor bell—no one has said anything to the contrary. Now, if we assume that he had decided the only way out was to commit suicide, he was given an opportunity to do so in a way which would look like an accident; because on the Sunday night they rang the bells down so that the steeple-keeper could put a new rope on one of them. It is highly dangerous to go near the bells, unless they are down; if you touched one when it was up, you could get crushed.'

'Why did he not commit the alleged act by doing just that?' asked the coroner.

'Because, as an experienced ringer, he ought to know better, and it would not appear accidental; after all, he had no possible reason for going to the bell-chamber.'

Sir Rufus grunted sceptically. 'Go on.'

'He may have contemplated it for months,' said Bragg. 'It was obvious enough that the day would come when he would not be able to pay. Anyway, the opportunity came when he heard the bells being rung down. He went to the conductor of the band and particularly asked if he could ring the tenor up again, on practice night. He said he was quite willing to hand over to the regular ringer, once that was done. The conductor—a Mr Pettit—had great respect for the dean as a ringer, and they all got on well with him; so you can imagine that they indulged his whim readily enough. In fact, it was arranged that he would ring throughout the whole of the practice.'

'He was a member of the Ancient Society of College Youths, was he not?' remarked Sir Rufus, with the air of counsel condescending to make a point for the other side.

'If that is what they call it, yes . . . Then, between the Sunday and Tuesday nights, the dean took the necessary keys from the cabinet in his virger's office. He removed the slider from the tenor bell, and with a chisel from the ringing room, he made a deep cut along the grain, on either side of the pivot hole. Then he put it back. In that condition, he could be sure that it would split, if the bell stay hit it really hard.'

'Then, why did it take so long?' demanded the coroner. 'You said you had been listening to the ringing for five minutes, before it stopped.'

'Because, while you are ringing up, the stay does not come into contact with the slider. It was only when they started ringing rounds, that there was danger of its splitting. But he could not allow it to split unless the rope was right for his purpose. These accidents seem to happen on what they call the backstroke, when there is a lot of rope coming down to the ringing room floor. Pettit gave me the real clue. He said the Dean's timing was rusty; he was late, then suddenly early. I reckon he was late because he was checking the bell early, so that it would not hit the slider too hard.'

'Why, then, become early?'

'That was when he did it. He gave it a real good pull on the backstroke, and got a loop of the rope round his neck as it came down. The bell stay hit the weakened slider, broke it, and the bell went over the top, jerking him upwards, and breaking his neck.'

'I won't have it, Bragg,' Sir Rufus said fiercely. 'It would never stand up in court. Dammit man! Do you know what it would mean? Thank God we no longer mutilate our suicides and bury them at the cross-roads; but, even so, he could no longer receive any of the rites of Christian burial. Do you realize, Bragg, that if I were to bring in a verdict of *felo de se*, he would have to be dug up from the crypt of St Paul's, and reinterred in unconsecrated ground? . . . It's unthinkable! Unthinkable!'

'Suicide is a crime, sir,' said Bragg stoutly.

'Rubbish, Bragg! An absurd remnant of medieval ecclesiastical law. I don't care tuppence for that . . . I shall not call you at the inquest. I shall take evidence of identity, hear what Burney has to say, and call this Pettit man to say briefly what happened. Then I shall bring in a verdict of accidental death . . . Yes, that's it . . . And you are to cease your enquiries into the matter forthwith! Understand?'

'I understand, sir,' said Bragg quietly. 'However, I should tell you that the Commissioner has ordered me to press vigorously my investigations into the blackmailing.'

CHAPTER ⸻
⸻ FOUR

Violet followed her aunt into the hall of Devonshire house, and almost gasped aloud in delight. On every side were banks of flowers, while garlands of ribbon and flowers coiled through the wrought iron balusters of the staircase. Myriads of electric lights were reflected from mirrors and polished marble walls, until the whole sparkled like the inside of a jewel casket. Poor Mr Edison! How crass his display seemed, compared to this.

The ladies gave their wraps to a footman in green and gold livery, and began to ascend the staircase. Ahead of them was a slowly moving procession of women in exquisite gowns and men in black evening dress. The contrast seemed to emphasize the presumption that, socially at least, women were infinitely superior to men. If only James had been here! He had promised to come. Surely he could have got away in time to escort them? A gaggle of four ladies was very conspicuous . . . She stifled the burgeoning reproach as they gained the top landing.

The Duchess of Devonshire received them graciously, then Lady Morton led them into the lavishly decorated ballroom and they settled themselves in gilt chairs near the door.

'It will become very hot, later on,' she commented. 'There will be more air here. Besides, I like to see the later arrivals. Since, in their own estimation at least, they come from the highest reaches of society, they are sure to be wearing the very newest of Paris fashions.'

'Excuse me, Lady Morton.' An elegantly suited young man, who had been on the reception line, bowed gravely. 'My mother has asked me to introduce two of the gentlemen to the young ladies. Would that meet with your approval?'

'The duchess is most charming,' said Lady Morton with a smile, and two young men, who had been standing deferentially a pace or two away, moved forward. There was a murmur of conversation, then Emily and Violet were drawn into the swirl of dancers.

Amelia smiled with satisfaction. 'They are at least starting well,' she said.

'Yes. It is so infuriating that, even at what is probably the most elegant ball of the year, the young men prefer hanging around the refreshment room, or smoking in the garden, to dancing. See how many of the girls are dancing with really quite mature men.'

'I imagine that the men, at least, are enjoying it!"

'Perhaps. But how is one to marry off a daughter, when the eligible males insist on congregating in a huddle to talk about race-horses?'

'Well, I am not concerned to marry off Violet,' said Amelia lightly. 'In fact quite the reverse.'

'Surely you would not have her an old maid?' exclaimed Lady Morton.

'Of course not, Charlotte. I brought her over in the hope that, after a season here, she would know her own mind better.'

'I do not follow you, Amelia.'

'Since you are probably the last person I should discuss the matter with, I shall want you to respect my confidence.'

'Of course,' said Charlotte, leaning forward with a smile of anticipation.

'You can well imagine that she has had no lack of admirers in Boston—some of them very pleasant boys. Although she clearly likes one or two quite well, she refuses to allow a serious relationship to develop . . . I think that, through the years, she has developed an ideal of manhood that is altogether more refined than she is likely to encounter in America.'

'I would not have said that Joshua is exactly boorish,' exclaimed Charlotte.

'No, of course not. I would not have married him, else. But, as you know, our men subscribe to a different ethos from the Europeans. There is so much to be done, such great opportunities. I am sure they find it very exhilarating and satisfying, but in the process they can become a little rough and inconsiderate.'

'Even in Boston?'

'Oh yes, even in Boston! Of course, one could say that the women are part of that way of life also; that they should accept it and civilize their menfolk as they go along. After all, that has been our role down the centuries! . . . But because of our frequent visits with you, and you with us, Violet has acquired a notion of how men should behave, which is essentially English.'

'I find that incomprehensible,' Charottle replied. 'Our families have not spent so much time together.'

'True, but they were always the special times, the highlights one looked back on, and compared with hum-drum everyday life. You know how, as a child, she admired Henry.'

'Henry?'

'Of course! You sound surprised.'

'I am.'

'But think of him when she was growing up—quietly authoritative, considerate and endlessly patient. I can still see them now, going down the long walk, hand in hand, when she was seven. And he has not changed through the years.'

'I suppose not—it is so hard for a married couple really to appreciate each other.'

'And as Henry has grown older, James has become her paragon.'

'James is hardly *a verray parfit gentil Knight*,' said Charlotte ruefully.

'Oh, but he is —in Violet's eyes. And until she makes up her mind about him, one way or the other, I doubt if she will ever settle down.'

'I see,' said Charlotte reflectively . . . 'But surely you would not approve?'

'The best I could wish for her is a happy marriage.'

'But they are cousins. What about their children?'

'It is not as if they had been born in a backwoods town in the Catskill Mountains, where everybody has been related to everybody else for generations.'

'And what would Joshua say?'

'I think he would welcome it. Your brother Thomas's son is the only male Harman of the next generation. I think Josh would be delighted if James were there to take over when he retired.'

Charlotte sighed. 'Well, I am sure that we should leave them to work things out themselves. James made it clear, several years ago, that I must not interfere in his choice of a wife . . . I only hope that Violet is not hurt in the process. James can be very ruthless, at times.'

The music stopped, and Violet and Emily were escorted back to their chaperons.

'How many dances was that?' asked Lady Morton archly.

'Two, aunt,' Violet gasped, her face suffused with excited pleasure. 'I just could not miss the polka!'

'Obviously your partner had no difficulty in persuading you! Was he nice?'

'Yes, in a stiff kind of way.'

'Who was he?'

'I did not catch his surname. He just bowed and said, rather abruptly, "I'm Rutherford", and that was that.'

Emily gave a giggle. 'That was Lord Rutherford,' she said. 'Peers are known only by their title . . . We will look him up in *Debrett*, when we get home.'

'No!' cried Violet, 'I don't want to have anything to do with that dreadful book! . . . Who was your partner, anyway?'

'Rueben Smith.'

'Is he not a duke?' Violet rallied her.

'No.'

'Not even a lowly lord?'

'He was very pleasant,' said Emily huffily.

'Good evening, ladies.' James, immaculately dressed, came

up to them and bowed. 'I am sorry that I could not get away in time to escort you here. I am afraid that I was detained at the office.'

'It sounds as if someone locked you up in your own cells!' exclaimed Emily.

'Sergeant Bragg needs do no more than look disapproving, and my resolve melts away. Have I missed anything?'

'Nothing that we have not missed also,' said Amelia.

Morton turned to Violet. 'Then may I have the pleasure of this waltz?' He led her to the edge of the dance-floor, and they were soon lost to sight.

'Are you enjoying yourself, Emily?' asked her mother.

'It's marvellous,' she replied, 'but I do wish someone would ask me to dance. I love waltzing.'

'Don't look round, dear, but a gentleman is crossing towards us now.'

Moments later, a young man halted before Lady Morton, smiled and bowed to her, then turning to Emily, asked her to dance.

'Well, at least they all seem to be having a good time,' Amelia remarked with a smile.

'Oh, look! It's the Prince of Wales!' Lady Morton pointed to the door with her fan. A short, rotund man stood by the door, surrounded by acolytes. His hair was grey and thinning, he wore a grey pointed beard, and his heavy-lidded eyes gave the impression of world-weariness. Meticulous in etiquette, he took the floor with the Duchess of Devonshire, but his eyes were constantly on the other women, exploring, appraising.

'Lady Morton! What a pleasure it is to see you here.'

A grizzled thick-set man was bowing to her.

'Why, Gordon, how nice! May I present my sister-in-law, Mrs Harman, from America. Colonel Wellstead is in command of the Life Guards, Henry's old regiment.'

Wellstead bowed low over Amelia's outstretched hand, then turned to Charlotte.

'Is General Morton not here this evening?' he asked.

'No. I could not drag him away from home.'

'A pity. We see all too little of him.' Wellstead turned to

Amelia. 'There may not be much of this waltz remaining, ma'am, but it would give me great pleasure.'

Amelia rose with a gratified smile, and Lady Morton was left alone.

Catherine Marsden followed her mother into the ballroom with some trepidation. It was her first really big dance, and she was worried lest she should not live up to the challenge. The duchess had been most kind, greeting her warmly. Quite surprisingly, her mother was taking the whole affair calmly, and seemed to know a great many more people than Catherine had expected. She acknowledged one greeting after another, as she made her way towards Lady Lanesborough—and seemed to be receiving an embarrassing number of invitations. Goodness! Even the Prince of Wales was here, chatting to acquaintances at the other end of the ballroom.

'You look quite radiant, dear,' Lady Lanesborough greeted her.

'Thank you. What a splendid ballroom this is.'

Catherine felt a light touch on her arm.

'May I be the first to pay homage to society's latest queen?'

'James! What are you doing here?' she exclaimed.

'You seem surprised to see me, Miss Marsden.'

'Surprised—and gratified.'

'I confess that this is not my natural habitat, but my family is here; mother, Emily, my aunt Amelia and my cousin Violet, from America.'

'Lovely! I must go and greet them.'

'But not, I hope, until you have given me the pleasure of this dance.'

'Why, James, how *galant*!'

She placed her hand on his arm, and stepped on to the dance floor.

'What is it like, to become the toast of London?' Morton asked with a smile.

'I think London must have gone off its collective head.'

'Nonsense! They have just realized what I have known for years, that you are the most beautiful young lady in England.'

'You should not flirt with me, James. It is not seemly.'

'If not here, then where?' he asked lightly.

Lady Lanesborough watched them with an approving eye.
'She looks quite beautiful, Harriet, and pale blue is so much
more tasteful than these clashing pinks and yellows . . . You
will have to give a dance for her, you realize that?'

'Oh, good heavens! I could never do that.'

'Of course you could, my dear. If you did not wish to put up
with the bother of holding it at home, you could have it at an
hotel. It would be perfectly proper, everyone is doing it these
days.'

'I suppose I shall have several invitations to reciprocate,'
Harriet assented feebly.

'That will be the least of your worries. Leave it till the
middle of the season, and all London will be fighting for
invitations . . . Here they come. Who is the young man?'

'The second son of Sir Henry Morton, from Kent,' Harriet
replied flustered.

'Never mind, dear. I am sure she will find a good match, in
time.'

Morton delivered Catherine to the protection of her mother,
bowed, and departed.

At the same time, with due ceremony, Violet and Emily
were returned to their parents.

'Who was your last partner?' Violet asked.

'An earl's younger son from Shropshire—and he danced like
one!' said Emily ruefully.

'I danced with Lord Rutherford again.'

'For the third time! You should not dance another with him,
or people will talk!'

Violet tossed her head. 'What do I care? He is really very
nice, once you get through his shyness. I even found out his
given name!'

'What is that?'

'Hugh . . . And he is a captain in the Life Guards.'

'Papa was colonel of that regiment, till he went on the army
staff.'

'Who was the girl James was dancing with?' Violet asked
casually.

'Oh, that was Catherine Marsden—you know, her portrait
was the sensation of the Royal Academy Exhibition. She is a

reporter on a London newspaper,' Emily went on enthusiasti-
cally, 'and she gets involved in all kinds of exciting
happenings. We all hope that she and James will marry.'

'And will they?' asked Violet flatly.

'Who knows? I think they are both too independent ever to
submit to each other.'

'Does a man ever have to submit?'

'The man Catherine accepted would have to—and then she
would no longer want him!'

At that moment, with Lady Lanesborough's encouragement,
Mrs Marsden was broaching a sensitive topic with her daughter.

'You have so many invitations, dear—to dances and dinners,
drums and picnics, teas and garden parties . . . I have a very
pressing invitation for you to help at a charity bazaar, next
Friday. It is a very worthy cause.'

'What time is it?'

'Three o'clock.'

'But I shall be working.'

'Must you dear? Lots of other girls will be there, behind the
stalls. It will be quite an event. The Princess of Wales has
promised to attend.'

'It is quite out of the question,' Catherine replied sharply. "I
work full time, and that includes every Friday, charity bazaars
or not.'

'But surely, dear,' Lady Lanesborough cut in, 'you will give
all that up now. You will not have time to work, with all the
engagements you will have.'

'Full time also includes May, June and July, Lady Lanesborough. If there were any question of choosing between the
one and the other—and I do not for a moment concede that
there could be—then I would not give up a hard-won,
responsible job, to play at shop-girls to fill an idle moment.'
Catherine spun on her heel, and came face to face with the
Prince of Wales.

'Ah, my dear young lady, I wonder if you would honour me
with the next dance.'

Catherine dropped a curtsy. 'Delighted, your royal highness.'

He held out his arm and escorted her on to the floor. She felt a strange sensation of elation and trepidation, as the crowd opened in front of them, making an avenue of animated and curious faces.

The waltz began and, as they danced, the crowd drew back to give them room. For a time the prince observed her without speaking. Then he smiled.

'You are very much the young lady of your portrait,' he said. 'I went to see it, you know—on the afternoon of the private viewing . . . Did you enjoy the account of it in *The Times*?'

'It was very flattering, sir.'

'And very perspicacious.'

'Perhaps.'

For some time they danced in silence, then the prince remarked casually: 'Your father is an exceedingly talented portraitist.'

'Thank you, sir. I think so.'

The prince laughed. 'With such a daughter to speak for him, it cannot be long before he is accorded the honour which is his due.'

The music stopped, and the prince, his arm still round her waist, escorted her to the corner of the room. Then, suddenly, he was whispering into her ear, his fingers, under her elbow, probing her breast.

'You are a very beautiful young lady, do you know that?'

'I have been told so,' replied Catherine, trying to keep her voice level.

'Why do you not come and have supper with me—in, say, half an hour. You see Fritz there?' He pointed with his disengaged hand. 'He is my equerry. He will be able to smuggle you into Marlborough House.'

'Alas! I fear bed is calling me.'

'You are also unusually forthright, my dear!'

'I have to get up early to go to work,' Catherine blurted out in confusion and embarrassment.

'Whatever kind of work is that?' the prince asked indulgently.

'I am a reporter on a newspaper.'

The prince released her abruptly. 'Then I will most certainly

allow you to go,' he replied coldly. 'I cannot say that I count
members of the press amongst my friends, nor would I wish
to.'

Major Walker, the Metropolitan police Assistant Commissioner, was a thick-set man with greying hair and a military
moustache. He was wearing a frock-coat and a silk cravat. He
waved Bragg and the Goodge Street Inspector to sit, then,
taking a pencil in his smooth tapering fingers, he leaned back
in his chair.

'I understand, Sergeant Bragg, that you have made a formal
reference under the liaison system to the effect that you wish to
enter the premises above the tobacconist's shop in Cleveland
Street. That reference has, very properly, been passed to me by
my people.'

'Yes, sir.'

'What is your purpose?' asked Walker.

'To search them, and to question anyone I might happen to
find there.'

'I am afraid that that would be quite impossible. I do not
have the authority to permit it.'

'Then who has?' asked Bragg tersely.

'All I know is that the Home Office put a stop on the
premises, three years ago. I suspect that you would have to go
very much higher than a departmental clerk, however eminent.'

'What possible reason could there be for that?'

'I am not prepared to go further, sergeant.'

'But criminal offences are taking place there!' said Bragg in
exasperation. 'Not only are you turning a blind eye to that, now
that you are hindering my enquiries you are bloody conniving
at it!'

'I take great exception to that remark, sergeant,' said the AC
hotly.

'Then why are you protecting a bunch of stir-shits?'

'We have had no complaints,' replied Walker, mastering his
anger. 'We have no official knowledge of what goes on there.'

'Well I have. A man on my patch used to visit there. He was

being rented, and when the money ran out, he committed suicide.'

'Does the City police detective department still investigate suicide as a crime?' asked Walker with a sneer. 'We have more important matters on our hands.'

'Blackmail is important—and it is going on in Cleveland Street.'

'I believe it is a common feature of such establishments.'

'Then why is it being tolerated?'

The AC hesitated. 'Because of the class of persons who frequent it,' he said at length.

'Upper-class bum-boys, are they?'

'Yes.'

'I shall enjoy turning that over,' said Bragg sardonically.

'I tell you there is a stop on it!' Walker exclaimed.

'None that the City police have heard of. I will take some lads down tonight—just in case the Home Office should suddenly realize that they haven't informed us.'

Walker bridled at the implication. 'You must know,' he said angrily, 'that any such action on your part would prejudice the *modus vivendi* at present existing between the two forces.'

'Well, it isn't achieving anything at this moment, is it?'

The AC threw his pencil on to the desk, and cleared his throat irritably. 'Very well . . . but I want you—and you Inspector—to understand that you are to forget entirely what I am about to tell you. Is that clear?'

'Yes sir,' they said.

Walker considered for a moment, gazing out of the window at a string of barges moving slowly up river. Then he turned to Bragg.

'The stop was put on by the Home Office, at the request of Marlborough House,' he said portentously. 'There were suspicions that the premises in Cleveland Street were being visited by the Duke of Clarence.'

'Christ Almighty!' exclaimed Bragg. 'But he was the Prince of Wales's eldest son, and heir to the throne after him!'

'I see you well appreciate the delicacy of the issues involved.'

'It sounds like a damned good reason for closing it down, to me,' said Bragg robustly. 'Anyway he has been dead for a year and more. Why is the stop still on?'

'Consider what would happen if we took them; and let us make the improbable assumption that we obtained evidence to found charges under section eleven. How are we to prevent reference to the Duke of Clarence and his friends being made during the proceedings? Think what the gutter press would make of that!'

'I would have thought the judge could handle that. I've seen them shut a witness up pretty quickly, at times.'

'No one would be prepared to take the risk involved—not even you, sergeant.'

'And are you content to let them go on committing these disgusting offences, with impunity?'

'I am not content, no.'

'Well, Duke of Clarence or not, I cannot just close down my file. In the strictest confidence, the victim was the late dean of St Paul's. The coroner insists on proceeding with the investigation. Sir Rufus has friends in high places and is not a man to brook interference from any quarter. If I drag my heels, he is quite capable of going down there himself. God knows what would happen then.'

'These damned coroners!' exclaimed the AC testily. 'They have too much power for their own good.' His gaze drifted over to the river again. Then he stood up abruptly.

'Very well,' he said. 'You may enter the premises this evening. The Inspector will get the necessary warrant. He must be with you at all times, and he will wear plain clothes. You must confine your investigation to the individuals engaged in running the establishment. You must neither question clients, nor ask questions about them. Above all, there must be no charges laid. No charges whatever. Understand?'

'Now don't forget, lad, as soon as you get inside, you hold the door so that we can follow.'

They were huddled in a dark entry in Conway Street. Morton was in full evening dress, a silk top hat on his head, a carnation in his buttonhole.

'I have been involved in some thoroughly disreputable

enterprizes, during our association, sergeant,' he remarked, 'but this is by far the most repugnant.'

'Get away with you! You look every inch a swell—if a bit left-handed!'

The Met inspector sniggered, and Morton gave him a baleful glance.

'Once inside, we dash upstairs, secure any exits and grab the principals.'

'But not clients, Joe. That was the deal.'

'I know, Bill. So long as we are agreed that the dean of St Paul's can't be a client, because he's dead.'

'But why on earth should they admit me?' asked Morton. 'They have never seen me before.'

'I should hope not,' said Bragg with a grin. 'You just rap at the door with your stick, stand back under the gas lamp where they can see you, and look as nobby as you can.'

'I only hope it succeeds, or we shall look exceedingly stupid.'

'If you are challenged,' remarked the Inspector, 'say that Lord Alfred sent you.'

'Thanks, Bill,' said Bragg. 'Who's he?'

'He's abroad—fled the country.'

'We will be close behind you, lad,' continued Bragg. 'We shall be screened by the yard wall till we get to the gate, and there isn't a light in the yard. So we are only at risk once we are in the passage. There won't be anyone inside the shop, so the only view they will have, will be from the peep-hole. There should not be any problem . . . If there is, you're going to have to break the door down.'

Morton grinned. 'In that case, I will do my best to convince them.' He raised his finger to the brim of his hat in salute, then sauntered off. Bragg and the Inspector crept after him, keeping in the shadow of the wall. They saw him open the gate, hesitate for a moment, then walk into the yard leaving the gate ajar. They followed quietly, tip-toeing across the flags, and took up position just inside the back door.

Morton rapped loudly on the oaken door with his cane, then stood back. In the lamplight his features were aristocratic, commanding.

Then came a rattle as the peep-hole was opened, then for some seconds nothing happened.

'Well,' came Morton's voice, 'are you going to open the door, my man?'

The reply was inaudible.

'I was sent here by Lord Alfred. He said there would be no difficulty.'

There was a murmur, then the noise of a key turning in the lock. Bragg and the Inspector dashed along the passage, and flung themselves after Morton. In a second the dazed guard had been handcuffed and gagged, the door locked, and the key was in Bragg's pocket. They paused, listening, but the scuffle had been so slight, that no one had been alerted above.

'Right, lad, up you go,' Bragg whispered. 'And don't forget you are a gentleman usher of the back door!'

Morton grimaced, then began to climb the stairs with a firm tread. He reached the landing and, pushing open a door, entered a room that took up the whole of that floor. It was dimly lit with oil lamps, but the smell of paraffin was overlaid by the strong scent of incense. The walls were hung with dark red velvet, so that no windows were visible. The ceiling was painted a deep blue, patterned with golden stars and a declining moon. The floor was covered with thick carpet, and settees and low tables were set discreetly around.

As Morton stood in the doorway, a man walked towards him, and greeted him. There could be no doubt that it was a man, though he was dressed as a woman, in a fantastic black and gold dress.

'Hello,' he said in an affected voice. 'You are new here, aren't you?'

'Yes. Lord Alfred recommended your salon.'

'Oh! How nice! How is his lordship?'

'Well, thank you. I met him abroad last month.'

'It was such a pity . . . Still, he has found you for us . . . And how fortunate! Percy is in this evening. He used to be a special favourite with Lord Alfred. I must introduce you! Would you like coffee, or wine before you . . . er?'

'Wine, by all means,' agreed Morton, wondering anxiously what was delaying Bragg.

The fantastic creature minced over to a spiral staircase at the far end of the room and, peering upwards, called for Percy. In response, a slight youth appeared and descended the staircase slowly, his eyes fixed on Morton as he negotiated its curves. Reaching the bottom he advanced towards him, hands on hips, swaying voluptuously. To Morton, it seemed an obscene caricature of a Moulin Rouge *danseuse*. The boy was naked, except for tight-fitting breeches of black silk. His chest had been adorned with little gold stars and crescents. As he came closer, Morton could see long slits in the breeches extending from near the waistband, down the front of the thigh. They were braided with gold, and the flesh showed pink beneath.

The creature sidled up to Morton, and pressed against him sensually.

'Hello,' he said softly.

The greeting seemed so mundane, after the display of licentiousness, that Morton almost laughed.

'I hear that you were a good friend of Lord Alfred,' he said.

'Oh yes,' replied Percy. 'We had some good times, him and me.'

The transvestite pranced over with a tray, on which there was a bottle of champagne and two glasses. With a salacious smile, he bent over to pour the wine.

'Police! Stay where you are, everybody!' cried Bragg, bursting into the room. The Inspector ran past him and dashed up the staircase. In a trice, the boy and the transvestite were handcuffed and sprawling on the floor, while Bragg was racketing around the room, searching every nook and cranny. After five minutes, the Inspector came stolidly down the staircase.

'Anyone up there?' asked Bragg.

'No one that need concern you, sergeant. The boys would not know anything, anyway.'

Bragg glared at the Inspector, then hauled the transvestite to his feet.

'Right, you loathsome bugger, I want some answers out of you!'

'I don't know anything!' whined the man.

In answer, Bragg fetched him a blow across the face that sent him staggering back, till he tripped over the train of his dress and went sprawling. Bragg followed him like a terrier after a rat, and dragged him to his feet again.

'Don't make me soil my fist again, you revolting pervert!' he growled threateningly. 'Are you going to answer my questions?'

'Don't hit me!' the man cowered away.

'I am going to show you a photograph—of a man we know used to come here. I don't want you to name him.' Bragg took the photograph of the dean out of his pocket, and thrust it into the light of the oil lamp.

'But he's dead!' exclaimed the man.

'I know. Now, he used to bring an envelope with him sometimes. Who did he give it to?'

'How would I . . .' he flinched back from Bragg's raised fist . . . 'How can I tell you, if I don't know?' he wailed.

'What do you know?'

'I know you are right, because I once saw him put an envelope in the rack.'

'Rack? What rack?' demanded Bragg.

The man gestured with his manacled hands to a small desk by the door, with coat pegs beside it. Behind the desk were some pigeon-holes.

'The gentlemen leave notes there, for each other . . . It is a rule of the house that it must be done discreetly . . . Some men get awfully jealous.'

'What would they put on the outside of the envelope?'

'Either a christian name, or one they had made up for themselves.'

'And were these envelopes always picked up?'

'Yes,' a hint of malicious triumph touched the man's lips. 'But I don't know who took them.'

A disgruntled Bragg unlocked the handcuffs, then the policemen banged down the stairs and out into the street.

'My God!' said Bill, breathing in the clean air. 'I have never seen anything like that in my life! It made me want to vomit.'

'What about me?' complained Morton. 'I think you took sadistic pleasure in letting that vile youth paw me!'

'We had to wait till the nancy came back with the wine,' said

Bragg with a grin. 'You did well, lad. I see, now, you are every inch an aristocrat! But where the hell has it got us? . . . Come on, Bill, you could tip us the wink, if you would.'

'Well, Joe,' the Inspector said slowly, 'you used to be a literary bloke in the old days . . . The only client I could name is a man of no importance . . . Goodnight.'

'What is that supposed to mean?' Bragg asked of his retreating back.

'I seem to recollect,' said Morton, 'that a play called *A Woman of No Importance* is on at the Haymarket.'

CHAPTER —————
————— FIVE

Catherine had left church after morning service and was walking home, when she heard a voice calling her name. She looked round and saw Arabella Godfrey hastening towards her. Catherine sighed. She had been hoping to steal home, and clarify her ideas on what she hoped the editor might see as a topical article about the Worshipful Company of Fan Makers. Now she would have to join the Sunday parade in Hyde Park.

They walked slowly along, Arabella chattering feverishly about society's doings. It was not as if she really liked the girl, thought Catherine irritably. But with her entry into the tribe, she seemed to have accepted an obligation to converse endlessly and emptily with everybody. How absurd it all was! Yet she had to confess that she was secretly enjoying it. She had always thought herself ill-favoured. As a child she would look in the mirror and wish that she had a pretty, round face, like many of her friends. Her own had always seemed long and thin, and she had been automatically cast in the male roles in school plays. Now beauty seemed to have stolen on her unawares; the very things she had hated seemed to make her distinctive. She overheard people talking about her fine cheek-bones, her aristocratic nose. They were comparing her to Mrs Langtry, and papa had said that no one else had made such an impact on society, till now. 'The most beautiful young lady in England,' that was what James had said. It was something she would remember—she hoped that he would!

They crossed Park Lane and walked through Stanhope Gate towards the area where society forgathered. Catherine glanced back regretfully at her parents' house, where she could have been happily scribbling by now. Well, she would have to put a good face on it, and play the part that a whimsical fate had decreed. They walked sedately down the path, smiling and responding to salutes. The men, fresh from bestowing fraternal greetings on the Almighty, were dressed in dark frock-coats and silk hats. Their ladies were more prepared to acknowledge the brilliance of the morning, and although the colours were subdued, the materials were rich—*chiné* silk, grenadine, chiffon. Reluctantly, Catherine admitted to herself that it was gratifying to be at the centre of it all.

Then, she suddenly realized that her companion's voice had changed; that instead of the bright prattle, there was urgency in her tone.

'I am sorry,' said Catherine. 'Please start all over again.'

'I said I need your help,' said Arabella plaintively. 'I cannot think of anyone else to turn to. If I went to the family solicitor, it would only get back to papa, and I am desperate.'

'How on earth can I help you?'

'Well, I know you are friendly with that young policeman, who was so brave last year. I hoped that you might persuade him to advise me.'

'Goodness!' exclaimed Catherine. 'This is a very sombre conversation for a May morning.'

'I cannot help that . . . If I do not find a way out, I am ruined!'

A note of hysteria was creeping into Arabella's voice, so Catherine led her to chairs, set apart under a tree.

'Now,' said Catherine, when they were settled, 'whatever kind of trouble are you in? Is it financial?'

'Well, yes, that is part of it. I have to pay a considerable sum, and I do not have the money.'

'Is it your dressmaker?'

'No.'

'Surely you have not borrowed money, unknown to your family?' Catherine asked in a disapproving tone.

'Oh, how I wish I could do!'

'So it is worse than that?'

'Far, far worse! Oh, Catherine, please help me!'

Catherine glanced at her fob-watch. 'Very well,' she said decisively. 'If we take a cab immediately, we might catch him at his rooms.'

Arabella seemed to take heart, and during the journey essayed a few bright remarks about the events of the coming week; but as they neared Bishopsgate, she fell silent again. Catherine had a momentary twinge of apprehension. Was she not being foolish? James was so chivalrous, and here was a not unattractive maiden in distress . . .

The door was answered by Chambers, James's manservant. He ushered them up the narrow stairs into the hall of the apartment, then went to announce them. Moments later, James came striding out of the sitting-room, a broad smile of pleasure on his handsome face. Catherine glanced at Arabella, but, thankfully, she was too lost in her problems to respond. He showed them inside.

'What a delightful surprise!' he exclaimed. 'I seldom receive calls, at this distance from town—and never from beautiful young ladies!' His eyes met Catherine's teasingly.

'This is Arabella Godfrey,' she said shortly.

Morton bowed, and saw that the ladies were seated.

'Arabella is in some kind of financial trouble,' said Catherine. 'She has asked me to persuade you to help her.'

'I would be pleased to, if I am able. What kind of trouble is this, Miss Godfrey?'

'I have received a demand for money, which I cannot pay,' Arabella began tensely. 'I dare not go to my father for it, and I have no money left. Nor have I enough jewellery to sell, in order to raise it.'

'How much is at stake?' asked Morton.

'One hundred pounds,' replied Arabella in a low voice.

'Not a trifle, then.'

'No.'

'Have you explained to this person that you cannot readily find the money? Sometimes they will agree to an accommodation.'

'I do not know who it is.'

'You do not know? . . .' Morton was suddenly alert. 'Then this is not a sum that you owe?'

'No.'

'How was the demand conveyed to you?'

In answer, Arabella took a folded paper from her bag, and passed it over. As Morton spread it out on his knee, Catherine could see that the letter was printed, in capitals.

'Why did you not take this to the police?' asked Morton.

'I was afraid that they would not be discreet.'

'I see, but you believe that I will be?' There was a hard edge to the flippant tone.

'I hoped . . . ' Arabella's voice trailed off.

'As it happens, we have seen something like this before.' He glanced at the boule clock on the mantlepiece. 'I take it that you will not have to be back for luncheon until two o'clock; I suggest that we take a short cab ride to see my superior, Sergeant Bragg.'

When they arrived at Tan House Lane, Bragg was in the garden, spraying Mrs Jenks's rose buds with soapsuds to kill the greenfly. He answered her summons with his shirt sleeves rolled up to the elbow and collarless, and mounted the stairs to his sitting-room at the back of the house. He surveyed the serious faces of his visitors.

'And what can I do for you lot?' he asked, crossing to the mantlepiece for his pipe.

'This is Miss Arabella Godfrey,' said Morton. 'She has received a most interesting missive.'

Bragg waited until his pipe was drawing to his satisfaction, then held out his hand for the letter. He read it carefully.

'The sign at the top seems to be the same,' he remarked, returning it to Morton. 'Is this the first one you have had, miss?'

'I had a similar one, a month ago.'

'How much was that for?'

'One hundred pounds also . . . . I used up all my allowance to meet that. I have no money left.'

'What happened to that letter?' Bragg asked.

'I am afraid that I tore it up, and burned it.'

'I see . . . How did you deliver the money?'

'I sent it to a convenience address in Paddington, as instructed in the letter.'

'How do you know it was a convenience address?'

'I went to look. It was a newspaper shop, with advertising cards in the window. I went inside to ask if I could receive letters there, and the man said I could.'

'I see, well done!' A trace of admiration had crept into Bragg's voice. 'He was taking a chance. He could have found the police waiting for him when he collected it . . . Either that, or he knows you well enough to be certain that you wouldn't go to the police.'

'Knows her?' exclaimed Catherine.

'Is Miss Marsden in your confidence?' asked Bragg.

'Well . . . no.'

'I think she should be; partly because it is not fair of you to involve her, otherwise, and partly because she might be able to help. You can trust her, you know.'

'If you think I should . . . '

With a frown of disapproval, Morton held out the letter. Catherine took it, and opened it out.

I MIGHT BE ABLE TO NEGOTIATE A SALE
BUT I SHALL NEED £100 FOR EXPENSES.
BRING IT TO THE SHAFTESBURY MEMORIAL
AT HALF PAST FOUR ON TUESDAY.
COME ALONE.

'What kind of hold has he over you?' asked Bragg. 'Have you done something criminal, or just been a bit rash?'

'I assure you that there is nothing behind it, sergeant.'

'Then you have nothing to worry about, miss.'

'Oh, but I have!' She glanced at Catherine mistrustfully. 'I am about to make a very advantageous marriage. The engagement is to be announced next Saturday.'

'Then, you should be on top of the world. What are you afraid of?' Bragg asked.

'Malicious gossip.'

'Why not unburden yourself to your young man? If he is any sort of chap at all, he will stick by you.'

Arabella moistened her lips with the tip of her tongue. 'The world might believe that I had been indiscreet. His family would shy away from the least breath of scandal.'

'The police can do nothing against the spreading of calumny,' said Morton. 'Nor would you wish them to try. Their investigations would only serve to spread the rumour more effectively than ever.'

'I think you are worrying unnecessarily,' said Bragg in a fatherly voice. 'Baseless tittle-tattle will never be credited by them that know you, and them that believe it are not worth having as friends anyway. My advice is to go on as normal, and disregard this letter. If you have done nothing, then he can't do you any harm.'

With painful reluctance Arabella opened her bag again, and, taking out a photograph, passed it to Bragg.

'This was sent with the first letter,' she said.

'It was a snap showing two figures lying side by side, in the secluded corner of a garden or a park. The man was in the foreground with his back to the camera, he was in his shirtsleeves. The picture was good enough to see that there was a bald spot on top of his head. He was propped up on his left elbow, looking down at the girl lying beside him, It was Arabella, there was no doubt about it, and she was clearly enjoying herself.

'It was not at all as it appears,' she urged. 'It was at a picnic in Windsor Great Park. Many other people were there, just close by.'

'Then you may well know the person who took the snap,' said Bragg.

'I . . . I suppose so.'

'I want you to let me have a list of everyone who was at that picnic.'

'I can try, but it was a charity affair. There were hundreds of people there.'

Bragg looked at her sceptically, then handed the photograph to Morton. 'I can see why you are concerned, miss,' he said in a matter-of-fact tone. 'It looks just like it did when I saw the bailiff and the innkeeper's wife, down by the bluebell wood. He had his braces down, too.'

Arabella flinched. 'What can I do?' she asked.

'Well, one thing's for sure, you can't go along with it. If you pay this, there will be another. He would probably be quite happy for you to get married. He would think he was made for life. You would receive a letter every month, and you'd get in deeper and deeper. Nothing is worth that . . . Of course, you could help us to catch him.'

'Could I?' said Arabella eagerly.

'Well, I might be able to arrange for the money to be made available—not as a loan, but out of public funds. Then you could go to the meeting next Tuesday, and we would keep observation, to see what happened.'

'I would willingly do that.'

'Good! You had better not be seen in contact with us, so we will let you know the arrangements through Miss Marsden.'

'Thank you, so much . . . And the engagement will be able to go ahead as planned!' Arabella said buoyantly.

'That is up to you, miss,' said Bragg shortly. 'That is up to you.'

It was late afternoon before Catherine could leave to pay a call on Lady Morton, at Curzon Street. The stupid Godfrey girl had been bubbling with relief, and had confided her plans for the wedding at great length and in the minutest detail. She now had the details of Arabella's trousseau, down to the very embroidery on her nightdress. Catherine wondered sourly if a husband would ever see it. Sergeant Bragg did not believe her protestations of innocence, so much was clear . . . How did someone as vapid as Arabella ever catch a husband, never mind a highly eligible one? She was cheerful enough as a rule, but she was far from beautiful, with her deep-set eyes and low forehead. It must be the full, pouting mouth, Catherine decided. Now that really was sensual! She mounted the steps and was delighted to see Parker, the senior footman from The Priory.

'Afternoon, miss,' he greeted her in a broad Kentish burr. 'The ladies is at home. You will find them in the drawing-room.'

'How nice to see you again, Parker. Is your wife here with you?'

'Yes, miss,' he grinned. 'Helping out in the kitchen.'

'I am so glad. Perhaps I shall see you at The Priory, this summer.'

'I hope so, miss.'

Catherine went slowly up the grand staircase and into the drawing-room. There were still a few guests, despite the lateness of the hour, and heads were turned in her direction.

Lady Morton crossed over to her. 'My dear, what a success you are having!' she said. 'Your mother must be so delighted . . . May I introduce to you my sister-in-law, Amelia?'

'You live in Boston, do you not?' asked Catherine.

'Yes. Do you know it?'

'I am afraid not. My visits abroad have not extended beyond a few short trips to the continent.'

Amelia smiled. 'I see Emily is waving at you, over there . . . I am sure we shall meet again.'

Catherine went to the far end of the room. 'I am sorry to come at so unceremonious an hour,' she said. 'James rather interrupted my plans today.'

'This is Violet, my cousin from America,' said Emily. 'We saw you at the Devonshires' ball, and then you suddenly disappeared!'

'It was borne in upon me that I was a working girl,' replied Catherine, 'and that my job demands a few hours' sleep each night!' She turned to Violet. 'James tells me that you are having a season here,' she said.

'Yes,' replied Violet shortly.

'Uncle Josh has sent her over to capture an earl or a viscount!' said Emily, laughing.

'You promised!' cried Violet accusingly.

'Catherine doesn't count,' said Emily defiantly. 'She is almost one of the family.'

'What promise is this?' asked Catherine.

'As you might imagine,' said Violet, 'it is quite the opposite of what Emily suggests. I am only interested in enjoying myself, not in finding a husband.'

'But she has made a conquest!' exclaimed Emily. 'She will not let me look him up in the red book, but I believe he is a good catch!'

'Good or bad, I am only interested in him as a dancing partner.'

'But we think we will ask mamma to invite him to the opera, on the eighteenth.'

'Are you ready for your presentation?' asked Catherine. 'Have you practised your curtsy?'

In answer Emily got to her feet, and sank gracefully to the floor.

'That is very good,' said Catherine. 'When the Prince of Wales introduced himself to me the other night, I was so flustered that I almost overbalanced!'

'We saw you dancing with him. It must be wonderful to meet him.'

'It was an experience that I could have survived perfectly well without,' said Catherine ironically. 'Are you enjoying yourself, Violet?'

'Oh, yes! There is hardly time to sleep! I think that when I get back home I shall have to go into hibernation, to catch up . . . You do some odd things over here, though. This afternoon we went to Tattersall's auction ring. There was nothing going on; just a few horses being led around prior to the sale tomorrow, and yet the place was crowded with fashionable people.'

'That is really no different from the Eton and Harrow cricket match,' said Emily. 'Most of the people there care so little about cricket, they don't even pretend to watch. James positively refuses to go near it!'

'I sometimes think,' said Catherine, 'that if you put it about that fashionable people would be going to the gasworks at such and such a time, the whole of society would turn up, without knowing why.'

'Or caring,' added Emily stoutly. 'The whole idea is that you are showing you belong.'

'On the whole,' said Catherine, 'I feel rather relieved that I do not.'

'Oh, but you must!' cried Emily. 'How can you not? Everyone is vying to get you to their houses.'

'I thought you were at the centre of it all,' said Violet.

'Good heavens, no! I cannot claim any connections with the aristocracy, nor am I ever likely to. My father is a painter, my mother is the daughter of a country gentleman. We are no more than on the fringe of society, and that by courtesy of my father's talent.'

'But you are a beauty,' said Emily vehemently, 'and they have always been able to enter society.'

Catherine laughed, 'I suppose that if I worked hard enough at it, I might succeed. But I begin to doubt if it would be worth the effort. To be a "professional beauty" is surely not so much better than being one of the professional ladies who haunt the promenade at the Empire.'

CHAPTER ──────────
──────────── SIX

'You know that the coroner brought in a verdict of accidental death on the dean, I suppose?' remarked the Commissioner.

'I didn't know, sir,' said Bragg.

Sir William Sumner CB shifted uneasily in his chair. From his recent daily contacts with the Prince of Wales, Morton could see that the supposed resemblance of the two men was only superficial. Sir William was taller, slimmer, and did not have the Prince of Wales's heavy jowls.

'It seemed to fly in the face of the evidence, though,' the Commissioner said.

'I know, sir, but I went through it with Sir Rufus, and while it all hung together, it was circumstantial. It would not have stood up in a court of law.'

'I would not have called the letters circumstantial,' said Sir William gruffly. 'In any case, the burden of proof is not the same as in a criminal case.'

'I expect it was the best verdict for all concerned,' said Bragg mildly.

'No doubt . . . But there are rumours, Bragg, that he was a . . . hmn, a you-know-what. God knows where they have come from.'

'Indeed, sir?'

'They say it is round all the clubs,' Sir William went on. 'I wondered if the blackmailer had set them afoot, as a kind of revenge.'

'You could well be right, sir. If so, he is a particularly nasty kind of person.'

'Now, what about this request of yours for a hundred pounds from public funds? It seems a great deal of money. I cannot imagine what the Lord Mayor will have to say about it.'

'A young society woman has received this, sir.' Bragg laid Arabella's letter in front of the Commissioner, and he read it carefully.

'Not a charitable letter, this time,' he remarked, 'more a commercial one.'

'Yes, sir. He's a bit above your common or garden renter. He does try to dress his demands up as innocently as he can.'

'Why do you think he puts the insignia at the top?' asked Sir William.

'Well, he prints the letters, and he doesn't sign them. He would want his victim to know they are coming from the same source.'

'And what hold has he over this young woman?'

Bragg passed over the photograph, and the Commissioner examined it intently. 'I take it that the first letter offered to get the negative for her,' he remarked.

'I imagine so, sir.'

'She is about to announce her engagement to a sprig of a noble tree,' said Morton lightly.

Sir William cleared his throat. 'They say the camera never lies,' he remarked. 'I can see why she should be anxious to pay up. I am less sure about why she should be helped from public funds.'

'We want to be there, in Piccadilly Circus, when she hands over the money,' said Bragg. 'With any luck, we should be able to take him.'

'What makes you so sure that it is a man? It could just as easily be a woman.'

'I suppose so,' said Bragg, momentarily wrong-footed. 'Still, if it were a woman it would be even better. A society lady would never venture as far as the memorial without a compelling reason. She might get mistaken for one of the Haymarket girls! And if one did appear, young Morton, here, would be able to spot her in a trice.'

'Why do you think it is someone in society?'

'Well, sir, Miss Godfrey said that the photograph was taken at a charity picnic in Windsor Great Park. Nobody but the nobs would go to one of them.'

The Commissioner mused for a while, then looked across at Morton.

'I did not know that you were interested in society functions,' he said.

'To be frank, sir,' replied Morton, 'I am not.'

'Well, from now on I think you should be,' said Sir William decisively. 'Very well, Bragg, you shall have your money.'

Gibson looked up warily, as he realized that Bragg and Morton were standing before his counter.

'We would like a word, when it is convenient,' murmured Bragg.

'Very well,' replied Gibson with an impatient sigh. 'You will have to wait until I have dealt with the customers behind you.'

As before, Bragg and Morton kicked their heels in the ornate banking hall, until Gibson reappeared and took them down to the small interviewing room.

'What is it this time?' he asked.

'We want your advice on a technical matter,' said Bragg smoothly. 'We are setting up an operation, and we wouldn't want to muck it up for lack of expert knowledge.'

Gibson gave a gratified smile.

'We are going to provide some money to a member of the public,' Bragg continued, 'and he will then pay it on, in settlement of a debt. We would like to find out where it ends up.'

'I see. How much are you concerned with?'

'A hundred pounds.'

'A small amount, then . . . Well, you certainly would not trace it, if the payment were made in sovereigns. It would have to be in notes.'

'I see, right,' said Bragg encouragingly.

'We could issue you with ten ten-pound notes,' said Gibson. 'Then we would know the serial numbers.'

'But they would be all nice and new,' objected Bragg. 'I wouldn't want that . . . It wouldn't fit in with the habits of the man making the payment.'

'I am afraid that we never reissue a note,' said Gibson. 'Every note that crosses this counter is cancelled. You should go to a joint-stock bank. They will be able to give you some used notes.'

'Now, that would be a problem. For a start, the funds will be coming from the Corporation of London's account with you; then again, we wouldn't be able to trust one of these commercial bankers to keep his mouth shut.'

Gibson looked deprecating, yet intrigued. 'Obviously, I am too junior to bend the rules,' he said slowly. 'But, Mr May, the chief cashier, could. And since you saved his reputation last summer, he could well be disposed to do so. Wait here a moment.'

After what seemed an interminable time, Gibson reappeared and led them upstairs into the chief cashier's office.

'Good morning, sergeant,' May said genially.

'Good morning, sir.'

'I gather that you want us to do something unorthodox.'

'It would appear so, sir.'

'I would wish to be assured that it was a matter of importance. It would involve putting several people to some inconvenience.'

'There has been one death in the case already, sir,' replied Bragg amiably.

'Well, that seems important enough . . . No one we would know, I suppose?'

'I am not at liberty to say, sir.'

'No, I can understand that . . . Well, we certainly could

make an exception, and reissue some notes. Mr Gibson suggested tens. Is that what you want?'

'It seems a good idea to me, sir. They are more likely to turn up again quickly.'

'How long would it take you to accumulate ten moderately used notes, Gibson?' the chief cashier asked with a conspiratorial smile.

'Certainly I would have them well before the close of business this afternoon, sir.'

'Then, if you will come in at three, sergeant, you shall have them . . . Ask for me, would you?'

'Thank you, sir. And you will have a note of the serial numbers, will you?'

'Of course,' said May indulgently.

'How long will they take to come back here again?' Bragg asked innocently.

'I expect one or two might come back within, say, a week or two. Most will knock about in people's pockets, or the banking system, for a time.'

Bragg looked blank. 'I'm sorry,' he said, 'I thought they would come back straight away . . . We haven't that sort of time to play with.'

'Well,' said May, 'I suppose we could ask all the banks to keep an eye open for them, and report back to us as soon as they are received. If we make the request under normal conditions of banking confidentiality, their customer will be kept in ignorance of it.'

'Would they really do that, sir?' asked Bragg in amazement.

'Oh, yes, sergeant. I only have to ask, and they will do it.'

When they got back into Threadneedle Street, Morton began to laugh. 'You knew all that, from last year,' he said. 'You played them both like fat trout.'

Bragg smiled smugly. 'People like to help, lad. It's a great human weakness.'

'I wonder where the rumours about the dean's sexual proclivities could have come from,' Morton remarked.

'Oh, these things leak out like a fiddler's fart—always in the wrong key!'

Morton laughed. 'After such a graphic simile, I can understand why the Met Inspector called you a "literary bloke".'

They took a cab to Chelsea and walked to Oscar Wilde's house. They were shown into his study by a manservant. The playwright rose from his desk and, with an extravagant gesture, waved them towards the settee.

'I was just considering some emendations to *A Woman of No Importance*,' he declared. 'But who am I to tamper with perfection?'

He was tall and plump, with almond-shaped eyes, and a heavy jaw. He was dressed in a well-cut frock-coat, with a half-guinea buttonhole at the lapel.

'We just wanted a few words, sir.'

'Certainly, sergeant,' Wilde smiled complacently. 'Conversation is the catalyst of sensation.'

'We are interested in the tobacconist's shop in Cleveland Street,' said Bragg. 'Do you know the one I mean?'

Wilde pursed his lips. 'I have been known to buy cigars there,' he replied.

'You also use the club upstairs, I understand.'

'Yes.' Wilde smiled infectiously. 'I adore the smell of incense, it stimulates my imagination.'

'I can believe that, sir . . . It's a house of ill-fame, isn't it?'

Wilde pursed his lips deprecatingly. 'To the pure, sergeant, all things are impure.'

Bragg pulled out the photograph of the dean. 'Have you ever seen this man there, sir?'

Wilde gave it a cursory glance. 'Had I done so,' he replied, 'I should not have remembered him. He is not beautiful.'

'The boys are beautiful, though,' said Bragg curtly.

'Oh yes! They are the very pattern of joyous classical youth, they are like young gods, and I bring my tortured soul to worship at their shrine.'

'They are valets and stable-boys, are they not?'

Wilde gave a gesture of impatience. 'True beauty transcends worldly station, sergeant. To me they have the naked beauty of Olympic athletes, they are glorious Garibaldis at war with society.'

'You enjoy associating with these illiterates, do you, sir?'

'It is no matter.' Wilde waved his hands expansively. 'I have a passion to civilize the community.'

'Have you ever been rented, sir?'

Wilde laughed. 'I have been rended on many occasions, as well you know, if you subscribe to *Punch*.'

'I mean blackmailed.'

'Never!' said Wilde firmly.

'But you have given presents, no doubt?'

'No more than the fit homage of affluence to beauty.'

'Have you ever received threats?'

Wilde affected to consider for a moment. 'If I had, I would not have recognized them,' he said.

'Surely a man of your eminence would not be happy to consort with that lot voluntarily?' said Bragg roughly.

'I do not seek happiness, sergeant, but pleasure, which is much more tragic.'

'Pleasure with the dregs of society?'

Wilde shrugged. 'The true artist must have a certain *nostalgie de la boue*.'

'Be warned,' said Bragg. 'You can't hope to cock a snook at society, and get away with it.'

Wilde rose dismissively. 'While there is life, sergeant, there is despair,' he replied, and showed them to the door.

'I should have let you handle that one,' remarked Bragg as they reached the street. 'He was way over my head.'

'"A transcendentality of delirium,"' Morton murmured.

'What's that?'

'A phrase from Gilbert and Sullivan. Wilde was the model for Bunthorne in *Patience*.'

'I don't know about that,' said Bragg grumpily. 'What was it he said about nostalgy boo?'

'It is a French phrase, meaning a longing for the mire. I take it he was saying that an artist has to have a craving for abjection, before he can create anything worthwhile. I do not know whether he believes it, or not. It certainly does not find expression in his plays . . . I must say I enjoyed your baiting of each other; you with your wholesome earthiness, he with his much polished aphorisms. I have heard at least two versions of the remark about not tampering with perfection.'

'Well, he will tamper with it, and no mistake if he goes on like this,' said Bragg gruffly.

'The odd thing is,' said Morton, 'that Wilde's idea of male beauty is not so far removed from the strong, handsome, aristocratic-looking youth that our public schools try to produce.'

Catherine shuddered. 'I am glad that you did not go to a public school, then . . . I feel so let down. I thought Oscar Wilde would be something like you—acute, detached, slightly disdainful . . . '

'Thank you for the unsolicited tribute! If I remember aright, Aubrey Rivington is more than a little effeminate himself.'

'Don't be so unkind! He is sweet . . . but he is inclined to gossip.'

'Are you sure he is right for our purpose?'

'Well, he may not be much of a man,' replied Catherine chirpily, 'but he does know about cameras. I only hope he is not busy. However, the Queen is not holding a drawing-room today, so there will not be a queue of débutantes waiting to be photographed.'

In fact, the studio was empty, and Rivington advanced on them with open arms.

'Catherine, my dear,' he cried. 'How lovely . . . and the delicious young policeman too! This is my lucky day!'

'Stop your silly act, Aubrey,' said Catherine severely. 'We have come about something important.'

'Not getting married, are you?' he babbled. 'Oh dear, I shall miss you so. The others are such a dull lot.'

'No, we are not going to get married. Please top chattering, and listen.'

'Well, if you say so.'

'I want to consult you on police business,' said Morton. 'If you can help us, it could well lead to your giving evidence for the crown, in an important case. You might easily become the official expert on photography.'

'Oh, I say!' Rivington smiled with delight.

'But first, I must be satisfied that you will treat what I have to say in the strictest confidence.'

'Never a word will cross my lips, I assure you.'

'If that were untrue in the remotest degree,' said Morton sombrely, 'then it would be far better if you did not undertake the commission. We are dealing with a ruthless man, and the slightest hint of what we are about would certainly lead to your murder.'

'I won't give evidence, if someone is going to come looking for me with a knife,' exclaimed Rivington shrilly.

'The police will have caught the man before any court hearing, silly!' said Catherine. 'There is no danger, if you are discreet.'

'Oh, I am discreet all the time,' said Rivington.

Morton looked unsurely at Catherine, but she nodded her head.

'I am going to show you a snapshot,' said Morton. 'I want you to give me a technical evaluation of it—tell me as much about the camera as you can. Is that within your competence?'

'Of course it is,' snorted Rivington. 'Did I not take that gorgeous photograph of the girl outside the court for you, a couple of years ago? Who else could have done that?'

'I am sorry,' said Morton contritely. 'I was not questioning your professional competence. I am totally ignorant of the subject myself.'

'Yes, well,' said Rivington. 'Are you going to show me the photograph or not?'

Morton extracted the snap-shot from his pocket, and laid it on the table.

'Oh, I say!' exclaimed Rivington. 'That's Arabella Godfrey!'

'Aubrey!' cried Catherine crossly. 'That is just the kind of thing that could get you into trouble.'

'Since you have recognized the girl,' said Morton, 'perhaps you can tell us if you recognize the man.'

Rivington looked at it briefly. 'No. There is not much call for photographs of the backs of heads.'

'Can you say anything about the camera it was taken with?'

Rivington took the snap over to the corner, where a gas

bracket burned steadily. Then, picking up a magnifying glass, he scrutinized every inch of the surface.

'It is a very good lens,' he remarked. 'The detail is beautifully clear, and there is no distortion at the edges . . . It is the kind of result you would get from a portrait camera; but there are one or two folding cameras on the market that could equal it.'

'Do you mean that it could have been taken with a portable camera?'

'Oh yes, but a good one.'

'Now, this is very important. We are told that this snapshot was taken at a picnic.'

'Oh, my dear!' Rivington said with a snigger.

'Can you comment on that from the purely technical aspect?'

'Are you sure this isn't a hoax?' asked Rivington.

'Do you think that I would expose Arabella in this way, if it were?' asked Catherine.

'I suppose not.'

'And in case you should assume otherwise, let me say that Arabella has no idea that we have shown this photograph to you.'

'Oh, I say!' Rivington turned back to the snap. 'I suppose it was not posed?' he asked.

'So far as we are aware, it was not,' Morton replied.

'Only, people are so naughty nowadays.'

'For our purposes, assume that it was not.'

Rivington took up his lens again. 'I am surprised at the graininess of the print,' he remarked. 'It seems as if it was taken on a very sensitive film or plate . . . plate I think, and then enlarged. It could have been taken from a position near to the subject, with a lens of short focal length . . . say fifty; on the other hand, the lens could have a longer focal length, and the snap have been taken from some distance away . . . Yes, that must be it, otherwise that branch would be out of focus.'

'So what are we looking for?' asked Morton.

'Something that I have not come across myself, though I have seen descriptions of them in magazines. Let us suppose that the camera is a half-plate size, and that this snap is an enlargement. You would then be looking for a box about six inches by five, to take the plate. Then either bellows, or a tube, extending forward up to eight or nine inches . . . I don't think it is a folding camera any more, I think it is more like a miniature edition of my portrait camera. You could easily carry it in a small bag.'

'Why do you think it is a plate camera, rather than film?' asked Morton.

'Well, he has obviously been able to look through the actual lens of the camera, to get the focus absolutely right. He has caught them perfectly, hasn't he?'

On leaving the studio, Catherine reluctantly rejected an offer of protection from Morton and, making a detour along the busier streets, finally came to the house Arabella Godfrey's parents. It was about five o'clock, and she was received without undue formality. After a few moments Arabella smuggled her upstairs and Catherine handed over the envelope containing the hundred pounds. She hurriedly passed on Bragg's injunctions, then left.

She strolled home, enjoying the cooling breeze of evening, and went up the steps of her house. She had barely set foot in the hall, however, when she heard her mother calling her name in a curious half-strangled tone. She replied, and her mother came sweeping self-consciously out of the drawing-room.

'There is a man in there,' she whispered urgently. 'He says he was introduced to you at the Devonshires'. He has been here half an hour already, and shows no sign of going. It is all most irregular.'

'You can say that I will be down shortly.'

'Well, do not be long . I have quite run out of conversation.'

Catherine hurried upstairs, and changed out of the two-piece that comprised her working clothes, into a light afternoon dress. She tidied her hair, then went sedately downstairs.

A man in his early thirties was sitting on the sofa in the bay window, his hat and stick by his side in accordance with strict etiquette. As she entered, he rose to his feet.

'Miss Marsden,' he said in a pleasant voice, advancing to shake her hand. 'We were introduced by his royal highness at Devonshire House . . . Fritz.'

'Ah, yes. I remember,' said Catherine uneasily.

He drew back to the settee, and Catherine perforce went with him. Her mother, stranded at the other end of the room, walked out, ostentatiously leaving the door ajar.

'I come as an emissary,' Fritz said with a smile.

'And what is your mission?'

'To give you this,' he reached into his pocket, and brought out a small jewel-box.

'What on earth is it?' asked Catherine in consternation.

'I have no idea. I suggest you open it,' said Fritz.

With a troubled look, Catherine did so. Inside was a small pendant of garnets, set in gold.

'I cannot possibly accept this!' she exclaimed.

Fritz looked at the pendant appraisingly. 'From my experience, it is no more than a peace offering. I would suggest that the prince is merely acknowledging defeat with a good grace.'

'That is hardly the point,' said Catherine firmly.

'If you refuse, you will make my position exceedingly difficult.'

'I do not understand.'

'It was a lack of perception on my part that brought our lord and master such acute embarrassment.'

'Your lord and master—not mine.'

Fritz inclined his head, and smiled in acknowledgment. 'Had I pursued my enquiries beyond your parentage and education, I would have discovered the nature of your employment, and the contretemps would have been avoided.'

'So the gift is an apology for your lack of industry, rather than for his making improper advances.'

Fritz looked at her quizzically. 'Then you are the innocent of your portrait's title?'

'No, of course not.' Catherine tossed her head impatiently.

'You must understand that Prince Edward has, through his assiduity, acquired a reputation as a connoisseur of beautiful women.' Fritz's voice had an edge of amused disdain. 'Any lady with pretensions in that direction would expect him to make advances to her. She would feel insecure in her beauty, if it had not occurred . . . Why not see the incident as nothing more than a representative tribute from the most eminent of men to your transcendent beauty?'

'If I am honest,' replied Catherine with a smile, 'I was so startled by the prince's strong German accent, that I rather lost control of the situation. It was, at least partly, my fault.'

'His accent is hardly surprising,' Fritz protested. 'He had a wholly German father and a partly German mother . . . I have every reason to be grateful for it. You see before you Lieutenant Count Friedrich von Brandis RN, with a pedigree back to Charlemagne and a castle in Hanover only temporarily, I trust, in the keeping of our gracious Queen's grandson, Kaiser Wilhelm the Second.'

Catherine laughed at his bantering tone. 'Then I feel that there is no need for this apology,' she said.

'I would hesitate to pronounce on the matter,' said Fritz lightly. 'But if you will not accept it as a peace offering, then take it merely to spare me further abasement at my royal master's hands.'

'Very well,' Catherine closed the lid and stood up. 'I will accept it on those terms.'

Fritz bowed over her hand, took up his hat and cane, and went out of the room. Catherine watched from behind the curtain, as he walked quickly down the steps and strode down Park Lane. She started guiltily, as her mother entered.

'Who was he, dear?' she asked. 'He does not seem to have left a card.'

'Count Friedrich von Brandis,' Catherine replied casually. 'He is an equerry to the Prince of Wales.'

'Oh my goodness!' Her mother seemed totally taken aback.

Well, Countess Catherine von Brandis would sound quite splendid, Catherine thought musingly. But, of course, it would be Countess Friedrich von Brandis—stupid business! . . . Indeed, they might call her Countess Fritz! That was much too much like an operetta! Catherine laughed and, her sense of proportion restored, followed her mother in to dinner.

CHAPTER _____
_____ SEVEN

Bragg and Morton strolled down the shady side of Piccadilly. They had waited outside Green Park, until Arabella Godfrey had emerged from a side-street. Now they were shadowing her, in case an approach was made before she reached the circus. Through Catherine, they had emphasized that she must on no account look for them, but walk slowly and steadily along the street. She was carrying out their instructions to the letter, her eyes decorously on the pavement in front of her. From time to time, Bragg or Morton would glance around covertly, but neither could detect anyone following her.

She had reached the Burlington Arcade now. Ahead was a queue of people for the Royal Academy exhibition, spilling out on to the pavement. No doubt wanting to see Catherine's portrait, thought Morton wryly. He glanced around at the traffic, in case he should need to sprint across the street . . . He tensed as she came up to the queue, and was jostled towards the gutter . . . then she was past, resuming her steady gait.

'It's clear now, until the circus,' Bragg remarked. 'I think we can assume that the blackmailer will meet her near the memorial. There are any number of streets converging there, so we had better split up. What route would you take, if you were wanting to get away quickly?'

'Into Soho, without doubt,' replied Morton. 'There is a maze of streets there, and no river to hem you in.'

'Right, then you cover that side.'

'I would think that the corner of Shaftesbury Avenue would be the best vantage point. He would probably rush up there, to get a clear start.'

'Then, I will be on the south side. There is sure to be a crowd gazing at London's latest marvel, I expect she will be approached there . . . off you go.'

Morton raised his hat, as if taking farewell, then strode off. Bragg noted that Miss Godfrey was in a clear stretch of pavement, just past Swallow Street. Morton would be well in position, by the time she reached the circus . . . This was the tricky bit. She would be going round the north side, and he the south. There was bound to be a few moments when neither he nor Morton would be able to intervene. He watched her out of the corner of his eye, as she approached Regent Street and prepared to cross it. He hurried along to the south side of the statue and crossed the road to join the throng around it . . . A flying cupid was a funny sort of memorial, he thought, to the uncompromising old philanthropist. Whatever kind of love he had cherished for humanity, it was not that represented by Eros . . . Bragg worked his way round the fringe of the crowd. Now he could see Miss Godfrey clearly. She had stopped at the north side of Regent Street and was looking down at something . . . then she began to recross the road. Damn and blast it! It was ten to one that Morton hadn't seen what had happened either . . . She was still keeping up her slow pace, though, walking along the pavement, now turning . . . going sedately into the entrance of Swan & Edgar's department store. Well, one thing was sure, they were wasting their time here! Bragg began to shoulder his way through the crowd, to find Morton.

When Arabella felt the paper being pushed into her hand she jerked round, only to see an urchin scampering off. She unfolded it anxiously. It bore the same mark at the head, as had the others. This one directed her to walk through the household furnishings department of Swan & Edgar's, not to look round, and to have the money ready. She could not restrain a hurried glance round for the detectives. If only she could alert them! But the blackmailer was probably watching. She must do as he said, and hope that they would realize what had happened. If she kept up the same steady pace, it should be a signal to them. She turned into the store and looked at the directory of departments. Household furnishings were in the basement. She found the staircase and began to descend apprehensively. She paused on the landing to steady herself, then walked down the final flight. The basement began to open out before her, aisles intersecting, lengths of materials hanging from the ceiling impeding the vision. If the policemen had followed her to the staircase, surely they would be able to catch whoever it was . . .

She walked slowly along the central aisle, glancing neither to right nor left. It must look very odd to the other customers, she thought. Perhaps that was all to the good. It might happen that an onlooker would see the transaction, and be able to describe the blackmailer to the police, even if they did not catch him themselves. She passed the brocades, the laces, then the damasks . . . now she was nearly at the far end of the floor . . . What should she do when she reached it? Turn and go back again, or go down a side aisle? . . . As she passed into the cheniles, she heard a quick step behind her.

'Don't look round!' said a hoarse voice. 'Get the money in your right hand.'

Controlling her agitation, she undid her bag, took the envelope and allowed her arm to fall to her side. She felt the money being wrenched from her grasp, then heard a rush of feet. Her heart thumping, she walked on to the end of the aisle and turned round . . . There was nothing to be seen. She looked around her. At the far end was the staircase she had descended. People were casually coming and going, mainly women; there was no sign of the policemen . . . She felt at a loss. They had said that she must walk straight home again, if the transaction took place. That seemed to be the best thing to do, even though they had probably not seen what had happened. She went up to the ground floor and began to walk back home. She had almost reached White Horse Street when she heard a firm step beside her, and Constable Morton was taking off his hat as if passing the time of day.

'Keep walking,' he said quietly, 'you may still be under observation.'

'I got a note,' she said hurriedly, 'It told me to go into Swan and Edgar's.'

'Get it into your hand, and pass it to me as we say goodbye. Did you see the person?'

"No. It was a man, though, with a hoarse voice. He came up behind me and took the envelope from my hand.'

"Was it the voice of an educated person?'

'It is difficult to be certain. He said very little.'

'What department was it?'

'Household furnishings, in the basement.'

'That sounds rather risky,' Morton murmured, 'I would have expected something at street level.'

'You did not see him?'

'I am afraid not. His switch of plan foxed us, I'm sorry to say.'

'Perhaps I should have waited, and tried to find you.'

'Absolutely not,' said Morton. 'He was almost certainly watching you, and would have been warned off if you had done anything but simply follow his instructions. You did very well, Miss Godfrey. I wish that I could say the same of us . . . I will leave you here.'

They halted, Morton raised his hat, they shook hands and Morton turned back again, the paper in his pocket.

When Catherine and her mother entered the ballroom of Grosvenor House, they sought Lady Morton's party.

'You have not met my mother, have you, Lady Morton?' said Catherine.

'I am delighted to have the pleasure at last. Harriet, is it not? . . . May I introduce my sister-in-law, Amelia Harman.'

The formalities completed, the older ladies settled down for another long evening, while Catherine was snapped up by a young man and whisked away.

'Your young ladies are already on the floor, I suppose,' said Harriet.

'Oh yes,' Charlotte replied, 'Violet is dancing with a rather splendid young man with red hair, and Emily with that nice Smith boy.'

'What a beautiful room this is!' exclaimed Amelia. 'The mirrors, the drapes, the chandeliers—I am sure Violet will never forget it.'

'And I think the pastel silks and satins of the dresses are so lovely,' added Charlotte.

'And most of their wearers think that this is what life is about,' remarked Harriet amiably.

'It is partly what life is about,' said Amelia.

'Yes, and yet I cannot help thinking that it is wrong to marry girls straight from the schoolroom like this, when the extent of their involvement with a man has been the excitement of a highland schottische!'

'What would you have?' asked Charlotte.

Harriet sighed. 'Less haste, I suppose. More opportunity for the girl to make a mature choice.'

'Some people would say that giving a girl any choice would only increase the likelihood of an unfortunate entanglement,' said Amelia with a smile.

'Surely there is no more unfortunate entanglement than a loveless marriage?'

'I think Mrs Marsden is right to this extent,' said Charlotte. 'We do rather bring up our daughters in ignorance of . . . well, of their role in life.'

Amelia laughed. 'In America, when we were young, we were too much surrounded by animals to be left in much doubt about a female's function.'

'That is what these pampered young people lack,' said Harriet. 'Something to force them into contact with the real world.'

Morton arrived late at Grosvenor House. The preparation of his report on the Swan & Edgar fiasco, and their subsequent conference with the Commissioner, had lasted well into the evening. It had taken all Bragg's deviousness to persuade Sir William to back another subvention from public funds, if the girl received a further demand. As a result, Morton had had to dash home to change, and come out again without a meal. He decided that he would go first to the refreshment room, to fortify himself for the exertions to come. He took his coffee and cake to a small table in the corner. The room was empty, except for a group of young men who had obviously drunk too well at dinner. Morton tried in vain to shut out their loud conversation.

'What about her?' one was asking.

'They say the prince has already bedded her.'

'Lucky devil! If I could get her in my bed, I would show her my opening flower, all right!'

With a cold anger, Morton realized that they were discussing Catherine. He glanced towards the buffet, but the waitress was serving a newcomer, and feigned indifference.

'Hey! Rutherford, you are late!' called the ringleader. 'Does it take a long time to come from Shorncliffe?'

The man at the buffet ignored them.

'Why Shorncliffe?' asked another of the group. 'I thought the Life Guards were at Windsor.'

'Didn't you know? They mutinied last autumn, and were sent down to Shorncliffe, near Folkestone, for their sins. Now poor old Rutherford has to come all that way for a dance!'

Rutherford went over to them. 'I would inform you, gentlemen, that there was no mutiny. There was a case of minor indiscipline amongst the other ranks.'

'Pull the other one, Rutherford,' sneered the leader. 'There was a court martial, wasn't there? They dismissed eight NCOs—but they don't get rid of officers, they send them to Shorncliffe, instead!'

'I warn you,' said Rutherford stiffly, 'that though I can ignore your personal innuendos, I must defend the honour of my regiment.'

'I should not think it has much honour left to defend!' The ringleader lurched to his feet. 'But if you do, then I'm your man.'

'What shall it be, then?' asked Rutherford scornfully.

'Billiard cues at twenty paces?' He turned his back and began to walk towards Morton. As he did so, the other man lunged towards him, catching his arm and spilling his drink over his shoes. Rutherford swung round in anger and, grabbing his assailant by the wrist, twisted his arm behind his back.

'Stop it, both of you!' cried Morton, 'or I will arrest you for causing an affray.'

Rutherford released the man and turned away.

'Who the hell are you?' shouted the other, straightening his cuff. 'Damn you for interfering.'

'My name is James Morton, I am a constable and an officer of the Queen's peace.'

'So that's who you are?' He turned to his companions. 'I'm not staying here, if the Westminsters have started inviting outsiders . . . Why don't we go down to Soho, and find some tit we can touch?'

There was a chorus of approval and, with a deal of braying mirth, the group found its way outside.

'I am extremely sorry,' said Morton. 'What I said was exceedingly pompous and rather stupid. I am afraid that they had already made me angry by some remarks concerning a friend of mine. You withstood their provocation better than I could have done.'

'They are just idle louts,' said Rutherford. 'The whole affair is best forgotten.' He took a napkin from a table, and wiped the coffee from his shoes. 'You are related to Violet Harman are you not?' he went on. 'I have been dancing with her quite a bit, of late. She really is a cracker!'

Morton laughed. 'Well, why do we not go up and join them? I take it that that is why we are here.'

When they reached the ballroom a dance was in progress so Morton formally introduced Rutherford to the three ladies. He left him chatting to Amelia and his mother, and took the chair beside Mrs Marsden.

'You must be greatly delighted by your daughter's social ascendancy,' he remarked.

'Not in the least, Mr Morton. The more particularly, since it entails my spending a good part of most nights at functions like this, as her chaperon.'

'It is a wry situation, I would agree,' said Morton with a smile.

'You two seem very earnest,' exclaimed Catherine, appearing in front of them.

'I am sure that that is the last thing one should be, on such an occasion,' said Morton, rising. 'May I have the honour of the next dance?'

'But of course.' She took his hand and led the way on to the floor.

'You look quite as beautiful as your portrait, this evening,' he said in his usual rallying tone.

'Oh! Have you seen it?"

'Of course, Miss Marsden.'

'For goodness sake, call me Catherine,' she said impatiently, 'I call you James.'

'Because a lady condescends, it is not thereby proper for a gentleman to presume.'

'Don't be silly, James. How could I ever condescend to you?'

'But I am now a mere follower in your baggage train. You are like a beautiful comet that has soared beyond my sphere.'

'You are beginning to mix your metaphors!'

'Then perhaps we should concentrate on the dance!'

When they returned to their group, Rutherford and Violet joined them, and they chatted for a time. Then the music began again, and Morton took Violet on to the floor. Catherine expected that Rutherford would invite her to dance, but instead he excused himself and she had, perforce, to take a chair beside her mother. She watched as Morton and Violet waltzed, sensing their easy intimacy, piqued at their gaiety.

'May I have the pleasure?' Fritz Brandis was beside her. She assented eagerly, and was drawn into the whirl of dancers. Despite the crowded floor, she set herself to be graceful and vivacious. Oddly enough, there seemed to be many more couples now—either that, or they happened to be always where the crowd was. Fritz seemed constantly to be pulling her close to him, to avoid jostling dancers. It was faintly disagreeable, thought Catherine. At length the dance ended.

'Would you like some air?' asked Fritz.

'It might just save my life!'

He took her through a doorway at the far end of the room, which gave on to a large salon. Through a door to the right she could see the bottom of a great staircase, with couples stealing up it.

'There are obviously more important things than dancing,' Fritz remarked with a smile. He led her to the conservatory, where the doors were open to the garden, and placed two chairs so that they could sit in the cool air. After a while, he pulled his chair round, so that he could look into her face.

'Do you think it could be,' he asked, 'that a man might succeed where his master had failed?'

'I am sure that history would afford countless examples,' said Catherine lightly.

'I have a friend with an apartment in St James's,' said Fritz urgently. 'We could meet there secretly.'

Catherine sprang to her feet in anger. 'Your suggestion is offensive,' she said icily, 'and you are not a gentleman!' She stalked off in the direction of the ballroom.

Morton saw her enter, her face flushed with anger. He crossed to intercept her.

'I noticed that you were dancing with Fritz,' he said, 'and I suspect that he has made you very cross.'

'Oh, do you?' she said shortly.

'Fritz is a buffoon, and an outrageous flirt. I am sure that he meant no harm.'

'Knowing that, a gentleman would have protected me from humiliation.'

'But I also knew that you would be resolute in the preservation of your reputation. Besides,' he gave a sly smile, 'now that you are an acknowledged beauty, you are in a sense public property.'

'Well, if that means that I am open to improper advances from every lecherous lordling, then I would prefer to withdraw.'

CHAPTER _____

_____ EIGHT

Next morning, Catherine was at the Royal Academy as soon as the exhibition opened. There was already a small crowd of ordinary Londoners—society was no doubt cantering in Rotten Row, or still in bed. She went over to a uniformed attendant.

'Can you tell me where William Marsden's paintings are hung, please?'

'Why, they are scattered about, miss. Was you wanting a particular one?'

'The . . . the portrait.'

'Very popular, that one.' He looked closely at her. 'Why! Here you are in the flesh! It's a very good likeness, miss.'

'Thank you.'

'You will find it in room number six,' he said. 'I don't need to look that one up. Everybody is asking for it!'

She crept into the gallery. Her portrait was hung centrally, in the middle of one wall. It had acquired the distinction of having a rail put in front of it, to keep the patrons at a distance. Already there was a group there; admiring it, discussing the brushwork, the tints. Catherine tip-toed out again, lest one of

115

them should turn round and recognize her. She approached the attendant.

'What would I do, if I wanted to buy the picture?' she asked.

'You would have to go to the office, miss . . . Along that corridor, turn left, and it's the second door on the right.'

She found the room and walked up to the counter.

'I would like to buy the Marsden picture called "The Opening Flower",' she said, inwardly wincing at the title.

The clerk looked at her quizzically. 'Unless I am much mistaken,' he said, 'you are Mr Marsden's daughter, and the subject of the painting.'

'That is so, but I want to buy it nevertheless . . . as a kind of present to myself.'

'I see, miss,' said the clerk, placing a ledger on the counter. 'You don't happen to remember the catalogue number, I suppose?'

'Two hundred and thirty-four.'

He slowly turned the pages, then stopped. 'That is very odd,' he exclaimed in surprise. 'Originally the painting was marked "Not for Sale". That has now been crossed out, and "Sold" put in its place.'

'I see . . . Thank you.' Catherine walked off thwarted. Now there was no hope that the painting could be taken out of the exhibition before the end of the summer.

Bragg and Morton hurried along Cheapside to the Bank of England, where they asked to see the chief cashier. They were shown up to May's comfortable office, overlooking the garden court.

'Ah, sergeant,' he greeted them, 'I sent for you, because we have received intelligence from our West End branch that two of the notes we provided for you have turned up.'

'Indeed, sir,' said Bragg, with admiration in his voice. 'Do we know where they came from?'

'We can say, with confidence, that they were presented to be changed into sovereigns by one of our customers on Thursday morning. We cannot, of course, be certain that they have not passed through a chain of, shall we say, innocent parties, in the meantime; though the time may well have been too short for that to occur.'

'I understand, sir. Can you tell me the name of the man who changed them?'

'Yes, sergeant. He is Sir Alexander Rouse, of 16 Ryder Street, St James's . . . Do you want to know the serial numbers of the notes encashed?'

'Not at the moment, sir, but I would be glad if the notes themselves could be preserved.'

They took a cab to St James's, and walked down Ryder Street.

'Not all that fashionable-looking, is it?' said Bragg.

'I imagine that they are oldish houses, which have been converted into apartments,' replied Morton, 'Obviously, not everyone in this area has unlimited money!'

'You know, lad, there cannot have been time for those notes to go through many hands. They were only taken off Miss Godfrey on Tuesday afternoon, and they were paid into the bank on Thursday morning.'

'Perhaps Rouse is our man. I have seen him several times at country-house parties during my tour at Marlborough House. Since he belongs to that set, perhaps we should treat him with some delicacy.'

Bragg snorted sardonically. 'What do you know of him?' he asked.

'Nothing beyond that.'

'Well, this seems to be number sixteen. He'd better be in!'

They climbed the stairs, noting the cards by the doorbells, until they had reached the third floor. There they found a card reading 'Sir Alexander Rouse'. Bragg looked around. The landing was narrow and covered in brown linoleum, the paintwork was chipped and a dirty ring surrounded the gas pendant over the stairwell.

'Only the attics above this,' Bragg commented. 'You are right. They must be strapped for cash.'

The man who answered their ring was tall and well-built, with amiable good looks. He wore a light tweed lounging suit, whose check was fractionally too large for good taste. The whole impression was slightly raffish.

'Are you Sir Alexander Rouse?' Bragg asked politely.

'Usually known as Alec—that's me.'

'We are detective officers from the City of London police,' went on Bragg, showing his warrant card.

'A little off your beat, aren't you? Come in, come in.'

The sitting room to which he led them was cluttered with furniture, but there were no fine pieces. Copies of the *Lady* and *World* littered the settee, while in the corner was a pile of the *Sporting Life* and *Sporting Times*.

'Must apologize for the mess,' said Sir Alec, with a rueful grin. 'The maid is not very good . . . Have a snifter?'

'No thank you sir,' said Bragg gravely.

'On official business, eh?'

'That's right, sir. We are making enquiries about some banknotes, and we believe that you can help us.'

'Well, that's a surprise!' Rouse said with a laugh. 'Carry on, sergeant.'

'We understand that you exchanged two ten-pound notes for sovereigns, on Thursday morning.'

'Yesterday? Yes, I believe I did, come to think of it. Why? Were they stolen or something?'

'Let us say that they were illicit, shall we?'

'It's no use asking for the money back,' Sir Alec protested. 'It has been spent.'

'Our interest is more in how they came into your possession,' said Morton.

'They might have come from anywhere,' replied Sir Alec vaguely.

'Would you try to narrow that down, sir?' asked Bragg.

'What period of time are we talking about?'

'Let's say, this present week.'

'Well, it would not have come from my wife,' said Sir Alec reflectively. 'So I must have won it.'

'And how would you have done that, sir?'

'Oh, backgammon, cards . . . anything.'

'You are a sportsman, then, are you sir?' observed Bragg. 'Keen on the gee-gees?'

'I sometimes think I support my bookmaker single-handed!'

'You seem to take it very seriously, though.'

'You haven't a hope of making any money unless you do.'
He picked up a copy of the *Sporting Life* from the table. The
name of a runner in each of the day's races had been ringed in
pencil. 'See this?' he asked, pointing to one apparently
rejected. 'On its past form, this horse should win. There are
only two other good horses in the race, and it has beaten both
of them last year. Only just, I admit. But it has made a good
start this season and ten furlongs is its best distance, to my
mind . . . But it won't win.'

'How can you be so sure?' asked Bragg.

'Because it is running in the Ascot Gold Cup next month,
with a real chance. They aren't going to let it run its heart out
today . . . Besides, they might want the odds to lengthen a
bit, to get more money on. No, it will run well enough today,
but the jockey will ease it gently in the final furlong or two, and
it won't come above third.'

'But surely, the stewards are there to prevent just such
malpractice?' said Morton.

Sir Alec laughed. 'They may have their suspicions, but if the
jockey knows his business, there would be nothing flagrant
enough for them to take action.'

'With your knowledge, you must win a tidy sum on the
horses,' said Bragg.

'Not a bit of it! You can sometimes tell which horse won't
perform, but as for picking the winner, you might just as well
take a pin to the paper.'

'Were you at the races on Tuesday afternoon, sir?'

'No. My lady wife dragged me off to a garden party, at
Lansdowne House.'

'You stayed with her all the afternoon, did you sir?'

Sir Alec appeared somewhat embarrassed by the question.
'As a matter of fact, I did,' he replied.

'There would be other people around at the time?'

'There were indeed. Far too many, if you ask me.'

'You could not have got those notes from any of them, I
suppose?' Bragg asked glibly.

'No, sergeant, as your colleague will confirm . . . You
were with the Marlborough House people, until recently, were
you not?' he asked.

'That is true, sir,' said Morton . . . 'Of course, if it was a charity garden party, you might have been given them in change.'

'It was an ordinary, dull, society affair.'

'What did you do on Tuesday evening?' asked Bragg.

'Had dinner at the house of some friends, then went on to a reception at Spencer House.'

'I take it you would not have spent any money there, either, so you could not have got these notes in change.'

'Dammit, sergeant, ten-pound notes are hardly loose change, even around here!'

'Very well, sir,' said Bragg mildly. 'Now, how about Wednesday?'

'In the morning I drove down to Roehampton, with Charlie Beevors, to look at a horse he was considering buying. Just got back in time to escort my dear wife to a concert, in St James's Hall.'

'Did you lunch anywhere, sir?'

'We grabbed a sandwich in a pub—and Charlie paid.'

'And after the concert?'

'I was in the dogs' home, for being so late that I had to turn up at it like this, instead of wearing a frock-coat. So I filled in the time before going out to dinner, by being dutiful and domestic.'

'I see, sir. And where did you dine?'

'At Marlborough House.'

'And afterwards?'

'I played whist with the Prince of Wales and a couple of other people,' said Sir Alec in a matter-of-fact tone.

'Did you win?'

'Oh yes, I won.' He gave a crafty grin. 'But not too much . . . It wouldn't do.'

'How much?'

'Over the evening, you mean?'

'Yes.'

Rouse wrinkled his forehead. 'A hundred and fifty or so.'

'And did you settle at the end of the evening?'

'Oh yes. The prince is most punctilious about that.'

'So, it is just possible that you might have been given the suspect notes at that stage.'

'I suppose it is, sergeant.'

'Was it a whist party, or was there just one table?' asked Morton.

'Just the one.'

'Who were the other two people?'

'William Bullivant, and young Reuben Smith.'

'Do you know where we could find them?'

'Bullivant is staying at his sister's house. Just a moment.' He crossed over to a small bureau, and took out an address book. 'She is Mrs Charles Handford, and her address is 149 South Audley Street.'

'And Mr Smith?'

'He is something in the City. I do not quite remember what.'

Bragg strolled towards the window, turned round and surveyed the room. 'Not a very sumptuous apartment,' he remarked, 'for a member of the Marlborough House set.'

'I have an estate in the country,' Rouse retorted.

'Not much of one, if this is all you can afford in London,' said Bragg brutally.

For a moment Rouse seemed about to explode with indignation, but under Bragg's challenging gaze, his anger ebbed away.

'All right,' he said cynically, 'I admit I have gambled most of it away. What is left just about pays the rent for this desirable residence.'

'So, what do you live on, sir?'

'I sponge on my wife, sergeant. She has money that I cannot get at—fortunately so, I would think. She pays my tailor's bills, so that I will not let her down in society . . . I am my wife's pensioner.'

'I should not think that would lead to a very happy marriage,' remarked Bragg.

'Marriage?' Rouse echoed bitterly. 'She is what they call a "frisky matron", sergeant. She is part of the Prince of Wales's harem. Not only am I her pensioner,' he said in disgust, 'I am also her pimp . . . Still, the old Widow of Windsor cannot go on for ever, and then the good times will come back again—if my lady has not lost her good looks by then.'

Bragg and Morton finally ran Smith to earth at the Junior Carlton Club, in Pall Mall. He greeted them cordially, reminding Morton that they had been meeting at dances over the past weeks.

'Is there anywhere that we can talk?' asked Morton.

'I am sure that they could find us a room. Just a moment, I will see the secretary.'

'A fine-looking young chap,' said Bragg as he departed.

'Does that mean that he is not what you expected?'

'I don't like a joker in my hand, lad.'

'I have to tell you,' said Morton seriously, 'that this man has been making himself agreeable to my sister Emily—and she does not seem wholly indifferent, herself. I shall, of course, endeavour not to let it influence me; but if you feel that I am not handling the interview as I should, you must intervene.'

Bragg looked at him shrewdly. 'Then we shall find out whether you will make a policeman or not, shan't we?'

Smith returned and led them to a small room on the second floor. He was presentable enough, Bragg thought, with his dark good looks and his confident manner. Nevertheless he was a bit of an oddity; he seemed much too normal to be mixed up with the likes of Rouse.

'Would it be entirely inappropriate if I were to address you as James?' Smith asked, smiling at Morton. 'After my conversations with your sister, anything else would seem excessively formal.'

'I think "constable" would be both adequate and accurate,' said Morton.

Smith looked slightly abashed. 'Then, how can I assist you?' he asked.

'We are making enquiries concerning some bank-notes which were exchanged by Sir Alexander Rouse last Thursday, and which may be illicit,' Morton began.

'Ah yes?' Smith's grey eyes lit up with interest. 'This must be the Bank of England notice that crossed my desk on . . . was it Wednesday morning?'

'Very probably.'

'Does old Alec know?—that the notes are suspect, I mean.'

'We saw him this morning. It seems possible that he obtained the notes during Wednesday evening—perhaps at a whist game in which you took part.'

'At Marlborough House, you mean? . . . And you are wondering if he got them from me?'

'Precisely.'

'Well,' said Smith frankly, 'it is perfectly possible. Before we closed, I asked the head cashier for a couple of hundred, in mixed denominations. I am afraid that I did not concern myself with the serial numbers—it was tens that the Bank was concerned with, was it not?'

'Yes. Would there have been tens in the money given to you?'

'Preponderantly tens, if my memory serves me.'

'You say "head cashier",' remarked Bragg. 'Was that at your place of business?'

'Yes. I work at the Lombard Street branch of the bank—Smith Payne and Smith's, that is.'

'That would be owned by your family, would it, sir?'

'Yes, sergeant.'

'Would you know what happened there, when the Bank of England notice was received?'

'My concern is with the investment side of the bank's activities, sergeant; I needed only to be aware of the notice.'

'You see what I'm getting at, though—and I'm assuming your bank took the notice seriously.'

'Goodness gracious, yes! If the Old Lady so much as raises a finger, we all scurry to do her bidding.'

'Well, then, I can see that the cashiers would have their eyes open for the serial numbers, from Wednesday morning onwards. Probably they would look at every single tenner that they took over the counter. But what about the notes already on the premises? Did you shut up shop and go through them all? Or did you trust the cashiers to check them, as they paid them out?'

'I am afraid that I do not know the answer to that question, sergeant, and it would be improper of me to speculate. I will find out for you.'

'For the moment, then, we have to assume that the two notes could possibly have been in the money you had with you, that evening.'

'That is so.'

'Can you remember the details of the games?' asked Morton.

'I cannot now remember the run of the cards, if that is what you are asking. It is difficult enough for me to remember which cards have already gone, during the course of play.'

'Who was your partner?'

'We changed partners during the evening, so that each played with all the others in turn.'

'Did you play for high stakes?'

'Not high—moderate.'

'Did you settle up after each game?'

'No, at the end of the evening.'

'Did you win, or lose?'

'I lost . . . That is my function, constable,' he gave a mischievous smile. 'I lose with a good grace. I would not be invited, otherwise.'

'How much did you lose?'

'About a hundred and forty pounds.'

'Then, who won?'

'The prince and Rouse. The prince is an indifferent player, but Rouse is, I think, very competent indeed. I am beginning to learn enough about the niceties of the game to suspect that, when I am partnering Rouse, he deliberately underplays his hand to make sure that we lose.'

'So if the suspect notes were in the bundle given to you by the cashier, you could have passed them on to Rouse?'

'That is certainly so.'

'You have a funny attitude, if I may say so, sir,' observed Bragg. 'Are you asking us to believe that you do not mind losing money, night after night, when so far as I can make out, you don't even know enough about the game to enjoy it.'

Smith laughed. 'You are disconcertingly acute, sergeant. All I can plead is that it is for a sound business purpose. My father advises the Prince of Wales, from time to time, on financial matters. It is not generally realized, but the prince is in very straightened circumstances . . . You smile. But when you consider that, through her default, the prince and princess discharge almost all the functions proper to the Queen herself—not only as the leaders of society, but on state occasions, and visits abroad—you will realize that what he receives from the government is niggardly indeed. However, in addition, the prince enjoys the income from the Duchy of Cornwall. Together with a few other advisors, my father has managed to increase the income from the duchy considerably over the last ten years or so.'

'That doesn't explain why you should be content to lose large sums at cards,' said Bragg.

'It gives me the *entrée* to society, which is largely composed of the landed aristocracy. For the most part, they have succeeded to estates built up by their forefathers. They have neither aptitude for, nor interest in, creating wealth. Their consuming passion is to spend, and they indulge it recklessly . . . Yet these are difficult times for the land-owner, and with the opening up of vast tracts of America and Canada to agriculture, the position can only worsen. In addition, many of our great families have absurdly extravagant country seats—like FitzWilliam's place at Wentworth, with three hundred bedrooms! Not even they can afford to keep up such monstrosities.'

'So you are trying to induce them to retrench, and diversify their investments?' remarked Morton.

'Not only trying, constable,' said Smith with a grin, 'succeeding!'

CHAPTER _____
_____ NINE

Catherine came down to breakfast to find her father sitting alone, reading the newspaper.

'Is mamma unwell?' she asked.

'I think she is merely exhausted from the excesses of the weekend,' he replied with a smile. 'She will no doubt be down later.'

'Dancing makes me ravenous!' said Catherine, helping herself to kidneys and fried bacon from the sideboard.

'I have been asked to paint Millicent Duchess of Sutherland,' her father remarked. 'That is quite a coup, she is rapidly becoming one of our leading hostesses.'

'Papa,' Catherine said casually, 'I went into the Academy last Thursday.'

'Oh yes?'

'I wanted to buy my portrait.'

'Whatever for?'

'To suppress it, of course! Only, it had already been sold.'

'I do believe it has,' said Mr Marsden absently.

'Come along, papa! You must know what happened to it.'
'I really do not!'
'But it was originally marked "Not for Sale".'
'That is true. I wanted to keep it. I think it would have
looked rather fine in the drawing-room, on the wall opposite
the window.'
'Then, why did you change your mind?' Catherine asked.
'Sheer greed, my dear. I was offered fifteen hundred
guineas, which was an astonishing sum for someone unconnected with the sitter to pay.'
'So you took it.'
'No, I did not. I sent back a firm refusal. Then I received a
further offer of two thousand guineas. Perhaps they would have
gone higher, perhaps they would have withdrawn; we shall
never know. My cupidity triumphed and I accepted the
money . . . I can always paint another!'
'Who was mad enough to offer such a sum?' Catherine
asked.
'I do not know. The transaction was handled by Agnews, the
dealers. Just think! It might have been the National Gallery, or
Mr Henry Tate!'
'Agnews have exhibited your pictures often enough, papa.
Surely you could find out?'
'I have tried, you may be sure, but I have been met with a
wall of professional silence . . . Why do you wish to know?'
'By now, it has somehow become a part of me. It is almost
as if you were buying and selling me!'
Her father laughed and turned back to his paper. Catherine
crunched her toast irritably. Only the Prince of Wales would be
stupid enough to pay a fortune for her picture—or Fritz. The
thought of either of them being able to gaze at her, willy-nilly,
was almost as objectionable as having their lecherous hands on
her body.
'Papa,' she said abruptly. 'I am considering withdrawing
from society.'
Her father looked at her quizzically over his paper. 'If you
do,' he said at length, 'it will not diminish you. Society woke
up to the fact that you are a beauty; if it closes its eyes again,
you will still be beautiful.'

'Perhaps society has its own standard of beauty—as it has of honour and chivalry.'

'There is certainly nothing immutable about beauty. Compare a woman of Rubens with a Gainsborough, then with a modern—say, Renoir. All enchanting in their own way, yet quite distinct.'

'If I had become the mistress of the Prince of Wales, what would you say?' asked Catherine suddenly.

Mr Marsden regarded her steadily. 'I would be frankly astonished.'

'That it should be proposed?'

'That such a proposal should be accepted by you.'

Catherine smiled impishly. 'He hinted that he would get you a knighthood, if I would.'

'The idea of a title is not wholly unpleasing,' he said, returning her smile, 'though I would deny it vigorously to anyone but you. Nevertheless, I would not wish to purchase it, nor at such a price.'

'Would you be concerned if I withdrew from society?'

'I would be concerned if you were involved in anything which was uncongenial or repugnant to you.'

'I would not wish it to affect the flow of commissions to you.'

'My dear child,' said Mr Marsden expansively, 'I have made so many promises, that if I worked night and day for two years, I fear I would have difficulty in fulfilling them . . . All I would ask, is that you should not throw society's adulation back in its face, but let your involvement dwindle away. At twenty-one it is tempting to strike attitudes, but you may wish to return one day, and society does not forgive a snub.'

'Very well, papa.' Catherine picked up the pile of letters from the table. There was the usual number of invitations addressed to her mother, stiff and opulent with their rich cream-laid paper . . . Ah! here was one addressed to her. A large buff envelope. She tore it open in excitement and drew out several typed sheets. She ran her eye over them quickly.

'Papa, I have received a letter from a man called Sully. He says that, in answer to representations from bodies concerned with the advancement of women, he is undertaking a survey of the attainments of young women who have left school or university in the last ten years, with a view to preparing a statistical report on their achievements. Is not that splendid?'

'If all women forsook the pursuit of beauty for the privilege of working in offices and hospitals, I should be poor indeed!'

'This is serious, papa! Britain is lagging dreadfully, compared with other countries. In Ontario, women have now been admitted to the practice of law; and there is a bill before the New Zealand parliament to give them the vote. Think of that! And they say it will pass.'

Her father held up his hands in surrender, but remained mute.

'It is just the kind of thing we need, to make men accept that we are not fragile, weak-minded incompetents, but just as capable as they are!'

'And what is expected of you?'

'The analysis of the results will be done in Professor Sully's department—whatever that is—but the interviews will be carried out independently, to eliminate bias. He obviously knows my name, but the interviewer will not, nor will the information obtained by the interviewer be attributable to me.'

'Who is this Sully man?' asked Mr Marsden, crossing to a bookcase. He took down a copy of *Who's Who*, and thumbed through the pages. 'Here we are,' he said, 'Sully, James . . . the usual academic career . . . appointed to the chair of Mental and Moral Science at the University of London in eighteen eighty-nine. Well, it all seems genuine enough. No doubt you will derive a fine sense of satisfaction from striking a blow for liberty. I, being a free man, must needs begin work.' He put down the paper and went out.

Catherine was re-reading Sully's letter, when her mother came down to breakfast.

'I thought you would have gone to the office, dear,' she said.

'I am covering a memorial service at St Margaret's Westminster this morning. There seemed little point in going in first.'

Her mother picked up the pile of correspondence with a sigh. 'More invitations, I suppose, and this will go on till August, at least.'

'I think not, mamma. I have decided that there are more important things in life than society functions.'

'Good! These last few weeks have been so trying. What will your father say, I wonder.'

'I told him before you came down. He seems to approve.'

'Then I shall go and buy myself some new novels.'

'I shall continue to accept a few invitations, but only ones which you will enjoy also.'

'That is very considerate of you, dear . . . How is Mr Gladstone getting on with the Irish Home Rule bill? I hear he was booed last week, when arriving at a reception.'

Catherine passed the newspaper to her. Her mother really looked very handsome in her pale silk morning-gown, she thought warmly. It had been a real struggle, she was sure, for her to overcome her natural lethargy in order to act as chaperon. Her normal attitude to life was a vague tolerance bordering on the apathetic, though she could become incensed by unkindness or injustice, such as a sewing-girl being sacked for displeasing a crotchety dowager. The company of society matrons peddling their daughters could not have been congenial.

'Why did you not have any more children?' she asked.

Her mother looked up in surprise. 'Well, I suppose God disposes, and man . . . er, whatever man does, dear.'

'In the present context, it would be extremely indelicate of me to speculate!'

'I hope you do not make fast remarks like that to young men,' her mother said sharply . . . 'On the whole, I have no regrets; childbearing is such a physical business.'

'I am going to be part of a survey of women's achievements, mamma,' Catherine said excitedly.

'Oh yes, dear? What kind of achievements?'

'Academic life, medicine—newspaper work, obviously . . . I suppose, in any preserve that men have hitherto reserved for themselves.'

'That is nice, dear. When do you start?'

'I am to go along to King's College for an interview, any Tuesday afternoon before the end of May.'

'I see. Will you go tomorrow?'

'No. My programme for tomorrow has already been decided, but I will leave enough time for it next week.'

'Good . . . I would be glad if you would go through that
pile of invitations, and tell me which you want me to accept.'

'I will do that tonight . . . Oh, by the way, man proposes.'

Her mother looked up in evident delight. 'No wonder you
can withdraw from society! Which one is it?'

'No, no, mamma! Man proposes, God disposes.'

'And I was beginning to feel that all the inconvenience of the
past weeks had not been for nothing,' exclaimed her mother in
disappointment.

'Poor mamma!'

'You should be married, you know. I was, at your age; and
I would do the same again, emancipated or not.'

'But with three girls to every man,' said Catherine lightly,
'and most girls incapable of supporting themselves, it would be
unfair of me to have a career and want a husband also!'

'Perhaps I ought to have had another child,' Mrs Marsden
complained. 'Then I might have grandchildren before I am too
old to enjoy them.'

'Withdrawing from society will make no difference to that,
mamma,' said Catherine gently. 'The only man that I remotely
care for, would disdain to compete for my hand with feckless
idlers.'

Bragg and Morton were settling down to review the two
blackmailing cases, when a young constable poked his head
round the door.

'The Commissioner's compliments, sir,' he said, 'but would
you and Constable Morton go to his room?'

'Straight away, do you mean?'

'Yes, sir. He has a gentleman with him.'

They went up the elegant Georgian staircase, crossed the
anteroom and, rapping on the Commissioner's door, went in.

'Ah, Bragg,' said Sir William. 'This is Mr Francis Knolleys,
who is secretary to the Prince of Wales.'

Knolleys rose and held out his hand. He was in his early
forties, with fine hair thinning on top, and a moustache ragged
enough to rival Bragg's.

'It is a pleasure to meet you at last,' he said in a dry
measured voice. 'The prince was much impressed by your

exploits over the counterfeit notes last year . . . I already know Constable Morton, of course.' He smiled and nodded, then resumed his seat.

Sir William cleared his throat. 'Mr Knolleys has been sent by his royal highness, about a matter of great delicacy. He particularly asked that you should be present when he broached it.'

'That is so,' said Knolleys. 'A crime has been committed which could have extremely undesirable repercussions. It is important that the matter should be investigated with all urgency; it is equally necessary, Sir William, that any enquiries should be conducted sensitively and intelligently. The prince is of the opinion that these two officers possess the imagination and drive to bring the matter to a successful conclusion. An added advantage is that the constable is conversant with society and its ways. The first point, therefore, is to ask you, Mr Commissioner, if you will release these two officers for the purpose.'

'To which force will they be seconded?' the Commissioner asked with reluctance.

'They will remain under your control, and no other police force must be told of their enquiries.'

Sir William seemed mollified. 'There will be no problems with Home Counties forces, naturally; but there might be difficulties with other forces, if they became aware of what was going on.'

'If they do find out, then you may rely on the palace to smooth things out.'

'Is the Queen involved?' exclaimed the Commissioner.

'Hardly involved,' said Knolleys with a grave smile, 'but certainly aware.'

'Then, of course I am agreeable to these officers' undertaking the enquiries. They will put their other cases into suspension.'

'Good. Then the only other prerequisite is that steps should be taken to ensure that this affair does not become common knowledge throughout the City force.'

'Have no fear of that, Mr Knolleys. Sergeant Bragg will report directly to me, and no written reports will be made. I am sure that that is how the sergeant would prefer it, anyway.' A foxy smile crossed the Commissioner's lips.

'The prince might well, from time to time, desire to confer with the officers,' said Knolleys. 'For this purpose, he would no doubt call them to Marlborough House. I trust there would be no difficulties . . .'

'None whatever.'

'Thank you, Sir William . . . I now come to an aspect where my own views differed from those of the prince, and I was overborne. His conviction is that the matter is of such extreme delicacy, that even trusted officers, such as these two gentlemen, should be given no more information than is necessary to commence their task—I am by no means convinced that even I am aware of all its aspects.'

'I don't understand,' said Bragg. 'Are you saying that we shall not be told about facts that are already known?'

'No facts bearing directly on the crime will be withheld, sergeant. Of that I can assure you . . . May I present his royal highness's attitude in this way. A certain result is hoped for, which is not necessarily the apprehension of the criminal. If your activities produced that result without your becoming aware of all the surrounding circumstances, then that is an outcome which everyone would prefer—not least yourselves.'

'We can't investigate in blinkers,' said Bragg bluntly.

'You are not being asked to. No attempt will be made to limit the information you feel it necessary to acquire in the conduct of your enquiries. It is merely felt inapposite gratuitously to burden you with knowledge which may prove to have no bearing on the matter.'

'How can I be sure we shall get co-operation from the people involved, sir?' asked Bragg.

'The prince has written to everyone, to ask that they should be completely open with you, sergeant.'

'And if they are not?'

'That in itself would be significant, would it not?'

Bragg tugged at his moustache unhappily. 'I am a policeman,' he said gruffly, 'not a tight-rope walker.'

'I am sure that ordinary police methods will suffice.'

'You can't get a warrant, without laying information.'

Knolleys turned to the Commissioner. 'Should you come to the consideration of such a step, Sir William, I would be glad if you would refer to me, before coming to a decision.'

'Very well.'

There was silence for a moment, as Knolleys looked from one man to another, inviting questions.

'What was this crime, then?' Bragg asked.

Knolleys gave a deprecating smile. 'It was the theft of a letter from a woman.'

'Who is she?'

'Frances Greville, Lady Brooke.'

'And where can we get hold of her?'

'Her London house is 6 Berkeley Square.'

'Right, we will make a start, then.'

'I am sure I need not add,' said Knolleys, 'that the prince hopes you will prosecute your enquiries with the utmost expedition.'

Bragg and Morton secured an interview with Lady Brooke between a visit to her dressmaker and a luncheon party. She was a tall, striking young woman, with fair hair and dark blue eyes.

'His royal highness told me to expect a visit from you,' she said in a bright, assertive voice. She turned to Morton. 'You accompanied him to Easton Park, in the spring, did you not?—He said you were one of us.'

'This letter, ma'am,' said Bragg. 'Was it stolen from here?'

'No, indeed, sergeant. It was taken from my bedroom in Warwick Castle. My husband, Lord Brooke, is heir to the earldom of Warwick; we were visiting my parents-in-law.'

'Just family then?'

'No. They were holding a house-party.'

'I see. And when was the loss discovered?'

'When I got up on the morning of the third of May. I went to my dressing-table, and it was gone.'

'It was in your bedroom, then?'

'Yes, sergeant.'

'Where precisely was it?'

'I have a small morocco correspondence box, which was on the left of the dressing-table, near to the window. The letters inside were tied together with ribbon. That morning I discovered the box open, the ribbon untied, the top envelope empty and the letter gone.'

'Had you locked the box the previous night?'

'It is not furnished with a lock, sergeant.'

'Would it be possible for the box to have been reached through an open window?' asked Morton.

Lady Brooke smiled. 'I would not think it at all likely. I cannot even remember if the window was open. Perhaps it was, the heatwave had begun by then, had it not? . . . I think you should ask my maid.'

'May I ask why you took a box of letters you had already read all the way from London?' said Bragg.

'For their protection,' Lady Brooke replied with an inscrutable smile, 'and for my own gratification, sergeant.'

'Your husband would know of this box, I take it.'

'In a general way . . . He would never read my correspondence.'

'Is it possible that he could have picked the missing letter up, and mislaid it?'

'No, it is not. In any case, he had his own room.'

'Who else would have known you had the box with you?'

'My maid.'

'I would like to have a chat with her.'

'I take it that you will be going to Warwick?' she asked.

'In all probability, ma'am.'

'Then I will telegraph her to help you any way she can . . . You look surprised, constable, that while I am here in London, or at my country house in Essex, my maid should be in Warwick.'

'I confess that I am intrigued,' said Morton.

'It is simple enough. Freebody—her name is Agnes Freebody—was recently married to my father-in-law's valet. It was a very convenient match and, as the earl is now very frail, I decided to allow it. When I visit Warwick, I leave my current maid down here, and Freebody looks after me.'

'When did you last see the letter, ma'am?' asked Bragg.

'Late on the previous evening—the Tuesday. I re-read it after preparing for bed, then put it away. The next morning it was gone.'

'And who was it from?'

Lady Brooke narrowed her eyes and hesitated. 'It was from the Prince of Wales,' she said.

CHAPTER ——————
—————— *TEN*

For the first hour of the journey to Warwick, Bragg remained grumpily silent. When Morton tried to engage him in conversation, he buried himself in his newspaper. Eventually he folded it and laid it on the seat beside him.

'I don't mind telling you, lad,' he declared, 'it's not my idea of police work, chasing after letters pinched from ladies' boudoirs.'

'You seem to be the author of your own misfortunes,' replied Morton lightly. 'If it had not been for your outstanding work last summer, some Warwickshire policeman would have been given the task.'

'What I cannot abide is being told to drop everything else. We were just coming to grips with the Godfrey case. By the time this is finished, the trail will have gone cold.'

'I am sure your robust independence will allow you to continue that case also,' said Morton with a smile. 'Incidentally, I received a communication from Reuben Smith, by courtesy of my sister. He said that the bank did check all ten-pound notes in its possession, before opening on the Wednesday morning, to see if any bore the serial numbers in the Bank of England notice. None did.'

'He would say that, wouldn't he?'

'We could interview the cashiers, to find out if it is the truth.'

'Not now, we can't . . . I expect it is. I cannot see a ten-pound note getting from Piccadilly to a City bank in, say, a couple of hours—not in the ordinary course of business, anyway . . . It would be different, though, if the blackmailer had an account there, and had gone to pay in the lot.'

'But then we would have expected to find the remainder of the notes in the bank's possession.'

'Unless they had paid them out again to customers . . . No, lad, it won't do. Our blackmailer is in it for the money, not for revenge or perverted pleasure. He would not have given the dean such a long ride otherwise. And young Smith seems to have plenty, if he can throw it away as he does.'

'He might not have much money as an individual,' said Morton. 'Still, one can hardly see him stooping to blackmail.'

'So if Rouse didn't get it from Smith, where did he get it from?'

'I must confess to a rooted dislike of Rouse,' said Morton. 'A man who is prepared to accept a comfortable life as the price of his wife's infidelity, is hardly admirable.'

'And yet we have found some pretty unscrupulous people among the seeming-upright,' Bragg commented.

'I looked Rouse up in *Burke's Landed Gentry* last night,' said Morton. 'In the previous edition it showed him as having a country seat in Northamptonshire. The present edition merely claims a residence there. One would infer that the mansion house and the major part of the estate has been sold. That seems to bear out his claim to be sponging on his wife.'

'Granted he has need of money,' said Bragg, 'why would he draw it to our attention?'

'A double bluff, perhaps?'

'Maybe . . . I'd like to have a word with Bullivant soon. The Dean Hadley side seems to have come to a dead end, with that bugger Wilde being so cocky.'

'The most extraordinary part of this whole affair,' said Morton, 'is the Duke of Clarence and that revolting club.'

'Why does that surprise you? All this Hanover lot are either mad or bad. My old grandfather used to say that, once, the king and his prime minister were both loony at the same time.'

'But surely that all ended with Queen Victoria?'

'Why should it? The Queen's grandfather was as mad as a hatter, and none of his sons were any good. And on top of it she goes and marries her cousin. You wouldn't breed a prize pig that way,' said Bragg contemptuously. 'Now her litter is spread through all the royal families of Europe, and soon their children will be inter-breeding. If you ask me, it's time the whole shooting-match was swept away.'

'Do I detect that our present assignment is irksome to you, sir?' asked Morton, tongue-in-cheek.

'You bloody do, so stop roasting me.'

They took a trap from the station, through Georgian streets interspersed with groups of timber-framed houses. Now and again, the towers of the castle would appear, white against the deep blue of the sky. They came to the outskirts of the town and suddenly the castle was revealed entire, awesomely massive, impregnable, dominating everything around by its mere presence.

'I thought all our castles were ruined,' Bragg remarked.

'I seem to remember that the Greville family were on Parliament's side in the civil war. I expect that saved the castle from the usual fate.'

'Just look at the size of it! And they expect us to go over that lot in an afternoon.'

They paid off the trap at the castle stables, and began to walk slowly along the path which ran around the foot of the walls. Great towers jutted into the sky, their exterior windows mere slits; between them, unbroken masonry thirty feet high.

'I wouldn't like to climb that lot,' said Bragg. 'Would you?'

'Not without equipment, and probably not alone, either.'

The path ahead swung in towards the gatehouse and, as they neared it, a man in brown and primrose livery, with an impressive beaver hat, came towards them.

'Can I help you, gentlemen?' he asked.

'I am sure you can,' said Morton. 'Would you tell his lordship that we have come from the Prince of Wales, and will wait upon him shortly. We have had a rather uncomfortable journey and will take the air for a while.'

'Very good, sir. The earl himself is not at all well today; but I will inform her ladyship.'

They followed the path to the river and scrambled some way down the bank. Here the wall fell like a precipice to the Avon. From the battlements to the water, it must have been well over a hundred feet. This was obviously the domestic side of the fortification, for the wall was pierced by windows—some small rectangular casements, others mullioned gothic structures.

'You would never get in on this side,' said Bragg. 'Not unless you had someone inside to throw you a rope.'

They retraced their steps, then struck westwards following the wall. Occasionally the height of the fortification would lessen, as it straddled a low hillock. In two places the wall was pierced by entrances, whose strong iron gates stood ajar. Then, as they turned towards the river again, the path was forced away from the base of the wall by a considerable mound. Looking back from the river bank they could see that, from a squat tower, a section of wall ran up the mound. Its top formed a regular series of steps, and in places it could not be more than fifteen feet high.

'Go on, lad,' said Bragg. 'See what you can do.'

Morton clambered up to near the summit of the mound, where a small tree grew close by. A branch projected towards the wall, but it would not bear the weight of more than a small child. He continued to the top. Here the surface of the wall had been eroded by wind and weather, particularly along the joins between the stone slabs, giving it a rusticated appearance.

'Well,' Bragg gasped as he toiled towards him, 'give it a try.'

Morton took off his coat and hat, then, finding a good foothold, began to edge his way upwards. Finger holds were easy enough, but the toes of his boots were too rounded to allow a sure grip, so he had to proceed by pressing the inner welt of the sole into the cracks. It was exceedingly uncomfortable and precarious. He crawled his way up for some five feet, then a foothold gave under him and he crashed to the ground.

'Well, that's interesting,' Bragg observed, as Morton got painfully to his feet. 'You see where your boots have scored the surface as you slithered down? There are no similar marks on the wall, so far. However, I think we can say it could be climbed with a rope and grappling iron. It was worth a grazed shin or two!'

They descended the mound, keeping close to the wall, but found no evidence of attempted entry. Soon they came down to the path and walked round to the gatehouse again. There they were met by the gatekeeper once more.

'The countess presents her regrets, gentlemen. The earl is too ill for her to leave him at the moment. She says that you may see whatever you wish, and that the housekeeper will give you any information you require. She will join you herself, later, if circumstances permit.'

'That's very good of her ladyship,' said Bragg. 'You know what this is all about, I suppose?'

The man looked uncomfortable. ''Tis said something disappeared, when her young ladyship was last up,' he said reluctantly.

'That's right, and we have come to look into it. I suppose, as gatekeeper, you are responsible for locking up, and so on?'

'Yes, sir.'

'Is there a rigid pattern, or does it vary?'

'It might be different when there's a big charity do in the courtyard, or the estate supper after the harvest, but the rule is that the two gates in the east wall are locked at sunset, and this door is locked at ten o'clock.'

'Suppose that one of the family has been out, and returns after ten,' said Morton. 'What is the procedure then?'

'The coachman stops at my cottage by the stables, and I goes and lets them in.'

'Are you on duty from six o'clock in the morning till ten at night?'

'I have two breaks, at noon and tea-time.'

'Does anyone stand in for you then?'

'Yes—the gardener who looks after the courtyard. 'Tis part
of his job.'

'Where do you actually stand, when you are on duty?' asked
Morton.

The gatekeeper walked over to the inner extremity of the
passageway. 'I stand here. I can see both the gates in the outer
wall from here, so nothing nor nobody can get in the castle
without I see them.'

'Do you drop that thing too, when you lock up?' asked
Bragg, pointing to the spikes of the portcullis over his head.

'No! But we could do. It is in working order!'

'I would like you to come round the inside of the wall with
us,' said Bragg. 'We have to consider the possibility that an
intruder got into the castle and took the missing object.'

'Not while I was on duty,' said the gatekeeper emphatically.

'It would be dark about half past eight,' Bragg mused, as
they walked along the path towards the north tower. 'Are these
gas-lamps lit at night?'

'I light them as I go to lock the gates.'

'And who turns them off?'

'In the dark weather, I turn them off when it gets light in the
morning. In the summer, the watchman will turn them off at
first light.'

'What watchman?'

'Dick Bowman. 'Tis his job to patrol the courtyard and keep
watch all night, after the main door has been locked.'

'So the courtyard is lit throughout the hours of darkness, and
you have a watchman here,' said Morton. 'I notice that up by
the mound there is scrub and a few small trees, and that the
gas-lamps do not extend beyond the paths. Is there not a dark
area there, which could afford concealment?'

'There are dark shadows, right enough. But anyone getting
in there would have to cross the lighted part.'

'Let's climb the mound, shall we?' said Bragg. 'We went
round the outside of the wall and decided it could be scaled
with a rope.'

Reluctantly, the gatekeeper toiled with them along the wall
to the top of the hill, then down the other side. There was no

scrape mark on the surface, where a grappling iron might have taken hold.

'Thank you for your help,' said Bragg, as they reached the domestic quarters on the south side of the courtyard. 'Would you be good enough to tell the housekeeper that we would like to see her?'

'Mrs Roberts? Certainly.'

'It looks hardly likely than an intruder could have been responsible for the theft,' said Morton, as he disappeared.

'Maybe. I reckon we can forget about anyone getting over the wall. I'm not so sure about the entrances though. You noticed that the gatekeeper didn't call anybody to take over, when he came with us round the walls. And he certainly wasn't standing at his corner when he saw us coming along the path. I bet if we had wanted, one of us could have drawn him away, while the other slipped through one of the gates in the outer wall.'

'But even if that were possible, an intruder would have had to conceal himself in the castle for a considerable time.'

'You know more about these things than I do, lad, but suppose it was a young woman that took the letter. Wouldn't it be possible for her to dress like a lady's maid? There was a house-party on. I bet there were any number of strange people wandering about.'

'That is certainty a thought,' conceded Morton. 'Though whether she could have penetrated as far as Lady Brooke's bedroom, unchallenged, is another matter.'

'Well, we will soon find out.'

A woman in a black, high-necked dress was coming towards them. Her grey hair was drawn into a bun on the back of her head, her whole mien was one of intense disapproval.

'This is one for you, lad,' Bragg muttered.

'Good morning, Mrs Roberts,' Morton greeted her pleasantly. 'I'm afraid that we are going to be rather a nuisance to you.'

His upper-class accent clearly took her aback.

'Her ladyship said I should take you anywhere you wanted to go,' she said grudgingly.

'Well, I am sure that you have a great many important things to do in an establishment of this size. If you have to break off from time to time, we shall not be in the least incommoded.'

'Thank you.' She seemed on the point of adding an automatic 'sir,' but cut it off.

'Basically, our concern is to look at the rooms which were occupied on the night of the second of May, and to establish what people were in the castle—not only family and guests, but servants also.'

'There were no servants,' said Mrs Roberts shortly. 'All the domestic staff left at six o'clock; personal maids and valets had finished by dinner time, and the kitchen and dining room staff left as soon as the dessert had been put out.'

'Are you saying that there were no servants whatever left inside, when the gate was locked at ten o'clock, ma'am?' asked Bragg deferentially.

'That is correct,' Mrs Roberts replied, her tone warming slightly. 'They are all accommodated in the stable block or the row of cottages beyond.'

'I wonder if we might start at the room occupied by Lady Brooke that evening,' said Morton.

She took them through an arched doorway, up two flights of stone stairs and along a dark corridor. Then she stopped and pushed open a door. The room beyond was startlingly opulent, after the austerity that they had encountered so far. The floor was covered in rich Turkey carpet, heavy damask curtains were at the window and the walls appeared to be covered in figured cream silk. A double bed projected from one wall. Over it was a small canopy, from which drapes of white gauzy material fell, to be caught up in ties at the bed-head. Cupboards had been installed at either side of the fireplace, to act as wardrobes; against the far wall was a chest of drawers, while near the window was a dressing-table. Bragg strolled over, and opened the window. You would have to be a spider to get up that, he thought. And, anyway, the dressing-table was too far away to be reached. The thief would have had to squeeze through the window into the room itself. The whole idea was a virtual impossibility. He turned to the dressing-table.

'This is where the box was, then?' he asked, pointing to the left-hand side.

'It is no use asking me,' replied Mrs Roberts severely. 'I know nothing about it.'

'Ah yes, I remember, it's Mrs Freebody that knows about that,' said Bragg humbly.

'There was a house-party that evening, with several guests,' said Morton. 'Can you remember where they all slept?'

'Of course,' said Mrs Roberts tartly. 'It's less than a fortnight ago.'

'Lady Brooke was in this room,' Morton prompted.

'We had the Marquess and Marchioness of Salisbury—they were in the Chippendale bedroom . . .'

'Wait one moment,' said Morton fumbling for his notebook. 'This is obviously of great importance . . . The Salisburys in the Chippendale. Carry on.'

'The Prince of Wales was in the Kenilworth Room, next door. It has its own dressing room.'

'The Prince of Wales?' exclaimed Bragg in surprise.

'Yes . . . Then there's the Blue bedroom. That's my master and mistress's room . . . Lord Charles Beresford was in the Wolsley room, and Lady Rouse had the Chinese room next to it . . . That is the lot, here.'

'I thought Lord Brooke had a room,' said Morton.

'He was in the Watergate tower, Sir Alexander Rouse was in the Gatehouse tower, and Lady Gladys Curwen was in the Watergate, as well.'

'Is that everyone?' asked Morton.

'It is.'

'May we see the Watergate tower?'

'Have you finished up here?'

'Why?'

'Well, we shall have to go down to the courtyard to get to it.'

'I see. Is there no passage from here, to that tower?'

'No. Nor to the Gatehouse tower.'

'Then, for the moment we shall stay here. I think we can let you get on now, Mrs Roberts. Would you be good enough to send Mrs Freebody to us in ten minutes or so? . . . And thank you.'

Mrs Roberts gave a perfunctory smile, and went out.

Morton went into the passage, and began to sketch the

position of the various rooms in his notebook. Then he labelled them with the names of their occupants on the second of May.

'So the Prince of bloody Wales was here,' said Bragg wrathfully. 'Why the hell could they not say so, instead of playing these sodding games with us?'

'Perhaps this is where the views of the prince and Knolleys diverged,' remarked Morton.

'Well, I'm not going to be treated like a blasted puppet, lad. I'll get to the bottom of this, however much they try to obstruct us.'

'At all events, sir, it seems exceedingly unlikely that anyone from outside the castle is involved.'

'I wouldn't be surprised if that hoity-toity bit hasn't lost the letter herself, and is creating all this fuss for nothing.'

There came a discreet tapping at the door.

'Come in,' Bragg called.

A pretty young woman with a pert smile entered.

'Why, Agnes!' said Morton warmly. 'How nice to see you! We met when the prince came to Easton Park in February. Do you remember?'

'Of course I do!'

'Congratulations on your marriage!'

'It's worked out well, really. The old man won't last long, and then Daisy will be up here—brighten it up a bit. She's a card, she is.'

'Daisy?'

'Lady Brooke.'

'Ah, yes. She said that she would telegraph you, to tell you to help us all you could. Did she do that?'

'If that's what "co-operate fully" means, yes.'

'You know that we are enquiring about the missing letter?'

'Yes.'

'We were told that it was in a morocco box, on the dressing-table there. Did you see it?'

'Yes. It was there all right. She never goes anywhere without it.'

'Why not?' asked Bragg innocently.

'Well . . . !' Agnes gave a snigger.

'You know who the letters were from, then?'

''Course!'

'Have you ever read any of them?' asked Bragg conspiratorially.

'I wouldn't go that far,' she said guardedly.

'What do you know about this particular letter?'

'Well, it was me that found it—that it was gone, I mean. I drew back the curtains in the morning, and there was the box, with the lid opened and the ribbon all untied.'

'What did your mistress say?'

'She went mad. She had me looking everywhere, even though she swore it was in the box when she went to bed.'

'Who else knew that it had gone?'

'Nobody. She didn't tell anyone, and she said I mustn't either.'

'It was a funny sort of house-party,' Bragg remarked.

'They all are, if you ask me,' she said dismissively.

'Where do you sleep?' asked Morton.

'We have a cottage beyond the stables. It's lovely.'

'I was surprised to hear that all the servants—even those of the guests—left the castle before the end of dinner. Why was that, do you think?'

'Stop pretending!' she said archly. 'That's when they get up to their fun and games, isn't it? They ring the stable bell at six o'clock in the morning, just like at Easton, so everybody can get back to their right beds!'

'Get away with you!' exclaimed Bragg, egging her on.

'It's true! You know that we leave a plate of little sandwiches in the guests' rooms at night, in case they get hungry? . . . Well, when I first went to Easton, the ladies used to put the plate outside their door. That way, whoever they had fixed up with would know that they were alone. Then, one night, we had a foreign diplomat staying. He didn't know anything about this, and he was hungry. So he walked down the corridor, picking up the plates and eating the sandwiches as he went. There weren't half some long faces, next day!'

'I can't see Lord and Lady Salisbury getting up to any of them tricks,' said Bragg sceptically.

Agnes giggled. 'No, but the others would . . . I remember Mrs Roberts was all of a tizz, because she had to change the rooms round at the last minute. It seems the Prince of Wales wanted Lady Rouse next to Lord Charles Beresford.'

'Is that why Sir Alexander Rouse was put in the Gatehouse tower?'

'That's right.'

'Surely there were fewer women than men,' said Bragg, pretending to consult Morton's notebook. 'Who is this Lady Gladys Curwen?'

'She lives in Leamington Spa.'

'Fairly locally, then.'

'I heard Daisy saying that she'd been invited for Brookie,' Agnes confided, with a giggle.

'Brookie?'

'Her husband.'

'I see. That's why they were both in the Watergate tower . . . And who won the beautiful Daisy herself?'

'The Prince of Wales, of course!'

CHAPTER _____
_____ ELEVEN

Catherine was engrossed in writing an article for the Saturday edition of the paper, when the office-boy put his head round the door.

'A young lady to see you, miss,' he said.

'Bring her up, will you, Tom?'

Moments later, he reappeared and ushered Arabella Godfrey into the room. She seemed strained and agitated.

'Whatever is the matter?' Catherine exclaimed.

Arabella sat defeatedly on the chair opposite.

'I have had another,' she said.

'Another blackmail letter?'

'Yes. I have to take one hundred pounds to Covent Garden on Saturday afternoon. Obviously, I do not have it, and cannot obtain it.'

'Did anyone see you come here?'

'No.' Arabella gave a wan smile. 'I have not completely lost my head. I walked down Oxford Street to Marshall & Snelgrove's store. I went to the millinery department and looked at hats, until I was satisfied that no one was watching me. Then I went out of the back entrance and got a cab in Cavendish Square.'

'You are becoming quite resourceful,' said Catherine encouragingly.

'Oh, no.' She seemed on the verge of tears. 'I cannot continue in this way. The sergeant was right. I can see demand after demand, stretching for ever into the future. That business, ten days ago, solved nothing. It even seems to have encouraged him.'

'I think that we should try to find Sergeant Bragg,' said Catherine, putting on her coat and hat. 'If no one followed you from the West End, then there can be no objection to our calling on him.'

'But will he be able to help?' asked Arabella dolefully.

'One thing I am certain of, he will undoubtedly try.'

They strolled along Gresham Street, looking in shop windows, and conversing idly. Then they turned up Old Jewry and darted into the narrow entrance of the police headquarters. They found Bragg and Morton brooding over a large piece of paper, covered with names and scribbled comments.

'Good morning, ladies,' said Bragg genially.

'It is not a very good morning,' said Arabella. 'I have received another letter.'

'Sit down, then, and let me have a look at it.'

Arabella opened her bag, and passed over the fold of paper. Bragg read it, scrutinizing the printing intently, then passed it to Morton.

'I would say it is from the same source, wouldn't you?'

'The mark at the top is certainly the same,' said Morton.

'It niggles me, does that,' said Bragg thoughtfully.

'If you like, I could try to find out about it,' Catherine suggested.

'Well now,' Bragg replied with a smile, 'there are some offers a gentleman can't refuse . . . Get one of the other letters, lad.'

Morton crossed to the cupboard and extracted a letter from a file. He cut the top off it, and passed it to Catherine.

'I don't think there is any more to the mark, than saying the letter is from the same source as the others,' said Bragg. 'But I don't mind you spending a bit of time on it . . . Now, the question is, what do we do about this morning's demand?'

'I feel like doing nothing at all about it,' said Arabella. 'It will go on and on, just as you said.'

'Now then,' said Bragg in a fatherly voice, 'we can't have you giving up, just when your engagement has been announced. There's one thing,' he added in a harder tone. 'You mustn't expect mercy from him. If you fail to pay, he will certainly find a way to circulate that photograph. He has even set about destroying the character of one of his victims, after the man had died.'

Arabella shuddered. 'So, even if I withdraw from my engagement and from society, he will still pursue me?'

'I believe he will,' said Bragg quietly.

'So what must I do?'

Bragg turned to Morton. 'The Commissioner authorized that additional hundred pounds before our . . . er, trip to the midlands, didn't he, lad?'

'He certainly accepted your request, in principle.'

'That's good enough for me. You can slip round to the Bank this afternoon and ask May to repeat the process.' He turned to Arabella. 'Don't worry, miss, we will find the money. I will see Miss Marsden has it by Friday evening.'

'And I will bring it to you, as soon as I receive it,' said Catherine encouragingly.

'We will make sure we nab him this time, miss,' said Bragg. 'Now, what I want you to do is this. He said you are to be at the market at two o'clock. It should be nice and quiet at that time. I want you to do just what you did last time. Walk fairly slowly, and keep to the empty part of the street, where you can.'

'It is a not very salubrious part of London,' Arabella said dubiously.

'Don't worry, we will look after you. I want you to take a cab to Bedford Street, then walk the length of Henrietta Street towards the market. I will be at one end of the street, and the constable at the other—but don't look for us, just act normally. If you are approached there, we shall let him take the money, then arrest him. If he does not approach you there, then Constable Morton will draw back into the market, and I will follow you at a distance. We will keep an eye on you every second. You need not worry.'

'I do not see the point of it,' said Arabella listlessly. 'If you arrest the man, you will want me to give evidence at his trial. My reputation will be destroyed even more surely.'

'You can make that decision, once we have got him,' said Bragg persuasively. 'We have other, more serious things to charge him with. It is possible that your name need never be mentioned.'

Arabella sighed. 'Very well,' she said. 'It would appear that I have little choice but to agree.'

The ladies departed and Bragg tipped back his chair, staring at the ceiling.

'We have got ourselves amongst a queer lot, and no mistake,' he said at length. 'You have often said you tried society life for a bit, but couldn't stand it. I've never pried, till now, but frankly I do not understand the people we are dealing with.'

Morton smiled. 'I gave it up because it was wasteful and aimless,' he said. 'There are people in society who have so much wealth, that they can indulge any whim. As a result, they spend their lives in a constant search for pleasure, for novel entertainments, each more outrageous and extravagant than the last. They worship the same gods as our decadent friend Oscar Wilde, though they would disdain to write his plays.'

'And what about these funny parties we have been hearing about?' asked Bragg.

'They have simply suspended the moral code. Their creed is: "We can do as we wish, so long as we are discreet." '

'It's beyond me, lad. Daisy Brooke has the Prince of Wales in bed with her, and her husband's in a different part of the castle, stuffing a local tart.'

'You would be quite wrong to think that this is merely the result of the prince's influence, or that any dishonour attaches to such loose conduct in their eyes. Husbands and wives seem free to follow their own inclinations, without it being an affront to their spouse. Once a young woman has provided her husband with an heir, then she is regarded as fair game by the rest of the men. A young woman with only her looks to commend her is fair game, married or not.'

'It's not only a bloody disgrace,' said Bragg contemptuously, 'it's downright depraved.'

'Yet these affairs are conducted more or less openly. The only sin in their calendar is to cause a scandal.'

'You know, Lady Brooke once drove a four-in-hand from Essex to Land's End. Not many men could manage that . . . What a bloody shame!'

'I doubt if she would share your sentiment, sir.'

'So this is what Knolleys meant about you being conversant with society and its ways.'

Morton laughed. 'I suppose so.'

'It's no wonder there's blackmail around. They ask for it. Come on lad, let's see what this simple innocent flower has to say for herself.'

They took a hansom to Berkeley Square, and were received by Lady Brooke in her boudoir.

'I understand that you visited Warwick yesterday,' she greeted them. 'I trust that it was profitable.'

'It was, and it wasn't,' said Bragg gruffly. 'I want to have a word with you about that party.'

'As you will,' she replied coolly, taken aback by the lack of deference in his tone.

'It was a very odd party, wasn't it? There was you and your husband, an ex-prime minister and his wife, a sea-captain, the heir to the throne, a wastrel with a wife who is no better than she should be, and a local woman.'

'You obviously have a very plebeian view of life, sergeant. I had expected better.'

'Maybe you had, ma'am.'

'You clearly do not understand the function of a house-party.'

'I do believe you are right, ma'am,' said Bragg blandly. 'You see, with the exception of your parents-in-law, who don't seem to have appeared at all, and Lady Curwen . . .'

'Lady Gladys Curwen,' Lady Brooke interrupted tartly. 'She is a peer's daughter, it is merely a courtesy title.'

'Forgive my ignorance, ma'am. As I was saying, with the exception of those three, you could have all met in London, without any of the effort of going up to Warwick.'

'Some things cannot be achieved in the bustle of London, particularly in the Season. The serenity of a country house has often oiled the wheels of government.'

'But not this time, I think.'

'Very well,' she said irritably. 'I do not see remotely how this bears on your enquiries, but the party was arranged to patch up a quarrel between the Prince of Wales and Lord Charles Beresford.'

'I see,' said Bragg flatly. 'And how long had this party been arranged?'

'Some three weeks before; as soon as it was known that Lord Charles was coming home on leave from the Mediterranean.'

'So they had all known for three weeks?'

'With the exception of Lord Charles, yes. Really!' she exclaimed, 'I do not see what this has to do with the theft of my letter.'

'Because one of them took it . . . if it was taken.'

'But that is totally out of the question!'

'Well, ma'am, let's look at the evidence. When the letter went missing, there were no servants at all in the castle. Only your husband's parents, and the members of the house-party. All the gates and doors were locked. We are satisfied that no one entered the castle from the outside; if he had, he would have been seen by the watchman.'

'I know all this.'

'But you still say the letter was stolen?'

'I am certain of it.'

'I see.' Bragg reflected for a moment. 'When did you get that letter?' he asked.

'That same evening.'

'Who brought it?'

'It was pushed under my door, while I was dressing for dinner.'

'By the Prince of Wales?'

'I assume so.'

'Why would he do that, when he had been in your company most of the day and would be seeing you in the dining-room?'

'I take it that it was a happy impulse of friendship. It is by no means unusual.'

'May I ask if you spent that night in your own bedroom?'

Lady Brooke's eyes flashed. 'Your question is impertinent, sergeant. I will not be subjected to this kind of interrogation!'

'Well, now,' said Bragg smoothly. 'I was assured by the Prince of Wales, that everybody concerned would co-operate and would answer my questions truthfully. Yet you allowed me to think that the letter had been brought up by you from London, with the others.'

'What possible difference could that make?' asked Lady Brooke defiantly.

'Well, for one thing it reduces the number of people who could have known of its existence.'

'I tell you, all the people you have named are above suspicion.'

'Then all I am left with, is to go back to the Prince of Wales, and say that there is nothing to investigate; that it's either absent-mindedness on your part, or a practical joke of some kind.'

'No, please do not take that step,' Lady Brooke said in perturbation. 'I assure you that there was a letter, which, if it got into the wrong hands, could be misconstrued. The press has been consistently critical of the prince, and all his indiscretions have been magnified into deeds of evil.'

'And what was so special about this letter?'

Lady Brooke clenched her teeth, and her chin jutted out angrily. Then she strode over to her escritoire and brought out a red leather box. She took out a bundle of letters, jerked open the bow of ribbon and took the top letter from its envelope. 'There!' she said angrily. 'If you must see my private correspondence!'

Bragg took the letter, and perused it. ' "My own lovely little Daisy," ' he murmured, ' "my darling . . . my loved one . . . my adored little Daisy wife . . ." Yes, I can see what you are getting at. But this was not the letter that got lost,' he said, handing it back.

'Let us say that it was considerably more explicit. At all costs it must be kept from the public.'

'And what makes you think that it might get out?'

In reply, Lady Brooke lifted the bundle of letters again, and took out a paper from the bottom of the box. She unfolded it, and thrust it into Bragg's hand.

'That does!' she said vehemently.

The letter was printed in capitals, on good-quality paper. It was not signed.

SUCH AN INDISCREET LETTER. WHAT A PITY TO SPOIL THE WEDDING. THE EDITOR WANTS £10,000 COMPENSATION IF HE IS NOT TO PRINT IT. IF YOU WANT ME TO MEDIATE, PUT A MESSAGE IN THE TIMES PERSONAL COLUMN BEFORE THE END OF MAY.

'I almost missed one curtsy!' said Emily with a giggle. 'It must have been to one of the royal princesses. I cannot remember which. Anyway, my heel caught in my dress and I could not get down any further! I just had to incline my head even more and make the best of it! Thank goodness the Queen did not see.'

'And after all your rehearsals—to say nothing of my tuition!' said Violet teasingly.

'I should have practised in the dress. It is much more difficult, when you are moving backwards and having to manage a four yard court train in addition.'

'Well, I am quite exhausted,' said Lady Morton. 'That tedious crawl along the Mall, the coaches nose to tail . . . and when we got to the ante-room, there was so much elbowing and pushing . . . I am sure it was not like that when I was presented.'

'That is because everyone wants to get there before the Queen gets tired. It is not the same, to have merely been presented to the Princess of Wales.'

'And did you get to see the Queen?' asked Amelia.

'Oh, yes! Mamma went through them like a charging buffalo! Never has American vigour been put to so good a purpose!'

'You make it sound so indelicate, Emily,' her mother

protested. 'In any case, having delayed your presentation, it was as little as I could do to ensure that you kissed hands with your sovereign.'

'And was it all worth the trouble?' asked Violet with a sceptical smile.

'Oh yes!' Emily exclaimed. 'It was so thrilling, and so splendid! The rooms in Buckingham Palace are very grand, and the uniforms were gorgeous!'

'I wonder why soldiers seem so very impressive,' Violet remarked. 'Even Rutherford was quite transformed at the Guards' picnic . . . I suppose it is the sense of their power over life and death.'

'Only a woman has the power over life, dear,' said Amelia caustically. 'A man merely has the choice of whether to kill or refrain from killing.'

'Oh, mamma, don't be so withering!' Violet protested.

'I remember the Civil War all too well. It was not remotely glorious; just bestial carnage.'

'You would think women had precious little to do with giving life, if you went by the papers,' said Emily. 'Listen to this birth announcement.' She seized a copy of *The Times*. ' "On the seventh of May, at 15 Palace Court, the wife of Arthur C. Brockenhurst, of a son". There! who is the central figure in that episode?'

'The child, of course,' her mother observed mildly.

Emily crossed impatiently to the window. 'Where on earth is James?' she asked. 'He always seems to be late, nowadays, and we just mustn't miss the first scene of *Carmen*!'

'Be patient, dear. If need be, we will go without him. We must certainly not be so impolite as to keep our guests waiting.' She smiled fondly at the two girls.

'Oh, I nearly forgot,' cried Emily happily. 'Aubrey Rivington loved your diamond necklace! They sparkled so brilliantly under his lights. He said that he had never seen anything to equal it!'

'I imagine he said it just to make you smile, dear,' replied her mother in a gratified tone.

There was a brief tap at the door, and Morton hurried in.

'I am so sorry to be late. I had to see Miss Marsden, on the way here.'

'You are not yet late, James,' said his mother tartly, 'merely discourteously tardy.'

Morton turned to Emily with a grin. 'Did all go well?' he asked.

'Now, we cannot go through all that again,' said Lady Morton. 'Off you go, girls, and prettify yourselves. We shall leave in five minutes.'

The young women rushed upstairs, followed more sedately by Amelia.

'Who are our guests to be?' asked Morton idly.

'Lord Rutherford, and that nice Smith boy.'

'Reuben Smith?'

'That's right. He sent Emily the most beautiful orchid. She will be wearing it tonight.' She crossed to a side table, and picked up a card from beside a gilded flower-box. 'He wrote on his card: "The first of the season, for the best of the season". I thought that was so sweet!'

Morton took the card. The message had been printed in capitals, at the top of one of Smith's calling-cards. It might have no significance, he thought. It was difficult to make comparisons, as the printing was much smaller than that on the letters . . . Perhaps he had merely told the head-gardener what to put.

'Do you know who he is, mamma?' he asked.

'No, dear, but Hoddeston Hall, Buckinghamshire, sounds very promising. Perhaps, after this evening, I might ask you to make some discreet enquiries.'

'Very well. I will gladly do that.' He turned to the window, and slipped the card into his pocket.

At quarter past one on the following Saturday afternoon, Bragg and Morton arrived at Covent Garden vegetable market. They walked the length of Henrietta Street, and Bragg was well satisfied with his choice. There was no streets leading off it, and the entries were mainly closed with high wooden gates.

'If he tries it here,' he remarked, 'we'll have him.'

'I think I will take up my position behind those barrows at

the corner of the market building itself,' said Morton, pointing them out. 'I shall have a good view down the street, yet be well placed if Miss Godfrey gets beyond it.'

'Very well,' Bragg grunted. 'I could do with twenty officers for this job. But if I had asked the Commissioner, he would have told us to go and look for that bloody letter.'

'He will hardly be inclined to criticize, I trust, once we have caught the blackmailer.'

'Don't forget, it might still be a woman. That gruff tone could easily have been assumed by a woman, if she had a deepish voice.'

'Suppose you look for the man, and I look for the woman,' said Morton with a grin. 'I would find that much more congenial.'

'That's enough of that. It's a serious matter,' said Bragg shortly.

'Sorry, sir. Then I will take up my place.' Morton strolled across, his shabby coat and sweat-stained bowler giving him the air of a lowly-paid clerk.

Bragg turned and walked slowly back down the street. Of the two he seemed the more prosperous. His boots were well shined, his coat, though somewhat baggy, was well brushed. With his incipient paunch and bushy moustache, he could have been taken for a tradesman—a successful shopkeeper, perhaps. As he went, he scrutinized the features of the street again, till he was satisfied that he knew the danger-points. Then he entered the shop of an ironmonger, whose window commanded a view of the corner of Bedford Street. To his mind, Miss Godfrey's cab would come across Leicester Square, down New Row, and into Bedford Street at the top. He should be able to see her actually set down at this corner. If she were brought the other way, she would only have to cross the road to be in his vision. He strolled over to the counter and produced his warrant card.

'Do you mind if I hang about in your shop for a bit?' he asked.

'Suit yourself, mate,' said the shopkeeper with a smile. 'Here, you might as well feed the canaries. Save me a job.' He pushed over a small tray of bird-seed.

Bragg took it reluctantly and walked to the front of the shop. In fact, it was a sound suggestion. The middle of the window was filled with birdcages of various sizes, each containing one or two canaries. With the pretext of feeding them, he could be very close to the door and still not be noticed.

He pulled out his watch. Ten minutes to two. She should be arriving at any moment. He looked around. An oldish man was shuffling down the opposite pavement. Bragg tensed. You never could tell . . . He took a pinch of birdseed, and scattered it on the floor of one of the cages. The occupants flew down from their perches, and began to feed . . . The man had reached the corner now, and turned up Bedford Street. Suppose he was going to accost her as she descended from the cab? Bragg checked the impulse to sprint to the end of the street. Whoever he was, he didn't know she was coming this way. That was the whole point of the strategy, to let her walk slowly along a street that was in full view of the market, and draw him down towards her. Bragg took another pinch of seed, and tossed it into some of the other cages. It was now five past two. What the hell was keeping her? If she was more than a few minutes late, the blackmailer would scent danger, and be off. Bragg leaned forward between the cages, to get a better look; the street was deserted. He was becoming irritated by the cheeping of the blasted birds. They must be real canaries, for once, not just sparrows dyed yellow. He flung more seed around the cages, but the birds were losing interest. He couldn't feed them for much longer, that was for sure . . . Twelve minutes past two. Surely the traffic couldn't be that bad? Bragg suddenly realised that there was no traffic—not coming down Bedford Street anyway . . . He dashed to the door and sprinted down to the corner. A large van had become entangled with a hay wagon, some three hundred yards up the street, completely blocking the carriageway. The driver would have seen it and taken his cab across the top. He would have put Miss Godfrey down somewhere on the north side of the market!

Bragg hurried along Henrietta Street. As he approached its end, he saw Morton rise from behind the barrows, turn and saunter into the market. Bragg went to the opposite end of the buildings and began to search methodically. Between them, they criss-crossed the market several times. Then they went to the flower hall nearby, but in vain. Arabella Godfrey was nowhere to be found.

CHAPTER ———— ———— TWELVE

Sunday afternoon found Bragg and Morton in South Audley Street. After a brief conference with a mortified Mr Handford, they were allowed to see his brother-in-law.

William Bullivant was in his early forties, of medium height and slender build. His skin was pallid, and his carefully shaved cheeks already displayed evidence of a heavy beard. He constantly dabbed at his forehead and face with a handkerchief. It was hot, sure enough, thought Bragg, but not as hot as all that.

'We would like to ask you a few questions about some suspect bank notes that have been circulating,' he said.

"Ah yes, Sir Alec told me that you had been to see him.'

'Did he now?' said Bragg irritably. 'We have been trying to get hold of you for over a week.'

'So I gather. I have not been avoiding you.' His voice was light and pleasant, but the tension in his manner was reflected in it.

'Well, can we talk about that game of whist?'

'It is rather a long time ago . . . I seem to recall that the prince was particularly critical of any mistakes by his partners, that evening.'

'Did you win or lose?'

'I lost a little, on balance.'

'Who won then?'

'The prince and Alec.'

'Were you the only loser?'

'No. Smith lost . . . You are expected to, when you are buying your way into society,' he added with a sneer.

'Can you remember how much you paid, when the settlement was made?'

'Fifteen pounds, sergeant—so only one of your so-called suspect notes could possibly have come from me.'

'Why do you say "so-called", sir?' asked Bragg.

'For no particular reason.'

'So, even though it is a long time ago, you can remember the trifling sum you lost that night?'

'I would rather have won it, sergeant.'

'Suppose, for a moment, that Sir Alec had got one of these notes from you, where would you have got it from?'

'I have no idea, nor am I disposed to reflect on the possibilities. I understand that the burden of proof in these matters is upon you.'

'Good heavens, sir,' exclaimed Bragg genially, 'we don't think of you as a suspect! We are just making general enquiries.'

'Then please be content with my answers,' Bullivant said brusquely.

'You seem very edgy, sir,' Bragg remarked.

'If I wish for advice on my nervous state, sergeant, I will see my medical practitioner.'

'Very good, sir. Would you like to tell me where you were on Tuesday the ninth of May? . . . Or is that too long ago for you?'

A defeated look flickered across Bullivant's face. 'I remember very well where I was. I spent the day walking my estate in Surrey.'

'I see, sir. Then the bailiff, and so on, will be able to confirm that?'

'No, sergeant. I conferred with no one; indeed I do not recall having seen anyone I knew.'

'But you would have gone up to the house?'

'The house was empty.'

'Did you go down by train?'

'Yes, the nine fifty from Waterloo; and I returned to that station at about seven fifteen in the evening.'

'So the local station staff would be able to say that they saw you arrive and depart?'

'Possibly. I do not recall if there was anyone there. It is only a halt at Brookwood; my grandfather extracted it as the price for letting the line go through his land.'

'I see,' said Bragg slowly. 'I would have thought that, in the middle of the Season, you would not have had time for tramping around fields.'

'It was my last opportunity . . . The whole estate was up for auction, the following day.'

'Never mind, sir,' said Bragg. 'I expect you got a good price.'

'The bank got a good price, you mean.' Bullivant said bitterly. 'All I got was few thousand pounds.'

'That won't last long around here.'

Bullivant stared angrily back, without replying.

'But your family has always been wealthy,' exclaimed Morton, in surprise.

'Ah, but then, one does not publicize the growing mortgages on one's acres. I have now reaped that crop with a vengeance.'

'I am astounded!'

'You have no need to be. I am the victim of the perennial ingratitude of princes; or, more probably, mere thoughtlessness in his case.'

'You are speaking of the Prince of Wales?'

'Yes, constable. He is a man of few intellectual resources, with a horror of being bored. He demands to be constantly amused. When one diversion palls, he goes in search of another. His inadequacies are compounded by his small need of sleep. So, one finds oneself constantly rushing from country house to yacht, to grouse moor, to race-course . . .'

'But surely you had the resources to keep up with that way of life?' said Morton.

'I thought I had,' replied Bullivant, the bitterness creeping into his voice again. 'But I was wrong. The old aristocracy still cleaves to the court at Windsor; so the prince's extravagances bear very heavily on the comparatively small circle of his intimates. I have been favoured by his friendship—if that is the word—for twenty years, ever since I came into my inheritance. You would have to be very wealthy indeed, to survive that unscathed . . . I used to keep a shoot. But twenty thousand birds provide less than two weeks' sport for his circle.'

'Why did you not mention it to him?' asked Morton.

'What could he have done? He is not king—indeed I sometimes think the Old Lady will last longer than he. In any case, I could hardly do so without appearing to chide him. As I said, it is mere thoughtlessness on his part.'

'Or selfishness,' remarked Bragg.

'No, I cannot plead even that in self-justification. He assumes that anyone in his circle is in a position to indulge his whims—that is why they are there. He will descend on you with ten or so of his friends and their servants, his latest *maîtresse en titre,* his valet, a couple of equerries, his personal police; and they may stay for up to a week, before the fancy takes him to rush off somewhere else—with you in his train.'

'But surely you could just stop?' said Bragg.

'And what is there for me then? For twenty years I have spent my life trying to amuse him, being the butt of his laboured humour, the victim of his practical jokes. What function has a court jester, once he is cast out from the court?' he asked sardonically.

"You ought to marry a rich heiress,' Morton remarked, trying to lighten the atmosphere.

'I would rather shoot myself,' said Bullivant emphatically.

They took their leave and hailed a hansom.

'He's in a bad way,' remarked Bragg, as they rattled along. 'Though whether it's his insolvency, or something more interesting to us, is anyone's guess.'

'I suppose it was inevitable that Rouse would have told him about our visit,' said Morton.

'It's a damned nuisance. You may be sure that he has told all his acquaintances. Our blackmailer, whoever he is, will be on his guard now. I can't see those notes turning up, except through the big stores.'

'I suppose so—and that will apply to the second lot of notes we gave to Miss Godfrey.'

'Have you seen her since yesterday, lad?'

'No. I was on family duty at a dance last night. I will make enquiries.'

They paid off the cab in Eaton Square, and rang the bell of an imposing town house. They were shown into a sitting-room, while the footman went in search of his master.

'Captain the Right Honourable Lord Charles William Delapoer Beresford CB RN,' intoned Morton.

'Where did you get that lot from?' asked Bragg.

'I looked him up in the Navy List. He is quite a senior captain and, with any luck, he might expect to be made up to admiral before too long.'

Bragg surveyed the room. 'Well, not every younger son of an Irish peer is hard up,' he remarked. 'Unless the money came from the wife, like poor old Rouse.'

'I know she was a commoner,' said Morton, 'and is ten years older than Lord Charles; perhaps there was an inducement other than maidenly affection!'

There came heavy steps in the passage outside, and the door was flung open. A tall man, in early middle age, stood glaring at them. He had a high forehead, from which the sandy hair was receding; his complexion was florid and his blue eyes slightly protuberant.

'If it is about that young fool Crossley,' he said aggressively, 'he was trying to outpace my brougham on the public highway; damned lucky not to get more than a broken leg. The driver of the omnibus was in no way to blame.'

'It is not to do with any accident, sir,' said Bragg quietly. 'I just wanted a few words with you about an incident at Warwick Castle, on the second of May.'

Beresford's jaw dropped. 'In heaven's name, why should the police be involved with that?' he exclaimed wrathfully.

'Good God! It was supposed to be a meeting between gentle-men, and now we have the constabulary called in! Is there no end to it?'

'My concern is with the fact that sometime between, say, dinner and breakfast the following morning, a certain valuable object went missing,' said Bragg stolidly.

'I admit that I came back to London early the next day, sergeant, but I am not in the habit of taking the spoons with me.'

'It was not valuable in that sense, sir, it was a letter—from the Prince of Wales to Lady Brooke.'

Beresford gave a harsh laugh of contempt. 'Her and her damned letters . . . She ought to have been strangled at birth.'

'That is an unkind thing to say about a lady,' Bragg observed mildly.

'I do not need you to lecture me, sergeant. I have stood quite enough of that for one leave . . . That accursed woman has engineered the end of a lifetime's friendship.'

'That would be between you and the prince, would it, sir?'

'Yes. Our whole family has been close, ever since I can remember. My brother Marcus is the prince's Master of the Horse. You can imagine the position he is placed in.'

'I understand that the house-party at Warwick Castle was arranged so that you and the prince could settle your differ-ences.'

'Well, it did not succeed! Damn it, I have jeopardized my career in the navy to satisfy that man's whim! I even stood for Parliament, and entered the government as fourth sea lord, so that he could have my company. Now he treats us like this . . . Well, I have known Daisy Brooke far longer than he has, and he will find out that she is a dangerous, vindictive woman. She will land him in more trouble than she has already.'

'Already?'

'The newspaper reporters call her Babbling Brook, as you no doubt know. They say it was her indiscretion that made the Tranby Croft affair public, and ruined poor old Gordon Cummings.'

'You do not seem very cordial towards either the prince or Lady Brooke, sir,' Bragg observed.

'That is a considerable understatement, sergeant.'

'So the attempt to patch up the quarrel was a failure?'

'It was. That woman intended it to be so from the first. It was a complete waste of time. I told Marcus it would be, but he insisted on approaching the prince. If he and I could have sat down on our own, over a glass of champagne, we could have resolved our differences. But that bitch got him to insist it should be at Warwick. Well, I am sick of the whole affair, and my wife has been made quite unwell by it all. It has been purgatory for her, for the last two years.'

'May I ask how the quarrel arose, sir?'

Beresford's anger flared again. 'That was over a letter! This time, one that Daisy wrote. My wife was outraged by it, and Marcus was so shocked, that he advised her to take it to our solicitor, George Lewis . . . I was away at the time.'

'How did that involve the prince?' asked Bragg.

'I'll tell you how, sergeant! That stupid woman realized that she had gone too far, and actually appealed to the Prince of Wales to get it back for her. He became so besotted with her, that he routed George Lewis out of bed at two o'clock in the morning, and demanded that the letter should be destroyed.'

'And was it?'

'No. My wife refused to give her consent. But that was not the end of it. Daisy persuaded the prince to try again. He even threatened to cross my wife's name off his guest list! I was so furious, that I resigned from Parliament and went back to sea.'

'And the affair died down then, did it?'

'No doubt it would have done, if I had swallowed the insult. But I was getting letters from my wife, saying that she was ostracized, and pleading with me to allow her to sell this house and go to live in France. The whole position was intolerable. Society was split over it; Marcus was writing to me, pleading the prince's cause and saying how much we owed to his friendship; even the prime minister became involved. My wife was so distraught, that she telegraphed me to come home and defend her honour.'

'Which you no doubt did, sir.'

'Indeed, sergeant! I demanded an apology from the prince for his treatment of my wife. He refused to accept that there were any grounds for an apology—when all society had been gossiping about it for two years! We had another furious row; but in the end Lord Salisbury was asked to mediate, and we set our hands to a document that should have ended the affair.'

'That is why he was present at Warwick, is it, sir?'

'It is.'

'And how is it that the agreement did not restore harmony?'

'That woman is carrying out a vendetta against us. My wife has continued to be cold-shouldered, despite the prince's assurance. Daisy Brooke has no intention of letting the matter rest.'

Bragg brooded for a moment. 'Can I come back to the meeting at Warwick, for a moment, sir?' he asked.

'Of course.'

'Did you stay in your bedroom for the whole of the night?'

Beresford gave an unpleasant grin. 'I did, sergeant. After our so-called reconciliation meeting, I was in no mood to take advantage of the *douceur* they had so thoughtfully provided.'

CHAPTER ─────── THIRTEEN

Early on Monday morning, Bragg and Morton hurried to the Golden Lane mortuary. They were admitted to Burney's examination room and found the coroner there, legs astraddle before the empty grate.

'Good morning, sir,' Bragg greeted him deferentially. 'I have just sent a message to your chambers.'

'What about Bragg, what about?' asked Sir Rufus genially.

'The young woman they fished out of the river, yesterday morning.'

'What about her?'

'I would be grateful if you would appoint me coroner's officer for the case.'

'I would have thought that you were sufficiently occupied already,' Sir Rufus observed.

'I would particularly like that one, sir.'

The coroner peered at him suspiciously. 'And what is your interest, Bragg?' he asked.

'She was working for me,' replied Bragg shortly.

'What?'

'She was being blackmailed by the same person who blackmailed the dean.'

Sir Rufus shot an anxious glance in the direction of Burney, who was dissecting something unidentifiable at the bench under the window. 'How was she working for you?' he asked.

'She had made a payment to him already. Then she received a second demand, and came to the police. We were at the meeting place and hoped to grab him, but we did not succeed. The third time he fixed an appointment in Covent Garden. Constable Morton and I were there, but because of an accident in the street she would have come down, she must have gone into the market another way. However it be, we missed her.'

'Good God, Bragg!' exclaimed Sir Rufus. 'Surely you did not allow that young woman to act as your stalking-horse, without affording her adequate protection? It is utterly inexcusable!'

'We all do things that are expedient, without them being right,' Bragg observed lightly.

'I hope you exclude me from that observation,' retorted the coroner.

'We could not provide a watch at every part of the market, because I could not get the men,' said Bragg. 'The Commissioner has suspended the investigations into the two blackmail cases, so that we can concentrate on something new.'

'How dare he countermand the investigation into the hounding to death of Dean Hadley?' the coroner exclaimed. 'I will not tolerate it!'

'He is well within his rights, sir.'

'Rights! He has no rights, except to follow my instructions!'

'Ah, but if you remember,' said Bragg dryly, 'you brought in a verdict of accidental death.'

'But dammit, Bragg, we all knew that that was mere expediency!'

'Exactly sir . . . Anyway, we have been trying to keep the other cases going, unofficially. It was just bad luck that we lost track of Miss Godfrey.'

'Well, Burney,' said the coroner testily, turning towards the window. 'When you are quite finished, perhaps you will tell us the cause of death, then I can get about my more gainful business.'

The pathologist swung round with his slack grin. 'Oh, she was murdered,' he said. 'There is no doubt at all about it.'

'How?' Sir Rufus demanded truculently.

'From the bluish colour of the lips, and the petechial haemorrhages on the skin and in the organs, it is clear that she died of asphyxia.'

'Well, she would, if she was drowned,' interrupted the coroner.

'No expert would leap to such a conclusion,' said Burney admonishingly. 'You must hear me out.'

'Very well.'

'The cavities of the right side of the heart were engorged with dark-coloured blood, as were the lungs. Significantly, there was no froth or foam in the air passages, and no river water in the stomach.'

'So she was not drowned,' said Sir Rufus brusquely. 'Was she strangled?'

'No.' Burney gave a loose smile. 'There were none of the classic signs of strangulation. There was, however, an area of bruising and abrasion at the back of the head, which might well have been caused by contact with a hard, somewhat roughened surface.'

'A blow, do you mean?'

'Not a blow, Sir Rufus; more a steady pressure for some time. There were also large areas of bruising on the biceps muscles of both arms, and abrasions on the elbows. In addition, there were slight abrasions on the hands, indicative of a short struggle, perhaps.'

'Come on, Burney, get to the heart of it,' exclaimed the coroner irritably.

'The really interesting discovery, was an area of bruising at the point of the jaw, coupled with bruises on either side of the nose below the nasal bone . . . You see the significance, Sir Rufus.'

'You know, full well, that my medical experience went little further than passing the examinations.'

'She was burked!' said Burney with relish.

'I do not understand you.'

'She was asphyxiated by the method used by Burke and Hare in Edinburgh. She was brought to the ground, and from the marks on the upper arms, it is evident that her murderer knelt on them and sat on her chest, thus expelling the air from her lungs. Then he forced back her head by pressure on the jaw, so closing her mouth, and pinched her nostrils together. Death would supervene in less than a minute.'

'Hideous!' Morton exclaimed, glad that, for once, the post-mortem had been completed and Burney could not gloat over the body with his accursed probe.

'It must have been a man, you would think, sir?' asked Bragg.

'If there was only one assailant, then certainly.'

'Can you say anything about the time of death?'

'I understand that the body was discovered at dawn on Sunday, by a police constable patrolling just upstream of London Bridge, near the Old Swan Pier. It had been left on the mud, as the river dropped with the receding tide. From the slight waterlogging of the surface tissues, she had not been in the water for more than, say, six hours. On the other hand, rigor mortis was fully established, so she had been dead for considerably longer. The temperature of the body is not a very accurate guide in cases of asphyxia, particularly when the corpse has been immersed in cool water for some time; however, my view is that she was murdered at between three and four o'clock the previous afternoon.'

'That would fit in,' said Bragg morosely.

'It might assist your enquiries, sergeant, if I tell you that, from the lividity staining, the body was clearly kept in a supine position for some hours before being put into the river.'

'You have no idea where that might have been done, I suppose?' asked Bragg.

'You would be much safer with the opinions of the river police on that aspect. However, we did find what appears to be a message in the pocket of her coat. Just a moment.'

He disappeared briefly, then came back with a small piece of paper and handed it to Bragg.

'I regret that it was allowed to dry folded,' he said. 'So when

Noakes pulled it open, the surface was damaged. We soaked it again, in an effort to read what was on it—at that time it was our only hope of identifying the body. Our efforts merely completed what the river water had started, and I am afraid it is illegible.'

Bragg passed the paper to Morton. 'Here, lad, your eyes are younger than mine. See what you can make of it.'

Morton took it over to the window and scrutinized it. 'It seems to have been printed in capitals,' he remarked, 'as we would expect. The only word I can remotely guess at is this one.' He pointed to a group of marks near the bottom. 'I would say that was "RED", wouldn't you?'

'That is damned little to go on,' said Bragg crossly. 'Is there anything else, sir, that you think might help us?'

'Well,' said Burney, his mouth sagging open with a beaming smile. 'I do not know if it is of any relevance to your enquiries, but when her father came to identify the body, I gathered that she was of good family, and had just become advantageously engaged to be married.'

'That is true, sir.'

'I was, therefore, more than a little surprised. There was no indication of seminal fluid in the vagina, but the young lady was no stranger to sexual intercourse.'

'That has no bearing on her murder, though,' the coroner interposed sharply.

'No direct bearing, Sir Rufus. I shall not feel it necessary to refer to it in my evidence at the inquest.'

Sir Rufus grunted in approval.

'I would be glad, sir,' Bragg began hesitantly, 'if you could find a way to delay the inquest, for a time.'

'Why is that, Bragg? I hope you are not proposing anything irregular.'

'Not in the least, sir. I cannot go into details, but there is just a chance that we might have uncovered another blackmail plot, involving the same man. Now that your acquaintance and Miss Godfrey are dead, he will feel secure. I would like to keep it that way.'

'This other case is promising, is it Bragg?'

'It is certainly important enough for the Commissioner to have told us to drop everything else.'

'That is not necessarily the same.'

'But it might give us a chance of solving all three cases,' said Bragg.

The coroner pondered for a moment. 'Very well. I will open the inquest, and take evidence of identification and discovery only, then adjourn.'

'Thank you sir.'

'But I cannot keep it open for ever.'

'I understand, sir . . . And you will appoint me coroner's officer?'

'I would not have wasted my time with you, otherwise, Bragg.'

'Thank you, sir. Then, for the moment, I will let it be known that Miss Godfrey died as a result of a boating accident. That should give our blackmailer the feeling of security we want.'

'Girls of that class do not go boating on their own, sergeant,' Sir Rufus observed tartly.

'Ah, but then, Constable Morton is an eligible young bachelor. If it comes to it, he can say that he took her!'

When Bragg and Morton arrived at Marlborough House, they surrendered their hats to a scarlet-coated footman and were taken upstairs by a page in dark blue livery. They were shown into an ante-room and asked to wait there. Bragg was restless, pacing round the panelled walls and peering at the elaborate display of guns and swords. Suddenly a concealed door in the panelling opened, and Francis Knolleys appeared.

'It was good of you to come,' he said. 'The prince has just been dealing with some papers . . . Would you please come through?'

He led them into an opulently furnished room, where the Prince of Wales was sitting at a small walnut writing-desk.

'Ah, there you are.' He rose and waved them to a group of chairs in the bay window. 'How are you getting on?' he asked. 'I hear that you have been to Warwick.'

'I have, sir,' said Bragg equably. 'But I cannot say that I have been getting the co-operation I would have hoped for.'

'I do not understand that, sergeant. I wrote to everyone, as you are aware.'

'I do not know the terms of your letters, sir, but I practically had to drag from Lady Brooke the admission that she was being blackmailed.'

The prince gazed at Bragg with his hooded grey-blue eyes. 'As you will probably have deduced, this was the matter on which Knolleys and I disagreed. I had hoped that you might find the culprit without coming into possession of that knowledge. Obviously Knolleys was right, and I was wrong.'

'Since you were at Warwick Castle that night, sir, it would be helpful if this meeting could be more than just reporting what we have done,' said Bragg. 'But I am a policeman, not a courtier, and I shall have to speak what is in my mind.'

The prince smiled, and his heavy features were transformed with bonhomie. 'I think we can bear that, cannot we, Knolleys?'

'Thank you, sir,' said Bragg. 'Can I take it that you were aware of the identity of the other guests in advance?'

'I always approve the guest-list personally, sergeant.'

'It would appear that we need concern ourselves solely with the people who were actually sleeping in the castle; which means we can exclude all the servants, and so on, from consideration.'

'Yes, sergeant,' the prince nodded. 'Which is why it is so sensitive a matter.'

'I have to say that, in my view, the information we have received from Lady Brooke cannot be relied on. She says she read your letter just before going to bed, she stayed in her room all night, and in the morning it was gone. If that were true, there could have been no theft.'

The prince frowned. 'You certainly are forthright, sergeant,' he said coolly. 'However, I suppose we have accepted your terms . . . Since we know that the letter is in the hands of the blackmailer, you should assume that she is indulging in an innocent evasion, with the object of protecting . . . someone.'

'Lady Brooke said that she had given you the photograph of

the letter that the blackmailer enclosed with his demand. Are we to be allowed to see that photograph?'

'Only as the very last resort,' said the prince firmly. 'And that is certainly not yet.'

'You seem convinced that a newspaper editor would readily accept the letter as genuine.'

'According to the message, it is already in the hands of the press.'

'I don't believe that, sir. If he had gone so far, no payment of money would stop its publication. To my mind, the most he would have done is to mention its existence to one of the gutter press, say, *Reynold's Weekly Newspaper*; but I have my doubts about even that.'

'I hope you are right, sergeant. To answer your earlier question, my handwriting is characteristic, and the letter bore the initials A E at the foot. I do not doubt that its authenticity would be accepted.'

'Very well, sir. Now, we have to keep in mind the possibility that the person who took the letter and the blackmailer may not be one and the same person, but two people acting in collusion. Having said that, if we find the one, we should soon get to the other . . . On the face of it, only the people sleeping in the private apartments could have obtained access to the box with the letters in it. That means that, if we ignore the Earl of Warwick, who was too ill that night, we are left with his wife, Lord and Lady Salisbury, Lord Charles Beresford, and Lady Rouse.'

'It seems absurd to think that any of them could stoop to such an expedient,' said the prince firmly.

'Perhaps. Nevertheless, we have to look at it systematically. There is no lock on Lady Brooke's door, only a bolt on the inside. If the room was empty during the night, any one of them could have gone in and taken the letter.'

'I suppose so.'

'I spoke to the night watchman who patrols the courtyard. He swears that nobody could have crossed from the Gatehouse or the Watergate Tower to the entrance to the private apartments. But I've done enough night duties not to believe him.

So we ought to add to the list Lord Brooke, Lady Gladys Curwen, and Sir Alexander Rouse.'

'That is everyone,' protested the prince.

'All but three, yes, sir . . . Now we have got to ask ourselves which of those people had a motive; one that might lead them to theft and blackmail.'

'I suppose someone must have,' said the prince unhappily.

'Well, I think we can ignore the Countess of Warwick, and probably Lord and Lady Salisbury, for the moment; but there are two people who might have a strong motive.'

'Who are they?'

'Lord Charles Beresford was furious at the end of that evening,' said Bragg. 'I would not credit him with much self-control at the best of times. He might have allowed his anger to cloud his judgement and have taken the letter, with the idea of getting his revenge.'

'But how did he know of its existence?'

'I don't know, sir. Lady Brooke doesn't seem to stir anywhere without her little red box. Perhaps it is well known among the people she mixes with. It could be that our thief went into the room on the off-chance, and was just lucky to find the letter. After all, no one but you and she knew about it.'

'I suppose that must be true, sergeant, although it is known that I have a weakness for writing such letters . . . And who is your second suspect?'

'Someone who did know about the box . . . Lord Brooke might not be the complaisant husband everyone thinks he is,' Bragg said bluntly.

The prince's eyes flashed in anger. 'This is intolerable!' he exclaimed, his speech becoming more guttural. 'You were ordered to enquire into a crime, not make unwarranted judgements on moral issues.'

Knolleys intervened. 'I think the sergeant is, perhaps, overstating his case in an effort to come to grips with the central issue,' he said quietly. 'There has to be a strong motivation for what has happened.'

The Prince of Wales swallowed his anger. 'Very well,' he said. 'I suppose we asked for you, in the first place, because of these qualities; but, by God, I find them obnoxious!'

'I gather you do not think it likely that either of those gentlemen could have done it,' said Bragg.

'Beresford must be a possibility— Brookie, never!'

'There is a further person we should consider—or rather two. Lady Rouse was in the private apartments and, I gather, she was sleeping alone. She might have gone down the passage and taken it—though on the face of it, she had no motive, and I can hardly see her helping her husband to that extent.'

'Why should Alec become involved in something so despicable?' asked the prince.

'Money is a powerful motive, sir, and you must know that he is not over-supplied with it.'

'Well, yes. We all know that he is not rich, but he is a charming and amusing man. I cannot think that he could do such a thing.'

'In some ways, he seems the most likely to me,' said Bragg slowly. 'In the strictest confidence, Sir Alec is already suspected in connection with another blackmailing case.'

'I find that incredible,' the prince exclaimed, turning a troubled face to Knolleys . . . 'Perhaps we ought to take steps to distance ourselves from him.'

'We have recently had two other blackmailing cases, and they also involved letters printed in capitals,' Bragg went on. 'In the second one, the victim made a payment at our instigation. A very short time later, Sir Alexander Rouse changed two of the notes at his bank.'

'Perhaps he had obtained them from elsewhere,' suggested Knolleys.

'It is possible. One of the occasions where, to his recollection, he received bank-notes, was at a whist game here.'

'But he plays with me!' exclaimed the prince.

'He did so on that occasion, sir, together with Mr Bullivant and Mr Smith.'

'Well, shortage of money cannot be a motive for either of those gentlemen.'

'That is where you could be wrong, sir,' said Bragg evenly. 'From what he tells me, Mr Bullivant is practically bankrupt.'

'You are inflicting all kinds of unpleasant surprises on me,' the prince complained.

'I had known,' said Knolleys, 'that he was selling his Surrey estate, but I thought that he was looking for another. It is certainly the impression he gave.'

'But he seems to have no connection with the Warwick affair,' said the prince.

'It is not impossible that he might have persuaded Lady Rouse to go prospecting for him,' said Bragg.

Knolleys gave a dry laugh. 'If she had been a personable young boy, perhaps!' Then he checked himself. 'I wonder if we might not have a motive, nevertheless. Bullivant had formed an attachment to Lord Brooke's youngest brother. That young man recently, and quite suddenly, married an attractive young woman!'

'Now you are descending to the level of salacious gossip,' the prince said with distaste. 'There is no evidence which would link him to Warwick and, until some emerges, I shall refuse to speculate. Indeed, there seems no firm evidence to connect our problems with the other cases the sergeant spoke about. I very much fear that we shall be wasting time, by trying to link them.'

'Except in one respect, sir, the letters in all three cases are similar,' said Bragg. 'So far as we can tell, the printing is the same. And in the others, also, there is an attempt to represent the writer as an innocent middle-man. If they are from the same source, we might get a lead on the Warwick affair from the investigation of all three together.'

'Why do you not ask the Post Office laboratory to look at the letters for you?' Knolleys suggested.

'Post Office?'

'Yes, sergeant. They are experts in comparing handwriting. And we can be assured of their discretion.'

'Thank you, Mr Knolleys, I will certainly take your advice. It would help a lot if we could be sure.'

'In the meantime, what other steps will be taken?' asked the prince gloomily.

'We shall continue our investigations, sir, and I would advise you to put a reply in *The Times* personal column, as the letter required.'

'Ten thousand pounds is a great deal of money,' said the

prince. 'One could hardly expect Lady Brooke to find it; nor, in the circumstances, could one ask her husband to do so.'

'But the answer will buy us some time,' said Bragg.

'Yes . . . I agree. We have little enough as it is. If you are right about the newspaper concerned, sergeant, then publication would probably occur on one of the two Sundays preceding the sixth of July.'

'Why do you say that, sir?'

'On that date my son, Prince George, is to be married to Princess Mary of Teck. That is the wedding the blackmailer threatens to spoil.'

Bragg and Morton took their leave. As they went along the corridor. Morton heard his name called. He turned to see a slim, elegant woman approaching them.

'It is Constable Morton, is it not?' she asked with a charming, foreign intonation.

'It is indeed, your royal highness,' Morton replied with a bow.

'It is good to see you again. We miss you.' She smiled graciously, and passed on.

'Who was that?' whispered Bragg.

'Alexandra, the Princess of Wales.'

'She's wearing a damned sight better than her husband . . . And did you see what she had in her hand?'

'It looked like a very expensive and elaborate camera,' said Morton, raising an eyebrow questioningly.

'Dear God! . . . But it is unthinkable, surely?'

Catherine had finished the first draft of her article for the Wednesday edition of her paper, and, with another day before publication, felt that she could reasonably steal away for an hour or so. She strolled in the warm sun through St Paul's churchyard, down Godliman Street and turned into Queen Victoria Street. The warm brick buildings of the College of Arms enclosed three sides of a cobbled courtyard, with ornate iron railings fronting the street. In the centre of the block opposite the gates was an elaborate portico topped by the device of a sunburst with a Tudor rose at its centre and surmounted by a crown.

Catherine went up the balustraded steps and found herself in a lofty room running the width of the courtyard. The walls were panelled in mellow wood and hung with portraits. The most extraordinary feature of the room was a dais against the far wall, on which stood a richly carved chair. Below this throne, desks and chairs were huddled, and the whole area was enclosed with substantial wooden railings, breast high. A clerk was sitting at one of the desks, painstakingly inscribing a parchment.

'This is rather unexpected,' said Catherine, to attract his attention. 'What is it?'

The man looked up with a pleased expression. 'It is the Earl Marshal's court, where formal hearings on armorial matters are held.'

'Would it be possible for me to consult someone informally, without an appointment?'

'Indeed it would, madam. Rouge Dragon is in waiting this week, and I think he is free at the moment.'

'Rouge Dragon?'

'He is one of the Pursuivants of Arms.' He rose to his feet and pushed open a section of the railings. 'I will not keep you long.'

Catherine wandered over to a large portrait and examined it, then she heard a step behind her. A portly man with a shock of white hair and a cherubic face was approaching her. He was wearing an immaculate morning coat, and a rose was at his buttonhole.

'Rouge Dragon?' she asked with a bright smile.

'The same. Can I be of service to you, young lady?'

Catherine produced her *City Press* card. 'I am about to start a series of articles on institutions which are located within the City boundaries,' she said. 'I thought that I might start at the top, so to speak.'

'Indeed, indeed!' he beamed at her. 'So little is known of our work by the general public. I would be happy to give you any information you require. Come into the waiting room.'

He led the way into a smaller room off the court. Its walls were lined with book-filled shelves and cupboards. In front of

the fireplace was a large table, covered with papers and books
of reference.

'In what way can I be of assistance?' he asked, motioning
Catherine to a chair.

'I was hoping to give my article a more interesting slant than
the mere recital of facts—that is if I can induce you to
co-operate.'

'Then, you will have to tell me what you propose.'

'I know that you are experts in genealogy, and coats of
arms.'

'Yes, indeed! I could create a most interesting one for a
newspaper reporter. What a pity that, as a woman, you are
incapable of becoming an armigerous person in your own
right!'

Catherine laughed. 'I had something in mind which would
demonstrate your expertise considerably more than that.'

'Try me, try me!' he rubbed his hands together expectantly.

'Someone has marked a piece of paper with a sign. It is
deliberately indistinct. I would like you to examine it in any
way you wish, then I would ask you to try to identify to whom
it belongs.'

'Well, well! This sounds quite exciting. Your editor is
becoming quite innovative.'

'I have not yet put the proposal for these articles to Mr
Tranter. My hope is that he will find this one so interesting that
he will sanction them all.'

'Well now, let me see this mark.'

Catherine gave him the piece of paper that Morton had cut
from the blackmailer's letter.

Rouge Dragon picked up a large magnifying glass, and went
over to the window.

'It is undoubtedly heraldic,' he muttered. 'Clearly some kind
of sword . . . I will copy it, somewhat enlarged, on a sheet
of paper, and then we shall see.'

He went to his desk and took a piece of squared paper from
it, then carefully measured the dimensions of the mark and
ruled a border for his enlarged version on the squares.

'I think we will begin with the hilt,' he said. 'If I tidy up the
blurred edges, it should clarify things a little.' He made several

precise measurements and transferred them to his paper, then
he joined them up with a few deft strokes of his pencil.

'There you are,' he said beaming. 'Clearly a sword. And the
lateral smudge you see, rather like an Italian moustache askew,
is the knuckle-bow. Its shape is significant in itself, and I
already have a feeling for what will emerge, but we shall see.'

He drew steadily. First a curled guard appeared, one side
projecting down over the hilt to protect the hand, the other
jutting upwards to catch a slashing blow. Then the blade of the
sword grew; what Catherine imagined to be the sharp edge,
curving upwards towards the point. The other edge curved
more sharply, so that the blade widened considerably. Then it
acquired a distinct circular notch—perhaps another device to
prevent an enemy's sword sliding up the back of the blade. The
drawing continued, until the blade resembled half a new moon;
then, with a distinctly concave line, the back of the blade was
brought abruptly across to join the edge.

The man held the two pieces of paper at arms length, and
inspected them with satisfaction.

'I hope you will agree that this is an accurate representation
of the original,' he said.

Catherine compared the two. 'I would say that there could be
no doubt about it . . .   If it is a sword, it is a very curious one.
The point widens so quickly, that it would be useless for
stabbing.'

'Indeed, indeed! It was an eastern weapon, used chiefly on
board ship. It would have been wielded with a slashing action.
I confess that I have never seen one; however, the blade was
clearly fairly heavy and, with a sharp cutting edge, it could no
doubt wreak havoc. It was called a sea-axe, for obvious
reasons.'

'But why can you be so sure that it is a heraldic device?'

'That irregular bar running across, under the hilt, is called a
wreath and appears under crests. In an illustration, one could
see that it is like two bands of silk twisted together.' He drew
a signet ring from his finger. 'There, you can see them
distinctly in the engraving.'

'Ah, yes.'

'Now let me consider how your friend impressed this mark

upon the letter,' he mused. 'Yes . . . I think that must be it.'

He lit a match and applied it to a stick of sealing wax, allowing the molten drops to fall upon his piece of paper. Then he took his signet ring, and impressed it in the hot wax.

'That is my family crest—an eagle, and in wax all the detail of the engraving is reproduced. Now let us try an experiment.'

He took a fold of blotting paper and, lifting his inkwell from its stand, he allowed a large blob to fall. As it spread across the surface, he rolled his signet ring in the ink and then impressed it on the paper beside the wax.

'You see,' he said gleefully, 'there is the outline of my crest, framed in the ink; and, as you can see, the edges are blurred just as on your paper. That is how it was done! . . . Now to the second part of your test. Where is my *Fairbairn*?' He looked along a shelf, and took down a large tome. 'This gives illustrations of all the crests in English heraldry; and in heraldic terms, what we are looking for is a "seax erect proper".'

He riffled through the illustrations . . . 'Here we are,' he said triumphantly, and twisted the book so that Catherine could see.

'It is just as you have drawn it,' she said admiringly.

'Now to find out to whom it belongs.' He turned to the front of the book, where the pages were filled with columns of fine print.

'I cannot tell you exactly to what family the crest belongs,' he said in some disappointment. 'However, your friend must belong to the Belsted family—and there are several variations of spelling—or he is a Nottage, a Dalton, a Pearse, or a Rouse.'

Catherine smiled happily. 'That is the most impressive piece of deduction I am ever likely to see,' she said. 'I am sure Mr Tranter will be delighted.'

She took a hansom to Park Lane, and went up the steps to her front door. As she stretched out her hand it was opened from within.

'I saw you from the window,' her mother said conspiratori-ally. 'Mr Morton has called to see you.'

Catherine glanced in the mirror. She decided not to remove her hat; she was sure that he had not seen it before.

'James!' she said, advancing into the drawing-room. 'What a pleasant surprise!'

Morton rose and bowed. 'I am afraid that this is no social call,' he said gravely.

'Is it something about Saturday's operation, that I can publish?' she asked eagerly.

'In part, though not in any way that will satisfy you.'

'In the words of an old gentleman I have spent the afternoon with, "try me, try me"!'

'We would like you to feed the information to the press that Arabella Godfrey has been drowned, as a result of a boating accident.'

'The *Star* would be best for that . . . What is the reason behind this manoeuvre?'

'Unfortunately, we missed her in Covent Garden through a totally unforeseen traffic accident. She must have met her blackmailer and given him the notes I brought . . . Then, where we cannot tell, he murdered her in cold blood, and dumped her body in the river.'

'Oh! James, how dreadful!'

'We want him to think that we are unaware of the true cause of death to give us more time to catch him.'

'Hence your request?'

'Yes . . . We have no reason to suppose that the murderer is aware of any connection between you and Miss Godfrey. But if he got to know that you had acted as an intermediary between her and the police, you might yourself be in danger. Which is why, in defiance of the strongest prohibitions from the highest authorities in the land, I propose to tell you all we know . . .'

CHAPTER ────────
──────── FOURTEEN

The hansom had become firmly entangled in the afternoon traffic, so Catherine alighted and began to walk down the Strand. Ahead she could see the soot-stained bulk of King's College. Students were bustling in and out of the entrance, with books under their arms. All young men, of course. Well, perhaps today she would be helping to change all that. She went to the porter's lodge.

'I have come for an interview in the survey of the achievements of women,' she said.

The porter looked at her quizzically. 'Oh, yes miss?' He turned to his colleague. 'Mind the shop, Bert, will you? . . . If you will follow me, miss . . .'

He led her down a cobbled courtyard, enclosed by intimidating cliffs of buildings. It was as if the fabric of the college itself was hostile to her purpose. Well, she refused to be cowed by it. They went to the bottom of the courtyard and through a doorway in the corner. Halfway down a lofty corridor, they turned up a staircase. They ascended flight after flight of steps,

till Catherine's legs were aching; then they reached the top
floor. Here the corridor was little more than head high, lit by
grimy skylights every few yards. The porter took her into a
small room, with a table and a few chairs in it.

'Would you wait here, miss?' he instructed. 'I will say that
you have arrived.'

He disappeared, and Catherine walked over to the window.
Below her were the trees of the Embankment, with the River
Thames beyond. She tried to draw confidence from its placid
flow. That irresistible force must be a symbol of the inevitable
victory of women in their fight for emancipation . . . But
perhaps it was merely uncaring, immutable . . .

She heard quick steps in the corridor, and the door was
opened. The woman who entered was about thirty-five years
old, with black hair and dark brown eyes. She crossed to the
table and placed some files on it, then held out her hand.

'Good afternoon,' she said. 'You know, of course, that you
are not to give me your name, but I am Maud Stanford. Do sit
down.'

She had a warm contralto voice, and her smile lit up her
plain, studious face.

'I am sure that you would like to know a little of my
background,' she said. 'I studied for three years at Newnham
College, in Cambridge, where I became interested in biology.
Since it was not then possible for a woman to make a career in
medicine, I went to Vienna, where I spent some years studying
the functions of the human mind. I am now working at the
Salpêtrière Hospital in Paris, with Professor Charcot. He is a
renowned experimenter in the field of psychology.'

'That is a quite brilliant career,' said Catherine enviously.
'Beside you, I feel a failure! I hope that you are going to be
included in the survey.'

Maud gave a gratified smile. 'That would be quite improper,' she said. 'However, I was delighted when Professor
Sully approached Émile and asked if he could release me to do
the interviews for this survey. I feel that I am taking a small
part in your fight for recognition.'

'I had thought that it would be a desiccated old man,'
Catherine confessed.

Maud laughed. 'You may be sure that I shall be as objective as one. You have received a letter from Professor Sully, I take it?'

'Yes.'

'So you know that the aim of the survey is to tabulate the achievements of women, and also to chart the way forward by collating the views of the successful among us?'

'Yes.'

'Good. Now, in order to remove any lingering doubts in your mind, so that you will feel able to speak freely, I will just explain the system that has been adopted. Professor Sully has made the selection of people who are to be included in the study. I have not been involved in that process, but presumably it has been done on a basis that will enable the results to be applied to women as a whole.'

'Or at least to girls in the middle and upper classes,' said Catherine.

'Quite. The professor has provided us with a list of flower names, and we allot them to the interviewees in strict sequence.' She opened a file, and took out a list. Catherine could see that a tick had been placed by the first twelve entries or so. Maud ran the point of her pen down the page. 'So, you are "Bougainvillea",' she said.

'That sounds very exotic,' Catherine remarked with a smile.

'In fact, I have wondered whether it is a good system after all,' Maud said reflectively. 'Last week I gave "Allium" to a young lady. Unfortunately, she knew that it is a flowering onion! She was very unco-operative, and I am sure that the two were not unconnected!'

'I have no objection to "Bougainvillea",' said Catherine.

'Then all the sheets of your questionnaire will bear that name to identify them—but, of course, no one will be able to trace, from them, the person who was the subject of the interview. It is hoped, therefore, that you will be able to answer with complete freedom.'

'I certainly will do so.'

'The same questionnaire is being put to each person. You will see that the questions have already been written on the

paper, and I shall write your answers beneath them . . . Is
there anything you wish to ask before we commence?'

'No, I think not.'

'Very well. The first part of the questionnaire is aimed at
establishing your background, so that we can formulate a level
of expectation . . . To what social class would you say you
belong?'

'The upper middle class.'

'What is your father's economic position? Is he in a
profession, a trade, of independent means . . .?'

'I would say he is a mixture of artistic and professional.'

'Has your family private wealth?'

'My mother has expectations from her parents,' Catherine
said with a smile. 'But so far, our prosperity has derived from
my father's hard work.'

'Were you privately educated?'

'No, I went to school.'

'Which one?'

'Cheltenham Ladies College.'

'That is a good school,' Maud commented. 'We have had
another young lady from there, and she was very decided in her
views.'

'Whoever was it, I wonder?' said Catherine.

Maud looked at her list. 'I have an idea that it might have
been "African Lily",' she said with a gleam of amusement.

Catherine laughed. 'I should not have asked,' she said.

'How old were you when you left school?'

'Eighteen.'

'Did you go on to an institution of higher education?'

'No.'

'Do you regret that?'

'In principle, yes. In practice, no.'

Maud looked up with a smile. 'I think that answer will need
some elucidation,' she said. 'As it stands the two halves appear
to cancel each other out.'

'I believe that university courses must be beneficial, and
should be open to women. To that extent, I regret that I have
been excluded from them. In fact, I have obtained an interesting and satisfying career without having been to university.'

'I see.' Maud scribbled briefly. 'What career did you enter?'

'Journalism.'

'In London?'

'Yes—I am a staff reporter on the *City Press* and an occasional correspondent for the *Star*.'

'Are you indeed?' Maud's voice was tinged with admiration. 'Now we go on to the second part of the questionnaire, which I find the most interesting from a scientific point of view. In it we are trying to establish your basic attitudes to life so that, when we come to the third part, any necessary allowance can be made to correct for personal prejudices and experiences. In your case it is unlikely to be necessary; but some older ladies have acquired rather extreme views, because of the treatment they have received.'

'Why is the second part of more scientific interest?' Catherine asked.

'Because we adopt a technique which has been developed in Paris, in connection with mental illness . . . You need not worry! It carries no such imputation here. We merely ask you to answer each question quickly, without analysing it. In journalistic terms, we want your brain to supply the answers, before your mind has a chance to sub-edit them.'

'It sounds amusing.'

'Then let us begin. Do you admire the girls of your class, or not?'

'No.'

'Why not?'

'They are unambitious,' Catherine rapped out.

'Is money good, or bad?'

'Good.'

'What do you spend money on?'

'Clothes.'

'Which would come first, marriage or your career?'

'Career.'

'Would you ever marry a man of a lower class?'

'No.'

'Have you a personal antipathy towards men?'

'No, I get on well with them.'

'Have you ever had a close relationship with a man?'

'Only my father!'

'Have you ever had physical intimacy with a woman?'

'No! Never!'

'What kind of women do you admire?'

'Women who can hold their own with men.'

'Have you had, since your childhood, physical intimacy with a man?'

Catherine hesitated. 'Some involuntary intimacy,' she said.

'Has it affected your attitude to men?'

'No.'

'Have you any wish to marry?'

'At the moment, no.'

'If you could combine your career with marriage, would you marry?'

'I might.'

'Do you admire your mother?'

'Not a great deal.'

'Why?'

'She is too relaxed, too uncommitted.'

'Do you admire your father?'

'Yes, indeed!'

'Which do you prefer, your father or your mother?'

'My father.'

'Why is that?'

'It is inbuilt. He is one of the opposite sex, after all!'

'Where do you live?'

'At home with my parents.'

'Do you have a consuming ambition?'

'I want a successful career, but it does not consume me.'

Maud smiled. 'I detected more than a trace of sub-editing in that last answer,' she said. 'Still it was fun, wasn't it? . . . Now we go on to the third part, which is much more solemn. This is where we examine your views on the path that the women's movement should take. Do you think that it is right to demand total equality?'

'I confess that a bald statement, in those terms, troubles me,' Catherine replied. 'Men and women are physically complementary, not identical. It is clearly evil that women are employed in factories on heavy work, such as making chains.

Yet if we claimed total equality, then logically men could expect women to go back to working down the coal mines.'

'How would you define what the aims should be?'

'I think we should work to end the exclusions that are imposed by men. Why should women not be lawyers, engineers, chemists, parsons?'

'So you think we should concentrate on the professions?'

'Yes. If we achieve entry to them, all else will follow.'

'What were your favourite subjects at school?'

'History and English literature.'

'You were clearly able to build on them in your own career, but would you encourage the present generation of girls to follow in your footsteps?'

'Oh, dear,' said Catherine. 'This is difficult. In my view they are fundamental to a cultivated mind—and I would not wish the women of the future to be less cultured. Yet, if we are to challenge men on their own ground, we have to be prepared to become just as competent in science, mathematics, law . . .'

'Some men contend that women are mentally too fragile to absorb difficult subjects.'

'That is pure rubbish! They are afraid that if women are allowed to fulfil their capabilities, their cosy monopoly of power will be destroyed.'

'Do you feel that we should press for women to be given the vote?'

'Before anything else!'

'Well, that concludes the questionnaire,' said Maud. 'Would you sign the bottom of each page with your flower-name? Here is a pen.'

Catherine scanned the closely written pages briefly, then signed 'Bougainvillea' at the foot of each. 'When will the survey be published?' she asked, handing them back.

'That will be up to Professor Sully, but I know that he is under pressure to get his report completed quickly.' Maud stood up, and held out her hand. 'Thank you for coming,' she said.

'I am sure it will have an enormous impact,' replied

Catherine. 'I feel quite honoured to have been asked to take part; and apart from that, I enjoyed it!'

'You remembered to drop those letters in at St Martins le Grand?' asked Bragg, as the hansom turned into South Audley Street.

'Yes, I did,' Morton replied.

'Did they say anything?'

'The Post Office people are strange. They positively seem to discourage members of the public from penetrating into their headquarters. In the end I had to queue up at the public counter. Even then, no one would admit that their laboratory existed. When the clerk finally conceded that it was there, he was insisting that I should give the package to him. I had to use my warrant card, before I could have my way.'

'Did they look at them while you were there?'

'No. There was only an assistant in at that hour of the morning. But he did promise that they would be given priority.'

'Good . . . Pay off the cab, lad. Inspector Cotton is getting very suspicious of our doings. I want to keep my expenses down, or he will have an excuse to quiz me. Things are difficult enough, without him interfering.'

Bragg pulled the bell of the Handfords' house, and they were admitted. When Bullivant joined them in the drawing-room, his pallid face was drawn and there were dark circles under his eyes.

'We have had the Surrey constabulary checking on your story about going to your estate on Tuesday the ninth,' said Bragg brusquely. 'They have discovered that the Brookwood halt was manned for an hour either side of noon, and that no one saw you in all that time.'

'That is not in the least surprising,' said Bullivant listlessly. 'My train would have arrived there a few minutes before half past ten.'

'Furthermore,' Bragg went on relentlessly, 'they have talked to the people in the village. Not one of them remembers seeing you there, that day. Nobody has seen you for two months and more.'

'I am gratified that you have been able to obtain confirmation of what I told you.'

'Why not admit that you weren't there at all, sir,' said Bragg persuasively. 'It will save us all a lot of time.'

Bullivant sighed. 'I expected better of a City police sergeant,' he said with a faint smile. 'If you question the man who drove the train that morning, you will find that I asked him to stop at the halt.'

'But it's not just you that can use the halt.'

'No, sergeant, but I imagine that he will be able to give you a description of me. I tipped him half a crown.'

'And what about coming back?' asked Bragg.

'I sent a message with the guard of the outward train, to ask that the six thirty-five from Woking to London should stop at the halt.'

'Very good,' said Bragg urbanely. 'We will check that . . . Tell me, sir, do you know where Conway Street is?'

'Why, yes. It is north of Oxford Street, off Tottenham Court Road.'

'Do you know the area, sir?'

'I . . . I have been there on occasion,' said Bullivant uneasily, dabbing at his forehead with his handkerchief.

'Then you will know the tobacconist's shop in Cleveland Street?'

'I am afraid that I do not smoke, sergeant.'

'And the premises above it?'

'I have told you, no!' exclaimed Bullivant angrily.

'We have information to the contrary, sir.'

'Then your information is erroneous!'

'I see, sir. Can you tell us where you were last Saturday afternoon?'

'Afternoon?'

'Yes, sir; from, say, one o'clock to six o'clock.'

Bullivant thought for a moment. 'I was here, in my room.'

'Then, I am sure your sister, or your brother-in-law will be able to confirm that,' said Bragg genially.

'I would imagine not. They went to a luncheon party, on the river at Henley.'

'That's a pity, sir.'

'What is a pity?'

'Why, that nobody can ever confirm what you tell us.'

'That is exceedingly unjust, and you know it,' said Bullivant indignantly.

'What about that evening—say from eight o'clock onwards?'

'I went for a long walk—alone. I returned a little before midnight.'

Bragg gave him a long penetrating stare. 'I suppose no one can confirm that either?'

'I have had enough of your questions,' said Bullivant angrily. 'I told you last week, in confidence, of my financial difficulties, and now it is all over town. Thanks to you, I am being cold-shouldered by all my acquaintances.'

'We don't accept confidences from suspects, sir,' said Bragg coldly.

'What the devil is all this about? You are surely not making this fuss over Rouse's ten-pound notes?'

'You could be right there, sir. Do you know Lady Rouse, at all?'

Bullivant's lip curled contemptuously. 'Everyone knows Lady Rouse, sergeant.'

'Would you say she was a special friend of yours?'

'No, I would not!' he said violently.

'But you were a special friend of Robert Greville.'

'So that is it!' Bullivant sneered. 'Well you can tell them that they need not worry!'

'Would you like to explain that remark, sir?'

'No. It will become apparent.'

'I see, sir . . . There is one other thing. I would like you to give me a specimen of your writing—or your printing, rather.'

'For what purpose?'

'For comparison—so that we can, hopefully, eliminate you from our enquiries.'

Bullivant jumped to his feet. 'This is absurd!' he cried. 'No, sergeant, I will not give you what you ask. You may go to the devil!' He stalked to the door, and they heard him banging his way upstairs.

'Dear me,' said Bragg with a grin. 'Whatever did we do to upset him?'

'I suppose we shall have to check on the engine drivers,' Morton remarked.

'Yes, but first, let's see if we can raise a cup of tea.'

They went out into the hall and, pushing through a green baize door, found their way down to the kitchen. The cook was a tall, angular woman, with a disapproving manner.

'Good morning, ma'am,' said Bragg smoothly. 'We have just been having a word with Mr Bullivant, and he upped and walked out on us.'

'I'm not surprised,' she said sharply. 'He's a queer one, he is.'

'Is he a relative of the family, then?'

'The mistress's brother.'

'It must be difficult for you, having someone like him around all the time.'

'Oh, he's only been here six weeks, and if you ask me, he won't last much longer. According to the parlour maid, the master was telling the mistress that he had got to go.'

'I expect he was looking for somewhere, last Saturday evening,' said Bragg.

'I wouldn't know. We'd had a big dinner party on the Friday night, so the mistress gave us the evening off—they were going out.'

'How would Mr Bullivant be able to get in again?'

'Oh, he has his own key,' said the cook dismissively.

'But he was in during the afternoon, wasn't he?'

The cook thought for a moment. 'Well, he might have been, and he might not. At half past four, Alice took a cup of tea up to his room, but the door was locked and he didn't answer her knock.'

Abandoning any hope of a cup of tea themselves, Bragg and Morton took leave of the cook, and stopped a passing cab. They picked their way through the side streets; then, after a brisk trot along the Embankment, they became trapped in the City traffic. It was an hour before they were making their way up the scrubbed granite steps to the headquarters of the river

police at Wapping. A burly constable was sitting at a table in
his shirt sleeves, reading the *Sporting Life*.

'Is the Inspector in?' asked Bragg, showing his warrant-
card.

'Yes.'

'Could I have a word with him?'

The constable put down his paper reluctantly. 'Wait here a
minute,' he grunted, and disappeared down a passage.

'The river police appear to be a special breed,' Morton
remarked.

'They reckon they are the oldest police force in the world,'
Bragg replied. 'They didn't like being turned into the Thames
division of the Met.'

'I was referring to the general air of slackness.'

Bragg laughed. 'The lower ranks are all ex-sailors, and they
won't tolerate your spit-and-polish discipline. But they are
good at their job.'

'Where do the senior ranks come from?'

'The Met. It's the sort of job you get when you are not going
any higher . . . Inspector Dyson is too proud just to put his
feet up and say sod 'em. He has made himself an expert on
everything to do with the river. If anyone can help us, he can.'

Moments later they were shown into the Inspector's room.
He was slender for his height, with a trim moustache and
balding head.

'What can I do for you, gentlemen?' he asked affably.

'We are wanting you to look into your crystal ball, sir,' said
Bragg with a smile. 'We recovered a young woman's body, on
the bank near Old Swan Pier. We would like you to tell us
where it was put in, please.'

'Was that last Sunday morning?'

'Yes, sir.'

'I saw the report. What does the police surgeon say about the
time of death?'

'Well, sir, she was suffocated, not drowned, and he reckons
that the body had only been in the water for six hours.'

'Which of them was it?'

'Dr Burney. He is the professor of pathology at St Bartho-
lomew's hospital.'

'Ah, yes. I came across him once. He will be right, no question.'

'She was found at five o'clock on Sunday morning, by the constable on the beat. Her body was half in, half out of the water.'

'Why is it so important?' asked Dyson.

'Well, according to the pathologist, the body had been kept on its back for some hours after the murder. If we can pin-point the area we might find some clues.'

'So, she was put into the water at eleven o'clock at night . . . well, that sounds very reasonable. Where are my tide-tables?'

He opened a drawer in his desk and took out a small booklet, with columns of figures cramming its pages.

'That would be Saturday evening, the twentieth of May?'

'That's right, sir.'

'Halfway down the flood tide,' Dyson murmured. 'Were there any indications that the body had been caught in the pier?'

'Not that I am aware of. I was not present at the post-mortem, but Dr Burney would have mentioned it, if there had been any.'

'You see, sergeant, there is precious little land water coming down, after this dry spell. So we are almost left with the action of the tide alone to consider—the more so, as I seem to recollect that an easterly breeze sprang up that night, blowing up river.'

'Would that make a difference, sir?'

'Oh yes, particularly to something floating on or near the surface . . . I cannot understand how our people did not fish her out . . . She was adult, I take it?'

'Around twenty, I would say.'

'Well, sergeant, if the body was put in the river at eleven o'clock, it would be carried up river for a start, by the incoming tide. At slack water it might begin to come down, or stay where it was, depending on whether it was in or out of the stream. Then, on the ebb tide, it would come back again . . . It's not a high tide, so I cannot see it being taken up river further than, say, Westminster bridge . . . No,'

Dyson murmured, 'it cannot have been in the current, to end up by the Old Swan Pier. It would just have floated gently back with the tide . . . I reckon, sergeant, she was put in the river within a hundred yards either side of where you found her.'

'That would mean she could have been thrown in off London Bridge,' said Bragg disconsolately.

'Yes, sergeant, I would think that it is highly probable.'

Violet slipped off her shoes, and wiggled her toes in relief. This hectic round of pleasure was all very well, but it was very hard on the feet. Already today they had attended a breakfast party, walked round the shops, been to a picture gallery, and given a tea-party at home. Now, at a time when she would have been thinking of bed in Boston, they were preparing to go out to a reception! The English must be very bored for the rest of the year, if they felt it necessary to cram so much into the three months of the Season . . . Perhaps she could wear her other shoes, they were a little wider, and more comfortable. What matter that they were no longer high fashion? Anyway, she had been assured that there would be no dancing, so no one would see.

She walked over to the mirror and adjusted the diamond pendant on her breast. If her hair were a little darker, she decided, she would look quite striking. She pinched her cheeks and smiled coquettishly at herself, then burst into laughter. That would never do! It was more like a salacious leer! No, in a few weeks she would have her Paris gowns, and she could cultivate the bearing of a *grande dame*. It was Aunt Charlotte who had suggested it, of course. Mamma would never have thought of it. Probably the unspoken reason was that Emily might become engaged by the end of the summer, and would have to have some appropriately fashionable dresses. Anyway, it was good of her aunt to cajole mamma into letting her have some too. Lady Morton had already written to Jean Worth in the Rue de la Paix, and next week they would be going over on the packet boat, for a few days. Then, three weeks later, they would go over again and bear the gowns back in triumph! Mamma had pretended to be concerned at what her father would think about the cost. Seven hundred and fifty dollars seemed an awful lot to pay for a gown, even if Worth was the finest dressmaker in the world. But he would be proud of her, when he saw her wearing them.

The thought of her father, left to his own devices so that she could be indulged, made Violet feel guilty. She glanced at the clock on the mantel-piece. Twenty of ten, James should have been here by now, to escort them . . . Men were certainly different from one day to the next. Sometimes he was all attentiveness and charm, then he would be perfunctory, detached. And not only to her, but to his mother and Emily also. His excuse was always that silly job of his; but she had met no one else who had to beg leave of someone as lowly as a police sergeant, before he could get away from work. Perhaps papa was right. No man of calibre would be content with so subordinate a post . . . And yet she was sure he had felt more than a cousinly affection for her, last May . . . She heard a cab stop in the street outside and, squeezing into her smart shoes again, she picked up her wrap and went downstairs.

James was already in the drawing-room, being chided by Emily. He smiled ruefully at Violet.

'I am sorry, mamma,' he said, 'I honestly have been too busy, on other things, to investigate prospective brothers-in-law.'

'Really, James!' his mother exclaimed. 'Anyone would think that it is a matter of no concern to you.'

'I assure you that I regard it as of the utmost importance. I have not yet formed a view on Reuben Smith, and so any comment of mine would be premature. I did, however, have a conversation with him at his club, the other day.'

'And what did you find out?' asked Emily eagerly.

'He seems to have a healthily disrespectful attitude towards the aristocracy, which must be a point in his favour.'

'You must be useless as a detective,' said Emily pettishly.

'Well, I have found out that he works in a bank.'

'And at least,' Violet interposed, ' "clerk" has more letters than "duke" or "lord"!'

'Don't be horrid,' Emily said. 'I think it must be very interesting. I would not mind working in a bank myself.'

'Then perhaps,' said Morton, 'you might persuade him to

ask his boss if strings can be pulled. You might even become the first lady bank-teller. You would at least be decorative, even if you got the number of sovereigns wrong!'

'Stop squabbling,' said Lady Morton sharply. 'James, I suppose you have no idea where the card is that Reuben Smith enclosed with the orchid he sent. We cannot find it anywhere.'

'I remember your showing it to me,' said Morton carefully.

'Please stop fussing, mamma,' said Emily crossly. 'If I catch the man, I have no need of the card; if he goes on his way, the card would be of no significance.'

'Goodness!' exclaimed Amelia. 'How unromantic modern girls are. Sometimes, I can almost believe that they could hold their own against men.'

'Shall we go?' asked Lady Morton. 'Have you got a big enough carriage, James? It is not right for you to sit outside with the driver.'

'I am sure that it will be adequate. Ladies, your landau awaits you.'

The older ladies sat at the back of the coach, while James perched on the edge of the opposite seat, between the girls. Violet was conscious of the pressure of his thigh against her; conscious, also, that the contact created no excitement in her—nor, it would seem, in him. She was almost glad when the carriage came to a halt at the door of Spencer House.

After presentation to the hostess and host, whose names Violet promptly forgot, they made their way to the ballroom. This time, the decorations were more subdued, and although an orchestra was playing at one end of the room, it could scarcely be heard for the throng of people swarming everywhere. There must be five hundred or more, bowing, exchanging a brief word, and moving on. She was soon caught up in it herself, trading demure trivia for urbane inanities. It was with a sense of relief that she saw Rutherford pushing his way towards her.

'Hugh, please rescue me!' she said with a smile, 'I am beginning to wilt.'

He took her hand and forced a passage to the door, then led her down a corridor and out to a terrace.

Violet smoothed her dress. 'It is like a mad-house,' she

exclaimed. 'Everyone talking, no one listening. I was separated from the others within a minute of arriving.'

'Perhaps I ought to go and tell them where you are,' said Rutherford uncertainly.

'Not yet, Hugh, the air is so wonderfully cool.'

'I would not wish your mother to, er . . .'

'Don't worry so! Mamma well knows that I would always behave with the utmost propriety; and anyway,' she said with a smile, 'being American, we have different ideas about these things.'

Rutherford clasped his hands behind his back and cleared his throat nervously.

Violet gazed at his rigid, awkward posture in amusement, then tucked her hand under his arm.

'Just treat me as if I were one of your own sisters.'

'I, er . . . I have no sisters, Miss Harman,' he said gruffly.

'Have you not?'

'I have no family of my own at all.'

'Oh, Hugh!' she said in concern. 'I am sorry! Sometimes I think there are too many Harmans and Mortons in the world. But to have no relations at all, that must be dreadful.'

'I never knew my mother, and my father died when I was nine.'

'Were you an only child?'

'Yes. My mother was twenty-two when she died—not much older than you, I would suppose . . . I envy you your mother, Miss Harman.'

'My mother?' Violet asked with a laugh.

'You are such good friends. I have watched you together . . . I did not think such warmth was possible between mother and daughter. Over here, children seem to be regarded as a nuisance to be tolerated, not enjoyed.'

'I suppose you were not old enough to form that kind of relationship with your father.'

'From what I can remember, he was always a bitter, silent man. I do not believe that he cared whether I lived or died.'

'Oh, Hugh!'

'It is true. I think it was preferable after he had died, and my guardian was charged with my upbringing. I had a tutor who was interested in music and painting and nature. I was just beginning to understand his passion for these things, and feel a little of it myself, when I was sent to Wellington. That put paid to it for ever.'

'Wellington?'

'A boarding school, devoted to churning out soldiers and rulers of the empire. No room there for the fine things of life—all hard knocks and duty.'

Violet squeezed his arm. 'You seem to have come through the ordeal unscathed, at any rate,' she said.

'Do you think so?' he turned towards her and smiled hesitantly.

'I think,' said Violet firmly, 'that you are the only real gentleman I have met, since I landed on these shores.'

CHAPTER _____

_____ FIFTEEN

The Marquess of Salisbury received Bragg and Morton in the panelled library of his London house. His pate was bald and gleaming, while luxuriant whiskers and a beard bushed out from his heavy face.

'I hope that neither I nor my wife are suspected of this crime,' he remarked gruffly.

'If anyone is above suspicion, sir,' replied Bragg guardedly, 'then you must be.'

'I am glad of that, at least. Though it is the only crumb of comfort in the whole of this wearisome business. I hear that you have interviewed Lady Brooke and Lord Charles Beresford—not to mention his royal highness.' A gleam of amusement showed in his eyes.

'I don't mind telling you, sir,' said Bragg, 'that I find this swapping of stories behind my back very irritating. It's as if everyone involved—suspects and victims alike—are conspiring to keep me from finding out the truth.'

'That is how society functions, sergeant. If it were certain that no scandal would arise, no one would be concerned to identify the perpetrator. The present problem is a mere footnote to a *novella* that has been unfolding, more or less in public, for three years and more.'

'That's as may be, sir,' said Bragg.'But the characters are the same throughout, so I have to look at the whole for clues. I hope that you will be more forthcoming than the others.'

Salisbury smiled. 'That is asking a great deal of a politician, sergeant,' he said. 'However, I am prepared to help you so far as I am able—on the basis that most of what I know is in the realm of hearsay, and I would therefore not be able to testify in court.'

'I am surprised that someone of your eminence became involved in anything as squalid as this,' said Bragg brusquely.

Salisbury raised an eyebrow. 'I suppose that must be how it would appear to the evangelical conscience of the nation; which is why it is of paramount importance that this rather stupid letter is not published.'

'You have seen the photograph of it, then, have you, sir?'

'I have,' said Salisbury firmly, 'and I concur with the prince in his determination to retrieve it.'

'Why were you brought into it, anyway?'

Salibury laughed. 'It is one of the burdens of office, that the prime minister inevitably becomes involved with the prince's indiscretions. It is a source of unworthy pleasure to me that, on this occasion, it was Mr Gladstone who had to acquaint the Queen of the impending crisis, since he has gone out of his way to curry favour with the prince when out of office.'

'So you were drawn in, because you were prime minister?'

'Only partly, sergeant. My exertions were as much dictated by self-interest . . . You must understand that the great families of this country regard the Hanoverian dynasty as little more than parvenus—and inept parvenus to boot. My own family has been involved in the governing of the country continuously, for four centuries. During that time the direct line of the monarchy has changed twice. However, the revolution in France taught us that, inevitably, the nobility will sink or swim with the monarchy.'

'So your concern was to protect the prince's reputation?'

'That, yes. But also, I had to have an eye to the future. The Prince of Wales is interested in naval and military matters; Beresford is likely to rise to an important position in the Royal Navy. It would be in the highest degree undesirable that there should be personal animosity between a monarch and someone charged with the defence of the realm.'

'Your intervention wasn't very effective, though?'

'True, sergeant . . . I suppose that was inevitable, given the characters of the two protagonists,' Salisbury added reflectively. 'As you will have realized, Beresford is a very choleric man, and rational argument will only influence him up to a certain point. The prince, on the other hand, is used to having his way, as the arbiter of his court—if we may call it that without disrespect to her majesty.'

'You would think he would have more sense than to get caught up in something like this,' said Bragg bluntly.

'He is not wholly to blame,' Salisbury remarked equably. 'The Hanoverians have always mistrusted, and generally hated their heirs. The plain fact is, that our gracious Queen has lived too long. The prince is like an understudy who has not been allowed to learn the lines. As a result, what appear to be trivial matters are very important to him . . . But, of course, he became embroiled in this sorry business because of his predilection for pretty girls.'

'If you say that he was appealed to as arbiter,' said Morton, 'then the affair was already at an advanced stage.'

'Yes. If you want to trace the whole thing through, you have to go back to the early 'eighties. Frances Brooke is a high-spirited young woman, with considerable means of her own. She soon tired of her husband, whose idea of excitement is a good day's fishing. In the course of time, she and Beresford became lovers.'

'Was Lord Charles married at that time?' asked Bragg.

'Yes,' Salisbury smiled tolerantly. 'And in a curiously inverted way, that became important. Their affair was very intense, and there was talk of elopement and divorce. Fortunately, they were dissuaded from taking that step. Their association continued for some years, however, even though Beresford was aware that he was not her only lover.'

'But something happened to end it?'

'Yes, sergeant. Beresford's wife was found to be with child! . . . Lady Brooke was furious when she heard this. She wrote him a very unwise letter, reproaching him for not having kept his promise to abandon his wife's bed, and declaring that he was the father of her youngest child. She demanded that he should immediately leave his wife, and join her on the Riviera.'

Bragg gave a sardonic snort. 'It's something, when fidelity to your mistress is expected to count for more than the marriage-bond,' he said.

'As evil luck would have it,' Salisbury went on, 'Lord Charles was away when the letter arrived, and had instructed his wife to open any correspondence addressed to him. You can imagine Lady Charles's consternation and anger, when she read Daisy's letter. She showed it to her brother-in-law, and Lord Marcus advised her to place it in the hands of George Lewis, who is a solicitor well versed in handling such delicate matters. By this time Lady Brooke had begun to regret her impulsive reaction, and to realize that the incident could damage her in the eyes of society. She therefore went to see the Prince of Wales, and asked him to intercede and get the letter back for her.'

'And no doubt he did,' said Bragg.

'I have no reason to believe that, up to that moment, she had been anything more to him than a pretty face in the crowd. But from then on, he has been besotted with her.'

'And she with him?'

'Let us say that there is a certain cachet attaching to being the mistress of the heir to the throne,' Salisbury remarked with a smile. 'Be that as it may, the prince made strenuous efforts to persuade Lady Charles to give up the letter, or at least have it destroyed. She refused to do so, unless Lady Brooke was banished from court. This the prince refused even to consider, and riposted by threatening to exclude the Beresfords from society.'

'If I had been Beresford, I would have let him get on with it,' said Bragg.

'Perhaps, but to these people it would have been like a

sentence of exile. Beresford was every bit as anxious to have
the letter destroyed as was Daisy, but he was determined to get
an undertaking from the prince that he and his wife would not
be penalized. Accordingly, he went to Marlborough House to
seek that assurance. Beresford has never been able to keep his
temper and, inevitably, there was a bitter quarrel. Some say
that a blow was struck; at all events Beresford resigned his seat
in Parliament and went off to sea, appropriately enough, in an
armoured cruiser named *Undaunted*.'

'And did the fuss blow over?'

'Unfortunately not. And for that, the prince must bear at
least some of the blame. He was, I believe, punctilious in his
invitations to Lady Charles; but as he publicly flaunted his
friendship with Lady Brooke, it is scarcely surprising that she
felt unable to accept them. She seems to have complained to
her husband that she was being humiliated. Thereupon Lord
Charles sat down and wrote a letter.'

'Another letter?'

'Yes, sergeant,' Salisbury smiled, 'another letter. Indeed,
another unwise letter. Among other things it regretted that the
days of duelling are past, called the Prince of Wales a
blackguard and a coward, and threatened to publicize the
whole affair.'

'Did it now,' said Bragg thoughtfully. 'That was not how he
told it to us.'

'Well, the prince did not actually see the letter. Beresford at
least had the sense to send it to his wife, with instructions to
show it to me; so one could assume that it was primarily written
for my perusal.'

'Why did you not tear it up, sir?'

'I could hardly do that, sergeant. It was private correspondence! I did, however, prevail on Lady Charles not to forward
it to the prince—which was no doubt what Lord Charles
expected. It was at that point, that I became personally
involved.'

'What did you do?'

'Lord Charles was clearly out of order. No gentleman would
ever be the means of bringing disgrace on any lady, because
she had yielded to him. I expressed my views strongly to him

in a letter; and I pointed out that, whatever the rights and wrongs of the affair, a personal vendetta could only harm him and his family. He reluctantly agreed to withdraw the letter and send a less acerbic one, which would give the Prince of Wales the opportunity to apologize.'

'So that was where the affair had got to, before the Warwick weekend?' Bragg remarked.

'Not quite. There was another act of the melodrama to come. Lady Charles's own family were incensed at all this, naturally; and her sister, Mrs Gerald Paget, compiled a pamphlet for publication. She entitled it *Lady River*, and in it she set out, in considerable detail, the story of Lady Brooke's association with the Prince of Wales. Unfortunately, the silly woman was not content that society should merely know of its existence; she actually allowed typewritten copies of it to circulate around the salons. I would not claim that this was why the Tories lost the election, but it did not help our cause . . . There was, of course, a terrible furore and Lord Charles came back to England to protect his wife. As you would expect, this did more harm than good. He issued an ultimatum that, unless the prince apologized for his treatment of Lady Charles, he would call the press to his house and unveil to them the prince's private life in all its unedifying detail.'

'From our meeting with Beresford, I can imagine that,' said Bragg.

'It was perhaps the most anxious few days of my premiership,' said Salisbury. 'However, I was able to build on Lady Charles's original demand that Daisy should be excluded from court. The prince agreed that she should absent herself from London for a token period, then both men signed innocuous letters setting out their basic positions. That should have ended the affair. But Lord Charles expected that his wife would be welcomed back into society, as if nothing had happened. The prince is warm-hearted, I grant you, but it would need a saint to be so forgiving. Lady Charles still felt unwelcome, and Lord Marcus Beresford asked me if I would consent to mediate between the two men, when Beresford next came home on leave.'

'So that really does bring us to Warwick?'

'Yes, sergeant.'

'And how did things work out?'

'Badly, as you are aware. In one sense, the success of my earlier efforts hindered my purpose. Lady Brooke, having been seen to have shouldered the blame by agreeing to leave the court, was in no mood to repeat the process. The prince, also, was resentful of any suggestion that he had been less than wholehearted in welcoming Lady Charles back into the fold. Nor would he consent to a meeting with Beresford alone, even though he was assured that the letter which had started it all, had been destroyed. He went up to bed muttering that he would never forgive or forget the Beresfords' conduct.'

'And, early next morning, Lord Charles went back to London.'

'That is correct, sergeant.'

'We understand that Lady Brooke's room was unoccupied, for at least part of the night.'

'Indeed?' said Salisbury without surprise.

'Do you think that Lord Charles could have gone there, and stolen the letter?'

'It seems incomprehensible that anyone present that night could have done anything so improper. However, it is undoubtedly missing, and he must have had a powerful motive. Moreover, he is an impetuous man, as you will have realized.'

'If he had done so, sir, he would have had to pass your door. Did you hear anything like that, in the night?'

'No, sergeant. My wife and I sleep soundly, praise be to God. Neither of us heard anything.'

Morton led the way through the massive Grecian portal of the Post Office headquarters, then turned left through a door marked 'No Admittance'. At the end of the corridor they mounted a staircase, till they reached the top floor.

'Very trusting, these people,' Bragg murmured. 'We haven't met a soul yet.'

'It shows the power of the printed word,' said Morton with a smile.

'Let's hope your man has something for us on our printed words.'

'Do I deduce from the fact that he is suddenly "my man", that you are sceptical of the outcome?' asked Morton.

'I cannot say I care for these people who set themselves up as experts in reading the bumps on your head, and what not. They are all humbugs, if you ask me. What I want, is a man who can get up in the witness box, with a string of letters after his name and an established reputation. I had never even heard of the Post Office laboratory, till the other day.'

'Well,' said Morton, knocking on a brown-painted door, 'you will soon be able to satisfy your curiosity.' He turned the handle and they found themselves in a long room with tables and benches under the windows. Some were piled with parcels and documents, one had a mass of equipment such as would be found in a chemistry laboratory. At the far end of the room, a man was writing at a desk. He had thinning fair hair and wore tortoiseshell spectacles; a dead pipe was clenched between his teeth. As the policemen entered, he looked up in surprise.

'Sergeant Bragg, City Police,' Bragg said, showing his warrant card. 'We sent some letters across for you to look at.'

The man rose with a smile. 'Ah yes. My name is Murison. I am the chief chemist here.'

'I cannot help wondering what handwriting has to do with chemistry,' Bragg said sourly.

'Very little, I would agree,' replied Murison mildly. 'However, I have become fairly good at identifying writing over the years—enough for the courts to regard me as an expert witness.'

'Have you, indeed?' said Bragg. "Why are you interested in handwriting?'

'It arises out of the Crown exemption from postal charges. This franking is done by means of a superscription, placed on the letter or packet by the franking officer of the department sending it. So, if you can imitate the handwriting of that official, you can get your mail delivered free!'

'You would hardly think it worthwhile, to save so little,' remarked Morton.

'I can assure you that it is practised continually—not only by employees of the departments concerned, in reference to their private correspondence, but also by members of the public.'

'And you prosecute them, do you?' asked Bragg.

'Oh, yes. It is a criminal offence under section thirty-four.'

'I had never heard of a case, that's all.'

'Our own solicitor's branch carries out the prosecutions, so the police are not involved. I may say that the penalties are trivial in the extreme.'

Bragg grinned. 'I've never yet found anybody on the prosecution side who was satisfied with the sentence,' he said. 'Well, have you anything for us, yet?'

'I have done enough tests to reach firm conclusions. If, however, you were intending to call me to give evidence, I would have to carry out further work to round off my presentation.'

'So what is the verdict?'

'First, let me explain the way I have approached the task,' said Murison quietly. 'Only then will you have the confidence to accept my opinion.'

Bragg shrugged his shoulders. 'Very well,' he said.

'Following the information in your covering submission, I have considered the letters as forming three distinct exhibits; the first being the bundle of twelve letters and envelopes addressed to the dean of St Paul's. The second is two letters without envelopes, which I have called the "hundred pounds" letters. The third exhibit comprises one letter without an envelope, which I have called the "ten thousand pound letter". That covers all the documents, does it not?'

'Yes, sir,' said Bragg impatiently.

'Now, in making my examination,' Murison went on in his donnish voice, 'I have looked for evidence of similarities between the various letters comprised in exhibit one, and again in exhibit two. As the second stage, I have compared all the documents in the three exhibits.'

'I see, sir,' Bragg grunted. 'And what is the answer?'

'You must bear with me, sergeant. I get little enough opportunity to rehearse my evidence! In any case, your reactions, as a seasoned appraiser of facts, will be a useful guide to me.'

'Very well, sir.'

'I first examined the paper on which the various messages were printed. As you may have realized, three of the letters in exhibit one, one of the letters in exhibit two, and the sole letter in exhibit three, are on hand-made paper. I have made enquiries concerning the origin of that paper, and while it is obtainable in various cities in England, the only establishment in London which stocks it, is that of Charles Asprey & Sons at 166 New Bond Street—a somewhat exclusive establishment.'

'You got that by following up the water-mark, presumably,' said Morton.

'That is correct,' Murison smiled in appreciation. 'It is perhaps of interest to note that the hand-made paper appears in letters numbered seven, eight and eleven of exhibit one. The numbering being, of course, by reference to the date on the envelope . . . Are you able, sergeant, to tell me which of the two letters in exhibit two is the later?'

'The one mentioning Covent Garden,' said Bragg tersely.

'I see, the one not on hand-made paper . . . I do not have dates for the letters in exhibit two and three, sergeant. Can you supply them?'

'The first of the "hundred pound" letters was received in the first week of this month,' said Bragg, 'the second on the eighteenth.'

'And exhibit three?'

'Some time between the fourth and, say, the thirteenth of this month.'

'I see. So exhibits two and three are concurrent with each other, and immediately after the series in exhibit one . . . I did wonder if there was any significance in the alternation of machine-made, and hand-made paper. One would normally use one box of paper until it was finished, and only then begin another.'

'I suppose so,' said Bragg non-committally.

'What set me wondering,' Murison went on, 'is that there are at least four different inks used in the letters.'

'Really?' exclaimed Morton.

'Oh yes, young man. There are many shades of black!'

'That is odd. Ink lasts for a tremendous length of time! I

suppose that he could have written one at his office, another at home, perhaps another at his club . . . How do the different inks occur throughout the series?'

'The variations are all within exhibit one. Perhaps significantly, the letters in exhibits two and three are in the same ink as that used for letters nine and ten in exhibit one.'

'But not letters eleven and twelve, eh?' asked Bragg.

'No, definitely not.'

'You will put all this in your report, I hope, sir?'

'Indeed. Then, for the court, I would prepare a table setting out the characteristics of each document, and showing how it relates to the others.'

'At least, we have so far established that the writer of the letters is someone from a moneyed background, if he buys his writing paper from Asprey's,' said Morton. 'Though he may live a somewhat peripatetic existence.'

'I leave the interpretation of my opinions to you,' said Murison with a smile. 'I then moved on to an examination of the writing on the various documents. You must understand that script is much more individual than printing, which is obviously why the writer chose the latter mode. However, a person accustomed to cursive writing, inevitably becomes impatient with the laborious nature of printing.' He opened one of the files on his desk and extracted from it a letter which had been sent to Dean Hadley. 'See, the capitals on the first two lines are carefully formed, but lower down they begin to acquire some of the characteristics of script. Compare that B in the first line with the B in the penultimate.'

'I suppose you are right,' said Bragg doubtfully.

'I have taken photographic plates of several letters, and enlarged portions of them for the purpose of comparison.'

'Is it easy to do?' asked Bragg. 'I mean, to make a photograph of a letter?'

'Oh, yes. I have a special camera which will reproduce a page on one plate. That is big enough for most purposes. But you could photograph a letter with a smaller camera, and make an enlargement later.'

'It's just that a photograph of a letter was enclosed with

exhibit three. I wondered what equipment would be needed to produce it.'

"A good camera, and access to a dark-room with enlarging equipment, I would think,' said Murison. 'Though if the photograph was made purely, shall we say, to indicate possession, then a simple camera and developing equipment could well suffice.'

Bragg grinned. 'You are well up with the field, I'll grant you that, sir.'

Murison spread several photographic enlargements out on a table by the window. Each contained a portion of the printed text, four or five times the size of the original.

'You can see from the annotations at the top, that I have selected part of three letters from exhibit one, and all of the documents in exhibits two and three. I should add that each sample is taken from the lower half of the letter, where variations are more likely . . . Now let us look at the Bs again. Can you see how the top loop crosses the middle of the upright, goes upwards for a space, then sweeps back and down, forming an ellipse over the upright? Here you can see it again . . . and here, and here.' He pointed at different enlargements.

'It occurs within each of the exhibits,' Morton remarked.

'That is right. Then look at the Y. It is composed of one slanting stroke coming down strongly from right to left, with little more than a scratch to represent the left branch of the letter. That also occurs throughout the documents, as you can see. Then look at the exaggerated flourish on the pound sign in the examples.'

'Our man is used to keeping books of account, would you say, sir?'

'Possibly, sergeant . . . I have also found characteristic variations in the printing of the letters M, G, F and E, throughout the documents, which I shall be able to demonstrate to the court.'

'You seem very confident, sir,' said Bragg.

'I am, sergeant, I am.'

'So were the letters in all three exhibits written by the same person?'

'Indeed they were, sergeant. There is not a shadow of doubt about it.'

'What about the message on the calling-card?' asked Morton.

'The ubiquitous Mr Smith, you mean? No. I am sorry, constable. The printing there bears no resemblance to that on the other documents.'

'Well, at least that is something,' said Sir William Sumner, when Bragg and Morton reported back to him. 'Now we shall be able to take up the other two cases again, and run them all together.'

'So we shall, sir,' said Bragg warmly. 'I will clear it with Knolleys, shall I?'

'Yes, do that, Bragg. Now where do we stand?'

'In one sense, we ought to start again from the beginning. Miss Godfrey said that the photograph of her and that chap was taken at a society picnic, and we have assumed that the blackmailer must have come from that set. Once Dr Burney had reported that she was no virgin, however, it was obvious that the story of the picnic was a blind. The man who took the snap must have followed them and caught them at it. It could have been anyone.'

'But people do not carry cameras about on spec, Bragg; particularly cameras as elaborate as your photographer man described.'

'I agree, sir. I would accept that the person concerned must have known what to expect. I just wanted to make the point that he need not be the kind of person who would normally attend a society function.'

'So we might as well start afresh, eh?'

'Not quite, sir. I was struck by the fact that when our man wrote to the dean of St Paul's, he was meticulous in using the correct style of address.'

'How do you mean, Bragg?'

'He began the letters, "Reverend Sir", and addressed the envelopes to "The Very Reverend, the Dean of St Paul's". Your ordinary villain would not know that.'

'I expect anyone could get the correct wording from a book on etiquette,' said the Commissioner sceptically.

'Perhaps . . . But then, I ask myself why Miss Godfrey was murdered. On the face of it she was a meal ticket for life, marrying into a wealthy family.'

'It is possible he discovered that the police had been brought in,' said Morton cautiously.

'That could hardly be the reason,' said Sir William. 'You had been taken off the case long before she was murdered . . . I do not see why we need to assume that her death is linked to the blackmail demands at all.'

'It may not be,' replied Bragg easily, 'though we cannot think of any other circumstances which could have led to her murder.'

'What about the man in the photograph with her? He might have killed her to prevent the liaison becoming known.'

'I think that is hardly likely, sir,' said Morton. 'In those circles, it is only unmarried women who suffer by such relationships. If anything, the reputation of the man is enhanced by them.'

Sir William cleared his throat. 'Yes, well, I know nothing about that.'

'At all events, sir,' said Bragg, 'we know that the same man blackmailed her as the other two; so we ought to err on the side of caution and assume he murdered her.'

'I fear you may be misled by it, Bragg,' said Sir William doubtfully. 'We know that Miss Godfrey was murdered by a man, because Burney said so. But, unless I have missed something, there is still no evidence which positively establishes that the blackmailer is a man.'

'You are right there, sir,' Bragg muttered.

Morton came to his rescue. 'I think that only a man would have been likely to obtain the evidence on which the dean was being blackmailed,' he said.

Sir William glanced across. 'That club, you mean? Yes . . . I suppose that is true . . . So why, in your opinion, was Miss Godfrey murdered?'

'I think she discovered who was blackmailing her, sir,' said Bragg, 'and she was killed to keep her quiet.'

'But many victims know their blackmailer,' the Commissioner objected. 'As long as the hold is strong enough, the victim has to keep quiet.'

'It could, of course, be someone who would be personally vulnerable, once he was recognized,' said Morton. 'Society might condone adultery, but it would abhor blackmail.'

'Hmn . . . So we are back with someone who is in the upper class, are we?'

'It must be so, sir,' said Bragg. 'Or someone well versed in their ways. No outsider could have got anywhere near Warwick Castle.'

'You are referring to your theory that it might have been Lady Brooke's maid, Agnes Whatever-her-name?'

'Yes, sir. I grant you it is something of an outsider; and it would have needed a conspiracy between her and the blackmailer—and probably the watchman in the courtyard as well . . . Of course, if Lady Brooke was not telling the truth . . .'

'Why should she not be?' asked the Commissioner irritably. 'The damned letter has found its way to the blackmailer. She would hardly be conspiring with him!'

'I suppose you are right,' said Bragg smoothly. 'Then that certainly leaves us with someone who is in society.'

'So who are our suspects?'

'Well, on the face of it, no one can be tied in to all three cases. You remember Bullivant, who was at the whist game? He must be a prime suspect. He is very hard up, and has been for a long time. Someone like him would find ten thousand pounds very handy.'

'I did not think he was involved in the Warwick affair,' Sir William remarked.

'That is true, sir, but we can tie him in with the other two cases. He is a homosexual, we got that from Knolleys,' Bragg added. 'And he does know Cleveland Street.'

'And I thought the upper classes were all hearty Christian heterosexuals,' the Commissioner said with a foxy smile.

'Furthermore, he cannot account for his movements on the Tuesday that Miss Godfrey met the blackmailer in Swan & Edgar's store or, for that matter, on the day she was killed.'

'You seem to know a great deal about this man, Bragg.'

'We did happen to bump into him, last Sunday,' said Bragg airily. 'It was too good an opportunity to waste.'

'I suppose that Murison has retrospectively converted all your sins into virtues,' the Commissioner remarked sardonically. 'What else do you know about him?'

'He has been an intimate of the Prince of Wales for many years, though he hardly seems well disposed towards him. As he tells it, he has frittered away his fortune indulging the prince's whims.'

'That would suggest revenge as a motive for the Warwick affair, as well as gain,' the Commissioner said thoughtfully. 'But there is still no evidence linking him to it.'

'If we can leave that on one side, for the moment, sir,' said Bragg. 'I think we could say that his insolvency gave him a strong motive for all three blackmailing incidents. Furthermore, he probably knew about the dean's funny ways and perhaps, also, that Miss Godfrey was a bit sprightly. And, as I said, we have not been able, as yet, to corroborate his story of where he was on the crucial Tuesday and Saturday, in the Godfrey case. Moreover, he acts like a guilty man. He refused to give us a specimen of his printing, he was very uncooperative throughout our interview and he was obviously exceedingly worried.'

'I imagine that I would seem so,' remarked Sir William, 'if I were being questioned by two police officers in a public thoroughfare . . . Would this man be capable of smothering a young woman, do you think?'

'Oh yes,' Bragg replied firmly. 'He's not the nancy-boy kind of sodomite. He's all wound up inside; you feel he could explode at any moment.'

'I see. And how do you propose to link him with the goings-on at Warwick Castle?'

'He admits to knowing Lady Rouse, sir. She was sleeping alone that night, a few doors away from Lady Brooke's room. She could easily have taken the letter and, just as easily, passed it to Bullivant.'

'I take it that you did not explore that possibility, when you met him in the street.'

'No, sir,' said Bragg. 'But according to Knolleys, he has an additional motive in the Warwick case. It seems that he had formed an emotional attachment to Lady Brooke's brother-in-law. Some little time ago, that young man had the bad taste to go and get married to a young woman!'

The Commissioner sniffed with distaste. 'Not very edifying at the pinnacle of society, are they? And you may be sure that they make their tenants go to church twice a Sunday.'

'No doubt, sir.'

'Very well. If only because of the possibility that the marked bank-notes had passed through Bullivant's hands, we could hardly exclude him at this stage. What about the other men at the whist party?'

'I think we can exclude the Prince of Wales, sir,' Bragg said with a grin. 'Constable Morton obtained a calling-card of Mr Smith's, with a hand-printed message on it. According to Mr Murison, that was not written by the person who printed the other letters. What we have not yet established is whether Smith wrote the message himself, or not. Apart from that, he admits that he could have passed the notes to Rouse, but on the other hand he shows no sign of being a catamite, and his family seem to have money to throw away.'

'What about any connection with the Warwick business?'

'So far, we have found no motive in his case. No doubt he will know Lady Rouse, so it is possible he could have got the stolen letter from her.'

'But not likely, eh? Who is next?'

'Her husband, Sir Alexander Rouse. They appear to be on very cool personal terms. He makes out that it is because he has squandered all his wealth on gambling—and there is no doubt that he has done so. But, then, she might be equally put out, if his physical appetites had shifted round to the back door.'

The Commissioner frowned in repugnance. 'You have no evidence of that?'

'No, sir. We have nothing that could link him to the dean, apart from the sign.'

'Sign?'

'The mark at the top of the letter. The College of Arms man said that it was the crest of Rouse's family.'

'Did he, indeed? You have been busy, Bragg.'

'Miss Marsden found that out, off her own bat, sir. You will recall that she was aware of the letter received by Miss Godfrey.'

'I see.'

'The man said that it had probably been put on by pressing an inked signet ring on the paper.'

'Hmn. Ingenious. And why would he do that?'

'To identify the letter as coming from the same source, we think.'

'Then why not impress it on the head of the letter to Lady Brooke?'

'We suspect it is because she belongs to a titled family, sir,' said Bragg. 'She would know how to find out the owner of the crest.'

'We are back to the blackmailer being vulnerable within society, are we?'

'It is one explanation, sir. On the other hand, it could be that the ten-thousand-pound demand was going to be a one-off. It is a great deal of money.'

'I would have thought it very rash for anyone to put a mark that might identify him, on a blackmail letter,' the Commissioner mused.

'And yet, as you said, he is often known to his victim.'

'Very well, Bragg, go on.'

'Rouse is, of course, linked to the Godfrey case by reason of the fact that he changed two of the bank-notes we provided.'

'Have any more turned up, sergeant?'

'We have not been notified of any yet, sir.'

'Is not that surprising?'

'Not at all. Rouse seems to have gone out of his way to tell everyone that we had been to see him. I doubt if we shall get any further on that tack.'

'The candour of an innocent man?' asked Sir William, pursing his lips.

'Perhaps. But he could be bluffing. He is a gambler, and reckless as well, I would say.'

'At any rate, it is beyond question that he was in Warwick Castle that night.'

'As was his wife, sir. They could have been working together.'

'Anything else on Rouse?'

'Well, he says he was at a society garden party at Landsdowne House on that Tuesday afternoon. He could easily have popped down to Swan & Edgar's, taken the money from Miss Godfrey, and gone back there again.'

'And what about the Saturday afternoon, when she was murdered?'

'You suspended the investigation, if you remember, sir,' said Bragg stolidly.

The Commissioner glared at him. 'Anyone else in your rogues' gallery, Bragg?'

'So far as the Warwick case is concerned, Lord Charles Beresford had a very strong motive, as well as the opportunity to steal the letter. Moreover, he did beat a hasty retreat to London next morning. But he was not in England when the letters were sent to the dean, and there is no evidence linking him to Miss Godfrey.'

'I wonder if your earlier suggestion might be apposite here, sir,' Morton remarked diffidently.

'Which one is that?' asked the Commissioner.

'That the man in the photograph might have killed her. I noticed that Beresford had a bald spot on the top of his head.'

'You mean Miss Godfrey was Beresford's mistress?'

'He has a reputation as a womanizer, sir. He would think nothing of taking advantage of her.'

'Dear God! Give me ordinary criminals, any time,' Sir William said. 'Anyone else to consider?'

'No, sir.'

'So, what course of action do you propose?'

'Well, sir,' said Bragg amiably. 'You are a Justice of the Peace by virtue of your office. I would like you to give me warrants to arrest Bullivant and Rouse, and maybe Beresford as well.'

'That is impossible!' Sir William exclaimed. 'I have never originated a warrant in the whole of my time as Commissioner.'

'It seemed to me that this case is exceptional, sir, considering the sensitive nature of the matters involved.'

'No, Bragg. It would be quite improper for me to issue warrants. It would be seen as an abuse of police power. I will inform Knolleys of what we propose. Subject to what he says, you will have to go to the Marlborough Street court for your warrants.'

CHAPTER ———— ———— SIXTEEN

Bragg and Morton dismounted from their four-wheeler in South Audley Street.

'Wait for us, cabby,' Bragg called. 'We should not be long.'

He mounted the steps of the Handfords' house and tugged at the bell. A trim maid opened the door.

'We would like to see Mr Bullivant, please.'

'You were here on Tuesday, weren't you?' she asked chirpily.

'That's right.'

'Come in. If you will wait in the drawing-room, I will tell him you are here.'

Morton strolled over to the bookcase and began to read the titles of the volumes in it. Bragg began prowling round the room like a caged bear. After a few minutes, they heard hurried steps descending the stairs, then women's voices raised in the back of the house.

'I don't like this,' Bragg growled. 'Suppose he is slipping out of the back door?'

'It was a woman who came down the stairs, just now,' said Morton. 'I had assumed that it was the maid. Perhaps Bullivant is still in his bed. It is only half past eight!'

Then they heard the voice of the maid and that of an older woman in the corridor outside. The two women hurried upstairs, talking in low tones.

'There's something wrong, lad. I know it,' Bragg exclaimed. After a few more circuits, he could contain himself no longer and strode out of the room. A middle-aged woman was coming down the stairs.

'I am afraid that my brother is not here,' she said anxiously.

'What!' Bragg pushed her aside and rushed up the stairs, with Morton at his heels. At the end of a short passage they could see a half-open door and the maid hovering uncertainly.

'Is this Mr Bullivant's room?' Bragg demanded harshly.

'Yes, sir. Only his bed hasn't been slept in.'

'How do you know that he hasn't made it, this morning, and gone out?'

'What, him?' she sniffed. 'If he broke a shoe-lace he'd throw the shoes away.'

'When did you see him last?' asked Morton.

'At ten o'clock last night. He was in the drawing-room, drinking whisky—too much, if you ask me.'

Mrs Handford approached them along the passage.

'We are police officers,' said Bragg coldly. 'Where is Mr Bullivant?'

'I have no idea,' she said in a troubled voice. 'I thought he must be in his room. The door was locked and he did not reply, but that is by no means unusual. However, when he did not respond to being told that visitors were awaiting him, I felt it best to unlock his door with the spare key and talk to him . . . As you can see, the room is empty.'

Bragg went in, and made a rapid search of the room. The chest of drawers contained a plentiful supply of shirts and underwear, there were several coats and pairs of trousers in the wardrobe. In the corner was a valise and a large Gladstone bag.

'Is this all his luggage?' he asked.

'I think so,' Mrs Handford replied. 'I did not count his bags, officer.'

'When did you see him last, ma'am?'

'At half past ten, last night, when I was on my way to bed. My husband was with him in the drawing-room . . . I fear that they were quarrelling.'

'Where is your husband?' asked Bragg.

'He left for business, only moments before you arrived.'

'I see. And what were they quarrelling about?'

'I am afraid that William could be trying at times and, on occasion, my husband is a little intolerant,' she said evasively.

'Has your brother always lived with you?' Bragg asked.

'You know full well that he has not,' she said acidly. 'William told me what passed at your earlier visits.'

'I see. So you helped him get away from us, did you?'

'No, officer! I swear it.'

'You may find yourself doing just that. Where is he?'

'I do not know. Last night my husband told him that he had to leave this house by the end of the week, because he was . . . ' she bit her lip, 'he was bringing disgrace on our family. William would be quite capable of walking out, on the spot.'

'But he didn't, did he?'

'When Charles came to bed, he said he had left William sitting there, with the decanter . . .'

'Where could he have gone to?'

'As you are aware, he no longer has a home of his own.'

'Friends?'

'I fear that they have all deserted him in his trouble.'

'What relatives have you?'

'No close relatives, officer. Indeed, our only relative is our maternal aunt, Mrs Cicely Hargreaves.'

'And where will we find her?'

'She lives in Menton, in the south of France.'

Bragg made a grimace at Morton. 'Very well, ma'am,' he said. 'If he does come in, ask him to get in touch with Sergeant Bragg, at the City Police headquarters in Old Jewry. And if you have any news of him, perhaps you will do the same.'

The policemen tramped unceremoniously out of the house, and climbed into the growler again.

'Ryder Street, driver,' Bragg called, and slumped morosely

in the corner. 'This is a bugger,' he said. 'We left it too late.
If it hadn't been for Daisy bloody Brooke, we would have had
him in clink by now.'

'At least you have your warrant. We will be able to start
extradition proceedings,' Morton said quietly.

'We have to find him first.'

Bragg relapsed into a gloomy silence that lasted until they
reached their destination; but no sooner had they stopped, than
he was clattering up the stairs and beating a tattoo on Rouse's
door. As Morton came up to him, they could hear a stealthy
shuffling from within. Then the lock creaked and the door was
opened.

'God almighty, sergeant,' Rouse said, stifling a yawn. 'Do
you have to make such a racket?' A bath-robe had been thrown
over his night-shirt, and he was wearing carpet slippers.

'Sorry, sir,' said Bragg genially, pushing his way inside.
'We didn't want you to oversleep! I hope we did not alarm your
good lady.'

'My wife is in the country, visiting her parents,' Rouse said.
Morton could not decide if there was irony in his voice, or not.

'Have you got a camera, sir?' Bragg asked.

'Surely you didn't rout me out of bed, just to ask me that?'

'Among other things, sir.'

'My wife has a camera, somewhere. Do you want to see it?'

'Later . . . Would you mind holding out your hands, sir?'

With a puzzled smile, Rouse extended his arms, the fingers
splayed under Bragg's nose. There was no indentation around
a finger, no band of lighter skin where a signet ring might have
been worn.

'Thank you, sir . . . Does a "seax proper erect", mean
anything to you?'

'Why, yes. It is the heraldic description of my family crest.'

Bragg drew out of his pocket the piece of paper which
Catherine had taken to the College of Arms. 'What do you
make of that?' he asked.

Rouse took it over to the window. 'It is a rather crude
representation of my crest,' he said.

'Then I must warn you that your words will be taken down,
and may be used in evidence,' Bragg said gravely.

Rouse gave an uneasy laugh. 'I have nothing to hide, sergeant,' he replied.

'That piece of paper was cut from the top of a letter,' said Bragg. 'We have thirteen other letters with that same mark on.'

'What is that to do with me?' asked Rouse irritably.

'We are told by an expert that the sign was put on by inking a signet and pressing it on the paper.'

'What if it was?'

'Every one of those letters was demanding money with menaces.'

'Now look here, sergeant!' Rouse exclaimed hotly. 'I have been perfectly open with you. I have admitted that I am broke. But I am not having you pinning every stray delinquency you can find upon me.'

'I would call it a felony, sir,' said Bragg evenly. 'Penal servitude for life is the penalty.'

Rouse's face blanched. 'I tell you, it is nothing to do with me!'

'Then, how would you explain it?'

'I do not know. I . . . I lost my fob seal a long time . . . over a year ago. It was at Marlborough House, the March before last. You know how the Princess of Wales enjoys silly parlour-games. It was a kind of obstacle race; the men had to wriggle through hoops. Afterwards, I realized that my seal was missing.'

'Did you enquire about it?'

'I asked one of the footmen, when next I went there, but no one had seen it. I expect a servant found it and sold it for the gold.'

'Was it valuable, then?' asked Bragg. 'I would have thought you would have made more of a fuss, being so hard up.'

'It was not of great value,' said Rouse shortly.

'So you would like us to believe that whoever used it on the letters had bought it second-hand from a jeweller. Why would anyone do that?'

'I have no idea, sergeant.'

'You know, it won't do,' said Bragg evenly. 'The recipient of one of those letters went to the police, and we provided the money so that blackmail payment could be made. Two of those banknotes were encashed by you.'

'Oh God!' Rouse sank into a chair numbly.

'You were at a house-party on the second of May, at Warwick Castle, weren't you—with your good lady?'

'Yes.'

'You hate the Prince of Wales, don't you?' Bragg demanded, suddenly harsh.

'No!'

'He has made a strumpet of your wife and a lick-spittle of you. You would do anything to get back at him, wouldn't you?'

'It isn't true!'

'Oh yes, it is. That night, you stole a letter from an unoccupied bedroom, didn't you?'

'How could I? I was in the Gatehouse Tower.'

'So you know where it was taken from?' cried Bragg, leaning over him menacingly.

'No, I do not! I know that I was sleeping in the Gatehouse, alone.'

'Ah, yes. Your wife had been allotted to Lord Charles Beresford that night, hadn't she,' said Bragg contemptuously. 'Did you procure her to get it for you?'

'I cannot answer for her,' said Rouse stubbornly. 'All I know is that I did not leave my room.'

'Let us see what else you know, shall we?' asked Bragg, affable once more. 'Where were you on the afternoon of Tuesday the ninth of May?'

'The ninth?' Rouse repeated dully.

'Yes.'

'I . . . I was at a garden party at Lansdowne House, with my wife.'

'Did you stay with her all afternoon?'

'No. She went off with her cronies. I just strolled about from group to group chatting, until it was time to come home.'

'That is not what you told us before. You said you were together all afternoon.'

'We were together, in the sense that we were at the same function,' replied Rouse sharply.

'I take it there is nobody who can confirm that you were there all the time?'

'I would imagine not.'

'You see, in my book you left the party, walked down to Regent Street, took the blackmail money from your victim, and went back again.'

'That is not so.'

'The only mistake you made was to cash two of the notes.'

'I tell you, I do not know how they came into my possession,' said Rouse wearily.

Bragg gazed at him truculently. 'Where were you on Saturday the twentieth?' he demanded.

'Last Saturday? Let me think . . . Yes, my wife was away at a house-party in Sussex. I rose late, then took a steamer up the river to Hampton Court. I wandered around the grounds of the palace, then spent a couple of hours watching a cricket match in the village.'

'And then what?'

'I took a steamer back, had a bite to eat and went to the opera.'

'Did you eat here, or at a restaurant?'

'Not here,' Rouse said sardonically. 'This place is just for sleeping in.'

'Where did you eat?'

'I cannot remember.'

'What opera did you see?'

'*Faust*.'

'Who was singing in it?'

'I cannot recall. I do not care for opera all that much. I went merely to pass the time.'

'Could you not find anyone to play backgammon with?' asked Bragg sarcastically.

'I did not feel in the mood.'

'Did you see anyone at the opera?'

'If you mean did I recognize anyone, sergeant, the answer is no.'

'Where did you go afterwards?'

'I went to the Turf Club for a drink, then came back to bed.'

'Did you recognize anyone there?' asked Bragg.

'I could not now identify the men that I saw.'

'So out of all that busy day, you cannot find one person who can vouch for your whereabouts at any time?'

'I am afraid that is the truth,' said Rouse heavily.

Bragg drew a paper from his pocket. 'Sir Alexander Rouse,' he said, 'I have here a warrant for your arrest. You will come with us to Cloak Lane police station where you will be charged with extortion and murder . . . Constable, stay with this man while he dresses. I will have a look round the premises.'

Late that afternoon, Morton called at the Bank of England, in answer to an urgent summons. He was shown up to the chief cashier's office.

'Ah, constable,' May greeted him. 'We have tracked down a few more of your re-issued notes. Now, where is the list . . . ?' He began to rummage in a desk drawer.

'Have any of them been exchanged for cash?' Morton asked.

'No, I am afraid not. Ah, here it is! I will not bother you with the serial numbers. Two of the notes we gave you on the second occasion, have been paid into Grindley's Bank in Parliament Street by Wishart & Co., who are tobacconists. That occurred on the twenty-fourth—two days ago.'

'I do not suppose that Wishart's could tell us from whom they received them,' said Morton.

'It is possible, I suppose,' replied May. 'But in that kind of area, the payment of ten pounds for a box of cigars can hardly be a rare occurrence.'

'I suppose not.'

'I am afraid that I must plead guilty to contributory negligence with regard to the others,' said May. 'The joint-stock banks, with several branches, have caused any of the listed notes to be sent to their head office, so that a periodic report could be made from there, instead of allowing each branch to report to me direct.'

'In this case,' said Morton ruefully, 'if anything can go wrong, you may be certain that it will do so.'

'I am sorry. However, I suspect that my information would have been of limited use to you, even had you received it immediately. Of the first bundle of notes we provided for you, there were paid into the County Bank in Oxford Street by Messers Marshall & Snellgrove, on Tuesday the twenty-third of May. As you know, they have a large department store and, no doubt, the notes were part of their takings from the previous day . . . Then, a further two of the second batch were received by the County's branch in Regent Street, from Dickens & Jones, who have a similar store, on the twenty-fourth.'

'We rather expected something like this,' Morton remarked.

'The other report we have, is from Lloyd's Bank. Their Welbeck Street branch had three of the second bundle of notes paid in, on the twenty-third. This time the customer was Debenham & Freebody.'

'Another department store . . . Have you traced any of the others?'

'Not yet.'

'You have not had any report from Smith Payne & Smith's bank, then?'

'None. Would you have expected one?'

Morton shook his head. 'So, of the first ten notes, two were cashed by Sir Alexander Rouse, and three were received by stores in the ordinary course of business.'

'One would presume so.'

'I suppose that the other five are still circulating,' said Morton. 'It looks as if our man decided to convert the notes he still held by purchasing small items from these stores. Which suggests that he knew we could trace them.'

'It is possible.'

'And there are three further notes from the second bundle still untraced.'

'That is so. Do you wish us to continue pursuing them?' asked May.

'I think it would still be helpful, sir. You can be sure that I will inform you immediately, if we find that it is no longer necessary.'

Morton took his leave, and walked along to the offices of the *City Press*. He found Catherine engrossed in correcting her copy for that evening's print-run. She said that she would be free in an hour, so he sauntered down to St Paul's and sat in the churchyard for a while. Even in his light-weight clothes, it was exceedingly warm in the sun. It was oddly disagreeable to be hunting for extortioners and murderers in such glorious weather. But perhaps the hunt was over, with Rouse behind bars; though Bragg had not been as elated as he would have expected. However, he was now closeted with the Commissioner, going through the preliminaries, in case it was necessary to extradite Bullivant from France. Morton got to his feet, and strolled round to the west front. Even though he had warmed to the cathedral over the last weeks, he would never find it uplifting. It had been built by prosperous merchants to celebrate a God made in their own image. It was splendid, but not inspiring. He went into the nave and walked slowly around it, mentally sifting the evidence they had obtained, in the hope of finding a nugget which had been overlooked . . . No, 'beyond reasonable doubt' was the standard of proof they required, and so far as Rouse was concerned, they could discharge it.

He went down the steps into the crypt. The dean was safely interred, between the sarcophaguses of England's two greatest heroes; the newly-incised letters proclaiming his virtues. The Christian God would be mildly embarrassed by it all, thought Morton; but Zeus would have laughed till the heavens rang! He pulled out his watch, and began to stroll slowly back.

As he entered her office, Catherine rose and reached for her coat.

'Are you going to see me home?' she asked with a smile.

'For the pleasure of your company, if I may; not to protect you. We arrested Rouse this morning.'

'Thank goodness! But why Rouse? The way you have described him to me, I would not have thought him capable of murder . . . Blackmail, yes, but not murder.'

'There was a considerable accumulation of circumstantial evidence against him. I hope, with your help, to add to it.'

'How can I help you?'

'In this bag is a camera, which we took from Rouse's apartment. I would be grateful for your protection, while I get Aubrey Rivington to examine it!'

Catherine gave a gurgle of laughter. 'You would be quite

safe. I am sure that he is not a Cleveland Street type!' She shuddered.

'The thought of you in that horrible place makes me feel quite faint.'

'If you must swoon,' Morton said with a grin. 'please fall this way. I am not very good at catching people today.'

'I hope you would catch me!'

'I would most certainly try! . . . I was referring to the fact that Bullivant got away this morning, before we could arrest him.'

'Bullivant also?'

'Again, circumstantial evidence, though not so strong as in Rouse's case.'

'Then let us hope that you have the right man in the cells.'

They took a cab to Rivington's studio. As they dismounted, they could see his face peering out of the window. Then he caught sight of them and vanished. Catherine expected him to fling wide the door in his outrageously affected way, but no. Morton opened it, and she preceded him into the shop. It was empty.

'I am sure that I saw him,' she said.

'Perhaps he has popped out through the back door?'

'But I know that he recognized us.'

Morton pushed aside a curtain at the back of the shop to reveal a short passage leading to the back door. It was firmly secured on the inside, with a large padlock. Off the passage, to the left, was a door with a brass plate screwed on it, bearing the legend: 'Dark Room Keep Out'. Morton rapped on it and listened; there was no response. He turned the handle but the door was locked.

Catherine joined him. 'Why does he not answer?' she asked.

'I cannot imagine.'

'Aubrey, come out,' she cried severely. 'Stop playing your silly games!'

There was no reply.

She gave Morton a conspiratorial smile. 'Perhaps he has been taken ill in there,' she said in a loud voice.

'Do you think so?' Morton replied, taking his cue from her.

'It is possible. There are all kinds of noxious chemicals in there. He could have been overcome by the fumes.'

'Perhaps I ought to break the door down,' Morton suggested in a stentorian tone.

'So you think that you should?'

'It is my duty. He might lose his life!'

There was a scraping sound from inside the room, then a plaintive voice called: 'It wasn't me!'

'What was not you?' Morton asked.

'Arabella . . . it wasn't me.'

'I know you didn't kill her,' said Morton in exasperation. 'Open the door.'

'I didn't tell anyone about her. It wasn't my fault.'

'No one says it was your fault.'

'Have you not come to arrest me, then?'

'No. I have come to seek your advice. Come out.'

There was a rattle as the lock was turned, and Rivington emerged sheepishly, his large yellow bow-tie awry.

'It is true, you know.' he said urgently. 'I haven't said a word to anyone.'

'I believe you,' Morton replied quietly. 'I have brought a camera for you to examine. This is the photograph you saw the other day. I want you to tell me if it was taken by that camera.'

Rivington picked it up. 'They will not need photographers, soon,' he complained. 'The way this craze is going, everyone will be able to take their own.'

'Is it a good camera?' asked Morton.

'Oh yes. One of the best German makes.'

'Could it have taken that snap?'

'Well, it is a roll-film camera, and I expected it to be a plate camera . . . it all depends on the lens.'

'Will you test it for us?'

'I cannot do it now. Come tomorrow at this time, and I will let you have my opinion.'

'Very well.'

'Can I take it into the park, to try a shot or two there?'

'I see no reason why not,' replied Morton. 'But remember, it is a Crown exhibit in a criminal prosecution.'

Rivington shivered. 'She was murdered, wasn't she,' he said apprehensively. 'It was not a boating accident at all.'

'Yes,' Morton said quietly. 'She was murdered; but it would be unwise of you to proclaim the fact.'

'I won't, you may be sure!' Rivington exclaimed.

'Till tomorrow, then. And . . . be careful.'

Violet Harman looked in the mirror and patted her hair into place. A Scottish reel was apt to leave one somewhat unkempt; particularly if one's partner had been a dashing Guards subaltern. This dance was engendering in her a distinct feeling of *déjà-vu*. Nor was it wholly an illusion; it was true that the Italianate splendour of Dorchester House out-rivalled anything she had seen, but the scale of the entertainment was much the same as that at the other balls she had attended. Moreover, the throng here was composed mainly of the same people as she had met at other houses; she saw the same faces, occasionally even the same dresses! She would be glad to get away to Paris, for a change.

Emily, of course, had teased her when she had said as much, and accused her of lacking the stamina for high life. Well, her enjoyment of it was not wholly uncritical, and there was no point in hiding the fact. Emily would be equally glad to go to France, but for a different reason. Well, Violet resolved, she would not envy her one whit . . . Her cousin could hardly claim to be consistent herself! While they had been idling away the morning, she had asked Emily what would make her proud of a husband. She had expected her to say something like being a good shot, able to drive a four-in-hand or dance till dawn. Instead, she had answered without the slightest hesitation: 'his doing an important job'. She had indicated no scale of values, given no examples—such as prime minister or Archbishop of Canterbury— but on the principle she was definite. Well might she avoid the particular, for it seemed that she was intent on bestowing herself on a bank clerk—if a somewhat superior one. But perhaps if you were really in love with someone, whatever he did was important, so long as he did it to the best of his ability and it was useful . . .   That was possibly the clue to her own feelings

about James. She was very fond of him and admired him in
many ways, yet when one analysed the way he spent his life,
it was scarcely more admirable than the aimless idleness of
most of the men she had met . . . No, that was unfair to
James; and he certainly insisted that he was doing a useful job.
It was more that his abilities could have encompassed much
greater responsibilities. He could have entered politics, with
every expectation of rising to be a member of the government;
he could have gone into the foreign service and become an
ambassador. With his intelligence and charm he could become
anything he wished; yet, with incomprehensible perversity, he
chose to be a police constable. And, looking into the future, he
would some day inherit The Priory; then he would probably
spend his time walking the fields and patting the cows. Violet
sighed irritably. Papa had often said that James was lacking
ambition—for once, he would not be glad to be proved right.
With a final glance at her reflection, she went back to the
ballroom.

As she walked along the edge of the dance floor, she could
see James and Catherine Marsden waltzing together. They
deserved each other, she thought uncharitably; the unambitious
and the over-ambitious, locked in a contest that neither could
win. As Violet approached her mother, Rutherford detached
himself from a group of young men by the door, and came
towards her. He bowed to Mrs Harman and Lady Morton, then
turned to her with a smile.

'May I have the honour?' he asked.

'Of course, Hugh!"

His dancing was restrained, and yet her dress swirled out in
a very satisfactory manner. They must look an attractive
couple, from the side of the room; it was infinitely better than
being half-carried from one end of the floor to the other, in a
dozen strides! But then, the waltz was much the pleasantest
dance. Alas! a resonant chord signalled its end.

'What a pity!' Violet said with a brilliant smile. 'I enjoyed
that so much.'

'Good.' Rutherford looked down at her quizzically. 'Would
you like some air?' he asked awkwardly.

'I would certainly welcome a break from dancing.'

He led the way on to the terrace and they stood for a while by the balustrade, gazing across the silvered lawns and flower-beds.

'Are you cold?' he asked.

'No.'

'I could get your wrap, if you wished.'

'No, I am fine as I am. It is still so incredibly warm.'

Rutherford cleared his throat. 'Would you like to walk in the garden?'

Violet laughed. 'If I were home in America and you asked me that, I would have to scurry off to the protection of my chaperon!'

'But since you are in London . . .?

'Why, I place myself under your protection.'

She took his arm and they walked slowly down the steps, then along a gravelled drive. Here and there in the arbours, they could see the soft glow of a tulle skirt, and the gleam of a shirt front. Rutherford paused before an unoccupied garden-seat, screened from the house by azalea bushes, but in full view of the path.

'May we sit for a little?' he asked.

Without replying, Violet sat down at one end of the bench. Rutherford placed himself at the other, leaving a foot of space between them. A silence developed and Violet, amused and intrigued, allowed it to prolong itself. Finally Rutherford turned towards her.

'I have been promoted to major,' he said abruptly.

'Oh Hugh! I am so pleased.'

'Thank you.' He smiled briefly. 'There is only one problem.'

'What is that?'

'I am being posted overseas.'

'To where?'

'Bechuanaland.'

'Wherever is Bechuanaland?'

'In southern Africa.'

'Would you prefer not to go?' asked Violet sympathetically.

'It would be a very advantageous post, from the point of view of my career. I am being appointed military secretary to the governor.'

'What would you be doing?'

'I would advise on the defence of the territory—the deployment of our forces, where to construct strong-points and so on. In a sense, I would be totally independent. The governor is also governor of Cape Province, and lives in Cape Town. Bechuanaland is run by a chief magistrate, from Vryburg. He would be of equal rank to me. Moreover, I would be based in Mafeking, so that I would not even feel that he was breathing down my neck.'

'It sounds splendid,' said Violet warmly, 'what kind of country is it?'

'It is totally land-locked, with Cape Colony to the south, the Orange Free State and the Transvaal to the east, and German South-West Africa to the west.'

'And to the north?'

'Uninhabited scrub.'

'It does not sound very civilized!'

'It would be heaven on earth, if you were with me.'

Violet sat bolt upright. 'I did not know you felt about me in that way,' she replied, trying to keep her voice level.

'Oh, but I do,' Rutherford said earnestly. 'I have never met a girl who could remotely equal you. You are so good-humoured and gentle, and even-tempered.'

'You make me sound like a favourite pony,' Violet said with an uncertain laugh.

'I am sorry,' Rutherford said contritely. 'I have never been much good at expressing myself. I can only say that I have fallen in love with you.'

'But I have known you for so short a time.'

'Yes. And yet I am quite certain that I shall never meet anyone to match you. That is why I felt I must speak out now. It seems to me that there is not a position to which I might aspire, that you would not adorn with your charm and grace.'

Violet tried to steady the turbulent rush of her thoughts. A proposal of marriage was by no means as exciting as she had expected. In her day-dreams she had listened to words of newly-awakened love, from someone she had already chosen. Here, she was being subjected to a surprise frontal assault. It was not at all the gospel according to Jane Austen . . . Rutherford was looking at her anxiously.

'I am sorry, Hugh,' she said. 'You must feel that I am behaving like a callow girl.'

Rutherford laughed. 'I am afraid I rather sprang it on you. The only way I could bring myself to broach the subject, was to screw up my courage and blurt it out . . . I know you are bound to have reservations, and I would not dream of approaching your father until I had your tacit consent. So long as you can say that the idea of being married to me is not wholly repugnant, then I will gladly let you make up your mind in your own time.'

'You must know that I am not indifferent to you, Hugh. I would not be here, if I were.'

'Then, that is all right.'

'How long will you be in Africa?' Violet asked.

'The initial appointment is for three years. After that, it might be renewed, or I might be given a minor governorship somewhere . . . Of course, if you did not like it out there, I could ask to be posted back to the regiment.'

'Would that be something you would want?'

Rutherford studied the gleaming toes of his boots. 'Not really,' he admitted eventually. 'I do not think that I am staff officer material. If I came back, I would finish my days as a major in charge of a company. But if you could not put up with life in the wilds, then I would be content.'

'No, no,' said Violet quickly. 'I would never extract such a promise from you.'

'Of course, I could resign my commission at any time, and become a country gentleman. I am afraid that I have no claim to be wealthy, but I have two thousand acres in Gloucestershire, and a castle which Cromwell thoughtfully ruined for us! The manor-house is Georgian and reasonably small, so it is pleasant to live in. And if you were a thrifty housewife,' he added with a sly smile, 'we could perhaps afford to rent a house here for the Season—if that is what you would like!'

'I was about to say that I could manage very well without that,' said Violet with a laugh. 'But if I were to accept your proposal, I might feel quite sentimental about London.'

'Then I need not give up hope?' he asked.

'A wise man would suspend both hope and despair.'

Rutherford reached out and took her hand. 'It may just be a trick of the moonlight, Violet, but you look serene and beautiful, and quite captivating. How could any man not love you?'

'That is scarcely flattering, Hugh!'

'I am no courtier,' he replied wryly, 'but that does not diminish my feelings for you.'

'I shall have to talk it over with my mother, and I know that she will want to consult my father.'

'Of course.'

'I am sure that their plans for me never remotely envisaged the possibility that I might become the wife of an English officer—a redcoat, moreover!'

'I suppose not.' Rutherford fell silent. 'I can hardly blame them,' he said at length. 'It was really rather presumptuous of me to approach you . . . But I had to try.'

Violet laughed. 'Disingenuous humility sits very ill on you, Hugh; I prefer my resolute major.' She squeezed his hand gently. 'I shall listen to my parents' advice, of course; but I shall make up my own mind. I promise you that.'

CHAPTER

SEVENTEEN

Catherine came downstairs, to find her mother breakfasting alone. Her eyes were glued to a novel, which was propped up against the teapot.

'Good morning, mamma,' she said breezily.

'Good morning, dear,' her mother replied, without looking up.

'Where is papa?'

'He has gone to Tonbridge for three days, to do the sketches for a portrait.'

'Ah, yes. I remember.' Catherine poured herself some coffee. It was odd, she thought, that men should make such a show of abhorring Monday morning. She loved it. The other reporters on the *City Press* professed a reluctance to start another week of drudgery. She was longing to come to grips with it. Now that Rouse had been arrested, James had said she could go ahead with her article on the College of Arms. Today she would tidy up her draft and take it to the editor—but not until after lunch!

'Is there no post, mamma?' she asked.

'Yes, dear.' Her mother's fingers groped for her toast. 'I put it on the sideboard.'

Catherine crossed over, and picked up the bundle of letters. Amongst them was a large manila envelope, addressed to her. Strange . . . she was not expecting anything. She tried to guess what it might be. The address was typed, so there was no clue there. She looked for the postmark, but there was none, neither was there a stamp. So it had been delivered by hand. Curiouser and curiouser . . . When had she received an envelope like this before? she wondered. It was recently . . . Of course! Professor Sully. This envelope was identical. It must be something related to the survey. She tore open the flap, and drew out the contents . . . Suddenly she felt as if she had been kicked in the chest by a horse. There, on top, was an unsigned letter, printed in capitals on hand-made paper. In a sudden access of revulsion, she screwed it up and threw it away from her. Beneath it were two photographs of written pages. She was about to tear them up, when she saw that at the bottom of each page was the word 'Bougainvillea' in her writing. They were part of her interview questionnaire! She compelled herself to look at the pages. A thick pencil line had been drawn down the margin in three places. Hardly able to get her breath, she began to read them.

> Q. Have you ever had a close relationship with a man?
> A. Only my father.

> Q. Have you had, since your childhood, physical intimacy with a man?
> A. Some involuntary intimacy.

> Q. Which do you prefer, your father or your mother?
> A. My father.

> Q. Why is that?
> A. It is inbuilt. He is one of the opposite sex, after all.

Catherine felt sick, her mind was spinning uncontrollably—

the thought forming and re-forming in her brain . . . It was
supposed to be a survey . . . a survey.

'Are you all right, dear?' her mother asked in concern.

Catherine took hold of herself. 'Yes, mamma, I just feel a
little dizzy. I must be over-tired; I will lie down for a while.'
She retrieved the crumpled ball of paper from the fireplace and,
picking up the envelope and photographs, went up to her room.
For a while she lay on the bed, staring at the ceiling, conscious
only of her thumping heart. Then her mind began to pick at the
edges of her predicament . . . She had been so pleased at
Sully's letter, she thought in disgust, so proud to have been
selected . . . *Hubris*, that's what it was; arrogance on her
part, inviting disaster . . . How stupid she had been, playing
that woman's silly game—as if the first thing that came into
your head could ever be your real opinion . . . *Whom the
gods wish to destroy, they first make mad* . . . She had been
mad, without question, and just as surely she would be
destroyed. Catherine wanted to curl up between the sheets, till
the nightmare had passed. But this was no childish imagining.
Why? What was the point of it? What could anyone possibly
gain from ruining her reputation? . . . But perhaps it was no
more than a ghoulish prank . . . She picked up the crumpled
sheet of paper from her bedside table and, with repugnance,
smoothed it out. It was just like the letter Arabella had
received, with that obscene mark at the top.

*INCEST? AND YOU OUR LATEST BEAUTY! I WOULD
LIKE TO GET THE PAGES BACK FOR YOU. COME TO
THE TEMPLE CHURCH AT NOON ON WEDNESDAY.
COME ALONE.*

When Morton went into Bragg's room that morning, he found
it empty. He took some paper from the cupboard and carried it
over to his small table by the window. Usually he would have
made notes on interviews at some time over the weekend; but
with the Australian touring team due shortly, he had played
cricket on both Saturday and Sunday. It had been very
satisfying; he was feeling confident and in good form; with a
few matches for Kent under his belt he should be well

in the running for a place in the England team. All the same, he should have found time to jot down what May had said—and Rivington, if there was anything to record! He had been working for some time, when he heard heavy steps in the corridor and Bragg stormed in, his face flushed with anger.

'The buggers have done it again!' he exclaimed.

'What is that?' Morton asked.

'The Commissioner has just had me up, to tell me that Chief Inspector Forbes is going to interrogate Rouse . . . I had let him sweat till this morning, to take some of the cockiness out of him, now I can't get near him.'

'Have we been taken off the case?'

'No,' said Bragg wrathfully. 'We are graciously allowed to continue the investigation—which will be little enough, if Rouse cracks.'

'I do not understand,' Morton said in perplexity. 'The CI did not even know about the case.'

'They've got their heads together over the weekend, that's what has happened.'

'But why?'

'Because we had got too close, that's why,' said Bragg darkly. 'If it had been a valet or a lady's maid that had taken the letter, they would have left it to us. But with both main suspects being friends of the Prince of Wales, it cannot be left to common coppers like you and me.'

Morton suppressed a smile. 'Has the Chief Inspector been put in charge now?' he asked.

'No. If they did that, he would want Inspector Cotton brought in as well. Forbes always has to have someone to blame, in case things go wrong.'

'Then at least you will get the credit for making the arrest,' Morton said soothingly.

'If Rouse is our man, we should. But I wouldn't even bet on that . . . I have to ask you to make a full written report on the investigation so far. Forbes needs it for his interrogation. It must be with him by tomorrow night, so, if it will make it easier, you can write it at home.'

'Thank you, sir. Before I begin, I will go to see Rivington again, to get his opinion on Rouse's camera.'

'Very well.'

As Morton went out, Bragg felt in his pocket for his pipe. A smoke might improve his temper. It would be a *cause célèbre*, that was the reason; everybody would want to grab a chunk of the credit, now that he had done the donkey work. Well, it was not the first time; and if he was stupid enough to stay with this small-minded lot, it wouldn't be the last . . . He struck a match and sucked at the flame.

'Joe,' the desk-sergeant stuck his head round the door. 'There is a man called Lewis downstairs. He wants to see you, says he's a solicitor.'

'Send him up, will you, Bill?' Bragg knocked out his pipe, and walked over to the window. The church clock said half past ten. What a way to start a week!

There came a rap on the door and a middle-aged man entered. He was soberly but expensively dressed, a diamond tie-pin nestled in his black silk cravat, his finger-nails were carefully manicured.

'I believe that you are the officer who arrested my client on Friday,' he said, advancing into the room.

'And who might that be?'

'Sir Alexander Rouse. His wife has asked me to represent him. She saw his note on returning from the country last evening, and instructed me at once.'

Bragg waved him to a chair. 'Are you George Lewis?' he asked.

'Yes, here is my card.'

Bragg took it. 'Ah, yes,' he said. 'You are the one whose practice is largely made up of society folk.'

Lewis raised an eyebrow. 'How is that relevant?' he asked.

'I was just thinking that there are other people in this case it might be more profitable to represent,' Bragg said equably.

'That is hardly a consideration it would be proper for me to entertain.'

'No, of course not.' Bragg smiled sardonically. 'Well, what can I do for you?'

'I naturally would like to arrange bail for my client. I wish, therefore, to discover how far the case has progressed.'

'Bail? Your client has been charged with extortion and murder! You haven't got a hope!'

'Why on earth did he not send for me, as soon as he was arrested?' Lewis exclaimed testily.

'I gather he has no money . . . of his own . . . '

'Oh well, I shall have to make the best of it. Where is my client?'

'In Wandsworth prison. He was remanded, on Saturday morning, for seven days.'

'Perhaps I might get the hearing brought forward . . .' Lewis murmured to himself. 'Would the police be likely to oppose bail, sergeant?'

'If it were left to me, I would see you in hell first. Since it isn't, you had better go and see Chief Inspector Forbes about it. He's down the passage, the last door on the left.'

With a look of distaste, Lewis picked up his hat and walked out of the room. Bragg sat down heavily in his chair, and took up his pipe again. The nobs had got the crackers, he decided. Whoever had heard of bail, in a murder case? Either Lewis knew next to nothing of the criminal law. or else he just assumed that normal procedures would not apply to a friend of the Prince of Wales. Well, Forbes was welcome to this lot. He would enjoy dancing around them, smiling and touching his forelock. Let him get on with it . . . Bragg was just striking another match, when the door opened and Catherine came in. He took in her strained, worried appearance and hastened to set a chair for her.

'Whatever is the matter, miss?' he asked in concern.

'I have received one of those abominable letters,' she said tightly.

'You?'

'Yes, read it.' She threw a manila envelope on to the desk. 'It was delivered by hand, late on Sunday night, I presume. The maid says that she found it on the doormat, early this morning, before the first post had come.'

'Are you saying someone is trying to blackmail you?' Bragg asked in disbelief.

'You must tell me, sergeant.'

Bragg put his pipe in the ash-tray and took out the contents from the envelope.

'Good God!' he exclaimed. 'The seax crest at the top! But Rouse has been in custody since Friday morning!'

'I know, James told me about it.'

'I suppose he could have already arranged for it to be pushed through the door.'

'Please read it . . .'

'Incest?' Bragg raised troubled eyes to her face. 'Where did he get that idea from?'

'From me . . . No, I did not confess it,' Catherine laughed harshly. 'I was induced to take part in a survey concerned with women's achievements, which is being conducted under the auspices of Professor Sully of the University of London. I attended at King's College last Tuesday, for an interview. A woman went through a questionnaire, and took down my answers. The photographs you are looking at, are of two sheets of that questionnaire.'

Bragg picked up the photographs and read them, his face growing grave.

'What is this "Bougainvillea" at the bottom?' he asked. 'It is in different writing.'

'That is my pseudonym, sergeant. I wrote it on the bottom of every page. They said it would preserve my anonymity. Instead it is obvious to anyone who knows my hand, that I wrote it.'

'What does that prove?'

'I cannot pin my hopes on a denial, if that is what you suggest. It is perfectly clear, from the answers to the earlier questions, that I was the person being interviewed.'

'Hmn.' Bragg read through the pages again.

'Bougainvillea!' Catherine said bitterly. 'I looked it up in the encyclopaedia. Do you know what it said? . . . "A deciduous climber which is not reliably hardy in this country, and should be kept in a greenhouse". It seems an appropriate commentary on my naïvety!'

'Don't reproach yourself, miss. When young Morton comes back, we will soon get to the bottom of it.'

'No!' Catherine cried in alarm. 'He must know nothing about it.'

'But how can I keep it from him? He works with me.'

'You must! . . . Sergeant, I swear that what is suggested is not true. But if he were to see those photographs, the suspicion would always be in his mind. I would take any risk to avoid that.'

'No one who knows you would ever for a moment think it was true,' said Bragg warmly.

'I wish I could believe you, sergeant. But that kind of evil strikes beyond the rational. If it is rumoured abroad that I have had an incestuous relationship with my father, it will hardly matter whether it is true or not. I and my family will be ruined. I shall have my employment terminated, my father will receive no more commissions, we shall become social lepers. And all this, without anyone considering whether it has been proved or not.'

'Surely the best thing would be to catch whoever sent it?'

'Yes. But if Constable Morton got to know about this in the process, then I would have gained nothing.'

Bragg gazed at her. 'I thought it was imminent execution that was supposed to concentrate the mind,' he remarked dryly. 'So you think a lot of him?'

'Yes,' Catherine replied defiantly.

'Then, what do you want of me?'

'I want you to promise me that you will say nothing to Constable Morton about this. In return, I will do anything to help you catch the man behind it.'

'Let us hope we already have him locked up,' Bragg remarked. 'Very well, miss. I accept your offer.'

'Thank you, sergeant.'

'What do you think the blackmailer is after? It is obviously not money—or not at this stage, anyway.'

'I have not thought about it a great deal, but it is possible that he feels I have some influence in society. He would be quite wrong, as it happens, but I can think of no other explanation.'

'Hmn. How did you get to know about this so-called survey?'

Catherine pulled another envelope from her bag and passed

it over to him. 'This communication from Professor Sully was the start of it.'

Bragg read it carefully. 'The letter is dated the eighth of May,' he remarked, 'but from the post-mark, it was only posted at half past seven at night, on Saturday the thirteenth. That is a funny time to be posting a business letter.'

'It is all a façade,' Catherine said bitterly.

'Well, if you are right, someone went to a great deal of trouble.'

'I am convinced of it.'

'Then let us find out, shall we?' He picked up his telephone instrument and pressed the bell.

'Hello, Bert. Is the University of London in the directory? . . . It is? Good! Will you ring them for me?' He drummed with his fingers on the desk. 'Hello!' he said loudly, 'I want Professor Sully . . . No, Sully! . . . That's right . . . When will he be in? . . . Then tell him I will be there at twelve o'clock . . . Yes, Sergeant Bragg of the City Police . . . Very good.' He put the ear-piece back on the hook. 'If I had gone outside and shouted, I could have done as well,' he remarked. 'Right, let us see what Professor Sully has to say for himself, shall we?'

They took a cab to Bloomsbury, and found Sully in his office. He was a small man with thick pebble glasses and a sad drooping moustache.

'Sergeant Bragg of the City Police.' Bragg produced his warrant card, and Sully peered at it myopically.

'I trust that none of my students has been misbehaving,' he said in a desiccated voice.

'No, sir. Nothing like that. I just wanted to have a word about your survey on women's achievements.'

'My what?' he asked in astonishment.

'This young lady received a letter purporting to be from you. Here it is.'

Sully took Catherine's letter and read it intently. Then he handed it back with a smile.

'I know nothing of this so-called survey, sergeant; moreover, the signature on the bottom was not written by me.' He took a piece of paper, dipped his pen in the inkwell, and scribbled rapidly. 'That is my signature,' he said.

'It could not be a survey that is being done in your department, I suppose,' said Bragg, 'and one of your assistants has used your name?'

'No, sergeant, that is out of the question,' Sully turned to Catherine. 'I am sure that such a project is overdue,' he said kindly, 'but I am not aware of even the suggestion of one.'

'Have you heard of a Miss Maud Stanford, in your field?' asked Catherine. 'She said that she had studied in Vienna, and was currently working with Professor Charcot at the Salpê-trière Hospital in Paris.'

'I have not. Furthermore Charcot is not an academic, but a physician specialising in nervous diseases. He would not become involved in a survey such as indicated by the let-ter . . . I very much fear, young lady, that you are the victim of a more than usually imaginative hoax.'

'Bragg and Catherine left Sully, and took a cab to King's College, where they went into the porter's lodge.

'Which one was it, that you saw?' murmured Bragg.

'The man at the other end of the counter,' Catherine replied. 'The one speaking to those two young men.'

Bragg waited until he was free, then beckoned to him.

'Sergeant Bragg, City Police,' he said. 'I am making enquiries concerning a survey to do with women's achieve-ments.'

A flicker of surprise and consternation crossed the man's face. 'I don't know nothin' about that,' he said.

'Oh yes, you do,' Bragg said firmly. 'This young lady came to an interview here, and you showed her to a room at the far end of the courtyard.'

The porter passed his tongue over his lips. 'She was the only one,' he mumbled.

'So you admit it?'

'I don't admit nothin'. I was just asked to find a spare room.'

'Who asked you?' Bragg demanded.

'This woman. She came and said she needed a room on a Tuesday afternoon, for a few weeks.'

'What was she like?'

'Well . . . early middle-age, black hair, nice eyes.'

'When did she first come to see you?'

'Let me think . . . It was two weeks ago, last Saturday.'

'The thirteenth?'

'Yes, that would be it.'

'Was there anyone else with her?'

'No, she was on her own.'

'Have you at any time seen her with a man?'

'No, sergeant. I haven't.'

'What arrangement did you make with this woman?'

The porter hesitated. 'Well, I showed her where she could wait—in the library . . . If a young woman came to the lodge about the survey, I was to put her in a spare room. Then I would tell this woman where she was, so she could interview her.'

'How much did she pay you?' Bragg asked truculently.

The man looked around him furtively. 'Ten shillings,' he whispered.

'Each week?'

The porter nodded.

'I have to tell you,' said Bragg formally, 'that you may be charged as an accessory to a crime.'

'Cor Blimey!' he whined. 'I ain't done nothin'.'

'You have defrauded your employers, for a start,' said Bragg. 'That should earn you the sack. But I might be able to overlook that, if you tell me what I want to know.'

'As God's my witness, I don't know nothin' I haven't told you. She said there might be people comin' for the rest of May. But the only one that ever showed up was this young lady, last Tuesday.'

'Very well. If you help me, I will try to get you off. Tomorrow is Tuesday. If the young woman comes, I want you to show her into the library, as you did before. What time will she come?'

'It has always been around one o'clock, so far. I've had to eat my sandwiches early, to make sure I was here.'

'Right. I will be standing in the doorway of the church, over there. As soon as you have put her in the library, you come for me. I would like a word with that young woman.'

• • •

The following afternoon, Bragg was at his post early. He
squatted on the steps of the church, and pretended to be reading
his newspaper in the sun. It was a good vantage point to
observe the entrance to the college, although he was too far
away to intercept the woman, should the need arise. Still, that
was not the point. He wanted her to be lured into the library—a
place where she had no right to be. There would be no fuss
then. It was odd how the public took against the police when
they were arresting a good-looking young woman, who was
protesting her innocence. For a time Bragg waited contentedly;
but when he heard a clock chime three, he began to get restive.
It had always been on the cards that she would not show up.
Miss Marsden might well have been the only person invited. If
so, it would be pointless for the woman to come again. Bragg
acknowledged that he had been hoping to seize her, as an
alternative to using Catherine to entrap the blackmailer. As the
afternoon wore on, he became progressively more ill-
tempered. It was absurd to be buggering about like this. Left to
himself he would have squeezed Rouse dry by now; perhaps
got evidence implicating Lady Rouse, and arrested her as well.
As it was, Morton would not yet have finished his report.
When five o'clock chimed, Bragg left his post and went across
the road to the porter's lodge.

'Did she come?' he asked.

The man shook his head. 'No, she didn't—and I've been
here every second.'

'And this is the last Tuesday of the month. I don't suppose
she will come again, blast it!'

'No, and she didn't pay me for today,' the man complained.

'Think yourself lucky,' said Bragg grimly, 'your sentence
will be lighter.'

The porter looked startled, and turned away to deal with
another visitor. Bragg glanced at his watch, then strolled out
into the street and waved for a hansom. In twenty minutes he
was walking up the drive of Marlborough House. He was
ushered up the stairs and into the panelled ante-chamber. He
spent a few moments trying to find exactly where the concealed

doorway was, but decided that he could not succeed unless he knocked on the walls. That would hardly be seemly. He walked over to the window and gazed out across the garden, then heard a click behind him as Knolleys came into the room.

'It was good of you to come,' he said with automatic courtesy.

Bragg followed him into the study. The Prince of Wales was sitting in the bay window, smoking a large cigar. He waved Bragg to a chair.

'Lady Brooke has received another letter,' he said. 'She put a message in *The Times*, as you advised, and a reply was posted to her on Saturday night.'

'Where was it posted, sir?' asked Bragg.

'West London.'

'And what did it say?'

'It directs her to purchase ten thousand pounds' worth of government bearer bonds, and seal them in an envelope. They are then to be put into a second envelope, with a card saying "For Stanley Fortescue".'

'We have been unable to recall anyone of that name,' said Knolleys. 'We assume that it must be an alias.'

'No doubt,' said Bragg shortly. 'And where is it to be sent?'

'It is to be posted to the office of a notary, in Paris.'

'I have never had much luck with solicitors,' said Bragg pensively, 'particularly French ones. Have you, sir, got any strings you can pull?'

The prince's eyes widened in surprise. 'No, sergeant,' he said with a smile. 'My connections in France are gastronomic, rather than governmental.'

'Will we be able to trace the bonds at all, do you think?'

'We have discussed the possibility with one of the prince's advisers,' said Knolleys. 'We are informed that bearer bonds are freely negotiable, and would be just as useful for our blackmailer's purposes as cash.'

'He knows what he is about, then?'

'Yes, sergeant.'

Bragg turned to the prince. 'Did he say anything about your letter, sir?'

'It will be returned as soon as the bonds have been received;

which probably means, as soon as they have been successfully turned into cash.'

'Do you believe him?'

The prince shrugged, and spread his hands. 'You have more experience than I of these matters,' he said.

'Do you happen to know where William Bullivant is?' Bragg asked.

'No, sergeant. He has not appeared at any functions for some days.'

'We went to arrest him on Friday morning, but he had slipped away. We gather that he might have gone to an aunt in the south of France. We have alerted the French police to arrest him, if he appears.'

'Does not that mean that he cannot be connected with the latest letter?' Knolleys asked.

'By no means,' Bragg replied. 'He could well have stayed in London till Saturday night. He might have thought that the Channel ports would be watched. He could still be here, for all we know.'

'What about Beresford?' the prince asked with a curl of the lip.

'The magistrate would not give me a warrant on the evidence,' said Bragg gloomily.

'But you did arrest Alec Rouse,' Knolleys remarked.

'Yes. But if it was Rouse that sent this latest letter, then he would have needed an accomplice. We routed him out of bed at eight o'clock on Friday morning, and he has been in custody ever since.'

'His wife?' Knolleys suggested.

'It is just possible, but I doubt it. She is said to have been away, visiting her parents in the country. It is unlikely that she could have slipped back to the West End of London, and posted the letter to Lady Brooke . . . Anyway, there have been other developments. Another letter from the blackmailer was pushed through a door in London, late on Sunday night.'

'That could have been done by Lady Rouse,' said Knolleys.

'It could,' Bragg admitted, 'though I do not see her, or any woman, writing these letters, somehow.'

'Is one allowed to know the name of the addressee of this latest letter?' the prince enquired.

Bragg hesitated. 'It is a young woman named Catherine Marsden. She is a newspaper reporter.'

'I have met her,' the prince said with interest. 'Is this a blackmail letter also?'

'It is the usual offer to negotiate, though on this occasion, no money has yet been mentioned.'

'She was an exceedingly pretty and, I would have thought, upright young lady,' the prince mused.

'I would not disagree with that,' said Bragg. 'She was tricked into making some statements which could be manipulated to suggest impropriety.'

'My recollection is of a singularly direct and resolute person.'

'Well, she is the first to come straight to the police, if that is what you mean,' said Bragg acidly.

'And what course of action do you propose?'

'In relation to Lady Brooke's letter, you mean?'

'In both cases.'

'I would not take any steps to get the ten thousand pounds' worth of bonds for a few days, if I were you,' said Bragg. 'Miss Marsden is set on keeping the appointment with the blackmailer, and I am going to be nearby.'

'And when is that?'

'Tomorrow, at noon. After that, you may be able to rest easy.'

'I would not wish the young lady to run into any kind of danger on my account,' the prince said in a troubled voice.

'It won't be on your account,' Bragg said shortly. 'It will be for herself.'

CHAPTER   ————

———— *EIGHTEEN*

'What time is it, lad?'

Morton pulled out his watch. 'Half past eleven,' he said breezily. 'Not much longer to wait!'

Bragg finished his coffee, then resumed his scrutiny of the procession of carts and omnibuses passing in front of the teashop. It was pointless, of course. He had told Miss Marsden to go into the Temple on the stroke of twelve, even if she had to forsake her cab in the process. And as for the blackmailer, he would not show up a moment before he had to. Nevertheless, Bragg was anxious. They had been confident of success with Miss Godfrey, and look what had happened there . . . Well, they had taken every precaution they could, this time. He and Morton had walked round the courtyards that morning, and decided where they would station themselves. Miss Marsden would be in their view from the moment that she emerged from Inner Temple Lane. He had told her to loiter near Oliver Goldsmith's grave; that way, he and Morton could seal up Church Yard Court between them. Nothing should go

wrong. He glanced across at the constable, full of confidence
and good-humour. It would be a different story, if he knew who
the young lady really was. At first, the Commissioner had been
against his being involved, but Bragg had managed to persuade
him to change his mind. There was no sense in having a ring
of detectives around the place, all burly six-footers with
hobnailed boots. And if there were to be only two of them, then
Morton, young and athletic, had to be included. It was just a
question of how he would react, when Miss Marsden came
walking down the path. He should not have promised her that
he would say nothing to Morton. Policemen should never enter
into bargains. Anyway, he was sure that she was wrong about
him . . . Bragg sighed. This new breed of young women
were sometimes too determined for their own good.

'You seem inordinately gloomy, sergeant,' said Morton
lightly. 'Surely you are not contemplating the possibility of
failure?'

'Perhaps,' Bragg grunted.

'But with Rouse behind bars, this is a mere exercise. Our
latest blackmailee, Miss Perkins, is in no danger whatever.'

'So you think Rouse is our man?'

'By the time I had finished my report, last night, I had
convinced myself of it!'

'Even though it was not his camera that took the snap of
Miss Godfrey?'

'He borrowed one.'

'And despite the fact that two blackmail letters have been
delivered, since we nabbed him?'

'He gave some innocent person a shilling to do it.'

'Well, I hope you are wrong, lad,' said Bragg, 'Rouse was
released on bail, yesterday afternoon.'

'That is astonishing!' exclaimed Morton. 'But as it accords
with your evident feeling that he is innocent, I still do not
understand why you should be gloomy.'

'It is a murder charge, blast it!' exclaimed Bragg irritably.
'It's the principle of the thing that I object to. The magistrate
has not even considered the depositions, yet.'

Morton laughed. 'Perhaps they are experimenting with a

refinement of the medieval trial by ordeal,' he said. 'If Rouse can resist the temptation to flee, then he must be innocent.'

'He will be over the water by now, if he has any sense.'

'Then there is nothing to worry about today.'

'I tell you what, lad. If Rouse shows up in that courtyard, we grab him and ask questions later. No jury would believe that he could be there by chance.'

'Does the same procedure apply to Bullivant?'

'No, better not. Lady Rouse may do favours for a lot of men, but I cannot see her pinching a letter for a sodomite.'

'So if he comes, we wait for him to accost Miss Perkins and then arrest him.'

'That's it. Come on, it is time that we took up our posts . . . And remember, you are not to make a move unless I signal, whatever happens and whoever appears. Understand?'

'Yes, sir,' said Morton soberly.

'Right. Well, let's get it over with.'

They left the teashop separately, and strolled unobtrusively to their vantage points. Five minutes to twelve. Bragg began a systematic examination of the area. It was just possible, after all, that their man might already be there. He had selected the narrow passage by the north-east corner of the church, for himself. He would be near the meeting-point and he could stop any man on earth, trying to escape that way. Morton was sprawled on the grass at the top of the court, his hat tipped forward to shade his eyes, apparently asleep. The only thing that Bragg had miscalculated, was the constant stream of people coming by; bewigged barristers and their book-laden clerks returning from the law courts, solicitors and their clients arriving for conferences with counsel. He seemed to be the only person standing still; he must stick out like a sore thumb.

He heard the clock strike twelve and peered round the corner of the church again. There was no sign of Miss Marsden, and no one seemed to be loitering. As he drew back into cover, however, a man came up behind him, sauntering slowly along. He was well built and in early middle age; perfectly capable of subduing a young woman and smothering her. Bragg felt his muscles tensing as he mentally rehearsed how he would take him. The man strolled up to Goldsmith's grave, inspected it

briefly and turned back again. Bragg. memorised the man's
features as he passed him . . . But he was continuing round
the church, out of sight. Bragg crept to the south-east corner
and glanced after him. The man was just entering the passage
to Pump Court; in a moment he would be well away from the
church. Bragg dashed back again and scanned Church Yard
Court. There was no sign of Miss Marsden . . . Five minutes
past twelve . . . ten past . . . Perhaps Morton was right,
and the blackmailer would not come. But where was Miss
Marsden? . . . Quarter past twelve. Bragg poked his head
round the corner once more. There was no one in the court at
all, except for Morton. He was now sitting with his back to the
wall, looking across enquiringly.

'Are you Sergeant Bragg, mister?' piped a voice behind
him.

He swung round to find a messenger-boy, clutching a fold of
paper.

'Yes, son.'

'A young lady told me to give you this.'

'When?'

'About ten minutes ago. You wasn't easy to find.'

Bragg unfolded the paper. The message was printed in
capitals, with the usual crest at the head.

THE TEMPLE INCONVENIENT.
COME TO 7 RED BULL WHARF
ON FOOT AND ALONE.

Bragg beckoned to Morton, then turned to the lad. 'Where
were you to give her this?' he demanded.

'I was to watch the stretch between Middle Temple Lane and
Inner Temple Lane,' the boy replied. 'If I saw a young lady
getting out of a cab, I was to ask if she was Miss Marsden.
When I found 'er, I was to give 'er this paper.'

'You found her then?'

'Yes. She took one look at it, and told me to fetch it to you.'

Morton strolled up. 'What has happened?' he asked.

'A new message,' Bragg replied tautly. 'Who told you to
look out for the young woman?' he asked the boy.

'Another licensed messenger,' he replied.

'Did you know him?'

'I seen 'im around. I would recognise 'im if I saw 'im.'

'May I see the message?' asked Morton.

Bragg passed it over. 'Where can I find you, if I want you?'

'I 'ang about in front of the Royal Exchange, mister.'

'Right, off you go.'

'It is certainly like the printing on the other letters,' remarked Morton. He turned the paper over. 'Wait a moment! There is something written on the other side—in pencil. "Do not fail me!" . . . I know that writing,' he said, thunderstruck. 'It's Catherine Marsden's! She is your Miss Perkins, isn't she?' he asked angrily.

'Yes,' Bragg admitted.

'You know where Red Bull Wharf is, don't you? It's just above the Old Swan Pier. That must be where Arabella Godfrey was lured to . . . And now Catherine! You would sacrifice anyone to make an arrest, wouldn't you?' he said fiercely. 'If that girl is harmed, I will strangle you with my bare hands.' He thrust the message into Bragg's grasp and began running through the court-yards, towards King's Bench Walk and the Embankment.

Bragg lumbered after him. Once out of the Temple Gardens, he stopped a hansom and ordered the driver to hurry along Lower Thames Street. After half a mile they came up with Morton, still pounding along. Bragg stopped the cab.

'Jump up, lad,' he said grimly. 'You will need your breath at the other end.'

As Catherine paid off her cab, she felt a sudden sense of dread. It had seemed the only possible course of action, when she had been arguing it rationally with the sergeant. Now she was alone, going to face her tormentor. It had been easy, in Bragg's office, to insist that a dishonoured life would be intolerable. Here, her frailty wanted to cry out for protection . . . Perhaps if she waited here for the sergeant, he would be able to arrest the blackmailer without exposing her to danger . . . She looked back down Lower Thames Street, but there was only a van and a brewer's dray in

sight . . . She already knew the answer to her craven pleading. It was important that she should keep the appointment and
catch at least a glimpse of the man. Then, if he escaped, there
would be someone who could recognise him. She herself had
urged this on Bragg. It was straightforward and logical. But
she had taken for granted her own fortitude . . . and now she
was afraid.

The entrance to Red Bull Wharf was through big wooden
gates, now sagging drunkenly on their hinges. The new docks,
downstream at Tilbury, had destroyed the trade of the wharves
above London bridge and they had been left to rot. Catherine
could see a narrow lane running down between the derelict
buildings, its rutted cobbles strewn with rubbish. She screwed
up her courage and reluctantly began to pick her way along. It
was a forbidding place. The bars on the windows were rusting,
and every pane of glass had been smashed. The doors had been
broken open, some torn off their hinges, by gangs of children
or looters. Everywhere had been violated. She stopped, as a
piece of newspaper flapped lazily across her path . . . It was
so silent! Cut off by the high warehouses, the noise of the City
traffic was barely audible. She was gripped by sudden panic.
Where was Sergeant Bragg? He should be here by
now! . . . She opened her handbag and, taking out her
handkerchief, dabbed at her nose. The mundane action stead-
ied her nerve, and she walked on. Even if the sergeant were
here, he would not show himself. He would lurk in some
doorway, until she had left the lane and gone to keep her
tryst . . . Of course she could rely on him! He had promised
to rescue her, and he would not fail.

She stopped at the doorway on her right to decipher the
faded number. Six! She took a deep breath and looked at the
next building. It was lower than the others, with only two
storeys. A derrick stuck out over the lane like a gibbet, the
windows were menacing blotches in the sooty brick-
work . . . Nothing moved. No one seemed to be watching.
She fortified herself with the thought that the blackmailer
might not be waiting for her, after all; then picked her way
along the wall till she came to a doorway. The number seven
had faded, and someone had recently renewed the outline with

chalk. So much for her hopes! She pushed at the door and it creaked open, to reveal a small lobby and a flight of stairs leading to the next floor. She crept hesitantly upwards. There was a landing at the top, and a door standing ajar. The room beyond seemed empty, the floor thick with dust and fragments of window-glass. She pushed the door open. In the far corner was a pile of old sacks, but that was all. Catherine summoned up her courage and stepped inside. Suddenly she received a violent push in the small of her back, which sent her staggering towards the window. She looked round, in terror. A man was by the door, closing the hasp, and dropping a pin through the staple. He straightened up, and turned.

'Good afternoon, Miss Marsden.'

'Fritz!' Catherine exclaimed.

'You are surprised?' he asked pleasantly.

'I am flabbergasted . . . I would not have dreamed that you could be behind it. Was it you who arranged that interview at King's College?'

'Indirectly, it was.' Fritz laughed in delight. 'I thought that was a master stroke. Just the bait to tempt you!'

In an odd way, the fact that she knew the blackmailer had taken away some of Catherine's fear. She felt able to talk to him—converse if need be.

'I cannot believe that you would stoop to sending anonymous letters,' she said.

'Letters?' Fritz asked with a frown.

With a surge of fear, Catherine realised that she had made a bad mistake.

'Arabella Godfrey showed me the ones you sent her,' she said hastily.

'Ah, the voluptuous Miss Godfrey.' His voice sank to a caressing whisper. 'She was a foolish young lady. There was no need for her to do it. We could have maintained our relationship indefinitely. Her fiancé has ample money. He would not have noticed. But she said she had told the police! So stupid . . . She had to go.'

'Did you kill her?'

'Oh, yes. She had recognised me, you see . . . I had

outfoxed the police once, and it would have been folly to rely on her promise to keep silent.'

Catherine felt a cold shiver run up her spine. She must, at all costs, keep him talking till Bragg came.

'Did you take the photograph of Arabella, with that man?' she asked.

'Yes.' Fritz laughed. 'I borrowed one of the Princess of Wales's cameras, when she was away. They had no idea I was there . . . A pity—I might have made her my mistress, if she had not gone to the police.'

'If that is what you wanted, why did you ask her for money?'

'I needed money. You think that because I am a count, I must be wealthy! In truth, I am a pauper, a refugee from my country. When the Prince of Wales appointed me as one of his equerries, he gave me the social status I was accustomed to; but he would do nothing to help me recover my estates. And since, as an equerry, I was entitled to only half of my Royal Navy pay, I was in a dilemma. Even in my position of servitude, I was being drawn into the extravagances of his court; yet without his patronage, I was nothing . . . But that is almost behind me.'

'Why?' asked Catherine, feigning interest.

'I have very much bigger game afoot than Arabella Godfrey,' he said smugly. 'Thanks to the unbridled carnality of my master, I shall be able to begin a new life, away from this accursed country . . . These stupid people live in a dream world, where only their own desires matter. Bertie writes love letters to his mistress of the moment, heedless of the fact that some day he will be king. Well, one of his indiscretions will prove very useful to me—again and again.'

'Surely you would not blackmail the Prince of Wales?' Catherine asked in a shocked voice.

'Why not? He is nothing more than a doltish old satyr; and she a whore with a coronet . . . But you are altogether different,' he added in a lubricious tone. He began to advance slowly towards Catherine, hands outstretched.

'What do you want of me?' she cried fearfully. 'I have no money.'

'The only thing that my master desired and could not

obtain . . . your body. Take off your coat!' he ordered abruptly.

Terrified, Catherine fumbled at the buttons and slipped it off. His eyes ran gloatingly over her. Then he stepped forward and, gripping her arms, savagely forced a kiss on her.

'You must be more generous than that,' he said with a mocking smile. 'Now your blouse.'

'No I will not!'

She backed away from him and he followed, like a cat playing with a mouse. Her heel struck the wall. With an evil chuckle, he tore open her blouse.

'You should not hide your beauty from me,' he taunted her. 'Take off your clothes!'

'No!' Catherine drew her torn blouse about her breasts.

Fritz took a spring-knife from his pocket, and held the blade an inch from her eyes.

'Oh, yes, you will,' he said softly, 'or no one will ever want to paint you again.'

Catherine was numb with fear. Her brain was screaming at her to do what he said . . . anything to ward off impending destruction. He touched her cheek with the point of the knife. She felt it prick her flesh. Then suddenly he swung round, his head cocked. In relief Catherine heard feet pounding on the stairs. She screamed loudly and grappled with Fritz. She managed to get a hold on his knife arm, as the door shook under repeated batterings. Then he placed the heel of his left hand under her chin and thrust her away, as the door crashed open.

Morton careered into the room, and threw himself headlong. Fritz was smashed into the wall and dropped senseless to the floor. Morton stumbled, then fell on top of him.

'Hold on, lad!' Bragg shouted, rushing into the room.

'Watch his knife!' Morton gasped, and rolled away.

Bragg kicked the knife out of Fritz's nerveless hand, and handcuffed his arms behind his back.

'James! There is blood on your coat!' Catherine cried in alarm.

'I did not see the blade quickly enough.'

Bragg gently pulled up Morton's shirt. Blood was oozing

from a deep stab wound in his side. 'That looks bad,' he said. 'Stay still, and I will whistle up some help.'

Catherine took Morton's handkerchief from his pocket and pressed it against the wound, to staunch the bleeding. He looked up at her with a rueful smile.

'I owe you an apology, Miss Marsden,' he said painfully., 'I told you that Fritz was nothing but a buffoon . . ."

The next afternoon Bragg went to the police hospital in Bishopsgate, and was directed to Morton's bed. He was sitting up, propped against a mound of pillows and looking little the worse for wear.

'How are you lad?' he asked.

'It was only a flesh wound,' said Morton raising a smile. 'The point of the knife skidded along my ribs. It hurts like hell, but the surgeon has sewn me up and says I shall be back on duty in two weeks.'

'It looked terrible, I can tell you! You should have waited for me. He would have given up quietly, when he saw there was no chance of escape.'

'Are you carrying out the interrogation?' asked Morton.

'No. Forbes is. But, as a great concession, I have been allowed to sit in and prompt him from time to time.'

'Has Fritz confessed?'

'He's singing like a canary. It seems that he has always been hard up; for years he sponged on the Duke of Clarence.'

'Was he blackmailing him, as well?'

'I do not think there is an easy answer to that. They had known each other since Clarence was doing a spell in the navy, as a youth. They became close when Brandis was appointed an equerry. It's my guess that he knew what the duke was like, all along. However, when rumours started circulating, it was to Brandis that the Prince of Wales turned to find out the truth. It's my guess that he followed Clarence to Cleveland Street— he might even have gone in with him. Anyway, he saw Hadley there and recognised him as being the dean of St Paul's.'

'So, when Clarence died, Hadley was a ready-made substitute?' remarked Morton.

'Yes, though inadequate by comparison. Brandis had just

added Arabella Godfrey to his list, when the dean killed himself.'

'But, so far as anyone knew, she was a poor prospect when he wrote the first letter.'

'It seems that the Prince of Wales confided in him a fair bit; and her fiancé was a godson of the prince.'

'So that was how he knew.'

'It sounds as if Brandis intended to extort money from her, and have her as his mistress at the same time.'

'Enterprising! Still, Beresford and Rouse were essentially doing the same thing. What has happened to them?'

'Beresford goes back to his ship next week; Rouse's charges have been dropped, of course.'

'Poor old Rouse,' said Morton with a smile. 'You were rather hard on him!'

Bragg laughed. 'He did not seem to bear me any ill-will, when I went to tell him. The amusing thing is, that Rouse must have got the two bank-notes via the Prince of Wales. Brandis denies ever paying any money to Rouse.'

'That is what I call bad luck!'

'But for his becoming involved, we might have caught Brandis earlier. When Rouse broadcast to his circle that we had been asking about suspect notes, he was put on his guard. Once he had got rid of all the tenners, however, he felt safe again—though he did begin to switch the locations of the meetings with his victims, at the last moment.'

'Was it Rouse's fob seal that was used to put the mark on the various letters?'

'It was. Brandis has a quirky sense of humour, if you ask me.'

'What about the Warwick Castle affair?' asked Morton.

Bragg smiled with satisfaction. 'This one was to be his pot of gold. He reckoned he could make it last his lifetime . . . We were right all the time. It could not have happened as we were told it.'

'Then how did he get the letter?

'He was at the castle with the prince, of course; sleeping in one of the cottages. When he came to the prince's dressing room on the morning after the meeting with Beresford, he found the letter under a chair. Lady Brooke must have brought it in with her the previous night. He reckons the prince went looking for her, and she tucked it down her bosom. Then it fell out when they were undressing each other.'

'Did you manage to recover it?'

'We did. When we searched his room at Marlborough House, we found the letter and the photographic plate of it, in a valise with other papers . . . Strange that it was within fifty feet of the Prince's rooms all the time.'

'Did you get the negative for the snap of Arabella Godfrey?' asked Morton.

'No I expect he destroyed it, after he had killed her.'

'Who processed the photographs for him?'

'He would not say; though he assured us that there were no further copies . . . He seems very loyal to his accomplices. There was also a young woman, but he will not tell us where she is either.'

Morton shifted himself gingerly on his pillows. 'So now Bullivant will be able to come back from Menton,' he remarked.

'I am afraid not,' said Bragg soberly. 'They found his body in Brookwood, yesterday morning. He had shot himself on the front lawn of what used to be his house.'

'Good God! When did it happen?'

'I don't know. All I have is a telegraph from the Surrey police.'

'I am sure that it has but little to do with our enquiries,' said Morton reflectively.

'I am sorry, though. By and large, all the people in this case got what they deserved; but he got more than his shovel full.'

'Anyway,' said Morton with an attempt at joviality, 'you have once more achieved the impossible. When are you charging Brandis?'

'He has been charged, this morning, under the Post Office Acts.'

'Post Office? . . .' exclaimed Morton. 'You are having me on the stick!'

'No. It appears that he sent a letter to a certain young lady, not by post, but by a messenger. It seems that by doing so, he infringed the monopoly of the Post Office.'

'Is that a crime?' asked Morton in surprise.

'Oh, yes. The Home Office has been very ingenious,' said Bragg sardonically. 'You can send a letter by messenger without breaking the privilege, but it has got to relate to the private affairs of the sender or the recipient. The argument goes that the letter could not relate to the private affairs of the recipient since the allegations in it were untrue; on the other hand, a criminal act could not constitute a private affair of Brandis.'

'It all seems very obscure,' said Morton. 'I presume that it is in the nature of a holding charge.'

'Quite the reverse, lad. The penalty that crime carries is a five pound fine . . . Of course, the magistrate gave bail on the nod. I expect Brandis is on the channel packet, by now.'

Morton looked at Bragg in surprise. 'You do not seem as upset as I would have expected,' he said.

'Well, this way there will be no trial; the whole affair will be kept quiet. In the circumstances, I can see that it is right. For once, even Miss Marsden is not badgering us to let her publish the story.'

'I still do not understand how she became involved,' Morton remarked.

'She offered,' said Bragg laconically.

'Had I known, I would have tried to prevent it.'

'Why do you think you were kept in the dark? . . . No, lad. Once she sets her head, there is no shifting her. Anyway, no harm came to her, so you have no excuse to commit a battery upon me!'

There was a sudden commotion in the corridor, then the Prince of Wales and Knolleys came striding in. The prince shook Bragg by the hand, then went over to Morton's bed.

'I understand you will be playing cricket again soon,' he said. 'I have brought this to assist your recovery.' He placed a bottle of Chateau Margaux on the bedside table.

Morton grinned. 'I shall have to hide it from matron,' he said.

The prince sat down heavily beside the bed. 'I am still

astonished that it could have been Fritz,' he said in a
bewildered voice. 'I suppose it was, in some measure, my
fault. He kept asking me to intervene with the Kaiser to get his
lands back, but my nephew is a very difficult man to deal with,
and it never seemed opportune.'

'There could be no justification for what he did,' said Bragg
firmly.

'Well, I am very grateful to you both, as is the Queen; and
we are all indebted to the remarkable fortitude of Miss
Marsden. Indeed, the Queen has expressed a wish to meet her.'
He looked over at Bragg. 'It seems absurd, does it not, to mark
such a signal service to the crown by a mere expression of
gratitude . . . I could get you made a Commander of the
Bath, sergeant, if you would accept it.'

Bragg laughed. 'How would I explain why I'd been given it,
down at the pub?' he asked. 'Anyway they gave the Commissioner a CB last year. It wouldn't do for me to have one!'

'Perhaps we could promote Sir William to Knight Commander, Knolleys,' the prince murmured, then turned to
Morton. 'As for you, young man,' he said genially, 'you are in
a fair way to gaining the most coveted prize of the Season, if
what I hear about the young lady is any guide.'

'Well, sir,' said Morton with a mischievous smile, 'if the
lady spurns me, I shall be able to spend the rest of my life
looking at her portrait.'

EPILOGUE

Catherine walked in stately fashion around her bedroom, trying to get her twelve-foot train spread out in a straight line behind her. No, the room was just not long enough. She gathered the train on her arm and went out on to the landing. Draping the voluminous folds over the bannister, she walked slowly through the door again, towards the mirror. That was better; the train was fully extended now, and she could pretend that the receiving line was along the wall in front of her. She sank to the ground in front of the mirror in a graceful curtsy; then hitched her train over her left arm, and repeated the process two feet to the right. By the time she had come up against her bed, she had managed six curtsies without disgracing herself. She only hoped that she would manage as well at the presentation.

It had begun a fortnight after the dreadful business at Red Bull Wharf. Catherine had, quite unexpectedly, received an invitation to the Queen's drawing-room at Buckingham Palace, on the fourth of July. She had been nonplussed, particularly as the letters VRI had been written at the bottom of the card, in short imperious strokes. Because her mother had not been presented at court herself, Mrs Marsden could not now present

presented at court herself, Mrs Marsden could not now present
her daughter. At her suggestion, therefore, Catherine had taken
the card to Lady Morton, to ask her advice. James, asserting
that he was well past the walking-wounded stage, had just
called to see his mother, before going back to duty. He had
been delighted at the invitation, indeed he almost seemed to
have been expecting it.

A personal invitation from the Queen was so unusual, that
James had had to explain something of the events leading up to
it. His mother had been gratifyingly perturbed that Catherine
should have been placed in such a hazardous predicament. She
had asked if she could present Catherine, herself, and had
taken charge of all the arrangements. Catherine had been left
only with the problem of what kind of dress to wear. She knew
that she could not afford to compete with the elaborate Paris
gowns, that most of the girls would be wearing. So she had
elected to wear a simple dress of pale rose-pink silk, with the
mandatory white gloves and veil. Now, in a mischievous
impulse, she fastened the Prince of Wales's pendant around her
neck.

There was a knock at the door, and the parlour-maid came in
with unaccustomed respect.

'Lady Morton's carriage is outside, miss,' she said.

Catherine put her wrap round her shoulders and, gathering
her train on her arm, went downstairs. Her mother was
standing in the hall, with a mixture of pride and uncharacter-
istic regret on her face. Catherine kissed her warmly, then went
outside. James had insisted on providing the carriage; it was a
penance, so he said. If so he must be well on the way to
forgiveness, for it was the most splendid equipage that anyone
could wish for. A liveried footman handed her up, and they
began their stately progress towards the palace.

'You look quite exquisite, dear,' said Lady Morton.

'Thank you,' replied Catherine with a nervous smile. 'It
must be quite exceptional to make two presentations in the one
season.'

'Yes, but think of the advantages! I can remember where
Emily and I were pushed into an eddy for a quarter of an hour,
and can predict where we are likely to be trampled underfoot!'

'I find all this more trying than walking down Red Bull Wharf.'

'You need not worry, dear. After all, you may be sure that no one else will be there at the personal bidding of her sovereign.'

They drove along the Mall at walking pace, behind similar carriages. Knots of people stood at the road-side, peering in and commenting on their occupants. For Londoners, it was something of a spectacle, and on a glorious sunny day like this, they were out in large numbers to enjoy it. Eventually the carriage passed through the gates of Buckingham Palace, and deposited Catherine and Lady Morton at the entrance. There was a moment of panic, as Catherine forgot her bouquet and the footman scampered after her with it. Then they were crossing the great hall and ascending the grand staircase. There they were caught up in a press of young women and their mothers, all beautifully dressed and trying to conceal their harassment.

Lady Morton shepherded Catherine along the corridor, till they were admitted to an ante-room by a splendidly dressed gentleman-at-arms. There final adjustments were made to Catherine's toilette, then she went on alone. At the door of the picture gallery two gentlemen-at-arms took her train from her arms, and spread it out on the floor with their wands. She removed her right glove and, at a nod, crossed the gallery to the door of the presence chamber. She gave her invitation card to a page, who passed it down a line of servants to the Lord Chamberlain. Catherine waited nervously, as the two girls in front of her made their curtsies. They looked so cool and confident, she thought, as if they had been born to it. Perhaps they had . . . Well, she would not be outdone by anyone, on such a special day.

The Queen was seated in a gilded chair, her black dress relieved by a rope of pearls around her neck. A black veil fell from a small gold coronet, and she wore a diamond bracelet on her wrist. The Lord Chamberlain bent over and whispered to her, then straightened up.

'Miss Marsden comes next,' he announced.

Catherine, her composure belied by her thumping heart,

walked sedately across the floor, curtsied and kissed the
Queen's outstretched hand. As she rose, a brief smile of
pleasure crossed Victoria's face. Standing next in the line was
the Prince of Wales. His eyes immediately fastened on Catherine's pendant and he acknowledged her curtsy with a grin.
Then she was backing down the line, curtsying to the Princess
of Wales, Prince George and Princess Mary of Teck. At last
she reached the exit door and backed out of the royal presence.
She was looking for Lady Morton, when a page came hurrying
up.

'The Lord Chamberlain thought that you would wish to
retain this, as a memento, madam,' he said, giving her the
invitation card on which Victoria had written her initials.

'Thank you. Please say that I am very grateful.'

She found Lady Morton in the ante-room, and soon they
were back in the carriage, threading the narrow streets to
Aubrey Rivington's studio. He made a great fuss of Catherine,
while Lady Morton insisted on personally adjusting her train,
until she was satisfied that it was perfect. Aubrey took three
plates, in various poses, exclaiming each time that it would be
gorgeous. Catherine wished she could tell him that he need no
longer fear the blackmailer, but Bragg had forbidden it. Once
Fritz had escaped to France, it had been decided that total
secrecy should be maintained. James had averred that some
kind of bargain had been struck. Certainly, no one seemed
worried any longer, even though the marriage of Prince George
and Princess Mary was a mere two days off. So poor Aubrey
would still be kept in ignorance—but he would soon forget it.

After the traditional circuit of Hyde Park, where crowds had
congregated to watch the display, Catherine was set down with
due ceremony at her home. For the next two hours, she
recounted every moment of the afternoon for her mother's
benefit. Then she went upstairs to dress for the opera. It was to
be a state performance of Gounod's *Romeo et Juliette*, in
honour of the Tsarevitch. James had declared that it was really
in her honour, and had taken a box. Since Rutherford and
Reuben Smith were also to be in the party, and would escort the
other ladies, James had said that he would come for her
himself. After the affair of Red Bull Wharf, he had become

very attentive for a time. She had, of course, visited him on several occasions when he was in hospital; and while he was convalescing, he had taken to walking down to her office in the evening. He would drive home with her in a cab, then walk back to Bishopsgate again. He said it was good exercise for him, and would help him to get fit once more. Certainly, once he had gone back on duty, the practice had ceased and Catherine had seen little of him thereafter.

He arrived in good time, however, and, when he had paid his respects to her parents, they drove to Covent Garden in a four-wheeler. He was impeccably dressed and debonair, as he escorted her through the glittering throng in the foyer and up to his box. She ought to have been flattered, but there was something faintly proprietorial about the way that he had introduced her to various acquaintances, which piqued her. She began to wonder if she would really enjoy the evening. For one thing, she did not know the opera; for another, she felt somewhat out of place. Apart from her, it was a kind of Morton family party. Lady Morton and Mrs Harman were there, Emily was chatting gaily to Reuben Smith, while Violet and Rutherford were sitting glumly at the other side of the box. After numerous telegraphic consultations with Mr Harman, on the other side of the Atlantic, it had been decided that there would be no engagement at present. Rutherford and Violet were to be parted for a year; after which time, it was hoped, they would know their own minds. It seemed a ridiculous proceeding to Catherine; certainly neither of them seemed content, as the date of Rutherford's departure drew near.

There was a sudden roll of drums from the orchestra pit and the trumpets blared out a fanfare. The audience stood and applauded, as the Prince and Princess of Wales entered the royal box followed by the Tsarevitch; then cheering broke out, as it was seen that Prince George and Princess Mary were also in the royal party. The excited babble of conversation continued long after the houselights were dimmed and the overture began.

Catherine could not concentrate on the opera. Her mind was sifting through everything that had happened in the last two months. She had been brought face to face with dire peril;

indeed, she had recklessly invited it. Her cosy complacency
had been threatened, albeit by wholly spurious insinuations.
She was conscious that she would need to reassess the
assumptions on which her life had been based. But it was too
soon yet. She would wait until the humdrum pattern of
ordinary life had been reestablished; then she would know what
it was she really desired.

When the performance was over, she walked with James
down to the Strand, where, he said, they would find a cab more
easily. She was glad to get away from the others, away from
the unspoken assumptions; glad to relapse into the accustomed
friendly intimacy with James. He, also, seemed to be relieved,
and began to discuss the evening in his usual bantering way.
Then his voice changed, and became diffident.

'I would like your permission to raise a very delicate subject,
Miss Marsden,' he said. 'I would not, however, wish to
outrage your susceptibilities.'

'You are hardly likely to do that, James,' she replied with a
smile.

'I will desist at any time you wish.'

'You intrigue me. Go on!'

'Sergeant Bragg gave me the blackmail file, when I resumed
duty. Since I was not fully fit, he suggested that I should write
the final report on the case.'

'Oh, yes?' said Catherine, her heart sinking.

'In it was a transcript of an interview given on the subject of
women's achievements. The interviewee was, of course,
anonymous; which makes it possible to consider the ideas
contained in the document objectively. There were some
penetrating observations on the relationships between parents
and children. Having thought about them, I realise that they
illuminate my own experience . . . I would in no way
entertain the interpretation which Fritz sought to put on them.'

'Thank you,' Catherine said quietly. 'I realise now that
Sergeant Bragg takes the spoken word very literally. I enjoined
on him that he should say nothing to you about it. I should have
said that he should keep you in total ignorance.'

'He is a devious man,' said Morton lightly. 'Though what
his motive could have been is obscure.'

Catherine took his hand. 'Since you now know that I was "Bougainvillea", I must tell you that the physical intimacy I so rashly revealed, was the touch of his hand on my breast, last summer.'

'But that was an operational necessity,' said James blandly.

'And involuntary on both sides, without doubt.'

'Indeed! I had hoped that you would have forgotten it.'

'As you already have . . .'

Morton burst out laughing. 'I shall never be content, till I get the better of you,' he said.

'Why not aim higher, and get the best of me?'

'Could I ever be worthy of it?'

'You could but try, James,' she said. 'You could but try!'

221